Cary J. Lenehan is a former trades assistant, soldier, public servant, cab driver, truck driver, game designer, fishmonger, trainee horticulturalist and university tutor (among other things). His hobbies include collecting and reading books (the non-fiction are Dewey decimalised), Tasmanian native plants (particularly the edible ones), the SCA and gaming. He has taught people how to use everything from shortswords to rocket launchers. He met his wife at an SF Convention while cosplaying and they have not looked back.

He was born in Sydney before marrying and moving to the Snowy Mountains where they started their family. They moved to Tasmania for the warmer winters and are not likely to ever leave it.

Looking out of the window beside his computer is a sweeping view of Mount Wellington and its range.

**Warriors of Vhast Series
published by IFWG Publishing Australia**

Intimations of Evil (Book 1)
Engaging Evil (Book 2)
Clearing the Web (Book 3)
Scouring the Land (Book 4)

Warriors of Vhast Book 2

Engaging Evil

by
Cary J. Lenehan

Engaging Evil
Book 2, Warriors of Vhast
All Rights Reserved
ISBN-13: 978-1-925956-43-6
Copyright ©2017 Cary J. Lenehan
V1.0

Scene break illustration ©2015, 2017 Cassandra James
Maps' lettering and illustrations ©2015, 2017 Marjorie Lenehan

IFWG Publishing International
www.ifwgpublishing.com
Melbourne, Australia

Acknowledgement

It seems so long ago and yet only yesterday that I launched the first book in this series. Now, not only is this the second book, but the third should be out before the end of the year. As well I now have a website (caryjlenehan.com.au) and a dedicated group of followers on Patreon who get monthly stories from Vhast as well as recipes, Tarot cards, character details, town details and many other things. Their support is letting me spend more time working at extending the universe and adding texture to Vhast while worrying a little less about bills.

I would also like to thank the many people who have read iterations of this book. Most have been polite and said they liked it, but sometimes the readers have not enjoyed it and have been kind enough to say why, which has often told me things about my writing. Their criticism has been invaluable. Some have also offering some amazing insights that have led me to change sections and the way I write. In particular I wish to thank Pip Woodfield who has read this book so many times that she know it better than I do.

I would especially like to thank Marianne de Pierres (a lot) who encouraged me on this journey many years ago.

Once again I would like to dedicate this book to my mother, Eden and my beloved wife Marjorie, both of whom have shown incredible patience with me over the years as I have followed my dreams. I hope you both still enjoy it and are proud of how it has turned out.

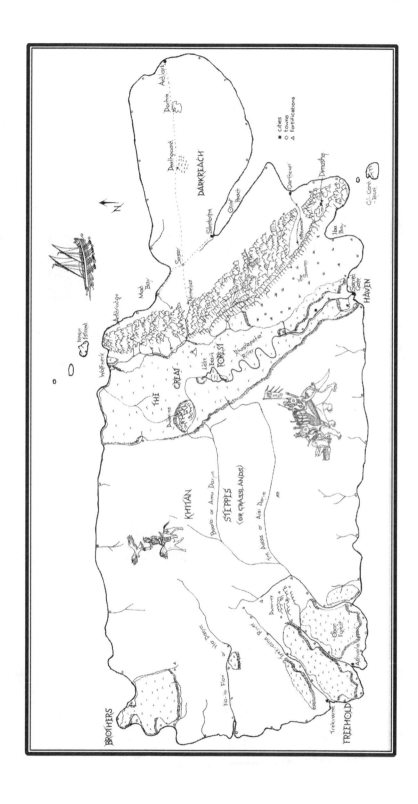

Map of the Lands
East of Lake Erave

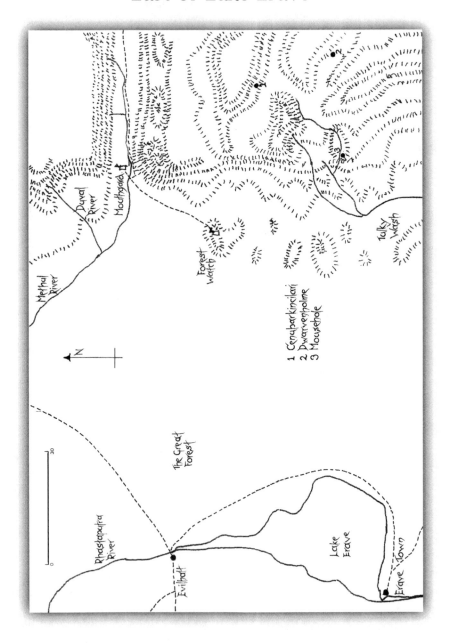

Travellers come swift from the west.
Find their way through forest and foes
Strike hard slavers deep hidden nest
With Mice now found, the mountains are free.
Dwarven leader they did depose
His minions they captured and slew
No more terror will bandits impose
With Mice now found, the mountains are free.
Freed slaves with new life now imbue
With hope that was torn from their hearts
Bright futures perhaps now may ensue.
With Mice now found, the mountains are free.
Who knows what the future imparts?
We all will give of our best
For me, a new life now starts,
With Mice now found, the mountains are free.

A Kyrielle
Ruth Hawker
on the occasion of her freedom

Chapter I

Hulagu

In a very literal sense, the sounds of conflict died quickly away. *I have now passed the final test of being an adult while I am on my wanderjahr. I have now killed a man in open battle. If I wish I may now wed.* In glee he let out a wolf-like howl of victory until Astrid held up her hand. He noticed her gesture and suddenly stopped in mid-cry. *Might there be others? I should have thought of that. She is intently listening to find out.*

Astrid

Astrid was re-assured. *Apart from noise from where my people are further down the creek, I can hear the faint noises made by some horses that are stirring. They are nervous about what they have been hearing; the sounds of spells, of screams, and of battle. The beasts don't seem to be kept all that far off, but other than the noise they are making there is no other sound that would tell of a survivor crashing through the undergrowth in an attempt to flee...That was a faint groan from somewhere among the fallen. One of them seems to still be, at least not yet, dead.*

The horses were not moving from where they were, and she heard one that softly whickered to another. *There is no urgent pounding of hooves. They are probably secure in a line. They can wait. I want to look over the battle site first.* She signalled Hulagu to give her cover in case there was someone left alive on the other side who could do more than groan, slung her bow over her shoulders, and leant over to pick up her spear. Soon she was wading carefully through the small stream. It was autumn and so the level came to just over her knees. *By the standards of home the water is still mildly warm. It will soon run a lot colder than this as it comes down from the hills and mountains with the onset of winter, but it is autumn and the sun is still capable of warming the water when its path lies in the sloping rays.* She could also see, from the marks on the bank, that it sometimes ran far higher than this, probably in spring after the melt in the mountains or after heavy rain.

It was not long before she had Hulagu join her on the far side, and together they started recovering shafts and checking that their opponents were all dead as their bodies were laid out in a row. One stirred briefly as they bent over him, but his eyes glazed even as Astrid bent to check his pulse. *All of them were men. I am sure that a couple are at least vaguely familiar.*

Stefan soon joined them, dragging a body, a gaping hole in it from the blast from an enhanced arrow, from somewhere nearer to the bridge. It didn't take long to get the remains of their enemies gathered together as more of their people joined in. They could then start to see what had been dropped or left against trees to be quickly grabbed. *By the appearance of this lot, their clothes and weapons, they were all used to violence. Several bear the scars that accumulate over time and the calluses of frequent practice. Their weapons are of good quality, but worn with use. Everything shows that we were lucky to turn surprise around on these men.*

Bianca

Bianca looked around. *My people are gathering on the other side of the creek and they are all ignoring their horses...typical.* She moved to gather the animals up and took them over the bridge. Cautiously, looking for a place to tie them up, she moved past the line of bodies already laid out. Behind a thick screen of a small tree with glossy dark leaves and the remnant of what could be sprays of tri-lobed brown seed cases, she found what she sought—two hands of horses already occupied it. Looking closer there were eight saddles sitting near the heads of animals while a small pile of pack frames stood beside the last four animals. She studied the campsite that stood a little further back from the animals when Astrid joined her.

"Seems they have been here at least a couple of days," Astrid said, as she looked at the well-set camp. "I had seen signs of movement on the road, but hadn't realised it was this recent. I guess that, if they came from Evilhalt, they left well before we did."

"T'ey be coming from Evilhalt," Stefan said, as he joined them. "I be a recognisin' most of t'em an four're local." He paused. "I be tryin' to remember when t'ey left...I didn't see t'em go, but I do remember t'at someone who was on watch made a comment about how t'contents of t'packs must be real valuable with only four pack horses an' so many to guard them. It would hast to be near two weeks ago. Unless t'is were accident, an' on t'is road t'at seems unlikely, t'ey hast been a waiting for us all of t'at time. Someone hast sent t'em ahead of us an' it be deliberate. It seems t'at t'ey do know we be comin' t'is way."

Bianca listened as Stefan and Astrid moved from where they were talking across to the fire pit and the bivouac. She added to the pair what she could see from the horses and they nodded sagely and soon started moving around the campsite. They talked back and forth as they thought aloud. *I wish I could see what they can see in footprints and broken branches. They are obviously seeing evidence of how long the men had been here, but it means nought to me.* Gathering the salvageable possessions and the food was only of secondary importance. Reluctantly they came to the conclusion that Stefan was right in his speculation. From what they could see it had to have been at least two weeks. The men must have left Evilhalt, acting under someone's instruction, and moved quickly along the path they were following and then waited. There was not even any sign that they had hunted while they were here. They had brought all of their supplies with them so that they were not distracted from their task. She could at least contribute something on how much they had brought and how much was left. As Stefan had thought, this meant that someone was expecting them to come this way. Someone knew, possibly better than they did, where they were headed and what they were doing and, what is more, their enemy wanted what they were doing stopped. According to the other two, it had been a well-laid ambush. If Astrid had not felt suspicious, then it was likely that they would all be dead now. As they gathered together what they found the two began talking about how they would have to learn to rely on their intuition. If they saw or heard something amiss, that was good, but even the slightest feeling that something was wrong could not be ignored.

Astrid asked Stefan, "What else lays ahead? What didn't they know about? Did the people where they were heading to already expecting them, or were these people sent by someone else?" *I like it even less than them if the people who are experienced in these things are so full of doubt. I need them to at least sound confident for me to feel safe.*

Chapter II

Gamil

*O*nce more the cycle turns, thought Chief Predestinator Gamil, *and now it is my turn to be in charge of our race's response to the plans of the Adversaries.* She sat in the cool breeze that wafted from the airshafts that were placed over her desk on her race's space station high above Vhast. Thousands of years ago her people had started this experiment and built the world that she could see through the window on the wall to her right. It was day below her at present and autumn in the northern hemisphere. Clouds raced along from the west to meet mountains that ran from north to south and so drop their load of water.

She turned and looked down at the work of her people. *Having built a world we had then peopled it in a way that should, if we are lucky, encourage the result we are looking for.* Gamil cast her mind back over the details of the task she had ahead of her, reviewing it all in her mind once more as she looked at the results of the decision she had made that would affect what was about to unfold.

Once more she studied the files and the ideas that her staff had assembled for her as they projected on her walls and screens. *Originally there had been details of well over twenty young people here, and a variety of suggestions were given that should motivate them to act. Some of them had seemed cruel, but it was hopefully only briefly so and the gain for the races below was far more important than any single individual's short pain. However, now the responsibility for success is mine and mine alone. I hope that I have chosen wisely among them, and, just as carefully, instructed the Motivators to construct the details of what I want to happen from my scripts. None could now over-rule me. The hope of my race in the struggle against the Adversaries sits on my shoulders. The die is cast and my chosen people have passed their first test as a group. How will they cope with the next? Will they divine what is happening and be able to interpret the hints I have left for them? As* her race tended to do, she sat back for a few hours and contemplated the future.

Coming back to her senses, as she stared at the unfolding planet from high in space above Vhast, Gamil shook her head and briefly ruffled her wings. No-one had disturbed her as she sat lost and far away in thought, even though a quick check showed that some time had passed. *I have done all that I can and now I watch time pass and spend too long looking down at my people. I need exercise and a long flight. The Adversaries had, throughout their history, always been far better at destroying than building. Building is what my people do, but this experiment can never be repeated. My race has taken people and creatures from various times and places and from so many different planets that seemed to form a plasm that could be moulded. We have taken the animals, the plants, and the people from anywhere we wanted that seemed to bring out the traits we wanted to create and enhance among the people on this built world of Vhast. These had been bred, gene-spliced, transmuted and set down. New animals and plants are still occasionally added when they are developed. Whether there were enough, or even any, suitable intelligent beings left behind in their original homes to start again is another question that is unlikely to have a positive answer. It had been hard enough to find their starting stock.*

Both of the races now competing for control of the experiment are very long lived. Our conflicts had been held, first directly until the Treaty had been put in place by the other races, and then in proxy across a vast swath of space. Legends of my people and our opponents and our seeming eternal war grew and flourished on thousands of worlds. Few of them resemble the reality that is.

Now what had to be nearly the final struggle had commenced as this project came to within a few thousands of years of completion. Wars had ravaged the project as proxy entities fought the battles that those outside could not themselves fight by the rules that had been imposed from outside. Then the un-looked for and unwanted plague of The Burning had come from somewhere—none knew where—to add another layer of destruction to their most advanced experimental area. None thought that it had been the Adversaries who had created that. It may

*have even interfered with their designs more than those of my people.
However, with that now in the past, once again, the Adversaries were
coming out into the open with their plots and their puppets and their
twisted evil and it was up to the players I have selected to foil them.
These beings who would hopefully act on my behalf without them
knowing why they did it were now in place, despite the efforts of the
Adversaries to stop them joining up. The free will of the chosen ones was
an important random factor in the unfolding events. The last time such a
crisis had occurred my predecessor had lost the proxy battle with her
selections. This time I hope to do far better. What is about to unfold
might be the last chance that I, and through me my race, would have to
regain sole control of the project. A loss now could be final, at least in
this, the main arena of conflict. The main game is about to start.*

Gamil had been preparing for this moment for many years. She
sighed and leant back in her chair again. Her wings fanned behind her
slowly with their tips raised in an unconscious gesture of triumph and
contentment. Around her, if she concentrated, the soft background
humming of the life support system could be heard and there was a
gentle breeze from an air return designed to play upon her comfortable
seat. *So far the most complex part my race's greatest piece of art is now
under way. Now it will be seen if what I have set in place will keep the
experiment going under the control of my people, or if I will fail.*

*Over ten thousand of the long years of this world, almost all of my
adult life, has been spent in service to the project of Vhast. I hope to
spend the rest of it engaged in the same way. The gamble is exquisite, the
workmanship is complex. The limits of intervention are well defined and
carefully prescribed by treaties and agreements that were many, many
millennia old. The Adversaries might break them, and had in the past,
but I will not. Now it is up to the chosen ones—and those that they will
choose to help them—to either succeed or fail. I have done all that I can
and all is going exactly as I have planned. It is certain that this will not
last. The unfolding is about to happen. I contributed, we all did, but I
had not been in a position to make final decisions on anything the last
time this had happened. The failure of her subjects then had cost my
predecessor her post. She had retired honourably, but far from here, for
at least total disaster had been averted. Everyone realised that this had
been more due to good luck than anything else, but it was the results that
counted.*

Now the Adversaries are starting to reach out again from the penalties that had been placed upon them. They are bringing new pawns into play and seem about to try again for a total takeover of the free area of the planet that was of most interest. I realised this in time. I hope that, to counter their moves, I have been more careful in the help that I have enlisted. I now have to hope that I have indeed been more thorough than they have and that my chosen ones will have more success in the task that had been set for them than my predecessor's did. In some ways I wish I could interfere more directly, but in other ways I am glad that the last decision has probably now been made. Unless I decide, at the last moment, to get the motivators to add more players on our side, which would most likely mean that my people are failing, all I can do now is watch and run my calculations as free-will, and chance, for better or worse, move my tools away from their optimistically allotted path.

Chapter III

Theodora

On the second night after the attempted ambush Theodora asked Stefan if he had any leather with him. "Of course," he replied. "I must be a prepared to fix anythin' t'at breaks."

"Then can you stitch and braid this copper and an amethyst into a necklace for me?"

"Easy, but why?"

Despite her efforts to fit in with the others, Theodora was still not used to them questioning her actions. When she replied she realised there was a touch of abruptness in her tone, "Tonight we will cast an illusion spell as you make it. It will mean that people using magic to see us will look at where we are and will see an empty path. They will see the path as it was a few minutes before we arrived there. Rani dear...I will need to draw on your mana again to increase the power of my pentagram, as I have never performed this spell before and neither of us will have anything left if we are attacked tonight, but it should work against someone who is looking with just their normal senses." Theodora explained to the others what would happen that night after dinner. Christopher insisted on taking part. As she listened to his short sermon Theodora realised why. Today was, coincidentally, the feast day of St Bartholomew. As the patron of leatherworkers he was a rare and un-thought of correspondence.

When the priest had finished what he had to say Theodora directed to Stefan to take over and he began to braid and stitch some leather he had started on earlier. As he worked, Stefan admitted to her that he had forgotten the Saint. At home he would have been reminded—there was even a small icon on the wall of his family's house, but being on the trail he had lost track of the days. As he began to finish up, late into the first watch, Theodora began to cast her magic. *Again, just as when I made the charm for Astrid, I can feel that I have a well-cast spell. It is almost like a small orgasm, warm inside of me.* She realised that she had a very pleased expression on her face as she took it over to Bianca. "You ride in the middle of us. You now need to wear this. We will need to ride much closer together now, and I fear that it may not cover Astrid, but she is on foot and so is less noticeable than the rest of us."

"I hope so," said Astrid dismissively. "Otherwise I would have forgotten most of my skill."

Astrid

N̲ow, during the night, the light chill showers made a faint southern promise of snow, particularly as they climbed much higher into the mountains. *I have tried to pretend that it would be just like winter at home, but I know that it won't be. For a start all of the trees are wrong and it gets worse as we climb. The trees are gradually changing to smaller, more upland, varieties; except in patches where the towering gums and some myrtle beech dominate. Here they grow taller than they do on the lower slopes and far taller than the more spreading deciduous plants of the flatter ground. Some of the gums reach up a full hand of ten paces into the sky or even more. Their leaves are clusters high in the sky. Now there is far less cover from the chill wind unless we are in one of the quiet moist upland valleys with their tall dense ferns three to four times my height. Off the path is mainly bark on the ground, with only occasional clumps of grass. It is a far different world to mine. Large lizards, two or three paces long, scuttle away from me, away from where they had been lying in the sun and, scarce slowing, run up the trees.*

Looking up at the sky she could see long-winged eagles and, once, some of the feathered flying lizards indicated that an eyrie of them must be nearby. Further down were flocks of bright-feathered parrots making the day noisy and moving around near the ground were a number of finches and small birds with blue patches of feathers and an upright tail the length of the rest of their bodies that she didn't recognise. They hopped around looking for insects and joined the pairs of forest doves in looking for seeds on the ground.

As they progressed the road turned towards the south and she could see, in the far distance to the east, the occasional tiny cold twinkle at night of Darkreach border outposts on the high ridges. Basil had shown her where they had already passed one, sited on a small mountain of its own, that lay between the road they were on and the one that went on to Kharlsbane. It had only been visible in glimpses through gaps in terrain and there had been enough trees around them that it was unlikely that observers there saw them unless someone knew of the road and their passage and was looking for them with a telescope. Perhaps it would have been different if this was a well-trodden and cleared path, but it must have been a long time since that had been the case. Even with the traffic of bandits paving was still pushed up by tree roots while whitey-wood, mountain laurels and other tall shrubs spread their leaves over the path.

Further east, behind increasingly higher ranges of foothills, towered the main range, the tall sharp peaks looking like a serrated knife on its back, their height emphasised by their covering of snow. No longer were there the campsites of the well-travelled road, although Astrid pointed out to the others where the brigands camped each night and suggested that they stay in the same spots, when they could do so, to leave no new traces. They had to push harder and to stop earlier to gather firewood and have their smokeless fires out before dark. The road was far narrower. It was based on what had once been a real highway, but now was only a track. The narrowness of their path now made it better for them to travel in single file. Behind them was strung an increased train of horses on lead ropes.

After a while the path took a turn to the south and widened. *We have joined what was once a proper road. It is both wider and one that was, although overgrown by grasses and mosses, still largely intact. The junction of the two is easy to make out. I now know that I have my people on the right path.* She kept finding many traces of the passage of large groups of people and horses—everything from their campsites and latrines to some discarded and lost items.

Each day they moved more and more cautiously. Travel went slower and slower. The feast of St Phocas came and went and then Pentecost, Holy Trinity and the celebration for St Pandonia followed. The nights were growing colder and the days were starting to go the same way. *Real winter is not so far off.* Astrid had taken up station moving several hundred paces ahead of the rest. Sometimes she would drop out of sight of the rest behind a ridge and they would take cover, waiting for her to re-appear and wave them on before she continued. *I am enjoying this. It is up to me to keep the others safe.* It was quite some time before this caution was rewarded.

One afternoon she moved over the rise and saw ahead of her the valley, just as the note from the Khitan had described. After having a good look for observers she went jogging back down the track to the others. "I've found the valley," she exclaimed. "It is just over the next rise and, where we stand now, we are all going to be clearly visible from what should be their watch point." She pointed ahead of them and up to the left. "That is, if there was anyone in it."

Rani had everyone move back along the path to where they would not be seen, while she moved forward and further up the hill with Astrid. Keeping Rani below her Astrid moved up the ridge towards the crest where she would be able to see the entrance to the valley and, what she thought was a watch point. She moved silently and delicately, just like her nickname 'stalking prey', as she picked her way through the brush. She snorted at the noise behind her and turned to discover that Rani was walking after her. "Get down, you silly woman, they may see you," she whispered urgently and loudly. Rani looked surprised, but dropped. *Rani is used to being in armies, not tracking prey, and, above all, she is used to being the one who gives orders.*

Eventually they reached the brow of the low ridge and Astrid positioned Rani where she could see, but still have some cover. "If I say so you have to move back down below the crest. Theodora says that she has hidden my magic from watchers. To them you will probably glow like a fire on the ice at night." They waited. Astrid looked around her to take in what she could see.

The entrance to the valley was only forty paces across. More than thirty was taken up by a fast flowing rivulet, its surface smooth with standing waves, but generally lacking any white water to indicate its depth. It split, foaming, around a great lump of stone, its sides steep but grassy, its top bare and black. On the top stood two stones, each near as tall as a man, while a third piece of worked rock created a table between them. It was either the work of giants or of a mage of power. A ledge, not much wider than the panniers of a heavy-laden packhorse or a small cart, ran up each side of the rivulet. It was a rough ledge at its start and looked to be more natural than man-made, perhaps deliberately so. The path ran four paces above the torrent and a cliff stood above it on each side, varying from forty to sixty paces high. They were perched on a high point of an out-thrust of the northern cliff. The southern cliff rose much higher and reached a peak directly opposite them. From the track that they had been following the great rock would block the view up the valley. The track crossed the river on a bridge—the first that they had seen on the path and one that was very old looking, possibly from a bygone age. Over the years it had lost a few stones from its sides. The bridge itself was intact but there was one gap at the downstream side that led straight down to the river below. The stones were covered in lichen and Astrid could see mosses growing around them. Ferns grew thickly on the steep slopes of the little river, some on trunks as tall as a person or even up to four or five times as high, their thick trunks buttressed and leaning over the water. Other ferns covered the ground beneath them and even grew on their trunks. *Yes, other types massed on the water's edge.*

The bridge was far wider than the track needed it to be. A dray and a small cart could pass each other with plenty of room to spare. The bridge itself was needed. Below it were cliffs and a steep-sided and rocky chasm filled with dense growth. The sides of the valley above the bridge were near vertical as far as Astrid could see and went around three hundred paces into the mountains before turning south.

After passing the rock upstream the ledges were both formed into smooth paths. Not only were the lower segments less formed but downstream of the rock they looked almost natural and were not obviously the entrance to anything. It suggested a deliberate act. Thord could not ride along the cliffs and climbing would be slow and dangerous. Astrid could see a faint path leading from the southern ledge up to the peak opposite—an easy ascent if you were careful, but again it would not be obvious from the road. Astrid pointed it all out to Rani and then settled down patiently to wait. *I am a hunter. I may not know exactly what I am stalking here, but waiting will tell.*

It was obvious when Rani grew restless beside her. *The bloody woman keeps shifting around; she makes noise constantly.* In time Astrid could see her patience rewarded. A man appeared, walking down the southern path. Astrid pushed Rani well down below the edge of the cliff where she could see nothing, but would not be seen either. When Rani protested Astrid reminded her, "Remember mages cannot see me easily, and he is a mage."

Rani ceased her protest and quietly admitted that, in the brief time before she was below the ridge, she had sensed the same.

Astrid noticed that, just like Rani, the man showed no caution as he moved, and seemed more concerned with his footing than anything else. If he had paid attention to what was around him he might have sensed the magic that Rani bore as she had sensed his. He soon reached the faint upward path and began his ascent up the cliff face.

"How did you know he was a mage?" whispered Rani.

"He wears town clothes in bright colours and although he wears a sword, it flaps around his legs nearly tripping him as if he were unused to it. He also carries wands, like you and your girlfriend wear, and almost as many as Bianca has knives. Lastly, he moves about as surely as you do. He has paid more attention to books than to woodcraft." She chuckled. "He tripped and nearly fell then...He had to grab onto the rock...Now he is looking at his hands. They would be soft and he may have skinned them...He is climbing again...No caution...He isn't even looking around...It looks like he expects to see nothing and is just doing this, a chore, because he was told to...He is at the top...He is very unfit. He is out of breath...Now he is taking something from a belt pouch. It is a telescope such as we use sometimes on the ships...He is using it to look at the track below him...idiot...he would see the track clearer without the scope...it is close enough...Now he is looking out over the forest...and to the north...and south...he probably seeks the smoke of campfires...he looks at the sky all around. Now he puts the telescope away...he is getting something else out of another pouch. I don't know what it is, but he is slowly turning around and looking at it, not at the surrounds. You had better hope that your spell works if it detects magic...it must, he just pointed it straight here and showed no reaction, but I felt the prickly sense. Now he is pointing it at the path below him. I will bet that he is checking to see if there is a spell in place. Now he points it at a different spot. Now he is pointing it below us...and again at a different spot...and again. There seem to be more spots on this side that he is checking. I noted where he pointed on the other side. I think that I will be able to find them...Now he puts the device away and is taking a look around. I wouldn't like to go hunting anything dangerous with him—he looks at all the wrong spots...Now he is going back down…His eyes are on the path only…one hand on the rock beside him…I will bet that they used to have someone up there all of the time, when they had more people. I think that I can see a small shelter built behind the lookout spot. Now they probably only check it a few times a day…If all those that are left are as bad at bush craft as this one is, a snow tiger cub could sneak up on all of them. If we pull back a bit up the track and hide, then I can take a day or two and I am sure that I can find a way in for the rest of you."

Rani thought for a moment demonstrated by her furrowed brow. "Good idea, but will you be able to find any traps that they have?"

"I will look at these ones now and see if I can see anything. How about that?"

Rani nodded and Astrid continued, "He is gone now. Which ledge do I use?"

Rani crawled clumsily up to the edge and peered over and closed her eyes and concentrated. Astrid could see her reaching a decision. "If I concentrate hard I think that I can sense magic there," she pointed, "and there…there…there…and there. Is that where he looked?"

"Yes," said Astrid.

"Well, Hulagu said we had to take the southern ledge, so the traps on that are probably only warning spells. Check the first one there. I will watch."

Astrid nodded and, putting her bow on her back and holding her spear, she headed back down to the path, making no noise as she left. She went down the slope to where she could no longer see Rani and then onto and across the bridge. She looked up the path. *If you knew it as a path it was obvious*, she thought, *but just wandering along it was less obvious…easy to miss.* Slowly Astrid moved up the southern ledge and looked up. Rani's head stuck up with no attempt to hide. She shook her head and concentrated on looking for physical traps as she moved along. She peered at the ground, the cliff and any plants growing on it. Eventually she reached the worked path behind the concealing rock and moved to where the first possible trap was. Carefully she studied the ground. To her chagrin, there was nothing that she could see. She looked up at Rani and shook her head.

Damn. She had been so sure she would be able to find something. *It looks like only a mage can sense it.* Then she had an idea. She found a loose rock on the cliff beside the track and, carrying it with her, moved back down the track. She looked up at the ridge. Rani was clearly visible. She gestured for her to get down. Eventually Rani got the idea. As the sky began to lose light it was not hard to find shadows to hide in further down the path. When she was sure that she was hidden, and with some cover in case something went wrong, she threw the rock onto the path and waited. She didn't have long to wait. A crow came winging down the valley towards where she was hidden. She drew deeper into the shadow. The bird circled the rock in the centre of the rivulet, luckily not rising high enough to see Rani. It landed on the top stone and sat there, moving its head from side to side peering down at the path. It flew down and peered at the rock and then up at the cliff. It looked all around, but didn't appear to see Astrid as she lay back against a fold in the rock. After a few minutes it gave a cry and sprang aloft, flying back up the valley.

Astrid waited for a few more minutes before moving, but it did not return, so she returned to Rani, explaining what she had done and seen to Rani's consternation. Together they went back to the others, where they were fussed over by their respective partners. *It is nice having Basil doing that...at least a little.* She noted that Theodora was covering the other mage in kisses. *It looks like she is not just going along with Rani's obsession any more. Anyone can see that it has quickly become her obsession as well. I am not sure that I have seen a couple so obviously infatuated with each other.*

Astrid set off to find a campsite for them all that she was happy with, which took until it was almost completely dark. She was pleased with what she had found and showed it off as if she had created it for the others. A thick stand of blackwoods and leatherwoods stood a hundred paces upslope from the road, tight against a small cliff. It was not until you were nearly through the stand that you realised that the cliff had an overhang fifteen paces deep and four high to give shelter from above. All of them, as well as the horses, could fit beneath the cliff and their watch had only to look out from the trees, down a talus slope that was bare except for small fallen rocks and some stunted scrub of red-stemmed mountain peppers, some bearing ripe fruit, and cheeseberries. The cave even had ledges and alcoves at the rear to sleep in. Not even the crow would see them in there and it was well back from where they could be seen from the lookout point, although the road below was not. *Someone has obviously used it in the distant past for the same purpose. There are the remains of a very old fireplace here and there are markings on some of the walls that may have been meant to be people and animals. Some were outlines of hands — all six fingers outlined clearly on most although some of the faintest — and so probably the oldest — looked very odd as they only had five fingers outlined.* Once the fire had been lit Astrid checked if it could be seen from outside and was reassured to find out that it could not.

They prepared a meal and set camp. That night, forgetting until too late that others might hear the purring, Basil and Astrid tenderly made love and held each other to sleep. The night was otherwise uneventful.

W ith the first grey light of morning just beginning to shade the sky with the promise of dawn, they broke their fast. Once they were started, Father Christopher caused much amusement by innocently asking if anyone on watch had seen any mountain lions around the camp, as he was sure that he had heard some in the night.

What did I miss? Oh my God. He is teasing me...my priest is teasing me. Astrid could feel herself blushing. "I am so sorry Father," she said contritely. *Why does it shock me more than a bit that my otherworldly cleric seems to have found an earthy side to him that has been long hidden and is just now coming out. Damn Basil, the upturned ends of his mouth tell me he picked up on it straight away.* She slapped his arm indignantly.

Before she set out to scout, this time with Thord, who was hung about with rope and various pouches, Father Christopher, who had held short prayers each day on the trail, declared that this was Krondag and before anyone went anywhere he was going to hold a full service. With the others looking on curiously he gathered her and Basil, Theodora and Stefan, and started. Astrid looked at the others. Bianca sat nearby, but apart from the other Christians. It seemed that she was unsure whether to sit with the Orthodox or with the other three. She must have eventually decided that her soul needed some consolation and, with evident trepidation, joined in on the end of the worshippers. Father Christopher said nothing but moved around slightly to include her better. It was a quick service and the whole group listened in to what he had to say in a short sermon about fighting evil, although he spoke in Latin and a few whispered translations had to take place. Even Astrid needed some help there. Once again she realised that her Latin was actually very poor. She muttered under her breath about that, but it had never mattered before. Except for blessings and benedictions, and everyone knew what to say there, services at home were mostly done in Darkspeech.

When the brief service was over, and with the sun still hidden behind the mountains, and the last stars were still in the sky to the west, Astrid and Thord grabbed a quick bite and a supply of dried food and headed off. She wanted to be in place before dawn fully arrived. The others settled in for a day or two of resting and mending. They would put the fire out well before dawn so that any accidental smoke would not betray their presence.

It was a different person who came to the lookout. This time it was Thord who was below the ridge and had to have everything relayed to him. *From his clothes and armour the new observer must be originally from Freehold. He is obviously a soldier and used to the outdoors, but from the noise he makes, no bushman. Although he is more thorough with his eyes, he is going through the same motions that the mage had and, again, not finding anything of interest. Again I can feel the funny prickly feeling. It looks like I will feel that whenever my protection works. He barely used the telescope and is obviously not expecting to see anything after his first quick scan.* He headed noisily back down the path but, instead of heading back up the valley, he turned left. When he came to the area where Astrid thought the second trap was he stopped and started checking the wall of the cliff at eye height. He obviously found something as he stopped and grunted. He then backed up before making a short run and leaping a pace and a half along the ledge. The armsman moved further down the track, again checking the rock wall before stopping and carefully leaning forward to pick up the rock Astrid had thrown. Standing erect he casually tossed the rock into the rivulet.

Having done that he turned around and moved to the upper trap, checking the wall and jumping again. Without looking back he continued up the valley, whistling tunelessly.

"We might just be able to walk in," said Astrid. "I am going to see if I can see those marks. Can you make some sort of noise if you see something?" she asked Thord.

"Will crow noise do?" he replied. "I'm no entertainer, but shepherds oft hear lot of crows."

"Good," said Astrid, as she quickly made her way down the slope and around onto the ledge. Just as she was where she thought the trap was she saw a mark. A faint 'X', almost like a fault in the stone, was visible on the rock. *How I missed it last time I do not know.* She backed up and jumped. When she landed she looked up at where Thord should be. She couldn't see him and heard nothing so she looked at the rock wall behind her. Sure enough, on the wall was another 'X' mark. More confidently she moved on to the next trap and repeated the process. She looked up. Unlike when she looked for Rani, there was still no sign of Thord. *Well, I am in now. I may as well see what lies ahead.*

She went up the path cautiously. On her right was the cliff while on her left was a drop of several paces to the fast-running rivulet. *A fall would be deadly. I suspect that, even if I could swim it wouldn't do me much good in that swift cold mountain stream. Luckily the path is wide enough.* Just before she reached the corner she started examining the rock wall beside her, but she saw no marks. The corner kept turning until it had gone through a full quadrant. Looking back, Thord was hidden from view.

Ahead she could see the cliffs opening up and she flattened herself around the rock, seeking shadows and trying to move inconspicuously while at the same time trying to look at the cliff for a mark. Her gymnastics were rewarded when, just before the opening, she noticed another 'X' mark and leapt to clear it. Again she found the second mark and continued. Suddenly, just as had been described, the valley opened up before her. The ledge led to a path, which led to some fields a hand of hundreds of paces away. Across the path, and obviously blocking the exit for stock was the prosaic sight of a wooden gate, looking exactly the same as one would find on any prosperous farm, only newer than most. *I can feel prickling. The gate must have a trap on it to detect magic.* She was careful not to touch it in case it had a trap for that as well.

Moving through the fields, and disappearing to the right, was the soldier. It looked like the village was where it was supposed to be. She couldn't see anyone else about. She carefully studied the gate. She couldn't see any traps on it, even though she knew at least one was there, but she couldn't see the other three. She felt the rock. *The cliff walls around the gate are very—indeed suspiciously—smooth. From the look of the walls they must had been smoothed...polished...with magic. There is no way over the gate without touching it or flying...and flying might set off the magic detection*. From here she could see that the ledge on the other side came around the corner, turned again abruptly in a promise of a cave into the cliff, and then ended in a smooth wall of stone. It was a dead end. The traps on it might be for something far more than just giving a warning. She took another look around, including, carefully, over the edge of the path into the water. *There is no way to go any further without touching the gate and without doubt that would at least set off an alarm. It seems that we will not get into the valley this way.* Carefully she retraced her route and re-joined an obviously relieved Thord. She described what she had seen.

"Perhaps I could climb t'wall near t'gate," Thord suggested.

"The wall is polished as smooth as glass. You would need to fly, and I think that they would detect that. When I was near the gate I had a funny feeling. I think it was my spell protecting me from being detected. We need to find another way in. Their village is only a few hundred paces south of the pass. There must be another way to get to it if we are careful."

"Well, let's move south'n' try'n' find it," suggested Thord.

Astrid nodded, and they moved off down the road. As far as they could see the way up the hill was difficult, more difficult than it appeared from below. *We would be in plain view from the lookout.* Eventually they chose a likely spot to start climbing.

"When they had more people and could have someone there all of the time, this would have been impossible," she said, when they were having a break. "It makes me think that they may have overlooked it now. Mind you, we need to keep an eye out for places to hide when they come to check."

"It's near midday," said Thord. "Do you t'ink t'at someone'll come t'en?"

"I would," replied Astrid.

"Well we can rest behind t'ere'n' see." Thord pointed out a small outcrop of rock with some small upland bushes with tiny sharp-pointed leaves on them. A last few tiny pink flowers lingered on some and a few others had a couple of different kinds of pink flowers, smaller than a grain of wheat. They moved to it as quickly as they could and Thord found a place where he could lie down out of sight. *Actually he is more resting than lying down. He is closer to standing as he is to being horizontal, but he has a firm footing and I can still just see the lookout position three hundred paces away.* They had a while to wait as the sun climbed into the sky. Both were drowsing a bit in a rare burst of sunshine through the grey sky, when a watcher appeared.

"He is here...the mage," whispered Astrid, giving Thord a nudge. Anxiously she looked north to where her lover was camped, but, although she could see the wind disturbing the tops of the trees in front of the cliff, there was no betraying sign of the camp. The mage went through the rituals of watching and headed back down the path. *We are at a slight westward projection of the mountains and a watcher, with the right equipment, should be able to see or detect a full day's travel north and south. It looks like the spells that Theodora cast have worked, or else we have been lucky—otherwise the watchers would not be so casual. I wonder if they even know of the ambush attempt on us.* She waited a few minutes before saying, "Let's go on. Do you think that we can get the others up this way?"

"I could ride up here," said Thord dismissively. "T'ey should be able to climb it, even t'mages."

It turned out that they didn't have much further to climb. The fold that Thord had been hiding in led towards a small dip in the rock wall behind them. The cleft they were following had a large slab of rock, seemingly split from the cliff beside it, which had fallen over it. By chance it formed a sort of small cave or tunnel several paces long and two wide. Although it was three paces high on one side it sloped quickly to the ground on the other forming a steep lean-to of stone. *Perhaps the tunnel might get them under any field that may be around the valley. It might not even be visible from below in the valley itself...at least the saddle that it forms has room in it for our whole group to rest in.* Astrid looked around. *It is even out of sight from the lookout and from below on the path. Unless the crow, or whoever sends it, flies directly over us, we won't be seen here. Even if they fly over, the saddle is deep enough that, unless they are using detection spells, the shadows and the fallen rocks will probably still hide us.*

Making Thord stay well back in the saddle, Astrid moved forward cautiously, looking for traps and waiting to see if anything made her prickle. *It is not likely. If the watch point were manned no one would be able to reach this place without being seen or detected. I seem to be right. I cannot see or feel anything untoward.* Getting close to the edge ahead she carefully put down her spear, took her bow off her back, and went down on to her stomach and inched slowly forward like a stalking cat.

Peering over the edge, but trying to remain in shade, her face took on the satisfied smile of a predatory cat seeing a fat unsuspecting prey sitting complacent beneath it. Directly below her was a small village sitting in a wide cleft in the rock wall. Its several rows of houses, each with a path extending around the valley, were built against and carved into the rock, and extended up both sides and the end of the small valley. The highest roof of the settlement was only twenty paces below her. From what she could see steps led from one row to the other. She could readily see that most of the buildings looked to be derelict and unused. Some of the lowest row had repairs done to them, work obviously carried out by an amateur—and one who was poorly equipped and didn't care. In the centre was a paved area with a spring surfacing at one end in a walled pool of water, emerging from the rock. From this spring arose a gentle splashing sound of constant water. Where it went to from there she could not see. *Perhaps into a drain.* People walked below her and she could see the watcher mage that she had seen from the gate coming slowly up a path from the fields.

Astrid settled down to observe the village with the patience of a hunter who stalks her prey. Most of the people had no weapons, not even knives. What is more most of them were women and girls, pretty ones, some even children, none looking happy and none of the children were playing. *These must be the brigand's slaves.* She could easily see a fortification across the mouth of the cleft. It was only a small wall about four paces high with a parapet facing out. It had a gate with two door parts in it set in a slightly higher and thicker section of stone in the centre. A watchman armed with a bow stood on the walkway below the top. Although it was made for defence from without, interestingly he was watching the village and the people in it. He didn't even glance outwards and he walked with an arrow nocked, but not drawn. *He seems to be more worried about rebellion than external attack.* Beyond the wall she could see where a number of stone walled fields were laid out. *From what little I know about such things it looks like someone in the village knows something at least about agriculture; a lot more than I do at any rate. I cannot even say what was growing. One large field seems to have grain about to be harvested and another has the grain already taken in and it is now only stubble with sheep grazing in it. Two other fields of around the same size have other things growing in them...I am not a farmer...green things and two more lie fallow and have cows in them. There were some fruit trees in an orchard and what looked like a hen house beside it, the birds still inside for the night. I can hear them. There are other signs of a prosperous farm. Beyond them, on the slopes that led away up the valley are a larger flock of sheep. From what I can see the usable area is at least as large as the fields that lie around Wolfneck, and this far south they will have far less snow to worry about. This could be a rich valley if they wanted.*

She saw a group of women slaves going out of the gate carrying tools, dressed just in very short leather skirts and aprons, their breasts bare in the chill air. A mounted archer...a Khitan...followed them. He was staying well away from their tools and she could see that he had a whip coiled around the horn of his saddle; a couple of women showed marks that could be from it. It seemed that the brigands kept tight control over their people. There was a big building like a tavern or a large house...another was possibly a granary or storehouse. There was a large barn outside the wall...a woman was driving pigs and geese out of it towards the fields, another released the chickens under the trees...there was a very big stable inside and two buildings built like barracks or perhaps a many-roomed sleeping hall and another that might be a public hall. One of the barracks buildings had its windows boarded up from the outside and was probably where the slaves were kept. The other would be where brigands stayed. There were also more than a few hands of houses and workshops. The houses are all derelict. Some of the workshops looked to be in better repair. They are the ones the skilled slaves use. She noticed that the few unarmed men all wore leg-irons or chains, so they were unlikely to be able to run either far or fast. The large building was finer and in better repair than the others. The mage had gone into it. It was a two storey building with a small balcony built under each window. Along the front of it was a long wooden veranda with a roof of slate above it. It had a guard in full mail sitting on a broad bench outside under the cover. Beside him was a helm and, leaning against the wall beside him, a great axe.

The main building was far enough away that she could see under the veranda roof. The guard was tall and blonde with braided hair and beard. *He looks like one of my people.* She looked closer. *His hands seem to have claws like a bear's on them, over the fingers. He must be from*

Wolfneck. Astrid reflected on this. *When I was very young there was a man called Thorkil who had looked like that...He had been outlawed ten?...twelve? years ago. I was a child then. What had he done?...How could I have forgotten?...A girl a few years younger than I was had disappeared while picking mushrooms. She was far too young to have been taken for marriage and the village had been in turmoil. A few days later Thorkil had also disappeared and men had gone out to bring him back but had failed.* If any had been in a position to see her, Astrid's teeth were showing more now, but her smile had completely disappeared. *I should kill him now. A person like him would explain why some of the girls below were so young.*

He sat there stroking his beard, looking at a young dusky-skinned girl fetching water. The girl saw him staring at her. A look of fear appeared briefly on her face and she quickly finished what she was doing and scurried out of sight.

I will try and kill him myself...or maybe to capture him and let Bianca do it. If what she has said is right then Bianca has some good ideas in that regard. Having made that compact with herself she returned to watching the rest of the village. Astrid lay there all afternoon counting heads and relaying what she saw back to Thord. Thord busied himself staring at the ground around him. He said that he was working out how to firmly fix rope so as to lower people onto the roofs below. Being a shepherd apparently gave him a lot of patience as well.

Towards the end of the day the guard on the wall rang a bell and the fieldworkers returned with their guard behind them. The gate guard counted them in and they immediately put their tools in a shed, which was locked afterwards. *It seems that these people are really afraid of their slaves in a way that no-one I have heard of is. Most slaves I know of have free run of their owner's houses and all that I have ever seen carry knives just like everyone else. One at home in Wolfneck even has a sword...but he will be freed soon and will surely settle into the village rather than go to his old home.*

Soldiers started coming out of the barracks and other buildings and slaves were gathering in the street in groups, and soldiers started to count them. Apart from the guard on the wall and Thorkil, there were three soldiers. Two men in houpelandes and one dressed like those from the Caliphate came out of the mage's house onto a raised platform; one of them was the man they had seen at the lookout. She also noticed the soldier they had seen at the watch point come out of the other large house. He didn't join the rest of the soldiers, instead went over and chatted to the three mages, all of them looking down on the others. Finally, emerging out of the same large building as the soldier came a dwarf. *This must be Dharmal, the leader of the brigands that the Khitan had talked about.* He was followed down to the platform by Thorkil, with his helmet on and his axe over his shoulder. Astrid could now see that he had a brace of small axes at his belt. His hands might look more like a bear's claws when they were clenched, but they had to be free to grasp the handles of his weapons. The soldiers came up to the Freeholder and reported to him. He, in turn, reported to Dharmal. They chatted briefly and then the man in armour turned around. From where she lay she could hear him softly but clearly, "After t'selection get on with your duties, t'ose who ha' no duties go to your quarters," he said in Hindi. He looked down at the soldiers. "T'ose off duty, if you a want a girl, get one."

A soldier headed off to the wall and the man that was there already came down when he arrived. It seemed that he and two others would be off duty. Astrid realised that one was female, while another was Thorkil. The three went over towards the slaves who waited in rows. They stood there in a dejected fashion with their eyes to the ground. Thorkil went straight to the clump of little girls, who all shrank back from him. He strode up and grabbed one. *A southern girl, perhaps the one he had been looking at earlier; at any rate, from her black hair and darker brown skin, she was from Haven.* He pointed at the barracks. *The girl looks terrified and the relief on the faces of the others is evident, even at this range.* The woman, who was dressed as a man in the clothes and armour of Freehold, chose a girl who looked like she came from the Caliphate. *That is curious, that the woman she chose looked as scared as the little girl did.* The other soldier, possibly also a woman, chose a Havenite girl. *She actually looks pleased.* The three chosen ones moved towards what appeared to be the soldier's quarters, while most of the others headed for the other barrack building. A guard, who reached up and removed a bunch of keys from near the door, followed them. *He must be going to lock them inside.*

Some slaves went to other buildings on their own account. This group included the men, and a small group went towards another building beside the main one, which appeared to be a large kitchen.

Another guard was going around the small buildings, locking them. *I wonder if those who are locked in will be fed.* The captain was walking out of the gate. *It must be his turn to be the watcher again.* The mages and the dwarf returned to their dwellings. At the last minute one of the mages turned and went over to the slave barracks. He disappeared inside and came back with a woman. Although she was not dressed like one, from her hair and the shape of her eyes Astrid had a feeling that she was a Khitan. The girl followed behind him by several paces, with her hands clasped and her eyes on the ground.

"Three mages, the dwarf and six soldiers. If there are no others and we strike fast then we have the advantage and can take them like a baby seal on the ice," Astrid said to Thord.

"If we strike and t'ere are more hidden somewhere we may have trouble," Thord replied. "We need to watch 'em for a day. If t'ere're others around we should find out during t'at time."

"Perhaps you are right," Astrid reluctantly agreed. "Now we look for ways to get to them. We must be able to kill some without the others noticing. Depending on how good their watch is I am sure that we can all get down onto the roof below us."

"Easy," said Thord. "If t'ey cannot climb t'emself, I can lower 'em from here. T'ere is plenty to brace against. All t'same, once we go in, we'd better be sure of success. Retreat wouldn't be easy."

They settled down to observe. Once the soldier's leader had returned the gate was closed and a bar put across the back of it. Under guard, food was delivered to the slaves, the barracks and the mages. Shortly after this the kitchen slaves were taken to their barracks and then, once the dishes were picked up by some of the little girls, taken into what must be a kitchen and they emerged and were locked up, the brigand village had settled into its nightly routine.

The leader of the soldiers had the first watch.

"They must be very short on men if he is drawing duty. They still have to stand guard during the day as well, when the slaves are out and about, so they must all be very tired," said Astrid. Tired or not, a series of sharp noises came from below, followed by short and pained cries, subsiding to muffled sobbing. It emanated loudly from the soldier's barracks, showing that at least one of the brigands was still taking cruel pleasure from a slave.

The single armed guard did not seem to have a fixed post. He wandered into the guardroom beside the gate, through the village and the slave's barracks, checking locks and barred windows. They climbed the wall and looking out and sometimes sat down near the front of the building below them, from where they could see the front of all the buildings in the village. Not once did he look up to where the watchers waited. Lights went out in the buildings, the last just before the guard changed. When he had roused the next person the guard leader stayed inside the guardroom, rather than return to the building he shared with the dwarf, and where the mages had also retired for the night. The guardroom must be where the guards on duty slept.

The night was quiet and Astrid and Thord were able to take turns to sleep and eat. Luckily for them, although the sky was covered completely in cloud, there was no rain. So, although it was chilly, at least they were not wet. Thord commented on the cold, but Astrid was dismissive of calling these warm southern nights chilly. A wind, blowing through the gap from the west, kept off any frost. That was more than enough.

Once the sky began to lighten the process of shutting the village down was reversed. The kitchen slaves were let out to begin work and gradually the village returned to life. The three slaves who had spent the night with soldiers crossed the street to their barracks. Two were naked and carrying clothes—the little girl and the Caliphate woman. The latter showed marks around her wrists and on her body and legs. She had been beaten hard enough to draw blood. It must have been her cries that had echoed loud last night. The Havenite woman stooped and picked up the little girl and carried her. The girl immediately threw her arms around the woman's neck and started sobbing on her shoulder. The Caliphate woman was obviously stiff and sore, but she walked erect and proud, as if she were fully clothed, ignoring comments from a guard as to what he would have her do the next time he had her.

A different mage went to the lookout—the one who had taken a slave to bed. The slave girl followed him out of the building, walking with her eyes down and hands clasped, and moved quickly down the street to the barracks.

"I think they are waiting for reinforcements," said Astrid. "There are too few of them to do anything and they need more men. If we can get them now, and then get their new men, then we will have removed this menace completely."

"You may be right," said Thord. "T'ey seem to be just pickin' at t'walls rather t'an doing serious digging."

That must be a Dwarven expression.

The guard commander was waiting when the lookout returned. He asked a question, Astrid could not make out what it was, but it was rewarded with the shake of the mage's head. They talked briefly and quietly before both going into Dharmal's building.

"See," said Astrid. "He was waiting to see if their reinforcements were arriving. They aren't coming now, but they are expected. Do we watch further or do we go back to the others now? Even a day's delay might be important."

"Let's go now," replied Thord. "T'ey have just done t'eir check, so we know t'at no-one is in sight. If'n we come back t'is afternoon we can attack tonight. Even if'n t'others arrive later today t'ey will be tired." Quickly they packed up and prepared to move down the slope. Before they went down, Thord, as quietly as he could with a muffled hammer and a cloth over the target, drove an iron spike hard into a crevice and left his rope under cover. This is where he would need it next anyway and it was better to do this work with the daily noise from down the hill in the village masking the blows. Astrid, still watching, could see no sign from below that anyone had noticed what the dwarf had done above them.

Chapter IV

Father Christopher

While he was clearing away after his service, Thord and Astrid had left. When he was finished it a watch had been set up by those left behind, with one person looking each way from the trees. Christopher went and peered out. It seemed that they could see quite some way to the north. At least an hour's march was visible in parts as the road weaved in and out, up and down. Less could be seen to the south—they could see just past the bridge—but if anyone arrived from that direction, they would be seen. Due to the shape of the rock they couldn't quite see the lookout, or the entrance to the valley itself, but they could see the track. *I suppose that is good. Anyone coming south along the track will have to pass within easy range of even my sling.* He went back inside the cave. The rest had set about making themselves at home. Ayesha even cleared a small patch of rock and washed it for her prayer rug. It was facing east. They only had to leave the cave to gather food for the horses and to fetch water. He realised that Astrid would have looked for water and there was a stream only a short distance away. About two hundred paces away, down slope to the north, and further back into the cliff, a small waterfall splashed into a pool screened by ferns and bushes and then wandered under the road to probably eventually join the larger stream. Basil attended to washing clothes, unconsciously digging into Astrid's pack as well as his own and the mages'. Father Christopher noticed that Basil kept looking south, to where Astrid was, and went over to him.

"Don't worry," he said. "I have travelled with her. She moves like a cat and seems able to disappear in the woods. She will be fine."

"What makes you think that I am worried?" asked Basil.

Father Christopher nearly laughed out loud. *Try as I might, I am not used to dissembling. My amusement must be evident on my face.*

Basil realised that his own dissembling was useless and continued.

"All right, I am worried. I have never had anyone that I worried about like that before. I mean, I know that she is capable and will probably be fine, but I still feel worried. Is that normal? Does that mean that I love her?"

"You're asking me?" asked Christopher with a smile on his face. "I have been raised in a monastery most of my life. What would I know? Mind you, I think that I now know why they make priests marry. If I was in love and married, then I might be able to answer you." Just then Bianca walked past with two leather buckets of water for the horse lines. "Bianca," asked Father Christopher playfully, "you might know more than me on this. If you love someone, do you worry if they are away from you?"

Bianca looked stunned. "I wouldn't know." *Is that a trace of bitterness in her voice?* "I have never had anyone to miss. The nuns, my horses...and Hulagu...as a brother you understand...are as close as I have ever come to loving anyone and having anyone care about me. Anyone else I have always lost, so I try not to get close to anyone."

"Don't you miss your parents?" asked Father Christopher curiously.

"I never knew them. How could I miss them?" replied Bianca.

Now it is certain that there is bleakness in her voice. I wonder what I could say to ease her pain. "I knew very little of mine. They died when I was only a baby," said Father Christopher regretfully, "but I still miss them. I miss the boys that I grew up with. I even miss my teachers." *I surprised myself a bit when I said that, but it is true.* He said, "Basil, you are lucky. Perhaps one day I might be like you and have a woman to love. I think that I am jealous." *I am getting more and more taken aback with myself in finding out just how serious I am sounding.* "Perhaps the Abbot was right and I do belong in the world. Oh well, if it is to be I will trust in God to provide me with a woman whom I can share love with." *This is all getting too serious. I need to try and lighten the mood a little.* "I think that I will have to spend a lot more time on prayer and contemplation about this matter now."

Basil laughed at his tone, and even Bianca smiled. Father Christopher went away smiling. *I know that I have done my work. Basil now felt somewhat better—as long as his woman comes back. I am surprised to discover that I really meant what I said.* He shook himself and settled down with his prayer book to rehearse a few prayers that he never had to actually use seriously before. *Battle is coming against the forces of evil and, if I fail, then people who I already care about and who are in my care will die. My role will largely be not to attack, but to heal them in spirit and body and so keep people alive and in God's grace.*

Hulagu

*E**ven though I am not on horseback, it is a fine afternoon to be on guard. The last warm days before winter are always to be treasured. I give thanks to the sky spirits for this sun.* Around him he could hear the others, in their own way preparing for the upcoming fight. *I notice that the mages have disappeared into an alcove of the cave for a while and everyone is pretending not to notice or to hear anything.* When they emerged and Stefan had taken over from him on watch, Rani took him aside and started making him work on mental exercises. *Why did I suggest this?* He sat cross-legged and thought about having a blank mind. *My sister is interrupting my thought. Under Ayesha's guidance she is throwing her knives over and over again. Bianca is determined to be as good as she could be. Now she is learning which of the knives seem to better than the others, whether due to workmanship or magic. These are the ones she will rely on the most.* Rani eventually released him and then it was a time for blades to be sharpened and arrows checked as they all sat around and chatted about their past.

Soon it was time for the Christian priest to hold yet another service. *Doesn't his God ever get tired of being talked to?* This time Hulagu noticed that his sister sat with the other Christians from the start and the Hindi mage came with the Christians and sat holding hands with Theodora, although she didn't say anything or join in. He moved off to take a watch as the day passed. Soon it was dark and the night proved to be as quiet as the afternoon, cold but with no rain.

The next morning started the same. Ayesha and Bianca went off to bring water up the slope and were returning when suddenly there was movement on the road to the north. Hulagu called out to them, "Hurry — and keep close to the cliff. Horsemen are coming from the north." The camp went into a burst of activity. *I can only catch glimpses of a hand of riders. They are still a long way away. We were very cautious coming along the same road.* "Coming as fast as that, it is unlikely they are innocents. What is more they are all armed as if they are warriors. Two are Khitan, one a Havenite and the rest are Freehold. I think they are headed towards their village in the valley and want to get there as quickly as they can."

He looked at Rani. *I am not the only one to do that.* There was a pause for Rani to realise this and think. "We should stop them," she said. "Of course there is a risk, but if they make it into the village then it will make our task there harder." She looked around and paused for a little while longer in thought. She pointed at the rocky slope. "I think from here we can take them all with either bow or sling with no risk."

"That will not stop their horses," said Bianca. "They might return home on their own, or stay around and be seen by their watchman. I can be down there quickly, with Sirocco and Firestorm, and round them up."

"But if one makes it through us, then you may be at risk," said Rani.

"If I go as well, then we will be safe," said Basil. "Besides, I have no long range weapons. I only throw my darts and I cannot easily reach them from up here."

"Can you get down in time?" asked Rani.

"Watch us," replied Bianca, springing towards the cave where the horses were and reaching for a saddle. Basil checked his weapons and then began moving down the slope without waiting for her return. *He was on foot. Bianca would not be.*

"Now go quickly," said Rani, when Bianca had come back. "Stay hidden until you hear us attack and only fire if you are needed. Your job is the horses."

Hulagu left his sentry post and moved further forward to the trees above the slope. Father Christopher and Stefan followed him. Behind him he heard a kiss. *That must be the mages.* "No magic," he heard Rani say. "Someone might feel it if we use it this close to their lair, so we both use bows only and make sure they are plain heads so there is no loud noise." Theodora made no reply, but he could hear them going back to the cave. By the time they had joined the others with bows Bianca and Basil had already met at the bottom of the slope and had moved towards a dip in the road and some trees. *They should be able to take cover there.*

The five that were left on the rise gained their positions. To the north the riders were just disappearing into some trees a hand of hundreds of paces away. To the south he could see that the two people had moved off the rocky slope and were already headed into some degree of hiding. *I can see them, but someone moving quickly along the path probably will not. The rise and fall of the road will see to that.* From behind him Rani spoke again: "Hulagu, you can surely hide better than I can. You give the order to fire. The rest of us will stay concealed until you say so."

Hulagu nodded and moved to a better spot. The rest went to ground behind trees and lapsed into silence. Gradually the keen of hearing would be aware of the sound of approaching horses and soon all could surely hear them. *Getting close to their home the bandits are growing careless and are paying no attention to either caution or concealment. They must have been safe here in their village for quite a while and perhaps these riders don't even know of their band's losses on the plains. Perhaps they expect to be under observation, which they are, but not as they would have wished.* The sounds they made grew louder. Hulagu peered around his tree. *These riders are riding for speed and comfort, not for battle. Their horses look tired. They must have ridden hard, perhaps even through the night.* The mail was held up from the front of the Havenite's helm and all of their shields hung from their saddles or backs rather than being on their arms. The first rider approached the rock he had fixed in his mind. "Get ready," he said softly. Four on the slope stood and took aim from behind their trees. Father Christopher had to stand clear to swing his sling.

Rani

Still speaking softly Hulagu said, "Loose". Four arrows and a bullet streaked down the slope while the people who sent them reloaded. All of the missiles hit. *Karikeya, God of Battle, I didn't co-ordinate our fire. I have made another mistake.* Three shafts hit the Khitan at the front and he immediately slumped sidewise, falling out of his saddle, dead before he knew it. The third rider, the Havenite, was riding with his camail held up at the front and sides and had been rewarded with a shaft into his neck. She had shot at him. It wasn't fatal and he began screaming incoherently and trying to claw it out. The last rider, a Freeholder, was leading the spare horses. By accident or design Father

Christopher's sling bullet hit him on the helm. Its force meant that it didn't need to penetrate and the rider slumped forward onto his pommel, dead or unconscious.

The second rider, also a Khitan, reached back and started to remove a shield from where it hung off his saddle as he looked wildly around. The fourth and fifth riders, both Freeholders, did not hesitate. Both dug their heels into the flanks of their horses, spurring them forward. The Khitan located the figures on the slope above him just as the second flight of arrows came in. A shaft took him in the eye and another at the base of the throat. He toppled backwards off his horse, his foot catching in his stirrup. Rani hit the fourth rider in the head. She muttered a curse as the shot glanced off his helm. Another shaft hit the fifth bandit in the body. The rider had a steel-armoured torso, but leaning forward to spur his horse on had exposed his armpit and the shaft took him there, but it did not stop him. Father Christopher's sling was slower than the bows, but surer in its effects. Out of mercy he had aimed at the wounded Havenite, who stopped screaming abruptly as the bullet took him on the temple.

The two surviving riders spurred out of the melee of plunging horses, trying to break out of the killing ground. Arrows hit them, others missed. None did vital damage. Suddenly, ahead of the bandits a mounted figure and one on foot appeared twenty paces from them. Rani noted that Basil had thrown a martobulli as he appeared and this took the lead rider in the face as he leant forward. He toppled, briefly clutching futilely at his face. The second rider's horse stopped dead as Bianca urged her horses to rear in front of him. The rider had to clutch at his horse to avoid falling off and this momentary stillness was all the archers on the ridge needed to drive home several shafts and bring him down.

I haven't had to say anything once it all started and now it was over.

There were no more targets to fire at as Rani lowered her bow and watched the two below at work. Bianca now had to calm her horses which, excited by the familiar sound and smell of battle, were primed to fight, before she could round up those of the bandits...but it mattered little. Sirocco and Firestorm blocked the way forward for the bandit's horses, rearing up and stopping their headlong rush dead. Basil moved forward and started to gather up loose reins as the rest of the ambushers came down the slope towards them. Two of the horses were pack animals, and there was a spare mount as well. The bodies were thrown over saddles and the arrows that had missed targets were gleaned. Rani got her lover to use her senses to make sure that no magic item was left lying around in the killing ground that might be sensed by the watcher and his device. Blood was soon covered up by dust and dirt as Hulagu was the last up the slope. As he backed up he swept at the ground with a small bush he had broken off to use like a broom. *I would not have thought of that, but it seems that this sort of thing is normal for the Khitan.*

By the time they had finished their task the horses had reached the top of the slope and were moving behind the trees. Hulagu resumed a watch while the others laid out the bodies behind the screen of trees. Stefan and Basil quickly and pragmatically started to empty the pouches of the bandits and strip their bodies of anything that might be useful. They put the money and valuables in one heap, their weapons in another, and other items in a third.

"Basil," Theodora said in a shocked tone in Darkspeech, "you cannot do that. It is robbing the dead." Rani realised that she had been thinking more or less the same. *Touching the dead is bad enough. Robbing them...*

"Pardon me, my lady," replied Basil, in the same tongue. "They don't need any of this now," he waved his hand towards the growing piles, "and we might. If we were at home this would all go into Treasury's coffers. Here *we* are the Treasury. Anyway, it was probably all stolen in the first place and we should be sure of what they had."

"That is right," added Father Christopher, changing the conversation to what passed as their common language of Hindi so that all could understand, straightening up from where he was saying prayers over the dead for their souls. "These men are bandits. Look at the money. There are coins from everywhere, some I don't even know, and their jewellery must be looted. Some are obviously meant for women and the styles are all different—even I can see that. See that cup," he pointed at a large ornate gold vessel with an even larger base. It had jewels inlaid on it, gaps where some were now missing and there was a large dent in it, "That is a chalice stolen from a church—not one of ours—I think it is from Freehold. If you have qualms about taking any of this then I suggest that you take your share and give it as alms for the poor. Of course, Astrid says that I am very poor and so is Bianca so you could just give it to us," he said cheekily. *Now that it is put like that...I suppose at home we would do the same.* The priest smiled and his infectious good humour broke the mood. Grins appeared all around and they resumed their tasks.

Once the horses had been stripped of their gear Bianca took them back to where the other horses were tethered. They had been restive near the bodies, but calmed down near the other horses and under her ministration. *She only has to tend one arrow wound and some other minor cuts before she can feed and water them.* Theodora and Rani began to check the bandit's gear for magic while others dragged the bodies down the talus-covered southern slope, away from the water, and out of sight of the watch point, and buried them under rocks so that they soon disappeared.

Just as the burial party were returning up the hill for the last time from their grisly task Hulagu softly called out from his watch, "I can see Thord."

"Just Thord?" asked Basil quickly and with worry plain in his voice.

"Yes, no sign of Astrid...wait he is well in the clear now...I can see Astrid now, I couldn't see her when she was moving in the woods. She must be a very good hunter."

They finished stowing away the useful items. *Ayesha is correcting me on one of the potions?* Rani sniffed again. *She seems to be right and I was wrong on my first guess. Hmmm.* It seemed that the bandits carried several different healing draughts as well as a large supply of dried betterberries. Several of the weapons they carried were magically enhanced as well. Those using horse bows were eager to divide up their arrows.

The group gathered on top of the slope as Thord and Astrid approached. Astrid paused briefly to look at where the bodies were buried before resuming her climb. As she neared the top she asked, "Who did you bury?"

"Bandits," said Basil, before losing his reserve and rushing down to greet her. *He has stopped on the slope so that they are the same height and seems to be looking her over to make sure she is unwounded. She is doing the same. Now they are reaching out and their heads are moving forward, so did hers. They are kissing. They are an odd couple, but they do seem fond of each other.*

Thord kept trudging up the slope before saying, a little breathlessly, "It is so much easier climbing when you are on a sheep. Better get back under cover. It is near midday and time for t'eir watcher to look around."

"We weren't expecting you yet," said Rani.

"We found a way in to t'em," replied Thord, "'n' we t'ought it best to get back to you so t'at we can attack quickly. T'ey are very low on numbers now, but seem to be expecting reinforcements at any time."

"They can expect all they want, but they won't arrive. You just passed their bodies," stated Rani. "Now, let us have something to eat and we can find out what you know and then work out what to do next."

Once they had exchanged their news, Rani concluded, "So, if we leave now then we can be in place to attack them tonight. Correct?" Astrid nodded. "And we can get into the village easily from the gap?" This time Thord nodded at her. "So how do we make the attack? We need to take out the watch quietly first, then neutralise the mages and then the soldiers. They are on their home ground and if we use magic on the watch the mages will probably have a chance to react." Rani looked around. *Everyone has gone quiet.*

"With Allah's grace I can get into the village quietly and take out the watch," Ayesha said in muted tones into the silence.

"Aren't you a runaway slave dancer?" asked Rani suspiciously. *Having been corrected on the nature of that potion I am no longer entirely sure that this is the case, unless the Caliphate woman is a very unusual slave indeed.*

"I am," Ayesha replied, "but it amused my master to train me in some other skills as well. It was by using them that I was able to escape the Caliphate. Get me above the village with a rope and I will get you the watch. If I can take a rope and a grapple with me I might even be able to get into the mage's building—but I won't know that until I see it."

Rani studied her, weighing up the slight figure in a new light. She thought about what she knew about the mountain realm that the girl hailed from for a moment before saying anything. "I notice that you pray even more than our good Father. Are you temple trained?" she asked softly. She looked around. *Only Ayesha seems to grasp the significance of that question. The rest are just looking blank at the exchange. Mind you, Basil always looks blank.*

Rani looked hard at the Caliphate girl's face. *That pause before answering is all I really needed.* Ayesha now nodded. "I am," she answered softly.

Rani nodded back and just said, "We will talk more later." She said to the others confidently, "Ayesha will take care of the guards." *Now the others look surprised at my more assured tone.* "Now for what the rest of us will do...Basil ..."

"I will be looking after my lady," interrupted Basil. "She will be casting spells and will not want to be interfered with by rude people with swords."

"I was actually about to suggest that. You are ill suited for open combat with your shortswords, but anything coming at her is likely to be close, and that you can deal with. For the same reason I will be keeping Bianca with me. Her daggers are meant for close work as well." She was turning from person to person now. *As the battle leader I need to be confident. Now, if the plan survives first contact all will be well.* "Father Christopher, you are our only healer. We need to keep you safe and you might not be able to defend yourself down in the village, so you should stay on the ledge. You can use your sling from there. Astrid, your spear is not suited to this work in buildings, but your bow is still needed. You can also stay on the ledge and keep an eye on things. You will need to keep a sharp eye out, as it will be your bow that will guard our backs and stop our enemy from moving around between buildings. Thord can come with us. Hulagu, you are more used to fighting mounted, but this time you will have to take Stefan and be responsible for their soldiers. There are six of them, as well as their leaders so, even if Ayesha can take all of the watch, you will still be outnumbered. There are two or three mages for Theodora and myself as well, so we must take advantage of as much surprise as we can. Astrid...do you think that we could get the slaves to fight?"

"Some might, if they were sure we were winning, but I doubt it," replied Astrid. "Most are women and young girls, undoubtedly chosen for their appearance rather than for a skill with weapons. There are many more of them here than there are bandits, but they do not seem to resist and they obey orders meekly—even when they are treated very badly."

Rani thought for a moment. "Then we will only take time to free them if a group has eliminated all the threats that are likely to come on them. Now, does anyone have any comments or questions?"

Bianca spoke up. "What about the horses?"

"We have to leave them tethered here with enough food and water and hope that they do not break lose and we lose them," replied Rani. "We cannot take them with us and we have too few people to leave someone behind to look after them."

"My horses do not like tethers. I never use them...and what about wild beasts coming and attacking them?"

Hulagu laughed and even Bianca glaring at him didn't stop him grinning. "Your horses," he said with an amused tone in his voice, "they may be pets to you, but normal people...even bandits...are likely to be scared of them and anything less than a dragon is likely to feel the same way. If you tell them to stay put and guard the rest of your dowry herd, I am sure they will somehow understand you. I am almost willing to bet that they will find a few more horses to add to your collection if we are away long enough."

Bianca tried to look indignant and failed.

"Then it is settled," said Rani. "Get ready, bring up fodder and water and then we will set out."

Chapter V

Rani

I *have never heard them all so silent as they don their armour and make other preparations.* She saw, as she was helping her lover armour up, that they were each turning to one another to be checked for anything loose or that might rattle or catch on things. Rani carefully noted that, after she had prayed, Ayesha had opened her pack and donned a pair of soft boots that she had not previously worn, that looked as if they would make no noise when moving. She changed her normal headscarf and veil to one that was much darker in colour and showed an irregular pattern in dark grey. She had also put on soft leather gloves and looped a light rope over her shoulders, adding a grapnel from Thord's saddlebag and winding cloth around its prongs to soften any sound it made in a very professional manner. She strapped scabbards with throwing knives onto her forearms and thighs outside her clothes.

She saw that Bianca was watching with interest and that she moved some of her blades around to the same configurations.

Next Ayesha undid her belt taking off pouches and putting a selection of different shaped blades from her pack onto her belt, moving them in and out of their scabbards smoothly. *I am sure that Ayesha has never been seen with these blades before and they are quite unusual and...specialised. One had a thin straight blade, t-shaped in cross-section. It was needle-sharp at the point and widened in a curve into a normal blade-width at the hilt. I have seen such blades before being worn by the devotees of Kali. They are designed to enter mail armour and open it up, even if it was riveted, while they felt for a vital organ. I was fairly sure before, but now I am absolutely certain where Ayesha has received at least some of her training. Why do we have an assassin with us? Her target must not be one of us. She has had ample opportunity to kill any one of us and still escape unharmed and she is now being quite open about her skills. Now that we are in the field and away from others it seems that the dancing girl has completely disappeared and been replaced by a silent killer in the night. After tonight I must take the girl aside and ask her. I won't worry the rest now by revealing what I know. But how should I dress?...Padding and helm, but no bow and lots of wands. Some of my arrows may, however, still be useful.*

She took five that she had enhanced for Astrid. "I know that my bow is weaker than yours," she said, "but it shouldn't be enough to make a difference in their flight. These arrows will explode in fire when they hit—loudly and strongly. One should easily kill any unprotected person. I made them myself and I know their power. I caution you though to only use them once the battle has been joined and noise will not be important any more. Do not use them lightly. I cannot make more of them easily here in the field."

I may not be used to horses, but it was easy to see that Hulagu is amused by Bianca's treatment of her horses. I was surprised at what she did and my Princess confided that she, being used to the ferocity of trained war animals, and also worried about leaving Esther tied up with the others, was amazed as Bianca casually treated hers as some palace girls treated their lap dogs.

After all of the horses had been fed and watered. Bianca slapped her animals on the nose and told them to stay and guard the others before heading off. They were headed down the slope when Bianca had to stop and turn and stamp her foot before she could stop them following her—and obey her they did. Eventually they stopped at the top of the rise and they remained visible there, along with her packhorse, until they entered the trees.

Astrid made them walk quickly, but allowed them a short break before they started climbing the slope. *Theodora has taken my hand! It still feels strange to hold the hand of a paradēśī, a foreigner. That it is a woman and I love her is almost trivial beside that.* They reached where they would climb. Astrid, as the stronger, went first. A rope was tied around her waist that led back to Thord at the rear. The others went between them. Theodora gave her hand a little squeeze before taking her place and letting go. *It was strange holding her hand, but now I miss it. It was just a simple gesture of affection, but I want her to take my hand again. I miss it already.* As they went up she took her place just in front of Thord. Rani noticed that most of the group had steadied themselves on the rope, but Ayesha walked free and moved up the slope with ease, helping others if they needed it.

They reached the cleft well before dusk and settled down to sleep and wait. Astrid edged forward towards the shadows at the edge and then came back to report a similar scene to that she had seen before. Eventually she whispered, "The watcher this time is a mage." Then, "It was three women who were chosen this time—no children." Later still, "The mage has returned and is very upset. The dwarf and the mages are arguing discretely. I'll bet they decide to send their carpet out to look for their people in the morning, unless Dharmal goes to his mineshaft. We will strike just in time."

However, it turned out that they were too late for the carpet and the mage on it. Astrid whispered back that one of the mages, a man who looked like he came from the Caliphate, took it out of the village, towards the gate, just before dark. They could not see the area near the valley entrance from here, but Astrid did not have its return to report.

*W*hile *we wait and rest above them, the village below is settling down into what must be its own form of quiet...one of the women who had been taken into the barracks cried out a few times in short involuntary bouts of pain that were quickly suppressed and then, while the guard walked rounds around the darkened buildings, all of the others below lapsed into sleep, or at least had gone silent. I need to see everything.*

After Astrid allowed a peak over the edge Rani surveyed the scene below. *I do not have to change the plan much. The best time to attack is just before the first watch change when the soldier on duty will be sleepy and still tired from his day.* When those among the attackers who had slept woke, everyone made final preparation. *By Dhatri, god of enchantments, I have forgotten to check my little fire pot...luckily it is still smouldering inside and quite warm on the outside.* She dug in a pouch and added some fresh dried paper-bark to the contents and blew into it until it glowed just a little bit more inside. *My lover is lucky to work with the element of air. It is all around her and she needed to make no such preparation.*

Bianca

Before he would allow them to attack, Father Christopher took Astrid, Basil and even Theodora aside one by one to quietly talk to them as they closed their eyes in prayer and the priest blessed them. Theodora even went back to her lover looking happy. *They have all just made confession. I might die unshriven with what I have done still on my conscience before God. My soul...what of my soul?* With horror she became conscious of an ache inside, not a physical hurt, but she could still almost feel the pain inside her. *All of my life I have been governed by the rules of the Church, and I have tried as best as I could to live by them, and now I fear dying with my sins still there to be perhaps answered for before God without me having made an effort to atone. The priest may be a heretic, but I still crave to go to him and do the same as the others.* Before she could make up her mind Father Christopher insisted on saying a quiet service over them all.

"Not all of you are Christian," he said quietly, "but you fight against evil. It will not hurt." Except for Ayesha the others submitted. Ayesha moved aside and made a prayer for herself and included the others in it. She had indicated earlier that for her they might be kāfirūn, unbelievers, but they were also halīf, allies, doing Allah's work.

"Except for Ayesha, who will choose for herself when she will strike, no one will attack until they hear noise from the main house," said Rani, as a final instruction to them when they were all ready. Bianca crossed herself a last time. *There is still an ache inside me over the peril my soul is now in. This anguish cannot be easily quenched.*

Astrid

When the guard was out of sight Astrid took Thord's rope and tested it. It was firm so she lowered it over the edge and gave the cable to the Muslim girl. Quickly Ayesha walked backwards down the cliff, her hands grasping the rope. When she had reached the roof she waved and Astrid pulled it back up as she lowered herself from the roof to the street. The last they saw of her was when she drew two blades and stepped into a shadow, where she seemed to just disappear. Astrid handed over the rope to Thord, kissed Basil and moved herself aside into the deeper shadow of a part of the cliff and stood up, stretching cramped muscles and readying her bow. *I needed that stretch. First a normal arrow.* She nocked one and held it down. *My support role has started.* The guard on duty — Astrid thought that it was one of the women — went in and out of sight. *I could probably take her.* Astrid flicked her eyes from doorway to doorway, looking for anyone coming outside. After what seemed to be forever the guard went into a shadow and did not reappear. In her place Ayesha stood, waving up at them, before again disappearing — this time towards the guardhouse.

Astrid gave a soft instruction and the rope was let back down and, after giving Astrid a quick return peck on the cheek, Basil lowered himself down the rope, not as neatly as Ayesha, but at least he moved under his own control, the rope rough beneath his hands. Next Bianca was lowered down on the end of the rope. She didn't trust herself to climb down safely. Once other people were on the roof of the abandoned building they moved to the edge and climbed or were helped down to the street. Hulagu was lowered next. *He is as elegant as a sack of potatoes once he is off his horse. I am worried about the noise he makes, but no one appears to have noticed.* Theodora was the first mage down. She was without her outer armour but with a sword at her side and a shield strapped to her back. She went down in the same fashion as Ayesha. Rani had to be lowered. *She makes Hulagu look like a mountaineer. She has tangled her sword between her legs...now she is about to hit the cliff with her helm.* Thord walked backwards down the cliff confidently and without fuss while hanging on to the rope...*He is a mountaineer...*and then it was up to Stefan to go down last...*clumsy under his own power.* Astrid muttered an instruction to the priest, who pulled the rope back up.

Basil

On the ground they fanned out, moving as quietly as they could, but without trying to hide. Stefan and Hulagu moved down the side of the street trying to stay in the shadows. Basil watched as they went to the door of the guard's barracks where they took position and waited silently, one on each side of the door. He moved towards the main house. Behind him were the mages; he could hear them, and Bianca was behind them. Thord went in front. If the door was locked and barricaded it was his job to open it and, after that, to take care of Dharmal. Thord had demanded that job if he could get it. Basil took a position to the side as he watched Thord cautiously try to turn the handle on the door. It was unlocked and swung open fairly quietly, easily and smoothly in front of the dwarf. *If it were his door he would have liked the hinges oiled.*

Light flooded from the room out to where they stood, spilling into the courtyard and outlining Thord. They waited for a moment but nothing happened. Inside it stayed silent. *The place smells like a tavern that has been carelessly looked after, a touch of the sour smell of vomit between planks and not properly washed, a little bit of spilt drinks, something of neglected dust and it is easy to imagine that there is more than a touch of despair. I have been in many taverns like it. They exist even in Darkreach.* Basil quickly pushed past the mages as they went to step inside, his shortswords at the ready. He saw that the light came from something that was hanging from the ceiling—a crystal candelabrum without candles. *It is obviously enchanted to give light all of the time; the light isn't coming from magic just cast.* He went further in and looked around as the others entered behind him. Walking as quietly as he could he could see that open doorways revealed empty rooms while a staircase climbed the wall to the right. *I guess that the residents will be asleep up there. Bedrooms are usually upstairs. I wonder if they feel secure enough in their village to not lock their doors or set any traps on the way up. There is only one way to find out and it should be me who does it.*

Feeling his way quietly on the wooden floor he headed slowly towards the stairs. *I have done this many times before in my work, but never against a house full of mages. At least this time I have strong magical support.* As he put his foot on the first stair he checked behind. Rani had pushed past Theodora to follow him closely; Theodora followed her and then Bianca, with throwing knives in her hands. Thord, the only one of them in full armour, brought up the rear with a war-hammer in one hand and a round shield on the other arm. The mages both had a wand in each hand, their swords still in their scabbards.

Carefully and stealthily he mounted the stairs. *I hope they don't creak. They seem to be of solid construction and, unfortunately for the inhabitants, give out no noise. I am relieved at their lack of caution. At least, behind me, except for the unmistakeably faint and inevitable liquid chinking noise of Thord's chain, my companions are managing to stay fairly silent. Usually when I do this I have other police to back me up and I know that I am with the stronger force. Now my best allies use stealth and surprise and we have no real idea about the opposition. My climb is taking a long time but as always, speed means noise.*

Reaching the top of the flight he discovered that, across a broad corridor, there were a further set of stairs ahead of him, which would logically go up to the roof. A balcony corridor ran to the left and to the right, going around a corner at each end to disappear behind a thin wall. Another light hung at each corner. Indicating that they should all stay still on the stairs he explored in both directions. Each of the other corridors ran back to the front of the house and each had a door just around the corner and another at the end. Damn. There were six doors, five targets and five of them in the assault. Listening at the three closest doors gave him nothing. *They are identical and it will be pure luck for the right attackers to get the targets that they are best suited for. Here is where the plan starts coming apart...* He stealthily moved back to Rani and quietly described what he had seen.

Rani

Rani nodded as Basil talked and thought for a moment. *Who would occupy which room?* She chose one of the rooms on the main corridor for herself and another for Thord. *These seem to be the largest, so hopefully they will hold the chief mage and Dharmal. It is half and half which room they are in.* She gave Theodora and Bianca one side corridor, the one towards the cliff, and Basil the other towards the front of the valley. Basil wanted to go with Theodora, but in whispers Rani pointed out that he was better at combat than Bianca and would have to deal with two doors and so possibly two people, until help could arrive. She would stand at one corner and Thord at the other. When she dropped her hand Thord would do the same and they would all count to three slowly to themselves as the two moved to the doors of the main rooms. On the count of four they would each try and open their doors and then they would attack. All of these instructions were given in quiet whispers as they all clustered at the top of the stairs. *If anyone comes out of a room then it will be us who will be surprised.* "Say your prayers and good luck to you all," she concluded. They moved to their positions. *I suppose they are trying to stay silent and stealthy, but it is with varying degrees of success.*

Rani looked around. Basil had chosen the end room first. *That made sense.* Thord waited at the other corner. The dwarf's hand with the hammer in it was raised. Basil was looking at her. *I was trained for battles between armies out in the open, not magical duels within knife fighting range inside a building. I hope that I don't look as nervous as I feel. I am their leader and I need to look confident so as to give confidence to the others. All is as ready as it could be. The longer I wait the more chance there is of something going wrong.*

She dropped her hand and saw Thord drop his hammer hand, as she started moving towards her door and Thord moved to the other. *One, and reach the door, two, reach for the handle and put my hand on it, three, pause now, four, and turn.* It was unlocked. *Open it.* Light spilt into the room. Ahead was a large bed with posts at the corners and a canopy. A dimly seen figure lay on it with its feet towards her. Peripherally she registered a case of books and a writing table, on the other side a chest or two. *I must have a mage.* The figure was stirring. She used her wand and the figure let out a muffled scream in reflex as a small ball of fire hit it and the agony of the explosion brought it awake. Again and again and again balls of fire struck leaving small charred wounds, the bleeding staunched by the flame. The figure twisted, trying to evade the blasts and trying to comprehend what was happening to him. Her ears registered crashes and screams coming from the rooms from around her. She knew not whose they were.

The figure is reaching out towards something that lies on that stand by the bed to her right. Again she fired. The figure screamed and grabbed something. *It is a wand.* Again she fired and the figure fell limp on the bed, dropping the wand. *Success...no...wait.* It convulsed briefly and most of the damage that she could see disappeared. *Damn him, the mage is at least cautious enough to have a contingency cure operating.* Again she fired. The figure reached for the wand again, but that was no longer on the table, it lay on the floor. The mage half leant and half fell out of bed onto the floor, receiving another bolt in the ribs as he did so. *By Lakshmi, he now has cover from my fire. I must move to the right.* The mage came into sight. This time he was raising his wand and they both fired. Rani felt a bolt glance off her helm and saw her ball strike home. Again they both fired and Rani felt a sudden explosion of pain in her torso and she went to fire again, but it was unneeded. The mage lay unmoving with eyes staring at her and a face distorted in a grimace of hate and pain—dead, unconscious, or faking it. *I need to be sure which it is.* Rani went over and drew her main-gauche, plunging it into the mage's body where she thought his heart should be. He convulsed once, perhaps a reflex, and then went limp. She straightened, removing her blade. Blood gushed briefly from the wound. *Only one contingency cure then.*

She smelled charred flesh and singed wool.

Bianca

"Holy Mary Mother of God, help me. Blessed St Ursula, I made this vow to you, please aid me in carrying it out." Bianca spoke her prayer softly as she looked at the dwarf. Thord's hand dropped and she nervously reached for the handle with her left hand. *One...What if the door is locked?...Two...I am an apprentice trader damn it, not a soldier...Three...Oh my God, it is about to happen...Four and turn and open.* Inside was a bed, its head against the wall. There was someone in it. On the carpeted floor to her right lay a naked woman. *Now I know that my duty is to rescue another victim and wreak God's revenge on the ungodly.*

Bianca felt determination flow into her. As hard as she could she threw the blade in her right hand at the person on the bed and advanced, quickly drawing and throwing another blade. A gurgled scream marked that her aim was good. A wet 'thunk' announced that her second blade had struck as well. Another muffled yelp of pain came out of the bed. The figure on the floor was moving. She ignored the woman, noting in passing that she was blonde and light skinned. A series of small explosions were heard from behind her. She threw again and went to draw her fighting knives. The third blade hit as she threw herself on the figure on the bed, a blade in each hand stabbing down into the body. A moment of resistance said that both blades seemed to hit and then the figure just seemed to vanish and she was stabbing down into the bed. "What?" she said. The girl on the floor was now aware of what was happening and was screaming and scurrying across the floor to sit with her back against the wall, cowering into it. *What did she think was happening?* "Shut up you stupid woman. Where did he go?" The woman kept screaming. *Maybe she didn't speak Latin.* She tried again in Hindi.

"Don't kill me," came the reply.

"Don't be stupid. I'm here to free you, now where did he go?"

The woman was terrified. All she could do was cower and babble, this time in Latin: "I don't know. Don't hurt me. I don't know. Please —"

"Damn," said Bianca. She felt in the bed. *My best throwing knives must still be in their target...wherever he now is. At least I still have my fighting knives.* She got off the bed and headed for the door. She left the woman, still huddled naked, behind her on the floor in a pool of dampness and still babbling incoherently in fear.

Thord

It starts, thought Thord, as Rani's hand dropped and in near unison the hammer fell. Thord moved to the door...*One, hammer hand on the handle, two...well I wanted an adventure...three...and off we go...four.* Thord pushed down on the handle but the door didn't budge. *It must be locked. This must be the room for the dwarf then. We are a cautious race.* Drawing back Thord attacked the door with his hammer. *Given time it might have been possible to make a quieter entrance. There is no time. At least the hammer is having an impact on the lock.* Around about could be heard yells and explosions and loud screams from a woman. *I think that I am hearing faint noises from behind this double-damned locked door. Someone is moving about.* Eventually the lock was a wreck and the door could be pushed open. Thord entered to see another dwarf picking up a shield from a peg on the wall.

"You must be Dharmal," said Thord. There had been time for Dharmal to slip on some armour and grab an axe and now his shield, but naked legs and feet peered out from under the unbelted mail hauberk. A stray thought went through Thord's head. *Given the hairiness of a dwarf's body, that had to be very uncomfortable.*

The two faced each other. *I may not be experienced enough for this. I guess that I will soon find out.* Both feinted and drew back, neither willing to commit readily. Eventually it was Dharmal who made the first move, advancing in a flurry of attacks. *About time he realised that time is on my side. Damn him to an empty mine, this one is a lot better than I am. My little adventure away from home may be far shorter than I wanted it to be.*

Thord gave up any idea attacking and moved entirely to being defensive. *Really I only need to stop Dharmal escaping to eventually win.* Dharmal must have realised this. Blow followed blow, some were turned aside by a shield that was having pieces chopped out of it. Some blows were avoided by Thord's footwork, but some impacted and, although Thord's enchanted mail gave some protection, the minor rents and the bruising were starting to add up. *I can feel blood starting to flow from several places. It is only a matter of time before he despatches me and gets his chance to escape.*

Dharmal seemed to realise this and redoubled the attack. *Defence seems to be forgotten. He is just attacking me. Now let us see...*Thord was forced down to one knee by a blow. He struck out hard at a low opening. Thord's hammer met the side of Dharmal's unarmoured knee under the bottom of the mail and before the shield could get down. A scream came from the bandit leader as the leg gave way, bending sideways in a way that it was not meant to bend in. Dharmal was still screaming in pain as he fell heavily to the side. Thord rose and quickly kicked the axe from Dharmal's hand before moving back out of a grab range and keeping an eye on the prisoner. *I won. A rich mine to tailings, but I won.*

Basil

*T*his is so much better when you have numbers on your side and know what is in the room. One...now I wait. At least Astrid is not here to worry about...two...I hope that the Emperor will understand if

Theodora is hurt...three...concentrate now and...four. Basil turned the handle and the light and Basil both entered an empty room. From what was lying around, someone, the Caliphate mage; lived here. *He is just not here now.* Loud noise erupted from behind him. *Great, unless whoever is behind the next door is a heavy sleeper, I don't even get surprise on my side.* He moved up the corridor. *Still, we work with what we have.* The next door was locked. *Damn, this is why we usually take an insak-div with a maul with us on raids. Let me see how good their carpenter is.*

He took a pace back to the other side of the corridor, before throwing his shoulder at the door. It creaked but held. *That hurt, but there was some give.* He tried again. This time there was a perceptible creak, but it still held. He weighed up his options. *If the door opened suddenly he might tumble into the arms of his opponent, but the more he waited the better prepared they would be.*

He charged the door again. *This time it gave a bit. I can hear noise inside the room now through the crack. Again...it almost opened.*

One last charge and Basil flew into the room, stumbling and trying to stop his headlong rush. He came to a halt close to the foot of a bed. To his right a man was turning around from a weapons rack with a sword in one hand and a shield on the other. *He has not had time to don anything else and it is obvious that he sleeps without clothes.* He was tall and broad with a full square cut beard and a dark expression on his face.

"You aren't a slave!" he exclaimed in Latin in surprise.

It is best to delay things as long as I can. "No and I never have been. I am Basil, and who are you?" He replied in the same language.

"I am—" the naked man started to say. Just then one of the background explosions echoed into the room. "What the...you are attacking us...then die." He charged at Basil, who only just got his blades up to catch the sword as it swept down, before Basil could free a blade to take advantage of their closeness the sword swept around to snap at his head. Basil got a blade up to block, but still couldn't use his other sword as it was blocked by his opponent's shield. The bandit's longer blade was moving fast, as fast as Basil's shortswords were and much faster than a broadsword should move, and his opponent was skilled at both attack and defence.

The speed of the sword negated the advantage of rapid cuts that a shortsword normally gave. *He is either very, very good or the blade must be magically changed in some way. At this stage being naked is an advantage. The bandit can move quickly around without the hindrance of any coverings. It was only if I manage to hit him that he will have a problem...I show little sign of being able to hit him.* It didn't stop Basil from trying though. The two danced around the room, blades intersecting in metallic clamour. Cuts started to appear through Basil's padded leather jacket. Basil managed to get one good slice along his opponent's side — unfortunately he had aimed it as a disembowelling thrust, but the bandit dodged aside at the last moment. *None the less it is bleeding and must be painful.* The dance continued. *It is only a matter of time before I am defeated. The best I can do is occupy the bandit, stop him escaping and hope that someone will come along soon...preferably a mage.* Basil tried to keep his back to the doorway. He saw the window on the wall near the bed open. *What is happening there?* Unfortunately even this slight a distraction was something he didn't need. The bandit swept his sword up and Basil was too slow to bring a shortsword around in response. The last thing he remembered seeing was the sight of the sword about to hit his head as he desperately tried to block it with crossed blades.

Astrid my —

Theodora

Theodora stood ready at her door. The dwarf stood at the corner and, between Thord and Theodora, Bianca stood ready. *I wonder if the door is locked? I would if I were him. This will need careful timing. Luckily opening locks is an air specialty...and particularly for my monkey sign. This would not take long.* She didn't realise that she was smiling as she began to quietly chant the phrases that she needed. She saw Thord's hammer fall, but could not interrupt her chant to count. Theodora finished her spell and was rewarded by hearing a soft 'snick' noise. *So it was locked.* She looked up. Bianca was still standing there. She waited until she saw Bianca start into her room before opening her door and starting in.

There was a bed, a desk, bookcases and a cupboard inside. The bed had an occupant, who dozed in ignorance. She raised her first wand. It had powerful air bolts enchanted into it. *Unlike my lover, who has to be careful with fire bolts not to start a blaze or cause an explosion that will damage her, air bolts have little in the way of side effects.* Theodora struck. *My opponent has little chance. That first bolt surely woke him...at any rate it has picked him up from where he lay and flung him back against the head of his bed and his eyes are now open.* The second bolt made his tongue protrude and his eyes bulge and his chest almost collapse as his rib bones were broken. The third finished the job and crushed him and blood flew out of his mouth. Theodora cautiously moved over to where he lay.

Suddenly she was under attack. The crow Astrid had talked about was pecking at her head and eyes and raking at her with its claws. *Its claws are not a problem, but my eyes are vulnerable to its beak. Luckily it is flying.* She batted it aside. It flew away to come back at her and she fired an air bolt. It was only a pace away from the wand and she could not readily miss with a bolt meant to seriously damage a person. The bird gave a rude sounding and despairing 'squawk' and ended up flung against the wall as a limp bundle of feathers.

She turned to look at its mage, or whatever he was. He was now stirring faintly. *He had a cure in place then.* At a range of only two paces, just out of reach, she let loose another bolt at him, aiming carefully. *It left his head a shattered and bloody ruin.* She waited for a while. *I wonder if he has another contingency cure in operation. It doesn't seem so. He seems to be quite dead and intent on staying that way.* She checked the bird. It now lay at the foot of the wall as a feather duster, the mark of its passage a bloodstain on the whitewashed wall. *No contingencies on it then. I even have one on Esther. They must really have felt secure in their valley.*

Theodora turned and moved quickly towards the door. The sounds of battles echoed through the corridors. She could hear Rani's smaller bolts exploding around the corner. Theodora moved up the corridor towards Bianca's door she could hear screaming from that room and then babbling in Latin...*I hope that isn't Bianca...no, the voice is too high a pitch.* As she came level with the door Bianca flew out and the two tangled, luckily without damage to either.

Ayesha

Ayesha moved down the quiet street, keeping to the shadows as much as she could. *Luckily the village is in a valley and the moonlight only hits the left hand side of this single street.* Quietly she headed past the mage's house using the veranda for cover. She came down from that. *Under my feet in my soft boots, I can feel the worn cobblestones of the street, still there is good footing. No lights show from the inside of any of the buildings and it is quiet.* She looked back. *I can see nothing that would reveal where the rest of my companions wait. Astrid must have found enough shadow to hide in.* Ahead she could see the guard on duty move from the wall and down to start checking the locks on the outside of houses of the favoured slaves sleeping in their own buildings. The sentinel was also going around the sides of the building, probably to check on the bars over the windows. *These slaves might be favoured by having their own houses...but they weren't trusted.* The guard was not attempting to hide as they moved around their own street.

I approve of the guard checking everything. It makes them predictable. It will make my task so much easier. In her ears she could hear the pounding of her pulse. *I might be acting like a confident professional to the others, but this is, after all, my first real mission. Up to now everything, even if I might have died while I did it, has been training or tests. May Allah, the Strong, be with me. Here it seems that many people, not just my companions, but also the slaves and perhaps others as well, are depending on my actions. It is exciting, but I am feeling nervous. At least my teachers would approve of this task. These people we are attacking are not only heathen, or pagan, or worse, but are also outlaws based near the Caliphate. They need to be quickly brought to Allah's Judgement, praised be his Justice. As far as I am concerned, and I am sure the imams will agree, this means me. Tonight I don't need a written fatwa to prompt me to act as I wished.*

The guard crossed to Ayesha's side of the street to begin checking that side. *They are wearing mail. I know what I need to do. At least it is mail. It is so much harder to despatch someone quietly if they are wearing a plate torso.* She put her fighting dagger away, but kept her pesh-kabz—her stabbing blade—in an underhand grip in her right hand. When the guard was checking the side of a building, she moved quickly towards the building two up from her. She had gained cover before the guard re-appeared. *It is a woman, not a man, who I will first kill as I was trained. Astrid mentioned that at least one of the brigands is female and apparently she likes giving pain to at least one Caliphate slave. That confirms what I was thinking before. It can be a pleasure doing business and this perverted and evil woman will die as easily as any man.* Unconsciously she was smiling.

Ayesha saw the guard check the lock and move down the side of a building. From the smell it might be a smithy. Ayesha was in the next alleyway. The soft footfalls of the guard became audible. *Not noisy, but not trying for stealth either. This is a person who has walked many guard rounds on quiet nights. She is confident of the safety of her village and careless in small things. She is further betrayed by the inevitable soft metallic rustling of chain. It made it easier to tell where she was, whereas I move quietly in my soft boots and supple leather.* Ayesha drew further back against the wall at the corner so that she would be passed by as the woman turned in. A pottery downpipe from the roof provided that extra bit of shadow to hide in. She heard a cough, the bandit woman was clearing her throat, and a spitting noise as the steps approached. The woman started a low humming. *Did she have to make it so easy?* The lane darkened as the guard turned in. *I am a part of the wall and just a shadow in the night. In the darker lane the guard is not seeing me, but then, most people do not notice what they are not expecting.*

The guard passed and Ayesha slipped behind her, matching her pace as she reached up to the taller woman with her left hand. *Allah, the Just, be with me.* She quickly covered the guard's mouth with the hand while, at the same time, she drove the pesh-kabz deep into the woman's vitals. The blade slipped neatly between the rings, using its shape to open them up and allow her to go deeper into the torso. The guard tried to scream and turn around, hands grabbing for something but Ayesha's grip was firm and her training good. After she had driven the blade home she rotated the point widely so that it cut a cone through the liver and a kidney before pulling it out and plunging it into the other side of the body to take the spleen and another kidney. The guard's attempts to get free quickly grew feebler as Ayesha held on and rapid and massive internal bleeding took its inevitable toll. She was soon slipping into unconsciousness. Eventually Ayesha removed her blade and, reaching up, plunged it again into the body, this time at the base of the skull into the spine and through into the brain. The dying woman shuddered once and finally died and Ayesha had to scramble to keep her from making a noise as she fell.

Ayesha let her down and wiped some blood from her hand onto a sleeve before feeling at her victim's belt. *There is a steel ring there with keys hanging from it.* She removed this, wrapping it in cloth so the keys would not make noise, and placed it in a pouch in her belt. Moving to the mouth of the lane she looked around. *No one is in sight.* Ayesha moved out into the street and waved. It seemed forever, but was probably only a few heartbeats before Astrid eventually stepped out of the shadow and waved back. She waited until she saw the rope appear and the first of the group coming down before she moved off, again in the shadows and quietly, to her next target—the guardhouse.

When she arrived she tried the door. *It is locked. They have some caution at least.* She quietly removed the keys from her pouch. The lock opened on the third key that she tried. Cautiously she opened the door. They had a well-oiled and silent lock on the door, which opened with an almost inaudible noise of well-tended hinges. Looking inside she saw that a globe hanging from the ceiling lit the room. The room had cases of weapons, barrels of arrows, a desk and some benches and chairs just like any other guardroom. A doorway was on the other side. She re-locked the door, being careful to make no noise and leaving the keys in the lock. *Now no one from outside will interfere and any noise from there will be muted.* Cautiously and quietly she moved to the doorway and looked through. There was another door on the other side of the room and two bunks, one above the other, on each side. Both bottom levels were occupied. *That is considerate of them.* There was another globe above her head, but it had a night cover over it, something metal and pierced with holes that muted its light so that it did not shine too brightly into the eyes of someone trying to get to sleep. *Patterns of light like little stars are playing on the walls and roof as the light faintly stirred with the breeze from my opening the door.*

The guard on the left was lying on his side with his back to her. *He is snoring.* The one on her right was lying on his—or her, she wasn't sure which—back. Ayesha drew back and exchanged her pesh-kabz for a kindjal—a broad-bladed, parallel-sided heavy dagger with a short point. It was long for a knife and almost a shortsword. She held this underhand in her left hand and moved towards the sleeper on her right. Simultaneously she laid her right hand hard over her victim's mouth while she drove the kindjal into her head. *It is the second woman.* A thrust through the nasal gap and straight through the base of her brain severed her spine. *Her eyes are staring at me...it is just a dying reflex... her mouth is trying to scream or bite me...I must stifle any possible noise.* The body quickly spasmed as the stench of opened bowels filled the room. *At least I was told about that. Phew.* Heels briefly kicked the bed and one leg ended on the floor. She quickly looked around. *The other sleeper is still snoring on.* She felt no pity for the guard, merely wiping the kindjal on the bed and replacing it in its sheath before drawing an old-fashioned fighting knife—a kukri—from the back of her belt. *This is ideal for the task at hand, but I was taught that you rarely get to use it this way.* She took it into her hand in an underhand grip and drew her pesh-kabz in her left hand in an overhand stabbing grip. *This sleeper not only snores, but he is untidy. The floor near his bunk is littered with boots, belt, pouches and weapons, all lying wherever they have been dropped. I have to tread carefully.* When she was in place beside him both hands moved as one as she stood above the sleeper like an avenging angel. She plunged the pesh-kabz down through the temple into the brain while the heavy bladed kukri she swung in a chopping motion at the neck like a butcher slaughtering a goat. The neck was nearly severed. This time, as he died, the sleeper tried to make a noise. What should have been a truncated scream emerged from the windpipe as a wet and burbling moan. His body tried to reach up before slumping back on the bunk in death. Blood fountained out onto the pillow as the heart pumped its last and Ayesha had to step back quickly to avoid getting splashed.

Ayesha took a while to wipe blood off her blades. *I will need to clean them all properly after this. Thanks be to Allah, the Victorious, for guiding my hands tonight. Praise and honour also to my teachers. May Allah, the Wise, bless them.* Next she moved to the door at the rear. The key to this was in the lock, but it was not needed. The door was unlocked. Opening it she saw several cells with bare floors and some staples set into the walls of each at floor and incrementally higher to chain a prisoner to. *There is no one in them.* Ayesha turned and went back to the front door. Taking her pesh-kabz in hand she unlocked the door and peered out. *I can see Hulagu and Stefan have taken up station at the barracks to my left, but nothing else is visible. The others must be moving into the mage's house already. I am too late to go in there by the front door now*. She moved out of the guardroom into the shadows and left the building, re-locking the door quietly but leaving the keys in the lock. Quietly she moved up to where the two waited and paused, just out of sword range.

Very quietly she said, "It is just as well that I am not a bandit."

Stefan, whose back was towards her, turned around with a start, peering at where she stood deep in the building's shadow.

Hulagu merely looked surprised as his eyes widened. "Where did you come from?" he asked inanely in a soft whisper.

"The guardroom," she replied. "If Astrid had the count right then there were seven armsmen all up. There are now four of them plus the dwarf. I think she said that their captain slept in the mage's house as well. That leaves three for you two. Do you think that you can handle them or would you like me to stay and help you?" she asked cheekily. *Hulagu is looking down at me and his mouth is opening and closing with no sound coming out. The wheels are going round as he thinks through what I just said. He will get here.*

He eventually was able to say, in a soft mock-serious voice, "You can get on and see if you can find something useful to do. We will call for you if we find that we need your services." He smiled.

Ayesha smiled back. "May the blessings of Allah be on you."

Stefan came back with "God be blessin' you," while Hulagu managed an awkward sounding "May the spirits of the clan be with you." *It seems to me that he is not used to asking for the blessing of his spirits in earnest.*

Ayesha moved past them, vanishing once more into the shadows. She reached the mage's house and assessed it. *Nothing is happening here yet, but it won't be quiet for long. This is where the battle will be decided. The soldiers outside are deadly but they are, after all, only a sideshow. I wonder how to best act.* Ayesha looked up at the balconies. *It was with them in mind that I have the rope. I can get up there easily. The question is, can I move from one to the other. If I can then I can move from window to window and attack from behind as needed...I can do it.*

She unwound the rope and whirled it around before casting upwards. It landed on the balcony above her with a faint noise. She listened. *There is no reaction.* She tested its grip and moved up the rope, grasping it with her hands with her feet on the wall. She was just about to reach up to her destination when she heard sounds of combat erupt from within the building. She quickly swung herself up and peered through the shutters ahead of her. *The windows here are just frames with no glass or oilskin in them and the curtains are not drawn. The door to the room is open and the room is vacant. Should I enter?* She decided not to and coiled the rope, tossing the grapnel up to the roof. This time it made more noise. *Speed is more important here.* She tested it and swung across to the next balcony. Again the window was shuttered, but this time a curtain stood in the way of her seeing anything. *I have to pry open a shutter. Curse the bandits to Shaitan; this room has glass as well. I have to pry that open before I can even move the curtains aside slightly.* She looked through the gap.

Inside she saw Basil defending himself desperately against a huge naked man with a sword and shield. *No one should be able to swing a sword that fast and he is good with it as well...very good.* Basil was having to use both of his shortswords to simply defend himself, often bringing them together in a cross shape, against the power of the man's blows. The man's strength was evident, his overhand blows oft-driving Basil nearly to his knees as he blocked. *Basil is good as well...but not good enough. It is only a matter of time before he is killed.* Ayesha decided to enter the room and see what she could do. She pulled the shutters open and pushed the window open.

She moved the curtains apart and entered the room. *It is too late.* The bandit captain swung his sword at Basil's head and Basil was slow in blocking it, only getting one sword up fully and it was batted aside. He fell. The bandit captain gave a loud roar and reversed his sword, preparing to drive it down into Basil's body. The roar disguised the noise of Ayesha's move as she, without thinking, leapt and plunged the pesh-kabz and her rapidly drawn kindjal into his body. The kindjal was aimed towards his spleen but this time the pesh-kabz was aimed directly at the bandit's heart. Its shape allowed it to force its way through the bandit's ribs from behind as easily as it did through mail. The naked giant roared again and spun around. *His bearded face is a study in hate.* Ayesha had to stifle a laugh. *He is mighty only in his height, skill and strength. How did I think that?* As he spun she lost her grip on her kindjal. It stayed in his body as he moved, unfortunately plugging the wound that she had made. *It is a wound that would probably kill him eventually, but not quite yet. Allah's Grace, I was able to keep hold on the pesh-kabz and to withdraw it.* She skipped backwards smiling. *I am sure that I have gotten his heart. With Allah's aid it will be the right spot. If I am right, he dies. If I am not, then I, most likely, will be doing the dying.* The giant chased her briefly roaring in pain and frustration. She crossed lightly over the bed as she pulled out another blade. The hilt of the kindjal was protruding from his back. Suddenly, instead of following, he stopped. He dropped his blade. His shield slipped off his arm to clatter on the floor and he clutched at his chest. His voice hushed. A look of pained surprise appeared on his face and his mouth opened and closed silently a couple of times before he toppled forward and fell on his face on the bed. *The thin blade has done its work. It has punctured the heart and, when the giant moved and pulled it out, has caused it to collapse like a punctured air-squid. His blood flooded through the ragged hole into his body cavity instead of the next chamber of the heart. Praise Allah!* Ayesha leapt back onto him and, replacing her new drawn blade, removed her kindjal from his body.

Quickly she moved to where Basil lay still.

Hulagu

Hulagu watched as Ayesha appeared to melt into the shadows on their side of the street. *In the middle of a fight she had been teasing him just as Sparetha did to Togatak.*

"Be she killed all t'watch?" asked Stefan in a whisper.

"I'd say so," replied Hulagu equally softly. "Did you see or hear her moving? I didn't and she has just disappeared in front of us again. They were not expecting to be attacked. Would you have expected someone like her if you were bored and walking the walls of your stone town? At least on a horse it is harder for someone like her to get to you—but she can ride as well. May the spirits help me avoid having her angry with me. Now we just wait and do our part. She has culled part of the herd, but these bulls here will be awake and angry. We need to be alert in case there is another way out, but if they come through this door there may be three of them, but there is only room for one of them at a time and there are two of us."

They returned to waiting. Suddenly, from the mage's house, there was an eruption of noise—explosions, a prolonged scream that rose and fell, and the sound of wood shattering and then the clash of steel on steel with more explosions and cries in the background. They could hear nothing from within the barracks ahead of them.

"Be t'ey deaf?" asked Stefan.

"Perhaps they are used to such goings on," suggested Hulagu. He put his ear to the door to listen better.

Eventually, as the sounds in the mage's building started to die down, their patience was rewarded. From inside he could hear the sounds of people coming down stairs as a last loud explosion came from the main battle.

"They are not complete fools," said Hulagu, moving away and motioning with his mace. "They have stopped to put on some armour. I can hear them rattling."

Both moved closer to the wall. Hulagu had his mace raised, but he had to stand more squarely to the wall than Stefan, who had his back to it. *Luckily the door hinge is on Stefan's side and the door opens in, so they are not likely to see me unless the door is opened back on itself. The door is opening...about half way into the building. Whoever is inside must be looking to see what is outside. Perhaps they are expecting untrained slaves.* Neither attacker moved. The floor inside creaked. *I can hear some whispers.*

By now all noise had ceased in the mage's house—except for one woman who was loudly crying and sobbing. A Khitan stepped rapidly out of the doorway—his shield held high. It would have stopped a sword blow at the head from his right, but Hulagu brought his mace's shaft onto the shield forcing it down flat and allowing the mace head to hit the man's helm through it. Still, the shield took much of the power from the blow. At almost the same time Stefan snapped a shot at the man's chest with his broadsword. Unfortunately for the Khitan, Hulagu's blow had caused him to duck and, what was meant as a chest shot, passing under the flattened shield, took him directly in the neck. *Stefan has been waiting and he must have put all of his strength into that blow. I am impressed.* With a shower of blood, the head flopped back almost severed. The body stood erect for a moment before crumpling forward out onto the street as blood cascaded from the neck. The fall completed the damage and the head rolled free to the left and his helm bounced down the stairs with an unnoticed clatter.

While he was assessing things there was a roar and two men

jumped out between him and Stefan, using the death of their comrade as cover. *By the Spirits, we should have expected that. One is the northerner that Astrid described with the axe and the bear's hands; the other is a Freeholder in part plate and with a sword and shield.* Both ran into the middle of the street and Stefan and Hulagu went to follow them, instinctively changing positions as they ran. *I need to face the tougher armour of the Freeholder with my mace.*

For a moment they faced each other two against two. The northerner roared like a bear and charged Stefan. Hulagu was just about to charge his man when an arrow came from the cliff and hit the bandit in the armoured back. *I saw it flick in. It must be enchanted. It should have bounced off the iron at that range. It has exploded.* The man was knocked forwards and almost to his knees by the impact as the armour took up some of the force of the explosion. *Not passing on that.* Before his foe had a chance to recover, Hulagu had brought his mace down from his shoulder and back up again in a continuous motion. The bandit, as he was quickly standing erect again, was struck a swift rising blow between the legs, where his armour could not properly cover…With a shrill rising scream he fell back to his knees, dropping his sword and clutching at his groin as if his hands could fix the ruination there and hold it together. Instantly he became temporarily oblivious to the rest of the world around him as all of his thoughts narrowed down to focus on the excruciating pain he felt between his legs. Hulagu strode forward and, with a downward blow to the head, made his oblivion permanent.

He turned to where Stefan fought.

Stefan

The man moved forwards roaring. Stefan waited until the axe-man was drawing his weapon back and was ready to give his blow and then dashed forward. *A blow from such a weapon could carve me into two and I am not going to trust my armour to save me. He is trying to intimidate me into inaction. I am best getting inside the blow.* He did. As he ran he stepped slightly to the right and raised his shield to try to tangle the axe haft as he thrust forward with his point, his weight behind it. He felt his shield slide along the haft of the axe and catch the blade before it could hit. The bandit had a helm on with just a nasal to protect his face. *It is not enough.* Stefan's sword point took the man in the face and left it a bloody ruin as it went into the skull and beyond. There was a loud explosion from where Hulagu was. Stefan tugged hard to pull his sword free from where an eye had been and shook his shield arm to free the axe. He turned to see Hulagu despatch his opponent as his man fell to the ground.

"Well, t'at be easy," he said. "Be we get any more?"

Astrid

Once everyone had gone down into the village Astrid took a stance and held her bow down. *I won't need silence now.* Quickly she changed shafts so that she now had an explosive arrow nocked, but not drawn. *If I have the distances right, all the likely targets are well within middle range. I could do quite good work, even without these enchanted shafts.* Except for the one on her bow she had leant all of Rani's arrows against the cliff face beside her where she could grab them without moving her feet. *Normally I would put the points into the dirt for the speed of using them...but these are explosive shafts and I cannot be sure what will set them off.* She watched her people spread out; *Hulagu and Stefan to the barracks, the others to the mage's house. Those at the house are inside quickly.* A quick glance showed that Father Christopher stood behind her, sling in hand. She could hear him praying. She faced forward again. *I hope that he has his eyes open while he prayed, but I still find it reassuring. I can hear his quiet murmur, and only partly understand it. I need to learn more of the Church language...after all I might have some wedding vows to say in it soon. Above me the sky is nearly clear...only a few small clouds. Panic is only at a quarter and waning but Terror is still half full. There is about half their brightest light, more than enough to clearly see all if it was in the open.* Briefly she saw Ayesha appear, talking to Stefan and Hulagu, before she again melted into the shadows.

Suddenly, from the mage's house, there erupted a cacophony of sound: first came the breaking of timber, then muffled explosions, screams and the sound of physical combat. She glanced briefly at the barracks. All was quiet there still, so she focussed on the mage's house.

Is that a naked man who has appeared on the roof? He has started gesturing. He looks to be wounded and has the skinny look of a mage. He is definitely a man though...not one of us then. She loosed and reloaded. He was moving his hands down when the arrow took him in the back. There was a loud explosion and he fell forward. It looked like most of his torso was just...gone. *He isn't going anywhere.* His body fell loosely and then, seemingly erupting from the roof, came a strange mist that glowed palely red in the night. There was a noiseless shriek in her head. The mist hovered briefly over the roof and the body, as if it were choosing what to do next. Eventually it chose, and it rapidly began to rise straight up and disappeared into the night sky headed north. *What was that? Like a little girl in a big thunderstorm...I am praying. Oh...Father Christopher is doing exactly the same behind me.*

Nothing else appeared at that building and the noise was dying down. Suddenly there was noise and motion at the barracks and she could see Stefan and Hulagu hitting someone who fell. Before they could hit again two people pushed past them out into the open. *Bad move. The first one out is armoured like a Freeholder. He has his back to me and looks far too much for Hulagu.* She loosed and reloaded again. The arrow took him in the back. *The armour must have taken a lot out of the force of the explosion, because he is only staggered...Hulagu has taken care of that.* She had to wince at what he did.

Astrid turned her gaze to the second bandit. *Damn, it is Thorkil. I should have shot him first. Will Stefan be able to deal with...oh yes...it is either a lucky strike, good thinking by Stefan, or else Thorkil has gotten reckless or desperate. Whichever of those it was, the result is good, very swift, and very, very, terminal.*

Ayesha

*B*asil is alive...just. *The one shortsword that he had managed to get in the way of the blow has deflected it enough so that it has hit the side of his head instead of in the centre, so he is still breathing. I can see inside his skull to a pulsing brain.* She thought quickly.

She called out, "Theodora...Rani...come quick...someone get the priest here fast." She dropped her blades and gently closed the hanging flap of skin and skull. Looking around she grabbed the nearest cloth she could see...*It is a fine linen shirt*...and tried to staunch the bleeding. *Shaitan, I wasn't able to bring a medics bag with me from home and I forgot to buy one in Evilhalt. I haven't seen anyone else with one either...unless the priest has one in his pack.*

"Hurry," she yelled.

Theodora

Theodora was all tangled up with the western girl. *My right wand is tucked under a knife scabbard on Bianca's arm and on the off side our two arms are linked like dancers. I want to giggle. Mustn't giggle.* "Mine just disappeared. He is wounded," blurted Bianca, as they pulled apart. At the same time Ayesha was calling for the priest from somewhere ahead.

"We'll get him later. Ignore it. Get the Father," said Theodora. "Someone is injured." With that she ran to the left where Ayesha's voice had come from. *How did she get there?*

She dodged around Rani. "Bianca's man has teleported" she said, "don't know where." Rani turned to the stairs. *Why did Ayesha call her?* thought Theodora. *Next room...On the bed is a naked man. He isn't moving. Ayesha is crouched on the floor over Basil holding his head in a blood-soaked rag. Damn. I am the closest healer. Healing is a water spell. Rani was a fire mage...a battle mage...she probably could only just heal herself if she was in a hurry.* Theodora reviewed her few healing spells. *It is too late to wish that I had actually practised some of them in the last twenty years. I won't have enough time to prepare. I will be snap casting. Basil looks almost gone.* She knelt and ran through the words in her head. *The best I can do is buy some time until Father Christopher arrives.* Laying her hands on Basil she began to chant.

Bianca

Still waving two bloody blades in the air Bianca ran down the stairs and burst out of the mage's house. "Father, Father," she yelled loudly heedless of who heard her. "Come quickly."

Astrid

Father Christopher looked around. *He doesn't have an idea about how he will get down.* Astrid dropped her bow. *Lucky the arrow did not explode as it fell.* She quickly pulled up the rope. A quick bowline round the priest and she threw him over the cliff, rapidly lowering him. While she did so, she could hear Christopher getting in a quick prayer of thanks. *At least I think that 'gratias' is thanks. He is clumsy with a pack on his back, but it will be needed. He has all his clerical stuff in it and his chirurgeon's supplies. He has often said that no priest leaves home without them.*

"Who is down?" Astrid called down, she could feel a sinking sensation in her stomach.

"I am not sure, but I think probably Basil," replied Bianca.

Without thinking Astrid grabbed the rope and slid down it, ignoring the heat in her arm wrapped around it. When she got to the bottom the priest was still struggling to undo the knot. Automatically she had grabbed her spear and, without realising the danger to Father Christopher, she had grasped near the head and used it to saw at the rope to cut him free.

"Go," she urged. Christopher ran towards the house, but she quickly passed him. She ran up the stairs. "Which way?" she called.

Ayesha replied, "Here," and Astrid turned left.

Rani

R ani thought for a moment and started muttering to herself, "If I were to have a set emergency teleport from here, where would I go? It has to be clear—the roof—of course—there was a noise up there earlier." She ran to the other set of stairs and up them. There was a trapdoor at the top and, haste overcoming caution, she threw it open and peered out. In front of her was a naked body, or at least most of one, lying on a pentangle. *Hopefully that is the escaping mage and not someone else. Astrid must have hit him when he appeared with one of my arrows. Blood is pooled around the body, obscuring the design, but actually less than I would have expected. Hopefully the design had not been charged...or if it was, hopefully the disruption is over.* She looked around cautiously—there were no manifestations that she could see. *Freed and unconstrained mana can do strange things—particularly in these circumstances.* From where she stood on top of the building she could see that Bianca was in the village courtyard and Astrid and the Christian priest had come down from the ledge. Two bodies lay out in the street and Stefan and Hulagu were just standing there looking around. *There seems to be no more resistance.*

Quickly she went down into the building.

Thord

T hord heard screams, cries for help and movement, but no more combat. *I can kill Dharmal easily, but the others seem to be in control outside and this Dwarf must have information they want...like where the map is. I will concentrate on the bandit chief. I just have to keep out of Dharmal's reach and keep him contained. I don't have to keep him unhurt.* Dharmal kept trying to scuttle around the bed to the corner. *There must be something useful there. An ungentle tap from my hammer onto a bare foot or one knee or the other stops the tentative moves. It is not doing too much more damage and it has Dharmal twisting around like a forest lobster out of water and trapped by a waving torch giving out amusing yelps as he does so.*

I am hurting and revenge is fun.

Father Christopher

Astrid had passed him quickly and now Father Christopher rushed up the stairs and followed to where the noise was coming from. He rounded a corner and entered a room. Theodora was straightening up from where Basil lay on the floor. Ayesha, her hands covered in blood, was clutching a rag to Basil's head. "His pulse is weak," she said.

Astrid is already kneeling at Basil's side, clutching a hand. I can see the pain in her face. He knelt down. *The bleeding has mostly stopped and, what was a major wound to Basil's head is, although raw and bloody, mostly healed enough to stop the bleeding.* "Theodora, you have cast a cure already?" he asked.

"Yes, I have done the best that I could for the moment. I thought it would hold him until you arrived." Without saying anything Astrid began to weep.

"It has. You may have saved his life, but he is still slipping away. The damage is bad." While he spoke his hands were moving over Basil, checking his pulse. Ayesha was right. He searched for any other wounds. "Quick," said the priest, "I need something to draw with. Clear a space on the floor where there is plenty of room and away from the blood....Stop crying child. If we act now we can save him. He needs you to be strong for him." Theodora swept aside a Caliphate rug that covered most of the floor and reached into a pouch, pulling out some chalk. She handed it over. "Now we lift him. Ayesha, you will keep hold of his head. Astrid—pull yourself together girl—he needs you. You and I will lift him by belt and leg. Everyone take hold, on the count of two, ready...one...two...lift. Basil was moved into the cleared area. "Ayesha—keep hold there and note his pulse. Tell me if he gets worse." Now that Father Christopher was in his area of expertise he had lost his diffidence before the others and was quick to act and take charge. *They can kill things, but I am a healer. I speak with the authority of the Lord and others move.* He started to draw a figure around himself and the three on the floor.

People began to arrive and a glance up showed Theodora and Rani holding hands in the doorway. When the symbol was complete, Father Christopher took off his backpack and, placing it outside the figure, began pulling items out. He handed Theodora an incense burner and, without asking, Rani lit it. He gave her his open prayer book and she automatically held it as close to where he stood as she could without stepping on the pattern. *Good I can make out the words.* Out came his icon of Saint Christopher, which he kissed and placed on a bare spot in the symbol. He removed an asperser and filled it with Holy Water and, starting to sprinkle it over them all, began to chant in deep and sonorous Latin as he read. He concluded with "In nomine patre, filis et sanctu," and rose weakly, staggering as he did so.

Basil began to breathe more freely and opened his eyes to have his mouth closed by Astrid's.

"Let him breathe girl. He will live now and you can bear his children later."

She drew clear and began to stroke his brow.

"Astrid," Basil whispered.

Christopher moved to a chair and sat down heavily. "I hope no more is needed. I have done more than I should normally do, otherwise he was lost. Now, someone make this bed clean to lay him in. Astrid—no you are useless here—Ayesha, if you would not mind. The rest of you, see if the others need help with anything else." Looking up he could see that his words had made the two mages realise that they were not all here as they started and looked at each other. *Half our group is missing. Thord has not appeared…nor have Hulagu and Stefan…Bianca has not returned either. I hope that they are all well and not in need of prayer as there is little that I can do at present without risk to myself. I wonder if I should see to that girl who is still crying hysterically a few rooms away. I will see if one of the others is with her first.*

Hulagu

Hulagu looked at Stefan and Stefan looked back at him. Weapons in hand they both started looking around the paved area in the middle of the village. *I am starting to shake a little with a reaction to killing that man. I think Stefan is doing the same. There is a wailing in the mage's house, surely not one of our women, and lots of noise in the slave's barracks, but all else seems quiet.*

Suddenly Bianca came bursting out into the courtyard crying out for Father Christopher and then the priest and Astrid were running into the house. Bianca stayed outside. "I lost mine. I wounded him but didn't kill him, and he just left," she said.

"T'ere was just an explosion on, I be thinkin', t'roof," said Stefan. "It might have been one of t'arrows t'at Astrid had—twas only one—so it probably worked. What do we do next?"

"We wait," said Hulagu. "The others are busy. We can see from here if anyone else is hiding somewhere or if someone has survived and is trying to escape. Bianca, get out your sling." Once she had her sling out, Hulagu moved to the guardroom and opened it. He saw what Ayesha had done and gave a grunt of appreciation. *She would be good in a raid if she could work outside as well as she did in a village.* He sent Bianca up onto the low wall where she could see any movement, while he and Stefan began checking all the shadows. *With the dying of sounds of battle the slaves have quietened down, but I can see glimpses of the occasional face trying to peer out through barred and shuttered windows.*

All of the doors to buildings were locked and they eventually came to the conclusion that there were no enemies left outside. "Now we check the barracks. I think we should all go." They moved in. Although there was a common eating area and a bunkroom, it appeared that most of the bandits had their own rooms. Some showed no sign of recent occupation, but others indicated where the guards they had killed lived. Two had women in them. One had a Havenite girl who was huddled, terrified and naked in a bed clutching a sheet to her bosom. The other had a big-breasted black-haired girl with very pale skin lying tightly bound in an uncomfortable position face down over a chest, but curiously calm. They took the two with them.

Bianca shuddered when they went into one room, obviously, from the clothes, a woman's. There was a frame set up on the wall and a selection of whips hung beside it along with a crude apparatus of leather straps combined with a huge and cruel-looking leather phallus on a peg. *I know now why Astrid had said that one of the women had been so terrified that she was the girl the woman bandit had chosen.*

In the end they concluded that no one else was alive in the building.

Bianca

Going back outside Hulagu grabbed Stefan and started to collect the bodies and lay them in a row while Bianca sat the two girls down and tried to comfort them before fetching the girl from upstairs in the mage's house. *I am glad that she fell silent when I held her. It seems she has regained her composure and even had the presence of mind to get her clothes.* "It will make it easier for the mages to see if there is magic," she could hear Hulagu tell Stefan, as she returned, "and this way the slaves can tell us if anyone is missing and still hiding." He looked at the three Bianca had with her. "That is if that one can find the courage to stop crying...city dwellers," he muttered in Khitan.

The other freed girl from the barracks glared at him and hugged the crying one. "Then get us something to cover us so we can get warm and not feel so...exposed," the calm one said in a velvet voice in the same tongue.

"Do you have clothes back in there?" *I am fairly certain I have it right with what the girl had said, but I had to ask in Hindi.* The girl nodded. "Then I will take you in and we will get them." Taking the others by the hands, Bianca took them into the building. She looked at the calm girl beside her. *Although she is short, she was very well built and attractive. Oh...she is as naked below as Theodora is.* She glanced back. *Both of the men are following her walk with their eyes. Well, it looks like I am always going to be the plain one around here...I'll bet she can dance as well.* Aloud she said: "I am Bianca and I want to hear your stories, how you got here, and what it has been like."

"No you don't," said the quiet one bleakly.

Thord

Thord had just hit one of Dharmal's feet again and the Dwarf on the floor was clutching it with one hand while he tried to grab his other knee as well. *It looks quite funny from here. I wonder...if I hit the other foot next which extremity will he grab?* Rani and Theodora came in. "Eventual remembered t'Dwarves did you?" he said. "I pulled t'is

74

snake's fangs for t'moment, but he keeps tryin' to get to something in t'corner."

Both of the mage's walked over to the spot. "I sense magic," said Rani.

"Several items," said Theodora. "Let us get him out of here where we can talk. Can you carry him, since you have prevented his walking?" she asked Thord.

"He doesn't like me very much. He could hop..."

Dharmal glared at him. "You'll be dyin' for t'is," he hissed.

"But I'm a just startin' to live. If'n you don't mind I'd rather it be you who died." *I know I have a grin on my face, but fuck him and his sheep. I am the one who will live.*

He could see Rani looking at the Dwarf on the floor. "Thord is going to carry you downstairs. If you try and hurt him or grab him or do anything that he does not like I am sure that he would like to drop you down the stairs." Thord found himself nodding. *She is right.* "So do what you are told and do not give him a chance...Thord, give me all of your weapons to remove temptation from his reach."

Thord did what he was told. *I wonder why the woman held them as if they could explode or hurt her...later.* Thord made Dharmal take off his mail. *It is just as uncomfortable to wear without padding as I thought it would be...and even worse to take off when I helpfully pull on it. It turns out that Dharmal is male.* With the mages following Thord carried him down the stairs. *Dharmal is lucky they are wide and there is little opportunity to run into anything.*

"Put him on that bare ground," said Rani.

Why should I be gentle? He just dropped him, and was rewarded with a shriek of pain.

"Right, now see if you can find some rope and something to attach it to. We will need to keep him still while we talk to him." Once this was done she addressed Dharmal. "You are going to stay here tonight, looking at the bodies of your bandits, and thinking about...things. We will guard you and in the morning we will all talk."

Hulagu

*T*ypical, *the People always get left guarding things. At least the mages have decided to leave the slaves who were locked up still confined until morning. I agree with Rani's logic that this way there will be less trouble. They might even settle down during the night. Rani has even hung that light thing from around her neck up so everyone can see what we are doing.*

At least, *being the guard, I don't have to collect all of the bodies, half a body in the case of that one from the roof. Bianca is pulling blades from it and inspecting them. One has a handle that was a bit scorched and its blade is a trifle blackened. It must have been near where the arrow hit.* He asked what was happening inside. It seemed that Astrid and Father Christopher were staying with Basil in the room of the dead bandit captain tonight while Bianca and Ayesha would take turns comforting and gaining the trust of the girls who had been outside the barracks. *They would be in the downstairs room.*

Once it was all set up the two mages, Thord, and Stefan started sharing his watch over the night and their captive. Sleepers went into the room with the freed girls to occupy a couch. After a while Hulagu gave a grin. *When Ayesha is not in sight, I have taken to looking over my shoulder occasionally. By the Spirits, the girl was good.*

He looked down on their captive. *Luckily for him, although it is a chill night, what with the approaching winter, it is not raining. Unluckily for him his last night will be spent in pain and he will not be allowed to sleep.* If he looked like drifting off to sleep someone would prod him with a blade or kick him until he was awake again. *It is a bit disturbing to find that, despite his discomfort and injuries, he soon seems to have regained at least some of his composure.* He mentioned this to Rani and she just shrugged and muttered something about it being temporary.

Chapter VI

Verily I Rejoice In The Lord Tiller

The night that she was freed, the night she had hoped for, the night that she feared would never come, Verily sat in the bandit's common room drinking a mug of brandy and milk with Naeve Milker and Lakshmi, two other freed slaves, and poured out her story to two girls who had always walked free. She was warm and for once she was not in fear, but she was still filled with uncertainty and, to an extent, with self-loathing.

She said in Hindi, "I was named Verily I Rejoice in the Lord Tiller. My name is a cruel irony, and I was born to a slave woman in the place that outsiders call the Brotherhood. It seems that in other parts of the Land the child of a slave is born free. That is not the case where I come from. It is only after seven generations of slavery that a child is born free. I was of the seventh generation and my children would have been born free. My master, who I think was also my father, decided that he had a good use for me. Rather than spend money to raise me, he sold me to pay his tithe when I was six years of age."

She paused and swallowed a little nervously. *I am about to say things that I have thought about and brooded over to myself, but that I have never told anybody. Such openness is new ground for me. What will happen to me if I speak in this way to my new owners who I don't know, but now I am not sure that I care. At least these are women and they seem to be gentle so far.* "He is the first man that I wanted to kill, because he knew what would happen to me. Although I did not understand until later what was meant by this, he assured my buyer, who now lies dead outside, that I was a virgin. My buyer brought me here and I was a virgin on and off for two more years. I lost my virginity in pain every few nights—and then was given it back by healing. Think what happens if you have a cruel man who can heal and what he can do. I notice that he also lies dead outside. Now...the warlock from the

Swamp…the one with the crow…It is a pity he is dead. Is it possible that you can resurrect him for me? Him and the bear man both? I want to have them at my mercy for a long time…so do others." She inclined her head towards the barracks. She looked at the two women from among those who had freed them. *They are shaking their heads at what they were hearing. It looks like their faces are masks of horror. It seemed that nothing had prepared them for this. I was perhaps right to be open.* "Oh well, it would have been good…very good. When I was eight I used a knife to cut myself after they had healed me and, although it hurt me a lot and I bled and bled. When they found out what I had managed to do to myself they beat me badly. I survived. At least it was too late for them to 'heal' me when they found out what I had done. They liked it that I never grew hair, even when my time came."

"Most children who are brought here die. These beasts kill them, or they kill themselves, or they lose the will to live and just die. The few of us who survive grow hard and learn to survive. I think it is easier for the girls who come here when they are grown. More of them live."

My voice is growing bitterer in tone as I speak. Perhaps now I can afford to be more honest with myself. Perhaps it will not get me killed. Perhaps that no longer even matters. Perhaps one day the dreams will stop. She could feel a wave of relief run through her and yet leave her…empty. "You would not understand. You grew up free with families who loved you. You have not seen and lived the horrors that we have every day here." Naeve and Lakshmi had recovered now and sat clutching each other for support. Both were nodding at her. *They want me to continue.* "We are always tired and sore. We get little rest. By day we work in their fields or in their mines, we feed them, we mend their clothes and we work to make them comfortable and at night, unless you can divert them somehow, they reward us by having sex with us in any way they want. If we protest we are beaten. If we kill one of them we die — very, very slowly and publicly. If we get too old or lose our looks — for any reason — we die. When we die they do not bury us, they just throw our bodies away like rubbish into the river. We each try and learn something special…something that we hope will make them value us more. I entertain…Naeve looks after the animals and milks them, and Lakshmi…well let us just say that she knows how to make the most tired and drunken man respond using her mouth. Sometimes this works to prevent them from being cruel. That is the most we can hope for. Sometimes it does not. Tonight it did not work for me and I am very sore. I hate being taken that way. I am sure he would have preferred it if we were all boys." The other two nodded again.

"If I am now truly free I might even leave this valley and see the world. I don't know. I have been here most of my life and there has not been a single day that I could call happy until just now. What little I can remember from before I was sold was bad, but this has been ten years of the hell the Brotherhood preachers ranted about and promised to all sinners. I was a child. I had done nothing to deserve this." With that Verily finished her story and sat back, crossing her arms. "Now tell me about your lives. I want to hear about families and people that have grown up happy."

With that the other two women told their stories to her. The first, Bianca, told of being an orphan and of the nun's of St Ursula who had loved her and raised her in their own way and how they cared for her. She told of her work and the city and how she had got here. *I wish that my life had been like hers. A quiet life of hard work with a lack of excitement and a safe place to go to at night, it sounds great.* She looked at Naeve and Lakshmi and saw the wistful expressions on their faces. *They are feeling the same.* That changed when the girl started to describe the attack on her caravan. *Now we all get grim again. Most of us here knew all about that.* As she continued with the tale Bianca told them in detail about what she had done to Koyonlu. *That is the first really good news I have heard in ages. The man was an animal.* To her surprise Verily found she had jumped up and hugged the woman in gratitude. *I didn't mean to do that. Naeve is even worse...covering her in kisses as if she had been given the greatest present ever...actually, in a way, she had been. Hearing what the Khitan had passed on about their captives was even better.*

The next girl took a while to begin her story. Once she started it became apparent why. *It all sounds like a fairy-tale...a childhood as the last and youngest daughter of a sheik. It looks like the other rescuer girl have not heard this story before either, as she was as entranced as the rest of them.* Ayesha then told of being chosen to train at Misr-al-Mãr as a ghazi, a Holy Warrior, the first woman to do so. She told of what that meant and of what she learnt and she told how she got here. Verily looked at the faces of the other two. *I wonder if my eyes are just as wide. Again, it seems to be news to Bianca that one of the mages is a real*

Princess, from Darkreach admittedly, but still some sort of Princess. What does all of that mean for us now? Will it change my situation? What does this woman's story mean to me? The Caliphate is nearly as bad as my home in keeping women from doing things. If this...little princess could become a...ghazi, what does that mean for me? Now, if I am free, could I stop being a prostitute or even a servant? Can I change my life into something completely different?

"If you can do that, I can do anything," said Verily. "I only know what to do with a knife from practicing on my own. I can throw one, I think acceptably, but that is the only weapon I have. Can you teach me to use things properly? There are many magical weapons on the dead and in their rooms. I can learn to use them."

"How do you know that about the weapons?" asked Ayesha.

"I have been all around this valley in ten years and I can, sort of, smell magic. I have told no-one, but I think that is what it is that I can do. Fire magic smells like spicy cinnamon, water magic like fresh cut hay, air magic is sort of tingly and earth magic is like a damp rich field that has just been ploughed. Is that unusual outside?"

She could see Bianca and Ayesha look at each other in surprise. "We may be training you in knives, but I suspect our lady mages will want to spend a long time with you as well," said Ayesha. "I admit that I have heard of people having this ability before, but it is a very rare talent."

"It is as well you are all women. Although the women bandits were bad, they were not as bad as the men...and there were less of the women and they only started paying attention to me recently. I do not think I will be able to stand to have a man touch me or be near me...even one who had rescued me...for many years. My beauty is my curse and I would not want to be near someone who looked at me and thought of me like that. I would have disfigured myself, but then they would have killed me. I might trust a blind man...but that is all."

"I am sure it will be good if you talk to Father Christopher," said Bianca, who spoke up and then, for some reason, looked surprised as she said, "I will sit with you when he does but, although he is not the same as my priests or yours, he is a wise and holy man and I think you will find him," she paused and searched briefly for the right word, "calming."

I may listen to her words, but I doubt that I will ever trust a man again. All men, and even some women, want to do is possess her beauty and use it and use her. I cannot believe that a man could look at me in any way except as an object of his lust or as something to take his pain and anger out on.

After all of that Lakshmi, always the practical one, started dragging rugs and blankets down from storage cupboards and upstairs and they made a type of nest from them and went to sleep together. There were men, and even a Dwarf, coming in and out of the room, but they had not touched any of the girls yet and they had had many chances.

I suppose that I have to trust them not to rape or kill me out of hand at least…at least for the moment.

Chapter VII

Rani

Rani looked out over the village square. *I hope that I am doing the right thing.* Her eyes tried to avoid the one patch of grass with its staked out prisoner, and even more so the row of naked bodies that were the pathetic remains of the bandits. *Everyone is still looking at me, even my lover.* She scanned the broader landscape. *The morning has dawned bright and clear, but there is a light frost over everything— including the hair on Dharmal and the bodies. Everyone is standing back so that I am in front of the group as we gather. The three slaves who were already freed are torn between tormenting Dharmal and trying to hide from him, so they stay back as well. Being at the front cast me in the position of leader doesn't it?*

Dharmal looked up and calmly addressed her. "My masters should be along to free me soon. T'ey have promised me t'at t'ey have seen my future and I'll be t' King in Dwarvenholme when t'ey leave t'ere. If'n you release me 'n' agree to serve me, and t'em, I am sure t'at you will be forgiven."

"I intend to release you…" said Rani "from this coil of existence so that you may be reborn as, say, an earthworm or something even lower and more unclean. You will spend many, many cycles of existence expiating this one before you are again reborn as a sentient. First however, I want information. But even before that, I want your former slaves to see what has happened to your ruffians and to watch what will happen to you." She addressed her companions, "Can we let the slaves out please and gather them over here." She indicated the front of the mage's house beside the grass, and turned to the three freed girls. "Can you please reassure your companions that we mean them no harm and that we are here to free them, and can you help us gather them together?"

Verily, Lakshmi and Naeve nodded and went with Ayesha and Bianca to unlock the women's quarters. Ayesha then gave the keys to Stefan, who went to unlock the male slaves.

The women and girls were gradually brought out and chivvied into a group by Ayesha, Bianca and the three women who had been freed last night. *From their looks and skin they came from all over, except Dark-reach. The young ones were either held by the older women or stood tight beside someone hanging on to skirts or hands. They were all obviously afraid, despite the assurances of the women who ushered them out. They kept looking from the row of bodies to Dharmal staked out before them, to various members of the party, particularly the men. Some of the older slaves made tentative moves towards Father Christopher. She noticed that he was wearing his crucifix and his icon openly on his chest, something he had not done when they were travelling. Perhaps they expected there to be a priest among their rescuers and he must either have looked priestly to them, or maybe the least warlike, as he sat on the veranda with Astrid and a still weak Basil, but others pulled them back into the group. Looking around it was obvious that all of the women in the village were very attractive.*

Bianca had commented on this to Verily within her hearing. "Yes," she was told, "they rape and kill anyone else on the spot. If anyone loses her looks, even if it is because of beatings by them, she is disposed of. Some of them like taking a pregnant woman, but they kill all babies out of hand, so we try and avoid having them. It does not always work. I have lost two." Her voice dripped bitterness.

When the men were released it was apparent that one was a large man, who walked with a limp that told of a broken foot, and who had already rid himself of the chains on his legs, although he still bore the rings they were attached to. *He is looking a bit nervous about what he had done.* "You would be the smithy then?" asked Rani. She had seen him approach and had gone over to him.

He nodded.

"We will get you to do the same for the others when we are finished here if you do not mind."

He again nodded and this time smiled.

"Stefan and Hulagu, can you please go to the watch tower at the gate and see that we are not interrupted. Keep your eye on the sky and the gap for the river."

She addressed the whole group in Hindi. "I am Shri Rani Rai, and these are my friends. They will tell you their names later and we will learn yours." She waved a hand around. "Following omens and prophesies...and for other reasons, we set out from all over the Land. Almost all of us were attacked by evil beings, which we now believe were trying to stop us from meeting. We followed more omens and information to come here after these scum attacked a caravan that one of our group was a part of. They looted and destroyed the caravan and raped the women, except for Bianca here..." who she pointed to, "who escaped, but I am sure that many of you are familiar with that part of our tale from your own experience." There were some nodding of heads among the audience at this. "They were after something that the caravan carried and they got it. We now want that same thing and we want to...indeed from the omens we have received...we must...bring these scum to justice.

"We want to find out why we were attacked. We want to find what the omens point us towards and we want to fulfil our geas. We are some of the way towards this. Many of the bandits have died, most at the hands of the Khitan, some at our hands in different places. We now hold their secret fastness and have Dharmal, their leader, at our mercy. If there are any others left we will track them down and find them and kill them, and Dharmal is now about to help us by telling us all about what he has been doing and why."

During this speech Dharmal had been looking up at the sky and to what he could see of the ridges.

How annoying. It seems that he really is expecting to be freed. Rani moved to stand beside him and gained his attention by lightly kicking his damaged knee. Dharmal gave a yelp of pain. "One problem." said Rani...*I need to talk partly to the captive dwarf and partly to the rest of the audience...*"With serving evil is that evil has no sense of being loyal to its followers. It keeps them until they are no longer useful and then it discards them. You have served your purpose and now that you have failed you will be discarded. Speak to me now and I will grant you a quick and easy death." There were some groans from the women. "Try and hold out and it will be harder for you."

"You have heard all you will from me," said Dharmal. *It is obvious that he is a bit nervous now. I can hear bluff and bluster in his voice.* "Ahmed has taken t'map to t'Masters 'n' you'll not be able to find 'em now. You would have worked t'is out for yourselves. If I were to tell you more I'll not be rescued now, nor will t'ey find my body 'n' bring me back if you kill me 'n' I'll be in agony in t'afterlife. You might as well kill me now." *He is trying to sound confident but, lying there naked and staked out in the open, with one knee at an angle, despite being bound, and a foot completely broken, he looks and sounds more pathetic than brave.*

"Generous of you to give me your life, which is already in my hands," said Rani, "but you are wrong. We have found another map and already know how to get to Dwarvenholme. We just wanted to see what book was worth the life of a whole caravan. You will talk. Today, tomorrow, some time later, but you will. We will find out all you know of those whose dog you are and of their plans. Will you speak now?"

Dharmal remained silent.

Rani gestured at Bianca, who moved forward. "Have you met Bianca? No, that is right, it was her caravan you destroyed and yet she managed to escape you and then kill her pursuers. Do you know how hard it is to get Khitan to talk about their business? She killed Kitzez outright and then captured Koyonlu and broke his will before killing him herself. From him she found out all about you and the book and this place...aren't you curious how this little girl did that?"

Now Dharmal is starting to look a little nervous. His eyes are locked on Bianca. He is trying to work out how the small, plain girl, laden with knives but seemingly no threat to anyone could be so dangerous. I can see the expression on his face as he tries to work out how she could defeat and question his men.

Give him time to stew and consider what I said...Bianca has smiled at him...That little smile has made him far more nervous. It is a shy smile. Even I can see that it is a nervous one. Why is Bianca looking at the priest? What did my Princess tell me about confession and sin? Now Bianca is looking from Dharmal to the priest to me. We will see if I read this right...Rani nodded at Bianca and the girl moved towards the priest. Rani followed. Maybe I should have talked this out last night.

"Father, you are not my priest, but you are all that I have." There was despair in her voice as she spoke quietly. Rani looked back towards Dharmal. Basil had moved down and was keeping his attention away from what was being said. "Father, please," she quietly spoke, "should I do this. I did it before, but I was not quite myself then and I am still not shriven from that."

Father Christopher paused before replying. It seemed that he was trying to think about his answer, to avoid the glib. "Your Dominicans would be better able to answer that than I as they use similar practices on my kind," he said wryly. "Many who are far wiser than either you or I have thought about this problem. Can you do evil in service to good? Is it justified? Does it taint the user? I am sorry, but I do not know the answer. My opinion, and it is only that, is that if you realise that what you do is wrong...and you abhor what you are doing...and you confess and are absolved as soon as you can...such deeds may, and I stress may, be forgiven by God. He is merciful in His wisdom. Having said that, and having given you this advice, some of the blame has now shifted from you to me and, although you are of the schismatic faith, I will still take your confession as a believer who holds to the Nicene Creed. I have no-one to confess my sin to. You have a hard choice, child. I hope you choose wisely." He gave her what Rani assumed was a blessing and she turned again to Dharmal, crossed herself, and took out her thinnest and sharpest blade and started toying with it. Christopher gave Rani a look. *I think our priest may not approve of what I am getting Bianca to do.* She moved back to her place. *It is, however, needed.*

Dharmal had twisted his head around and tried to watched and hear all of that was being said. He may have even heard a little, although it was not hard to guess what it had all been about. Now he was looking very nervous. "I'll not speak," he said, his voice beginning to betray uncertainty.

Although we could enchant him and force him to talk, we have no idea what threats may still face us today, those that may require magic. If we can I am determined to proceed by physical, rather than magical means, unless I have no choice. Now for the next part of the play; at least I prepared this with Theodora last night. She gestured Theodora forward. "You may not have noticed my lover," she said. "Look at her eyes. Do you know what they convey?" The true look of fear appearing in Dharmal's eyes showed that he did indeed know.

Theodora spoke up, her voice taking on as grave a tone as she could. "You fear your eternity now. Are you really willing to take the risk that, if I am not happy with what you say, I cannot arrange for far worse to happen to you? If you are, then I truly admire your courage and you will come to regret your stupidity."

Almost instantly the sweat started to stand out on Dharmal's brow in the chill morning sun and his eyes began to flick from Theodora's stare to Bianca's knife to the surrounding cliffs and back again to the start. Suddenly Bianca came to life. She knelt down beside him and reached for his flaccid organ with her left hand. Rani had already noted that, although Dwarves may not be able to have children with humans, it seemed, from her limited experience, that at least the men were built roughly the same. Bianca gave a playful squeeze of the sack beneath and was rewarded with a yelp. She smiled again and waved the knife around over Dharmal's body, gently applying pressure, but not yet breaking the skin.

"Please don't talk," she said confidentially to Dharmal. "Rani wants you to, but I don't...I swore an oath to St Ursula for Rosa, who you had tortured, raped and murdered and I had to watch as your people did it to her. I want Rosa to look at us from above this day and have cause to smile." It could be heard when she gave another, slightly harder and longer, squeeze. She was rewarded by a shrill and prolonged scream as Dharmal tried to shrink into himself. "Father Christopher will not heal you for us, as he is a holy man, but I am sure there are herbs and potions here. I think you will be stubborn, and we will be delayed in this village for some time while we prepare for the next part of our quest, so I will have all winter to play with you. You will not have to sleep; one of us will keep you awake like this all of the time." She squeezed his genitals. It must have been quite hard as this time Dharmal writhed and cried out in now quite genuine pain. "What is more I saw some fine toys in the room of one of your women. I am sure that some of the women she used them on would love to use them on you. We can all stay busy for hours each and every day taking turns playing with you." She had a wistful looking smile on her face as she began to stroke his penis with the point of her knife. "What is more I am told that one girl here can make anyone rise to the occasion if she wants to. I will make a bet with you that she could do that and I could cut this off with one of my very sharp knives when you are erect and we could stop the bleeding and one of the embroiderers could sew it back and we could heal it again and I am sure we could do that at least once a day...won't it be fun?" Bianca was smiling broadly and digging a little deeper with the knife as she ran it over his skin around his shaft, catching in his hair and leaving little cuts as it broke free. "I wonder how long your mind will last. Do you think that you will be able to stay silent before you go mad?" *Mad? The expression that the girl had on her face is not entirely what I regard as sane. Her smile looked sewn in place and her eyes almost looked through him.*

Rani could see Dharmal look past Bianca at his former slaves and then back again to Bianca's face a few times and then he broke. Suddenly, and beyond his volition, he voided himself and began to weep. "Keep her away!" He lifted his head and said to Rani, "I'll talk, I'll talk...just keep her away from me."

Rani looked at Bianca. Her face had suddenly gone blank, and slowly a look of disappointment grew on her and she looked up at the former slaves. Rani followed her gaze. *Well, I can see many genuine looks of disappointment. Some of the women's faces have the look of a starving dog looking at a feast that is about to be given it. Others just looked hard and predatory. Some looked happy with that bright-eyed happiness that told you all was not well in their heads. It seems that what Bianca had been suggesting as a course of action is very popular with them. Maybe they were her real audience after all, not just Dharmal. I wonder what Dharmal is seeing written on their faces. I wonder if that is what broke him?*

"Please take t'is mad woman away," said Dharmal. "I'll talk. I promise."

"I think that we both know that she should stay there just in case your memory starts to fail," said Rani. "In the same way I am sure that if she just keeps running the knife around it will help you remember so much more." Bianca started, almost as if waking up, and the knife began moving again, tracing lazy paths in his body hair and around his genitals.

Dharmal swallowed and began, "I went a searchin' for Dwarvenholme with group of friends from Copperlevy 'n' other parts of t'North-West. Unlike most Dwarves who search we didn't just wander around looking at mountains. We decided that t'ere were spells of protection on t'entrance 'n' so we went lookin' for t'old roads 'n' followed 'em all 'n' found where t'ey all ended up. Most were at one place 'n', although we could not see it, we decided t'at t'is must be t'main gate. It was." He stopped talking and looked at Bianca, who smiled back and leaned a little harder on the point. Dharmal gave a yelp. "We sat t'ere for many days looking for way to open t'door 'n' t'en, almost by accident, one of our people said: 'I am a Dwarf comin' home'...and t'door opened. We went inside 'n' began to look around. It was quiet 'n' t'ere were just t'normal creatures 'n' animals of t'underworld t'ere. As parts started take our interest 'n' we began to find t'ings, we were split up. I was with two others when we was attacked by some sort of wraith. T'other two fought hard 'n' I used this to try to run back to t'others for help. I failed. My way was blocked by two others. I fought t'en. As I was fightin' I called out t'at, if'n t'ey spared me, I'd be t'eir servant forever. T'ey stopped 'n' drew back. I looked behind 'n' t'ere were others behind me. I was surrounded. T'ey started to move 'n' I moved in a circle of 'em. We came to a hall where t'ere was a magic diagram. T'ey moved me into t'centre of it 'n' formed circle round me."

"How many were there?" demanded Rani.

"One hand," said Dharmal.

Suddenly Bianca spoke up in a hard voice, one that had certainty in it. "He is lying," she said and, leaving her knife where it was, she used her other hand to reach down to him and give a very hard and long squeeze where it would have the most effect.

Dharmal screamed incoherently and shrilly until it tapered out to a whimper: "I was, I was, I am sorry," he said in obvious pain when he had regained his voice. "T'ere were t'ree hands or perhaps more of t'em, I t'ink." Rani looked at Bianca. *Could the girl somehow detect lies? Treachery? Evil? She had heard of people able to do all of those.* She nodded for Dharmal to continue.

"T'ey told me of t'is valley 'n' t'empty village in it...it's been empty since T'Burning...'n' t'ey told me how to gather people who would follow any order. T'ey told me t'at I would be given instruct-ions...in t'e mine is a locked area 'n' in it is a mirror mounted to t'rock. T'Masters can talk to you t'rough it..."

Bianca said, "That is not the whole truth is it?" This time she idly drew a line down Dharmal's stomach with the point of the blade leaving an oozing trail of blood in his hair and cutting across the lines of tattoos.

Dharmal was sweating and trying to wriggle away from her while whimpering with pain. He was bound too tightly to do that. "I am sorry, so sorry, no...t'ey do more t'an talk...t'ey take over your mind 'n' drain everything t'ey want from it. T'ey can hurt you or make you...very happy."

"Where is the map?" asked Rani.

"What I said about t'at is all true. I had instructions, whenever I found one, to send Ahmed, with the map, to 'em. I don't know why t'ey want it. He had to go again last night, again I do not know why or when he will be back. Sometimes he does other things when he is away. He sometimes says what, sometimes he does not."

"Is that all?" asked Rani.

Dharmal thought for a moment and then looked at Bianca, poised above him. Rani followed the gaze and saw the sweet and almost loving smile Bianca gave him back as she reached out and gave him a gentle squeeze of his balls as a reminder. With a short shriek he shuddered and swallowed and seemed to think about what he should say. Finally he came out with: "We have two recruiting men out. One was due back yesterday from t'north 'n' one is due today or tomorrow from t'south."

"Who gives you information in the towns and cities?" asked Rani.

"Many people do. I do not know all of t'ose who work for t'Masters. T'ey keep themselves secret. Mostly we just pay people or use magic to get people to talk. We get messengers."

"Are there any other ways into the valley other than the river?" asked Rani.

Dharmal shook his head. "Not t'at I know of…no. How did you get t'rough without us detecting you?"

Rani ignored Dharmal's question and was about to ask another of her own when she felt her lover's hand touch her shoulder as Theodora interrupted. "Do you raid into Darkreach or do you have people there?"

"I tried to go once, but we failed. Sometimes I t'ink t'at t'at is where Ahmed goes. Sometimes I t'ink it is back to t'Caliphate."

Theodora nodded. "I cannot imagine the Granther liking people who call themselves 'Masters', however wrong they may be…he would not be in league with them. He must not know about them…what do these so-called Masters want?"

"I don't know. We raid, we find t'ings, 'n' we kill t'people t'ey tell us to. Sometimes we are given magic to do a certain job with. Sometimes we work with…other beings."

"They must have some access to Darkreach, it would have been them who sent the roused dead to me," Theodora said to Rani. To Dharmal she asked, "Did Ahmed go east about a month and a half ago? Did he say he went to Darkreach?"

Dharmal gave a short reluctant nod, looking at Bianca as he did so. "He had to release some of the Master's servants, he said t'at much. He didn't say why."

"How do you open the gate without an alarm? Does it just alert you or does it have defences?" asked Astrid loudly from the veranda. *What a practical question. I wasn't thinking of that angle.*

Dharmal twisted his head to the side to look up at her and then back down to Bianca. She was smiling and nodding in encouragement at him, so he continued, "T'ere is a device beside my bed. I usually have it with me. If'n you untie me I will get it 'n' bring it back." This time it only took a slight jab from Bianca for him to add. "T'ere are many devices by my bed. T'is one looks like a spider. If'n someone touches t'gate or tries to cross above it t'ere is a small chirp. If'n you press its middle it opens t' gate. Otherwise anythin' t'at tries to cross will be blasted with spell and t'gate will not budge."

I am running out of ideas...Astrid may not be the only one with a good question. "Anyone else have any other questions?" Rani asked generally. "Do you have anything to add?" she asked Dharmal. "Remember that more than your life is on the line here." Bianca moved her knife and, drawing back, stabbed him sharply with her blade into his buttock. It broke the skin and sank in a few fingers deep. Rani saw her eyes widen. *It was probably further than she had meant to stick him, and it had him shrieking and pulling away until she pulled it out again leaving a trickle of blood to flow out. He kept up a low susurration of pain. He obviously had not noticed the expression on Bianca's face.*

Frantically Dharmal shook his head, but Rani was looking at Bianca. *She is quiet.* "Will you let me go now?" said Dharmal.

"Who said anything about letting you go?" Rani almost laughed. "You were given two choices. You could tell everything straight away and get a quick death or you could delay. You chose the second. Now you get to die." She stopped and addressed the former slaves. "He is now yours. Do what you want to with him." Dharmal began to whimper. "All that I ask is that you are finished with him before dark and that he is truly dead before then."

"Can't we take our time? I like Bianca's ideas," said Verily almost cheerfully. "I am sure we can keep him alive for a very long while... weeks before he loses his mind. I know about being hurt and healed." She approached Dharmal and kicked him hard in the groin. He screamed and tried to curl in on himself against his restraints in agony. She waited until he stopped making noise before asking, "Don't I, Dharmal dear?" Her smile on an otherwise blank face was even more terrifying than Bianca's had been.

"No, we need him dead in case we have to leave," said Rani.

"You cannot do that yet, we cannot protect ourselves," said another former slave.

"Yes," said Verily. "We need to learn things, and besides, if Ayesha is right then we may have things to teach you."

Rani considered her words for a moment before nodding and said, "We will all talk about these things tonight...now we need to prepare for Ahmed and the others. Goodbye Dharmal. I will think of you the next time I see an earthworm."

Dharmal began to scream as his former slaves closed in on him. He tried to struggle, but restraints made it a futile effort. Rani tried to close her ears to the sound but his screams and cries didn't stop until nearly nightfall, and his howls, his whimpers, his cries and his pleas served as a disturbing backdrop to the events of the rest of the day. His screams continued, gradually becoming more incoherent when he finally lost some of his tongue and then most of his mind. Former slaves moved about doing other things or re-joined the circle around their former tormentor.

Preparations were set in train. The mages went up to Dharmal's room to look for the amulet he had spoken of. It was easy to find. Beside the bed was a leather case. Rani prodded it and then cautiously opened it. It contained a telescope, a small rod and a small broach in the form of a spider with a pentangle with five garnets set in it on its back. "I will wager this is the rod they use to find magic," she said. Picking up the rod, she pointed it at Theodora. It gave a low buzz. "I wonder if the pentangle is for the warning patches," she mused. "I guess we will find out when the horses come back. We can search for the rest of his magic later. I suppose that it is too late to ask." She cocked her head. *Dharmal's screams confirm what I said.* They headed downstairs.

What do we do next?...Someone on watch with the detector and someone to fetch the horses. Astrid was sent out to the lookout with the telescope and magic-detecting rod and Bianca was sent to get the horses. "Do you need someone to help you?" asked Rani.

"What about Esther?" asked Theodora.

Bianca snorted. "I am already tending her and she has no problems with me; besides, everyone else will be busy. You need to strip these bodies and get rid of them. I only have to go for a short walk and then ride back."

"Well hurry, we don't want you caught out."

As they were about to leave Thord came running up. "I'll have to go," he said to Rani. "Hillstrider'll attack you if'n you try 'n' do anything to him without me t'ere." *Luckily he didn't see Bianca's face. She had nearly laughed at the idea that she would be in danger from a sheep...I guess that her warhorses could deal with it, even if she could not.*

Astrid gave Basil a kiss as he stayed on the veranda and the two girls and the Dwarf set out. Eventually the spider chirped, as if it was a cricket and Rani pressed it. "Hopefully he told the truth," she said.

Chapter VIII

Bianca

*I*t *is nice leaving the violence and the screams behind and to be thinking only about horses. It is temporary, but it is a relief.* Astrid interrupted her thoughts by showing her and Thord where to leap over the warning wards. *I wonder if this really necessary? The way Thord leapt you would hope not. The Dwarf's short bandy legs are not meant for jumping.*

When they reached the path to the lookout, Astrid said, "Wait here until I reach the top and look around for a bit. It is no use being on the road if the southerners are almost here. You would be trapped out there."

Bianca watched Astrid mount the path while Thord looked at the trail and the rocks. Astrid leapt up it rapidly and surely, pausing twice to look around and see if she was being watched. From below they could see when she gained the top and started with the rod. She checked it by pointing it at Bianca and Thord. They could only just hear its beep above the noise of the water. She then circled around. Apparently nothing was within range to set it off as she waved at them and put it away. Next she used her own eyes, and lastly the telescope.

Bianca was interested in her surroundings. *To my side and below by two good paces the small river rushes, deep and black coming around the curve to the valley, splitting around the rock, and disappearing under the stone bridge. On the other side of the bridge is a waterfall. I can hear that. The occasional twig or leaf shows how fast the water runs. I will need to make sure that no animal goes over when we come in. Anything that falls in that river will not survive the experience and one could drag others with it.*

Astrid

A strid waved Bianca and Thord on and, sitting and keeping a lower profile, she kept an eye on them, as well as checking the approaches and the air towards the mountains. As she waited she thought about the last few months. *I have fled home to avoid a loveless, indeed a detested, marriage and I have instead found love. I didn't realise it at first. I thought that it was just lust, but I did. Last night I nearly lost my love and I didn't realise the love until it was nearly gone. Father Christopher is right. In the old days this is how most Wolfneck marriages started. While I enjoy what we are doing, I don't just want the love-making. I have found a man I enjoy being with who enjoys me and I have decided that I am going to keep him. He makes me feel warm inside when he looks at me with his quiet smile and I sometimes just want to hold him. When I get back to the village I am going to tell Basil that we are getting married...and if he refused? I will cross that bridge if I come to it. I don't think he will, but he has this duty that he cannot tell me about and it might interfere. Now, time to stop gathering wool and get back to watching. Bianca and Thord are almost approaching the slope that leads to where we have hidden the camp and the horses. I'll bet Bianca's mind is firmly on the task.*

Thord

A s Thord walked and kept an eye around him his thoughts were simple and direct. *This is an adventure from the legends.* He knew that he was happy.

Bianca

A s Bianca headed off to the horses her mind drifted back to what was happening. *I can feel my mind losing focus and going back to the bandits.* She kept her sling at hand, but didn't expect to use it. Her eyes kept looking about, but what she was seeing was not really registering. *A few short months ago I was an orphan trying to start a career as a trader's apprentice. Now, what am I? Where I used to be a loner, I now have a group of people around me whom I care about at least a bit. Despite what I said yesterday, if I lost them, I would miss them. Hulagu I would miss a lot. Lord forgive me but I am sure that the Sisters would not approve of many of the things I am seeing each day, and what I am accepting, from these people. I have killed in battle...that is fine. However I have also deliberately inflicted pain on people under my control...admittedly it was only on people who deserved it, but that still probably doesn't excuse me. What will I do next? Instead of the mild animal handler I once was, there is a be-weaponed what?...The only way I have been close to a man's sex in my whole life was to hold it and then use a knife near it. I am still a virgin and even my apostate girl friend has a man...well, a part-man...but he seems to love her deeply and she certainly loves him. I really do need to talk to a priest and the Father is right. I need to confess. My soul must be in terrible shape by now. If I die unshriven at this moment...*she shuddered...*I would be lost and in hell for eternity. I have no choice about it. I must accept Father Christopher as my confessor now and, if I ever get home, square it with the nuns...somehow. I wonder if this was the sort of thing that the nuns used to do when they were out in the world...some of them were once warriors...St Ursula had a militant Order working for her. They never made their stories sound like this though. The blood and the pain and the hard choices were missing from their tales. It was all adventure and fun and travel. Even rain and mud were only mentioned if it made the story better. Had they really forgotten or had they actually been shielding the orphan on their knees from what life was in truth like?*

Bianca moved up the slope. *The wind is behind me. I will now see how alert the horses are as the wind carries my scent up to the camping area.* Sure enough as they came near to the crest her three horses, Sluggard between the two battle steeds, appeared as a welcoming committee on the top of the rise. She called them and they came down to her. After patting them and talking a bit she checked them over. *They have not suffered from the time I was away and they show no marks of having driven off any predators.*

"Now," she said to them, "let's go and collect the others, shall we?" As they moved down the rear to the picket line the two walkers had three large followers.

Thord went straight to Hillstrider, who put up more show of having been maltreated by being left alone than the horses had, but then he had been tied up.

Bianca started checking the growing herd of horses, not that they needed it. While she did that Thord prepared and saddled Hillstrider. He looked at her and she got him to collect all of the gear that had been left behind and start placing them beside horses. Bianca saddled the horses, put the armour on Esther, and loaded the pack animals...after having moved some gear that Thord had incorrectly placed beside the wrong animals. With only two people working, and a growing herd of over six hands of horses, it took a while to get everything ready, but at last they set off back to the village. Thord only had one animal and could fight from it so she got him to take the lead on his sheep. Bianca followed behind on Firestar with most of the horses trailing lead ropes, each attached to the saddle in front, and her other two horses walking where they would.

Thord went ahead on his own until he could see Astrid step into view on her platform. She signalled them on, but seemed to be indicating that they needed to hurry. They rode down to the main track, then over the bridge and up the ravine. Bianca had to tie the rope to the rest of the horses to Sluggard, allowing him to lead them on his own as her other two refused to move to the back and, in trying to crowd the path, almost pushed another horse into the water.

When they had reached the track down from the lookout they discovered that Astrid had come down to talk to them. "I think that we will most likely have visitors...probably in about three hours...find out what Rani wants to do to greet them please," she said. "I'll stay here in case anything changes. If you don't come back I will take them with my bow as they pass me. It'll be good hunting." She grinned. "Don't forget how to open the gate...don't force it."

"Get back up in your little nest where you ha' been avoiding honest work and hard exercise. We'll be back soon," said Thord.

They moved quickly up the path to the gate. Thord dismounted and touched the gate. Nothing seemed to happen, so he reached out again and shook it gently a bit. This time it gave a chirp back and he could push it open as it swung free. Thord stood aside to allow Bianca and the horses to go ahead while he closed the gate. Ahead near the village they could see activity and, by listening hard, could hear muffled screams from behind the wall.

"It sounds like Dharmal is still alive, then," said Bianca to the dwarf.

Chapter IX

Rani

Once Astrid, Thord and Bianca had left the village, Rani wondered what she should do next. *I am a battle mage and a warrior, not a village headman, but people are looking to me. My branches of the Kshatya caste are warriors, not rulers. I have no idea what I am doing, no training. What should I have done first? I have a village of people to take care of, a search to be made for magic and anything useful, bodies to dispose of, and a possible threat from these self-styled Masters.* She was standing there…wondering…when Father Christopher came over to her. *From his words, he seems to see my confusion.*

"You worry about this Ahmed and his carpet," he said quietly, "and how to defend the village, and I will take care of the rest that needs doing. I will be sending people to do things, if you need one of them, please check with me first…I will make sure that someone is on watch at the wall—don't worry." He smiled. "I don't want to be killed by a surprise attack either."

Rani felt a wave of relief wash though her, and sighed. "Thank you."

She watched Father Christopher take charge of the mundane…*the mundane that I have no idea how to organise. Some of the villagers are moving away from Dharmal, who by now, despite his desperate struggles, has been moved from the ground to a whipping frame that is permanently set up beside the guard house. He struggled so hard that they thought he might escape…so he was hamstrung. Blood is still running down his legs. They had then drawn lots as to who had the right to do what to him, and when, and some of the women have now left him alone until their turn comes. Others still just sit and watch. It is surprising to see how quickly Father Christopher has been able to organise people to get breakfast for them all and find a work party to strip the corpses and dispose of the bodies.*

Is it just him, or do people expect a priest to tell them what to do?

Ayesha

*S*everal people are leaving the strung up dwarf to the ministrations of others among them. One of those who left Dharmal is Verily. That is curious. She noticed the Christian priest moving towards the girl and went over to head him off. "I didn't think you would have had enough so quickly," she said.

"I haven't, but I was lucky," Verily said. *There is a tight look on her face that may have been meant to be a smile, but which fails completely to convey any sense of humour.* "I get to remove his balls and that will be right near his end, so I have some free time now. I thought I would see what is around that I can find. I have nothing really."

"Good, then you can help me do just that. I will make sure that you get some knives. Bianca will not need any more." Grabbing Verily's hand she went over to Rani and Theodora. "This is Verily. Verily, this is Shri Rani and, probably Princess Theodora." She went silent as she allowed what she had said to sink in. *It is taking a while.* Eventually Theodora looked aghast. "They are both nobles and they do not like men either...well at least they prefer each other," she explained to Verily. To the mages she said: "You will never believe what this girl can do. She has been kept here for ten years and they have never realised that she can smell magic and what type it is."

"Smell..." said Rani.

"Magic?" asked Theodora.

The look on your faces is worth it. "My most noble and illustrious ladies, you have only been together for a week and you already complete sentences for each other. My blessed parents took years to do that, I am told." She saw the two mages look at each other and then Theodora blushed and stared downwards...*with the coy smile of a very young bride.* Ayesha explained what Verily had told her the night before.

The eyes on both mages opened wide.

"We will start with these here," said Ayesha, pointing at the bodies laid out in the courtyard, "and then begin to work through the buildings. I will see if Father Christopher will spare me someone to carry things." *Father Christopher has his work cut out for him. At least the women seem glad to obey a priest. I can understand that, and it is possible that they will not actually listen much to anyone else among the men. The other males would remind them too much of their former owners.*

As she was waiting to get a man to help she heard the men introduce themselves—she had a Robin Fletcher with her while the others were Norbert Black, Giles Ploughman and Harald Pitt...*a polite introduction from them all.* As they went to work on the collection of items she heard the priest declare that they had to get a grave dug first.

As they left she heard a chuckle. "It'll be t'first hole I've dug since I got here t'at I enjoyed diggin'," said Harald in an accent that was as thickly Dwarven as Thord's.

Ayesha explained what they wanted to Robin and they began to gather things from the bodies and place them on the veranda. *With Dharmal and his cries as a disturbing background, the pile is beginning to grow.* They added mail, daggers, Thorkil's axe, swords, bows, arrows, and many other items as they began to go through the rooms—necklaces that smelt of fire to Verily, a lead amulet, a fire opal broach, a magnesium amulet, all of these from the mage's rooms, and so it went on. They even gathered a carpet up from the floor.

With what they were doing she and the priest crossed paths all of the time. *I approve of what he wants done. It seems his training has led to a better appreciation of domesticity and its requirements than I have. He has started some of the women on cooking. A Havenite woman called Lādi, one of the oldest here but still more than handsome, is the chief cook of the village. Despite protests she was soon dragging some of the younger ones away from Dharmal and setting them to work in the kitchen, making them wash thoroughly first...good.*

Ayesha and the priest arrived crossed paths again before a Caliphate woman called Sajāh who, it seemed, was the chief domestic. *Even while the priest is speaking to her, she looks at me as if seeking permission. Someone must have told her something.* The priest got Sajāh to start getting the mess tidied up in the mage's house. *Again she looks to me for confirmation. It all makes sense.* She inclined her head in a gesture that could be seen as confirmation if she was waiting on orders. *Even if we move out on our next leg tomorrow we will still need a place to sleep tonight and that is the most comfortable place here.*

*W*ork is proceeding well, and by the sun's position it is Dhurhr and time to pray. Taking her leave from Verily and Robin she took a place in the square. *I am a ghazi, a Holy warrior, after all, and no man is present, so it is up to me.*

She gave the call to prayer and, startled, several former slaves appeared before her. "We have not been allowed to pray," said Sajāh. "We have almost forgotten how and Allah has forsaken us."

"He has not forsaken you," Ayesha replied crossly. "He sent me, a woman ghazi from Misr al-Mār, here to free you. How much more a sign of His Love and Mercy can you ask for? You are no longer abd sacālīk, slaves of the bandits, you are free and I have helped do it—a woman from the Caliphate. It may be that no man will take you as a wife now, but it may be that they will; Inshallah. Anyway, you have your own Wadi al Qalca, Valley of the Castle, to keep you safe. You should give thanks for your freedom to Allah, the Merciful. It is time for prayer and I am going to do so. If you wish to join me, you may."

Ayesha washed at the fountain and went to a vacant part of the courtyard and began to pray. *My rug is still with my horse, but Allah will understand.* When she had finished she looked behind her and there were five women, including Sajāh, and two children eight or nine years old. *Those two should be home playing with dolls or learning to make carpets, not sitting here with haunted eyes being coached through prayer by the older women—older...*she snorted. *Sajāh is the oldest, thirty at the most, three others are as young as I am and I am just setting out in life. They are all now looking to me. It is my duty to take the lead in matter of faith.*

After prayer she went and started to learn about them before kissing them and going back to her tasks and sending the women and girls to theirs.

Hulagu

*H*ulagu was embarrassed. Every time he turned around he had two shadows. *Who are these girls? Their eyes and faces and voices tell me they are Khitan, although their clothes say no.* He faced them. They introduced themselves as Anahita of the Axe-beaks and Kāhina of the Pack-hunters. Even when he explained that he was a Dire Wolf and so could not take either of them as a wife, they did not leave him alone. "We were on wanderjahr when we were taken," said Kāhina, "now no-one of our septs knows where we are. It is long enough ago that our clans will have mourned us and moved on. We have no clans now unless we find a way to go back. We are impure, we need cleansing, and there is no shaman here to help us."

"I know your clan fondly," said Hulagu. "We were helped on our way by Malik, Tzachaz and Uzun of that clan and I know the rituals you need. My family are also shamen in our clan."

"Malik!" exclaimed Kāhina, "he is my cousin. He will thank you for my release from being a thrall, a köle, to these animals, but it is not just the rituals. You have taken us from the brigands as köle so now we are your köle. You need not marry us, indeed we know that you cannot, but we are yours now and you are responsible for us. If you want either of us as your leman, then that is fine of course, but otherwise we will still look after you. You wouldn't want one of these city men to have that task, would you?" She paused, thinking about what to say next. "You are lucky to find us. Girls of the tents do not last long here. We fill with hate for these men and women, and fight back and try to escape. Sometimes we kill one of them before we die. This is my second year here. I was going to die soon," she said in a matter of fact tone. "I had started to think about which one to kill so that I might die and return to the spirits. Anahita had around half a year after me before she would have made her try to escape and died...one way or the other. They do not take many from the tribes, unless we are beautiful, as we do not last long and we are not worth the trouble." She swayed towards Hulagu. "I am told that I am very beautiful...but I was the first here for several years."

Hulagu studied her. *She is correct about her beauty, and she has obviously been learning things from the other women. I am shocked at her behaviour, but then...Kāhina is also right about the more important matter. She is not of my clan, and has not freed herself so; by killing those who had taken her prisoner and made her a slave, I am now responsible for her and she is now my köle unless I find her a husband who will take her...we all freed them, but I am the only one of the People of the Tents here, so I am the only one who counts. If I do not take responsibility for them, then they can never return to the tribes and may still kill themselves. How would I explain that to Malik when next we meet? How will I explain the alternative to the others? How will I explain Bianca to the girls? That should, at least, be the easiest...easier at least than the other way around. I do not want to lose Bianca's respect on this, but I know now that these two will be coming with us when we leave.*

"I will not be marrying you. My destiny...I have a dire prophecy upon me." *They look impressed as they look at each other. I guess if you had to be a köle, then at least it should be as a köle to someone who the spirits have plans for. They stand a little straighter already. I wonder if such a fate for their master gave them prestige as well.* "As a part of it, my fate lies not with a woman of The People. That is, if I get to marry. The rest...we will see how it plays out." He thought for a bit. "If it must be, it must be. We can organise the fires later; in the meantime, see if you can find me a room from Father Christopher," he pointed at the priest. "You can stay in your own rooms or with me, as you wish...and get yourselves some weapons. No köle of mine will go unarmed so that they cannot protect themselves or me and mine...and get some real clothes. You cannot fight or ride in those dresses of the walled towns. You are not tavern girls now. Horses will come later."

The two girls scurried off to find what they had been told to find. *They are definitely standing straighter and are now moving with confidence. It seems that getting weapons and real clothes were a good set of first orders to give...for the rest we will see.*

Perhaps I can make some good come out of the latest change in their lives.

Stefan

Stefan was posted to the wall to keep a watch on the sky and the entrance to the valley. His eyes swept around, not failing to check where they had descended. *If we can do it, so can others. From where I stand I can see all that is happening below...although I try to avoid looking...there...but I cannot avoid hearing it. They are mocking Dharmal at this stage. Someone has carefully cut his stomach open, so carefully that there was little blood spilt and, to his horror, Dharmal's guts are spilled to the ground and spread out before him to contemplate as they pulse before him. They must have fed him a curative potion to keep him alive after doing that as his stomach is healed back around where his innards emerged. In Evilhalt, if such a man as the Dwarf had been caught the punishment would have been ruthless...hung in a gibbet to be mocked and to have things thrown at him until he eventually starved and died and with his body left there to rot as an example to others. It would be a harsh and condign punishment, but not quite this brutal and bloody. Everyone is scurrying around—Bianca and Thord should be back soon. The mages have disappeared...I hope to make magical preparations.*

*M*y stomach is grumbling...and plates and food are appearing down below. It would be nice if someone remembers and feeds me. Even *the women who are at work on Dharmal are now taking breaks to grab something to eat, although some have to be reminded to wash their hands. I don't want to leave my post, or even call out to give an order. That may be too harsh for the women under the circumstances.*

But wait...there is a girl coming up the stairs with a tray. It is hard not to notice her. She has red hair. It is the fiery colour of autumn leaves and she has outer clothes that are green with a tight embroidered brown leather bodice worn over them. From where I stand it is obvious that the bandits liked their women attractive and the dresses they made them wear to be revealing. It is a nice view. She looked up and caught his gaze. Stefan blushed. *Damn, I am as bad as the bandits.*

The girl smiled at him. "That is all right." She spoke in Hindi. *It is not her native tongue.* "I am used to men looking at me. I even used to wear dresses like this when I was at home. When I was much younger...a few months ago...I once used to think that I was blessed with my looks. Then it looked like I was cursed. Now, for the future, we have to see." She sat with Stefan while he ate..."To take the tray back down," she said.

He was told her story. She was Bryony verch Dafydd, the most recent of the girls to arrive, having only been here three months. She was a hunter from the Swamp, from the village of Rising Mud. *I shouldn't smile at that.* He failed. "We are used to that reaction, but it is the name we like. It amuses us as well. Our village is built on islands in a river and we control the only real crossing. The problem is that the islands are only made of mud, so we are always fighting the mud and the river to keep our homes. If you forget and sit back, the mud rises." She shrugged and went on to explain that she had been at her wedding party at her family's farm outside the village when there had been a raid by bandits.

They killed several of the people there and had decided to take her. Her new husband was in the way and so he was casually slain. "Once I was here I got lucky, I got adopted by one of the women—not Ekaterina, the one with the whips—but Miriam, the ugly one." She pointed down at the bodies, specifically at the sleeping guard Ayesha had killed. "As long as I gave her the release she sought, she was quite kind to me, like you would be kind to a pet rabbit. I am not sure that she knew that I was really human. To her I was just some sort of pet that gave her enough pleasure to wear her out and let her sleep at night. She had bad dreams. I know that. She would pat me and comb my hair and I gave her the little death. At any rate, I was widowed on my wedding night and, apart from a few times when they took me on the way north, it has not been as bad for me as for others—but I have nothing to go back to. They told me on the way north that they were there to kill my family and I am the last one alive. If I went back there now then all I would have are memories...very bad ones... Now tell me about yourself."

So Stefan found himself standing on a wall feeling the sun warm him and, as they both kept a look out, telling each other about their lives. *We have both had lives that were reasonably uneventful, and so fairly free of pain, until recently.* The tray sat empty and forgotten. Gradually the bodies were removed to outside the wall and put in a shallow grave. The place below started looking like a normal village except for the cluster around Dharmal.

Two women walked through the village dressed as Khitan with bows and other weapons at their waists. *Were they from among the slaves? Bryony is looking hard at the two as well.* Eventually Thord and Bianca came into view. *Bianca's horse is moving fast, with her other two running free beside her. Her big packhorse, laden lightly, is keeping up with the war horses, stride for stride, making the other horses, tied behind it, run as well. Something is up.*

"Someone get Rani," he called. "T'ey be a comin' back with t' horses 'n' seem to be in hurry." To Bryony he said, "Better be gettin' below. We could be a havin' trouble."

She nodded and gathered the tray and hurried down. As she ran to the kitchen while holding her skirt up high and showing near the full length of her legs, that they were...*good legs too...*

Chapter X

Theodora

Theodora started to take stock of this hidden place for magic and defence. *The roof, where Astrid killed the mage, has a pentagram painted on it, but it will have to be completely re-worked before being usable. Blood lies all over the design and crosses several lines. The design is not just broken...it is ruined. The blood makes sure that the pattern would more likely serve to kill whoever uses it rather than helping them, if it is worked with now.* She was thinking what to do when her lover joined her.

"This is important," said Theodora, as she waved her hands around the valley. "From here you can see a long way. It is the best place to defend an airborne attack. We have lots of areas like this at home. I will get someone to clean this mess up and then I will re-craft the pattern. There must be paint here somewhere–one of the girls will know."

She left Rani on the rooftop to inspect what she had seen, and to find an assistant. *I was just about to just grab this passing girl—just as I would a servant in the Palace at home—but I realise I am not supposed to be a Princess here. Father Christopher has said to ask him for matters such as this.* She went down to where the priest was and explained what she wanted.

Christopher nodded and headed back into the house. "Sajāh," he called out.

A head appeared near the top of the stairs.

"Is there anyone who would know where the paint for the design on the roof would be and who can clean it up? We may need it fast."

The woman, Sajāh, sized up the situation and thought for a moment and grabbed the smallest nearby child. *She is a tiny blonde girl who looks a bit like a baby Astrid without the teeth.* "Go to the Princess down there and do what she tells you. You can be her servant now."

The girl's eyes grew wide and she scrambled down the stairs. *All of the children wear only short skirts—long tunics really. She looks quite funny as she lands at the foot of the stairs and bobs what is obviously meant to be some sort of curtsey, perhaps something remembered from when she used to have a home. So much for not being seen as a Princess. What had Ayesha meant by saying that? How did she know? Of course…she must have met Miriam. I need to have a long talk with that girl. She was not what she had pretended to be. Rani seemed to know…something about the supposed slave girl…I should have asked my lover.* She felt warm inside as she thought the last bit. *I am getting to like that word.*

The girl said she was Fear the Lord Your God Thatcher. "What do I call you?" asked Theodora.

"Fear, if it pleases Your Highness. If it does not please you, you can call me what you please." The girl dropped her eyes and bobbed again. *She looks to be torn between apprehension and wonder.*

Theodora took her hand and heard her story as they headed off to clean and repair the roof. As she listened, she sometimes shook her head in disbelief. *Like that girl that Ayesha had found…Verily…she had been sold to slavers by her family from the Brotherhood and ended up here. How could anyone do that? Slaves are captives or sometimes criminals or even people who sold themselves to pay debts. You don't sell your children…particularly not to this sort of scum. Now she has experiences that she will never forget, or maybe…*her mind drifted a bit…*maybe she could…*Theodora shook her head…*this will be for later, but perhaps she can find a way to take away the memories and give the girl a childhood back.*

Father Christopher

Christopher looked around. *Everyone has been fed. The house is being cleaned. Dharmal still has his cloud of attendants, although some have moved away and others have joined in. There is even a large pile of weapons growing on the veranda under Basil's watchful gaze. A smaller pile has weapons and other items that are being added to it every time that Robin appears. Weapons are also going from the other pile. Two beautiful women dressed as Khitan, their clothes obviously having come from much larger men, came and helped themselves to bows and some other items.*

As they are testing the draw of the bows and flexing arrows they see him looking at them.

"We belong to Hulagu. He told us to arm ourselves," said one, and turned back to her task.

She obviously thought that this was a complete explanation. Belong to Hulagu? Had he hidden them in a saddlebag? We came to free these people hadn't we? If they belonged to him, why are they arming themselves so happily? He shook his head. Tonight I can see that there will be a lot of explaining to do...after I have done a service for those who want it and I have the Feast Day of St John the Baptist to celebrate as well. I saw Ayesha do the same for her people, but her times are more set. I thought that women couldn't lead prayer in her culture. At any rate it will be important for some of them that I do the same and I will certainly have a lot of confessions to see to. It seems that I have the flock that the Abbot said I would find. I am also finding out about the world. I would have been happier to have stayed in the monastery in ignorance of the very real evil that stalks the world. I have stopped being a monk. Must I become not just a priest, but one of the Basilica Anthropoi, the Holy warriors of God? Who would have thought? I might have to learn how to use a real weapon...at least I can be sure that someone here will be more than happy to teach me how to do that.

Rani

R ani looked up the valley and thought about what she had to do. *There are several distinct problems. First there are the expected arrivals from the south. That should be the easiest to deal with. If they are as careless as the others had been and if they do not arrive too soon they should be easy to wrap up. She mapped out some ideas as alternatives. The exact details will depend on how much the people of the valley want to help us and, indeed, whether they can help.*

The second issue was that of Ahmed and the carpet. *That is a bigger problem than a mere gaggle of armsmen. I will need a spell to take him out. She thought for a bit. Not one of my spells or even one I can manipulate is guaranteed to take out a person on a carpet in one quick strike—particularly since he would most likely have some form of protection...and not just the normal resistance that mages develop as they grew familiar with their craft. Perhaps my Princess will have something useful.* She still didn't know exactly how powerful her lover was, although Rani suspected that she was far more advanced than herself. *Luckily the entire battle in the village was carried out with stored magic and we are both fresh and full of mana. That diagram on the roof is becoming more and more important. Between us we should be able to boost a control spell of some sort with enough power to take out any protection that Ahmed might have. Mind you, we will only have one cast to do it in and we will be useless afterwards if anything else happens. I will need to see more about getting the pentagram repaired. There is no other choice.*

Thirdly, there were these Masters. *In the long run they are going to be the biggest issue. What are they? How will we defeat them? We are most likely only going to have one chance to do so and, if we go in without the right preparation, then we will all die. Many others have probably done so in the past. That is obvious and it is likely the Masters grow stronger each time they win. It looks more and more as if we are going to need to sit and prepare for some time. If we wait here, the Masters can unleash something else at us—a dragon perhaps, maybe one of the wild tribes or something else...anything really. They seem to like using undead and since The Burning there are a lot of unquiet bodies lying around waiting to be used. That would be the most likely for them. I wonder why more people don't follow the practices of my people. Burning bodies is so much more sensible. Nothing could easily come back from being made into scattered dust and ash.*

On the other hand, if we go somewhere else, we would not have the advantage of such a good position. Despite the ease with which we entered and won, if this position is properly held, it would be almost unassailable to anyone who did not come from the sky. It would be hard to find such advantages elsewhere and, what is more, if we do go and leave these women here then it is likely they will either die or become someone's slave all over again. We must block the way that we entered and start to look at the hills behind the valley. What if there are other secret paths up there?

I am being called...Bianca is coming back. Something is happening. Well, I guess we will find out about these southern arrivals soon.

Bianca

Bianca rode towards the wall. *Ahead, before the wall—that is a small patch of fresh turned earth with a pile of dirt on top. Three men are walking away with tools. That is where the bodies are already buried.*

She arrived at the open gate, most of the horses trailing behind Sluggard, and with Thord and his sheep struggling vainly to keep up at the rear. *Stefan stands above me on the wall, bow in hand and with a spear leaning against the gate post. Inside is...some sort of ordered confusion. The place is almost tidy, almost like a real village, except for the lack of men and the beauty of most of the women. Here I am the ugly one—the only ugly one. Before I left Freehold I was just plain, no plainer than others, but unremarkable. Here I really do stand out as if I am ugly. The women I arrived with and, even more so, the ones from the village, are all spectacular. Tall and dusky Rani is swaying down from the mage's house. Father Christopher stands on the veranda with Basil sitting near him. Hulagu and two Khitan women are coming out of what must be the stables. They have horses with them. Two women? Where did he find them? That is right. I saw some almond-shaped eyes among the women. Here it is. I thought that he is not interested in such things. I must be so plain. He hasn't made a single move towards her. Mind you I am not sure how I would have reacted if he had. I don't think of him like that.* It did not cross her mind that he might think of her the same way.

"They are coming from the south," she called. "Astrid wants to eat them all herself, but I think that she might need help."

Rani

Rani came down the stairs. *I think my plan will work. Hulagu has two Khitan women in tow. He already has them armed and with horses. A woman is hurrying towards the veranda, obviously to get a weapon. I have seen that red hair before, but she is wearing a large green skirt. She still has the same top almost on, but now runs freely in trousers she has found somewhere. I doubt they are hers. A woman that looked that beautiful would not, by choice, wear clothes that fit so badly that the hem of the legs is just quickly rolled up over her boots…and the footwear are not hers either. Others, still in their skirts, are starting to head for the pile. Even Dharmal has reduced his cries to a whimper. He has been deserted by his attendants. Everyone seems to be staring at me. Well, this is my job. This is my training. However I am used to doing it with the disciplined troops of Haven, not a conglomerate mob drawn from every part of The Land.*

"Stefan…go to Astrid. You and she are to let them in and then come down from the lookout. You will provide a stop to prevent their escape. Use your spears. Just stay in place and, if you force them there, do not advance past the gate until I tell you. They will not be able to easily turn around on the path and will have to stay ahead of you. Horses will not easily face spears on a narrow path with no build up from a charge behind them."

Stefan nodded and headed off. "I am going with him." It is the red headed girl in the trousers. She has a long spear in her hand already and has just stood up. It is obvious that she is seeking something else. "I am a hunter. I can use a spear." *Great, now we have some sort of southern Astrid as well.* She had another look at the girl. *I know where that pale skin and red hair freckles come from. The girl is obviously one of the unclean cattle-killers of the Swamp. One advantage of that…at least she will be used to making sneak attacks from the rear and three would be more useful than two.*

"Very well, but obey Astrid when you get there." The girl nodded and, making a final rummage, grabbed a large pouch and strapped it on before joining Stefan, who appeared to already know her. *First Theodora and I, then Basil and Astrid, now it looks like Hulagu has two women and lastly Stefan has found company. Is this really a military expedition following urgent omens or is it a mage's picnic and marriage agency?*

She addressed those left in the village, "The rest of us will not make contact with them. We want their horses and equipment, but we don't need the bandits. We will let them through the gate and then kill them. I will take a position on the hill beside the gate where I will not be seen. The horse archers will hide on the other side of the gate until I signal the attack with an arrow, and then come out.

"Basil," she said, "Take anyone left who can hold a weapon, close the gate, and hold it until we return. You have Bianca, the priest and any of these here to help you."

Basil nodded.

Addressing the crowd Rani finally said, "The rest of you. If you can use weapons, get some and join in. Draw only from that pile," she pointed. "Those are the weapons without magic. Until we know more about the magic arms it may be dangerous to handle them. If you are used to armour and have time, and I think you will, you should change. Any questions?" There was no reply. "Well...move."

The village is starting to look like a kicked ants nest as people begin to run in every direction. Soon Thord is headed out of the gate again on his sheep, followed closely by Hulagu and the two Khitan girls, along with Theodora and Ayesha, all mounted. Rani started to head out and discovered that she had been joined on foot by all of the men from the village, with bows and hastily grabbed spears and swords. They were weighing their new weapons and testing draws and feeling the balance as weapons were swung.

"Thou goest not out on foot on thine own," said one...*which one? He had been with Ayesha...Robin...that is right. He has a soft but very odd accent I have never heard before and he uses the Hindi words in a way that they are not usually used.* "We all doth be a knowin' which end of an arrow points at the enemy and we all be a having family to avenge."

Rani nodded in acknowledgement. *Good amendment, although later we need to talk about chains of command and how such a suggestion would have been a better one if it had been made a few minutes before. They obviously do not know what I am. It is touching in a way, but it seems that they think they will protect me.*

She reached the gate with Stefan and Bryony close behind her and let them out before going back and looking up at the steep ridge beside it. It grew steeper as it went closer to the little river and eventually became the cliff face against the road. *No-one would be charging up there in a hurry. It has been neglected and is covered in bushes, large and small, and even the occasional small tree. Looking further afield, there are some woods on our side of the gate, a little way up the valley,*

mainly on the left hand side, but also extending on to this side of the little river. The riders can hide there and they look like they are doing that. They will take a while to come into action but by then the bandits' attention should all be fixed on me and my men. They will be taken unawares from the rear. It will work. She moved back away from the gate to where she could get up the slope safely, and directed the men to find cover to fire from. They quickly scattered across the hillside. They then settled down happily to wait.

At least they will obey a straight out order.

Stefan

Bryony had taken the lead and went up the hill track first. Astrid appeared at the top and looked about to draw her bow on the girl until she saw Stefan behind her. "You have decided to join in. Good. Where is Basil?"

"He be back in t'valley in charge of t'wall. He can still do but little 'n' could do even less out here. With luck, he will only have to cope with village full of women. T'is be Bryony. She be hunter as well." Stefan went back to concentrating on getting up the path safely. *I must focus on why we are here and ignore the sight there ahead of me at eye level. It is way more than distracting. The trousers may not be hers, and may not fit well, but they fitted her more than well enough. She has a very nice butt.*

When they got up Stefan said, "Let me a take over from you. T'ey be not expectin' to see woman up here. T'ey will just think t'at I be new recruit, put out on borin' job." He explained the plan. "T'is be Astrid t' Cat," he said to Bryony, and had to smile when he saw Bryony's reaction to Astrid's teeth. He had forgotten his own. He took position and allowed Bryony and Astrid to sit out of sight and get acquainted. As he went Astrid dismissively told him, "It looks like we are just in time. There are six of them, all southerners, so they probably will have to dismount to use a bow. They will be here in less than half an hour and they will clearly see whoever is standing up well before that."

He took the watch spot. Behind him he could hear a stumbling conversation. *My God, it may be part Hindi, part Dwarven, but they both have awful accents.* His attention soon was on the advancing riders. *Was that my name? Why did they both drop their voices?* One of the riders spotted him and waved. He waved back. "T'ey be a comin' up to t' path," he muttered in a low voice. "Be ready."

The riders came up the path. They didn't expect him to come down as they blindly went straight past with another wave. *I hope that none of the riders look back.*

Stefan sprang towards the track down to the river path. "Come on," he urged the girls. "We need to be a gettin' in place quickly." The last rider had disappeared by the time they got to the bottom and formed a line. *There is not room for all three of us. Astrid does not like being second row.* "You be taller t'an me an' canna reach past me," said Stefan. "Neither of us could a reach out an' attack past you." Keeping together they began to advance. Before they had even taken a few steps they heard an explosion.

"That sounds like one of Rani's arrows," said Astrid. "They are very strong," she added admiringly. "That will probably mean that one of the riders is down."

Rani

Rani sat on the hillside behind a rock. *Everything is in place, now we just have to wait. I cannot see the gate from here, but if I cannot see it, then the riders will not see me either. They should assume that all is well and be totally off their guard. It is warm sitting on a rock in the sun...* The jewelled spider she had been staring at gave the little glows and a little buzz that meant that the path was being used. It suddenly gave a chirp and she pressed its centre. *My mind was drifting. Concentrate...we are on.* She stood and gestured to where the men were and saw them take their places. She nocked an arrow, but did not draw it yet.

The first rider came into view. *He is definitely Hindi, although in different colour; he is dressed just the same as Sanjeev's cavalry had been, but not looking quite as neat... The second and third are wearing something like Haven-style dress, but are not from there...they are probably from the independent villages along the coast. The fourth is from Freehold, by his armour, although he is riding with his helmet off;*

the fifth is from the Swamp, wearing the green stained leathers that are popular there, and the last is another Hindi cavalryman. The two Hindi have their chain veils held up by the nasal of their helms...I will shoot the one from the Swamp...at least there will be one less of them soon. The men are riding oblivious to us, the Freeholder is pointing around the valley, obviously showing the men their new home. They are paying no attention to the surroundings and are quite ignorant to danger. It is the perfect ambush. She drew. *My men are more alert than I thought. They have been watching her and did the same.* None stepped out, none loosed. *At least they have some discipline as well.* She waited behind her bush. *I have an explosive head on this arrow...below me and about fifty paces away...let fly...again...my men are firing as well...seconds for them. My first arrow hit...spectacularly. By the Gods, I forget things. I need to get the others back from Astrid...only one more left. Those I brought from Haven are still on my horse. At least this one is not wasted.* She had hit the man in the head and it is now gone.

The riders reacted. Four were clutching at arrows. *The last is the Freeholder and he is just looking around, his mouth open.* Rani obliged him by putting an arrow into it. *I was not the only one. One of the others has seen the same shot and taken it. Two down.* The Hindi cavalrymen, predictably, had reacted best. *Despite each having two arrows in them they are spurring their horses away from the ambush to get to where they can see what is happening. Unfortunately for them, the first thing they can see is a sheep and four horses charging towards them with archers firing at them. Now they have turned and are coming back— behind them the rain of arrows is still coming down. Now the other two riders are down.*

The men are looking at the gate. *What they see there seemingly convinces them to try going the other way. Astrid must be in place.* They tried to escape towards the village but discovered that now they were being shot at from both the hill and the riders. Splitting, they found that they each had two horses following them. On the flat ground it was obvious that Thord's animal was almost useless and he quickly drew Hillstrider up and began to head back towards the gate in case they made a break for there. They did try, but did not make it. Two of the Khitan, the women, quickly began to gather the horses. Seeing the result, Rani gestured her men down the hill. The gate beeped again. *I hope that it is Stefan and Astrid and...the other girl.* She opened it.

Soon they were all joined on the field, the bodies laid across their own nervous horses. They gleaned the field for shafts that had missed and, after Rani had checked with Astrid to see if there was anything else in sight, with the day getting late, she brought everyone back to the village.

There is a lot of cheering from the women on the wall. The bandits had not stood a chance. It is obvious that my trap worked well...even if they had any, not the slightest bit of magic was used by their opponents and all of the bandits were down in a couple of minutes.

It seems the women liked watching that.

Chapter XI

Rani

*W*e need to strip the bodies outside the wall and leave them to be buried. We can bring their gear in and add it to one pile or another. Luckily people are already getting used to me giving instructions. Dharmal is still alive—just—so he stays in place for the nonce. It is plain to the women that the new entertainment is already over and they are drifting back to Dharmal or to prepare a meal and do other work. I don't have to worry about the horses, the Khitan are already looking after that. I cannot believe that, even with those that were here for some time, and those who have arrived over recent days and weeks, there are still many empty houses. It is obvious, from the amount of empty space around, that this had once been quite a large and prosperous settlement. Rani began making notes on a wax tablet for watches. Ayesha is again about to lead the Caliphate women in prayer. This time she is even bolder. With women working all over the village, she has climbed up to the gate and called for them to come out just as loud as the callers-to-prayer do. Already startled heads are beginning to appear.*

"I have heard many at home make such a call," said Theodora to Rani quietly, "but never yet a woman. I wonder what her teachers will say to her if they find out. Now I must go back to the roof. We are nearly done there, but I haven't charged it yet. I want to know what we are doing next. So, when we work that out, let me know."

Rani watched the women at prayer and then, when it was over, approached Ayesha. "You have never told us your full name and where you are from—your real one that is, not the one you were going to tell us."

"I am really called Ayesha...Ayesha bint Hāritha al Yāqūsa. I am from a little town on the Khābūr Rūdh. That is all there is to tell really."

Rani nodded and moved away. *Even to me the names of the town and the father are significant in conjunction with each other.*

Astrid

A strid strode straight through the village gate and up to Basil. *Why am I nervous about what he will say?* Before he could say anything she leant over and kissed him and, as she moved away she put her finger to his lips. "I am getting married within a few days." He looked surprised. "You have until tomorrow to decide if I am going to marry you or if I have to find someone else." She took her finger away.

"You want me to marry you?" he asked. She nodded. "Even without knowing what my secret is or anything else about me?" She nodded again. "Then you can have the answer now. I will be your husband as soon as the Father is free to arrange it."

He rose and Astrid gathered him in her arms and kissed him...long and hard.

Bianca

H ulagu and Bianca entered the stables almost at the same time. Bianca was looking at the other two women who were following silently behind. *Who are they?*

Hulagu sighed. "Bianca," he said. "These are Anahita of the Axe-beaks and Kāhina of the Pack Hunters. You remember Malik. He is her cousin." He paused. *He looks unsure what to say next.* "They are now my slaves; we call them köle."

Well, that is...interesting. People think that I am one of them but, I really don't know much about the customs of the Khitan. Why are they slaves?

"It is our custom...oh, I don't really know how to explain it, but because of what has been done to them and the way they were rescued, if they do not become my köle then they can never go back to the tents. If I make them köle and then go and find them acceptable husbands, who come from a tribe that they can marry into, then eventually they will be able to re-join their families with honour. I cannot marry them." He stopped.

"So, you have adopted them? They are not your women?"

"No, they are my slaves and I may, or may not, sleep with them, but that is beside the point. I may not marry them, but this way they can possibly get their lives back."

Bianca turned to the Khitan girls. "You are happy with this?"

"He didn't want to do it," replied Kāhina, "but we demanded that he do his duty. What I want to know is why he feels that he must explain this to you...a town dweller? What are you to him?"

Bianca held her tongue. *That is a very good question from a slave woman. We have never talked about what we are to each other. I don't want to marry him and I don't want to bed him. What he does is his own business. I guess I am just shocked at the way all three of the Khitan take the situation, but they are supposed to be odd. I have a feeling that I will soon be jumping around fires again.*

Hulagu saved her the trouble as he spoke up. "This is Bianca of the Horse. She is from among the Latins but she travels under my guarantee and that of my clan. I speak for her deeds and she may be spoken to." *It is now the turn of the other two to look shocked. I think he has just introduced me as if I was one of them, not as a city dweller at all.*

"The Horse?" asked Kāhina.

Hulagu nodded. "Bianca, stand next to Sirocco or Firestar."

She did, patting Firestar's nose. *What is he up to now?*

"Now, Kāhina, you stand next to the other horse." She moved a little but halted. *She stopped when she was shown teeth. She just realised what he is.*

"You may have noticed that while she rode one horse the other two just followed. Several of these horses are hers and they are getting as bad as these three. Horses love her and these battle horses, which were not raised as hers, and even Theodora's battle horse, allow her to treat them as if they were little puppies. She may be a Latin, but at heart she is Khitan. She saved my life and one day you can ask her to tell you how she found out about this place and why she was chosen to question Dharmal. You will be impressed. She denies it, and she does not look it, but I think she is a Khitan foundling left in Freehold somehow. Your cousin accepted her and he likes her. You must do the same. I want you to treat her as if she were your sister. I do."

The other two girls came over and hugged her and kissed her on the cheek,

I knew it...there is no doubt about it...fires will be lit and there will be jumping around them. These two will want to be cleansed and they will insist that I join in. At least I now know how I stand with him...as his sister...damn Hulagu. I hope this fire business will not put my soul further into peril. I'll ask the Father when I talk to him tonight. If it will, I have to stop it. Anyway, why doesn't anyone say something about Ayesha and her horse? It follows Ayesha around just as much as mine do for me. Is it because hers is not a war-horse or just that I have more horses? Why does my new brother think of me as Khitan? I look nothing like them. I have blonde hair and blue eyes and only dress like one by accident.

Well, to be really honest, it is nice to belong and perhaps I am sometimes acting like one as well...sometimes...just a little bit at least.

Rani

*A*t least the freed women kept their promise. They kept it to the letter. Dharmal was finally despatched just as the last rays of the sun disappeared. Although I had thought that he had completely lost his reason when Verily unmanned him, and then stuffed his organs into his mouth and forced him to swallow them, he was still aware enough that he almost welcomed the knife that gave him peace in this world as he bled out through opened veins. The blood flowed down a drain nearby. It being too late for anything else he has been left hanging in the frame until the morning. The women thought that, seeing he had ordered it for so many others, it was only just that he should have the final honour of hanging there overnight as a lesson. I hate it, but it seems to mean a lot to them.*

Next to secure things...

Rani had the magic items all locked up in the inner room of the guard house until they could be looked at. She had the rest of the weapons and armour, those that no-one had already laid a claim to, locked in the outer room and ordered everyone to make ready for the night.

L *ooking at everyone, this night, perhaps for the first time in many, many, years, there is genuine rejoicing in this hall next to the main house. All of the women are here, not just the chosen playthings of the night and the servers. Some of the girls have even brought out musical instruments and begun to play. The cooks and servers will get to join in when they have finished and before they have to clean up.*

During the meal Theodora and Rani had a little girl serving them and bobbing up and down every time she approached. *Who is this child?* Rani was going to question Theodora about her, but was waved to silence. "I cannot get her to stop doing that," she said. "I will explain the rest tonight."

Rani nodded and then explained to her lover what she wanted from her for a spell to take care of the mage on the carpet when he was likely to arrive.

"Oh, I can do that easily. I have one that I can adjust—" She paused for a moment. "Yes that will do. If I do not have to use my mana tonight then I can charge my device as well. One of us must be on the roof to keep watch. As a matter of fact I think we should get everyone to do their watch from the roof. You can see everything from there. We don't have to keep a lookout on the wall for escaping slaves. We just need to watch the hills and the sky, and we can do most of that with the magic sensing device."

It is a good idea.

After the meal was over Rani asked for everyone to assemble. When they had gathered she climbed onto the small stage and shooing the musicians down, called for attention.

She spoke in Hindi. *It seems that most of these people know at least a little bit.* "I will be fairly brief, as some here have to keep watch, but I think it is important that we all get to know each other. It is possible that we may be here for some time and we are going to have to learn about each other. You will need to trust us and we will need to trust you, so I urge everyone to be open. I will ask all of our people to introduce themselves—by their real names and you can ask them some questions. I am sure you have them." She briefly paused. "I will start. I am Shri Rani Rai. I am a Kshatya and a battle mage from Haven and I have left there in answer to some prophecies. Some of them have already been fulfilled and they have brought us to you, so you have a place in them and may yet have more involvement."

She paused again and looked at each of the darker skinned women and girls watching her. *What I am about to say comes hard, but I have to say it.* "None of the women here are of my caste, I am sure of that, but you may talk to me and deal with me and we will all talk with the priests later. I suspect that we will all have a lot to account for in our karmic tally anyway. Lord Krishna will smile on such a little thing as talking to or touching the wrong caste as that is minor as far as the rest are concerned." *There are distinct looks of relief on the face of the few Havenite women and older girls present. Others look blank. I suppose that I could have, if I wanted, taken the other path and made them treat her as was her due, but it does not seem...right...somehow.*

Without waiting for her to say more, the girl who called herself Verily jumped up to her feet. "I was told that you used to teach people how to become mages when you weren't being a battle mage and that other thing you just said—the 'Khh' thing, didn't you?"

Will this girl always be this direct? What do I say? "The 'Khh' thing is my caste—if you like it, is sort of like the rank of my clan. It is not important to you, even if it is to those from Haven, but yes I did teach."

"Then...perhaps...Ayesha said you might be able to teach me. She is going to teach me how to use my knives better, but she said that you might be able to teach me to cast spells."

I thought that would come up. "That takes a long time," she replied. "If we are staying over winter here, and I am starting to think that this is a good idea, then I am already trying to teach Hulagu—any of you who think you might have talent are free to join us as long as it does not interfere with anything else that is going on. Does that keep you happy?"

From that fierce grin on Verily's face, it obviously does. She sat down.

Rani waved at Theodora, who moved to the front.

"I am Theodora," she said. "I am from Ardlark and I have run away from home to see the world and seek adventure. I am a mage of the air and also trained to fight as armoured cavalry, what we call kataphractoi.

I have overheard some of you today say that these bandits were in the pay of Darkreach. I can assure you that this is not so."

"How?" interjected one of the women. *I cannot see which one, but the voice sounds like it comes from the Caliphate.* "There is no way that you can know that."

"I know Hrothnog and he would not do such a thing. If he was going to conquer over the mountains he would just do it. He would not use such scum as these. At home they would be condemned and sent to the arena...with just knives to use against wild beasts or else used as incendaria, covered with pitch and set alight until they died...sometimes more than once. They would not have been allowed to flourish."

"How do you know this?" *I can see now who it is. It was the head domestic, Sajāh.* "I have heard you called Princess today. Are you?"

Now my Princess is thinking. Surely she realises that her secret is out now. Theodora just looked at me and smiled a little before her eyes flicked towards Ayesha. I wonder if she will bring up what I told her earlier. If she did it would spread the interest a bit so that she was not the sole focus of attention. "I am. Look at my eyes. Have any of you heard what golden eyes mean? Have any of you ever seen them before?" There was silence. "Ayesha, please tell them. You have met golden eyes before, haven't you?"

Ayesha looked surprised at how she had been ambushed, but she stood up anyway. "Yes I have," she said, "but how you knew I don't know." Addressing the crowd she said, "Seeing that I have been instructed to be honest I will tell you this. I am Ayesha, from the Caliphate. I am a Ghazi trained at Misr al-Mār. I am one of the first women to do so. That will only mean something to those from the Caliphate." The rest of the women looked at those from the mountains who were nodding. *It seems that the storyteller in Ayesha could not resist making her tale more like a story. She certainly has their attention.* "To the rest of you, I am one of what generally are called assassins. That is not our real name or indeed our main task. Mostly we act as guards and often as scouts. Only rarely do we stalk and kill the enemies of the Faith. Mostly we obey the Caliph, may he always be blessed, as the Voice of Allah, the Merciful, here in The Land. What he tells us to do must be done. I was told to obey Miriam in all ways. Miriam is one of our Princesses. She had married the third son of the most Benevolent Caliph. Before she married him she was a Princess in Darkreach. She is a granddaughter, I am not sure how many times removed, of Hrothnog. She has golden eyes and it is only the family of Hrothnog who have golden eyes. It is one of the ways that you know them. I was called before Miriam and instructed to leave the Caliphate and seek out her cousin, who was fleeing Darkreach to find adventure, and to protect her...and obey her...however long it took." Her hands, in almost a dancing move, waved sideways at Theodora. She sat down again.

Sajāh spoke again to Theodora, "So you are Hrothnog's grand-child?"

Theodora nodded in assent. *I can almost see people edging away from my lover. So does she—she is pouting like a child who is rejected. Surely she realises that, as these people have grown up, the name of Hrothnog has almost been the same as that of the devil. It was for me.*

There was an awkward pause. "Yes," she said. *She sounds defensive.* "But he is not quite like the stories. Well, he is in many ways. He may well be immortal, while I am only very long lived. I am already over one hundred and twenty years of age and I will, unless I can do something about it, have to see Rani grow old before my eyes and die, and yet still live many centuries without her. He can be scary..."

Out of the corner of her eye Rani noticed a quick involuntary nod from Basil, who was resting in Astrid's arms after his healing. *I wonder if Theodora noticed that. Basil appears to have met Hrothnog as well.*

Theodora continued, "But he does not drink blood or eat children or any of those other silly tales...I know that he would hate what was done here and beside, these people tried to kill me and I am sure he would not like that...Besides, I am not the only Princess here...am I, Ayesha."

She said it. All heads swivelled back to Ayesha, whose face had gone blank. She rose again. "That is not really true. I am not a Princess." *She is obviously trying to dissemble.* "No-one would call the youngest daughter of the third wife of a minor sheik a Princess. My full name is Ayesha bint Hāritha al Yāqūsa. Those from the mountains might know the name of my blessed father. To the others, what I just said is that I am Ayesha, daughter of a man called Hāritha. He is from the small town of Yāqūsa and, indeed, has the honour of being its sheik. I am not a Princess, and am not going to find a Prince to marry such a minor daughter...besides, all my brothers are dead and my uncle, my father's next younger brother, will be the next sheik when my father dies. I am just another ghazi." Ayesha sat down again.

I know what my Princess has done. She comes from a level they could not understand. Ayesha's birth is understandable and the women now give their attention to her instead of to the woman of vastly higher birth. I have to admire it. Now Basil is looking at Ayesha quite strangely. Does he have a dark secret as well? Oh this is getting deeper and deeper. Is Bianca the sister of the Queen of Freehold in disguise? That would top everything off. There are rumours that she has disappeared after all.

Rani was about to ask Father Christopher to speak when Theodora stopped her by placing a hand on her arm. She waved at Basil. *Well, the last guess had paid off; now to see if this one did.* "Now Basil," she said, "you can tell us your story now; including how you met my granther." *She surprised him by a flicker of surprise in his eyes. Who would have thought he could be caught out?*

Basil's faced slipped for a moment. Instead of his habitual lack of expression he might of have been chewing bitter herbs. He is weighing something up in his mind and now, as his face resumed its customary poise, has made a decision. With that delay all eyes are on him.

Basil stood and looked around. "My name is Basil Akritas. I am a part-kharl, or as we are called in Darkreach, insakharl. In my family I am known as Kutsulbalik, which is from the tribal tongue of my ancestor who married a human woman and it means Holy Fish." *He disarms with humour. I can see little smiles appearing on people's faces. It seemed that a Holy Fish is not as scary as a Princess.* He said to Astrid, "You are about to hear my secret that I could not tell you without permission. I have just been told to talk about it." He turned back to the wider audience. *He certainly has their attention.* "I am one of Hrothnog's secret men called the Antikataskopeía. I am just like a simple soldier in the army, but my job is to find criminals and to protect people. I can tell you directly that Hrothnog knows nothing of all of this. I met him a few months ago and he gave me the job of protecting his grandchild...for the rest of my life if need be and, if need be, for the lives of my children and their children. I was to pose as her servant...I have been a servant before, to investigate things, but this time it was to protect her. If Hrothnog had anything to do with what has been happening here he would not have allowed us to be here."

Well, that was a surprise. She could see from the faces around her that the Holy Fish is now a man to be scared of. Hrothnog is a terrifying figure out of their tales, but here in front of them is a man who has met him and who talks casually of the meeting. He also confirms that Theodora is his descendant.

He returned to his seat.

"Is that all that the secret is about?" said Astrid. "We will talk about our children later, but your task is fine. I have been set to guard the good Father myself." She gave Basil a kiss and stood up and started speaking as she moved to the front. *Her Hindi is still poor and she has to speak slowly.* "Seeing that my husband to be has spoken and is committing our children to something without asking me, I will speak next." She said to Theodora, "We will have words about this before I agree about my children."

Without even deferring to my leadership on this she has just started.

"I was once Astrid Tostisdottir. That means I am Astrid, daughter of a man called Tosti. I have been across the sea to the land of ice that lies north of The Land. I am from Wolfneck in the far north of The Land and, like Basil, I am partly a kharl." She smiled and, on seeing the reaction from those who had not seen her teeth before, she grinned broadly. *I suspect she will never stop enjoying shocking people.* "Now I am called Astrid the Cat. I have run away from home because I was being forced into a marriage to the ugliest man you have ever seen. He had green skin all over and a face like a pig and yet he was mostly human. He was very tall, especially when he was lying down. He was a drunkard, and, from what I saw in a sauna, his prowess in bed must have been more in his imagination than anything else. From what I hear he would have fit in well with the brigands here. One of our people was here already—Thorkil. I remember him being outlawed for the…murder of a little girl. My intended may have been another of the people that Dharmal used."

She waved a hand in dismissal and continued, "I fled that marriage and found Father Christopher lost in the forest and so have ended up here, fleeing one marriage to end up in another." She grinned again and with a little bow went back to her seat."

Before Rani could say anything the priest stood and turned to Astrid. "Is that my prompt to go on?"

She smiled and he went up to the front. "Hello everyone. If you do not know me, I am Father Christopher. I was an orphan who was raised by the Church and I wanted to be a monk. My Abbot and the Metropolitan had other ideas and they made me a priest and sent me off into the world for a time to discover my fate. I would have died in it after a couple of days if Astrid had not saved me by killing some evil creatures. That is really my entire tale, but, if anyone wants to see me after we have finished here, I will be doing confessions and, when everyone that needs them has been seen, I will perform a Mass. It may have been a while since you last had one. For those of you who are from Freehold, Bianca will tell you that I use the same Bible as you do and that you have not moved too far from the original worship yet. We both still hold the Nicene Creed that establishes a common faith. I think that my prayers will still be valid for you." He returned to his seat.

"My name was used. Does that mean I am next?" Bianca asked Rani.

"Yes, you may as well," she replied with resignation and a small sigh. *I may as well give up directing things, but it all seems to be flowing well as one of their stories runs into the next creating a whole tale for the listeners.*

"My story is very short. My name is Bianca, and I am not a Princess." *This brings a smile to many faces. I guess she is not the Princess Anne then.* "I am a foundling who was raised by the good nuns of St Ursula. I was learning to be a trader when Dharmal's men attacked our caravan. I escaped and joined Hulagu and we found our way here." She returned to her seat.

"I guess then that I am next," said Hulagu. He stood up and moved to the front. "I am Hulagu of the Dire Wolves and I am on my wanderjahr. I have a debt of honour to you all for what those of The People among the bandits did to you. I will repay this debt." *I can see looks of astonishment on many faces, that probably mirror what is on my face, but Kãhina and Anahita are nodding. He has a debt?* "I was given a prophecy and sent to the east. It is a major prophecy and there are many who would like to see me not fulfil it. You are a part of the prophecy. Bianca did not tell you all of the truth. She did not just join me, she saved my life from the bandits and I then joined her. We went further east and met Kãhina's cousin where we were all attacked by more servants of these so-called Masters. We prevailed and came to Evilhalt where we met Stefan and the others....Oh, and if you are in the stables, stay away from Bianca's horses. They are much more dangerous than she is, and you saw what she did to Dharmal." He stopped again and looked around. Rani followed his gaze. *There may be no questions coming in, but people are looking a bit stunned. Some are looking at Bianca, some at others. I suppose when you lay all of our stories out, it is a bit like the stories that storytellers, the less believable ones, tell at night.*

"It be my turn t'en," said Stefan. "I be Stefan. I be leatherworker from Evilhalt an' I wanted to see t'world. My younger brother be going to inherit t'business, he be much better t'an I be as leatherworker an' I wanted more, so here I be." He started to his seat, but turned to Thord. "T'at only leaves our sheep rider."

From his face it is obvious that Thord had been happily sitting there taking it all in. Written across it for all to see is that all of the stories that he had ever heard are coming true and he is in them. He shook himself and paused as if wondering what he could say. He stood on his bench. "I am T'ord. I am from Kharlsbane in t'Northern Mountains 'n' I am a shepherd. T'at means my sheep will, like Bianca's horses, attack you if you go too close to it. I was sick of seeing t'forests 'n' t'plains from my grazing pastures in t'mountains 'n' wanted to see more of t'em close up. I seem to have found my way back to t'mountains, but I am not unhappy. I t'ink t'at I will be one of t'ose who find Dwarvenholme 'n' will become a part of a legend."

He sounds smug and happy.

Chapter XII

Rani

After these revelations, the former slaves started to break up a bit. *Did it put a damper on them? Their faces show shock or surprise or, for some, fear. A couple even have a look of wonder on their faces. They talk to some of us, but there is a clear area around me and my lover. Perhaps we are too intimidating, although Princess still has that small child chattering to her. At least I can catch bits of what is happening. Some of the former slaves are clustered around one or another of us to ask questions, while others are being dragged off to do the dishes. The men have the most questioners. Father Christopher is already taking women aside to hear their confessions. There is a queue of women waiting for him and all four of the men. The cattle-killer girl is fending off several women who have come close to Stefan. Really? What is happening here? She still has the same top on, but the heat of the common room seems to have prompted her to unlace it a bit more. I wonder. Apparently Astrid has decided that Basil should marry her. Was there something about this place that prompts the women to be...forward...no that was the wrong word...eager...perhaps that is it. The local women are all eager. It could not just be the shortage of men. Surely they had had enough of that. Maybe they are following the lead of the women that had freed them...us. None of are shy types, well...not in that way at any rate. What do all of these women want? Was being free going to their heads? When he sits down it always seems to be on a bench near the wall where Bryony is quickly sitting close, between him and any others. Now she has two mugs of wine for them. I didn't even noticed when she left his side to fetch them.*

It could be an interesting night.

Father Christopher

I *am growing very weary. From little girls to women older than me there are the same tales. I listen and tell them all that they have done nothing wrong, their sins are only the little ones that everyone has, things that they do to survive in this hellish place. I absolve them all and tell them that they have done their penance already. The blame lies entirely with their captors. I must be doing the right thing. They arrive with tears in their eyes, but they are leaving with smiles, leaving their tears inside me.*

I must be about finished. I can start a mass soon. Fear, the little girl who is now Theodora's servant is my last freed girl. She is really from the Brotherhood. She is not even a Christian really, but she doesn't know that and I am not going to tell her. Telling her she is a lady in waiting to a Princess got her to leave with a smile. He watched her skip back to where Rani and Theodora were and give them one of her little bobs before going up and tugging Theodora's skirt and asking her a question before racing off somewhere else.

When he turned back Bianca was seated in front of him. She had a plate of cheese, some salami and pickled onions, and a mug of beer, which she handed to him. He took it gratefully in both hands and took a long draught. *It is good ale. I didn't realise it until I drank, but my throat is very dry. I needed this.*

"You look exhausted," she said, "and you are going to do a Mass. I know that you were a monk and used to long hours, but hearing these tales has put a look of horror on your face that I have not seen there before. You need food and drink before you collapse. I have brought you my Bible to use. I know that I am Catholic and you are not, but Father, will you hear my confession? If you are too exhausted then I will see you tomorrow. After all, I am not really one of your people."

"You are all my people, even Ayesha, if she chooses to talk to me. Three of these women are from Freehold. After we have finished I will show you which ones. They would love to talk with you and be reassured. I can only do so much. I am only a man and they have suffered too much from men. I will hear your confession if you will help me. How is that?" *I can feel smug at that. By making it sound like a trade I have made it easier for Bianca.*

She smiled back. "Forgive me Father, for I have sinned. Mea culpa, mea maxima culpa." *The familiar words themselves reassure her and she settled into the comfortable and accustomed routine. I will sleep easier tonight.* Christopher listened to Bianca pour out her doubts about herself, her fears of what she had turned into, even her jealousy of all the other women in the room. By the time she had finished, she was crying.

"My daughter, you have sinned, but you are aware of your sins and you suffer for them. You searched your conscience and did what you had to do. Now look around you."

Bianca did as she was told, lifting her tear-soaked face and scanning the room.

"See how happy these women are. See what has been done for them. I tell you now that none of this would have been possible without you and what you did. I would not say that good can always come from doing evil in the name of good, but in your case it has. This is a mystery and I suspect that neither you nor I are wise enough to understand it. I suggest that you pray on this mystery for the next week before you sleep. Let that be your penance. As for your jealousy...you are a beauty inside and you will someday make someone a loyal, strong and faithful wife. Some of these women are probably only beautiful on the outside. What is there to be jealous of with that? You look at their outside beauty and are jealous, and they look at your inner strength and are envious of you. Who is the winner here?" He absolved her and stood up and stretched before announcing loudly, "I will be performing a Mass now. Some of you may be offended by this. If that is the case I will go elsewhere. What I am going to say is, however, not a mystery, nor is it intended to offend anyone."

That is nice. Everyone is urging me to do my Mass here. The cook has even made some bread just for me...it is unleavened and still warm... and she has sent some wine...and she is Hindu...maybe one of her workers has gotten her to do this.

He went to fetch his equipment and when he returned discovered that the hall had been rearranged. *Bianca, of all people, is organising things. She has the benches moved around so that the hall now looked like many of the halls in small villages that were also churches on Sundays. Almost everyone is still here and most are seated. The pagans are up the back...Hulagu and his two girls...I still didn't have the story of that...a few from the Swamp who must be druids or witches and the Hindus, except for Rani. She is sitting down the front holding hands with*

Theodora with Fear at their feet. Next are the heathens: Ayesha with the girls from the Caliphate and on the other side of the room is Bianca with the girls from Freehold. The rest are down the front, except for Stefan who has gone to the roof of the house to start the watches and...has that red-headed girl gone with him? I will see them tomorrow. I have decided that, if this is going to be my flock they will not just see me on Krondag, as some villages do, but I will at least give them the chance of a service every day or even more than one. I have the story of St John to preach to today and I think that I have chosen my text carefully. After hearing Bianca's story of her first use of her Bible and what she had found, this may be a text that will do nicely for tonight. I can blend the two together as an example of the right times and actions.

He began with some words of welcome and prayers and then rolled into the familiar phrases. He hardly needed Bianca's text to read from, but he used it anyway. "For everything there is a season, and a time for every purpose under heaven..."

I have chosen wisely.

Ayesha

"See," said Ayesha to the women from the Caliphate in their own tongue, after the Mass. "He may not be a Mullah, but he was teaching mostly from the words of Sulieman. Even the Mullahs would approve of what he said. He does not have all of the parts of their holy book, so he only uses the part that we use some of and, although he is wrong in many things, he is always good at giving his sermon. As long as we keep our daily prayers, I think that this priest will be good for our souls with his sermons. He is a holy man. If I am wrong on this then Allah, the Just, will blame me, not you, as I have studied the Qu'ran and you have not."

Bianca

It has been too long. I missed the consolation that Confession and a Mass gives to my soul. No longer do I have what I did to those men hanging over me.

Bianca went to sleep almost happy for the first time in over a month.

Hulagu

When Hulagu found his room, after his watch was over, he discovered that his bed was already occupied. He turned to go elsewhere and heard two deliberate coughs behind him. *It looks like my köle are not going to give me a choice...again. I would have thought that they would never want to see another man as long as they lived. I wonder if it would be any good to actually order them out...although I have heard that you should never give an order unless you are sure that it would be obeyed, and with this one I have severe doubts.*

Maybe, if I am lucky, they will just let me sleep.

Stefan

It was nice of Bryony to sit through my watch with me, but now it is over she has kept talking all the way to my room. It looks like I am going to have company tonight. I wonder if I should assert myself and, if I don't now, will I be able to later. Look at Basil. He is looking more than a little stunned. However he also looks and sounds happy. While he was wondering this he realised that Bryony had removed her jerkin, leaving a very see-through chemise, and had turned around to face him.

Well, my body likes her idea. Let us see what happens next.

Thord

*W*ith Rani and Theodora in one room, Basil and Astrid in another, Bianca and Father Christopher with one each, and Ayesha and Hulagu in the next two, rooms are running out. That only leaves one room for Stefan and me. Much as I like the Human, I don't want to sleep with him and I suspect that Stefan may not sleep alone anyway. I will make my home in the soldier's barracks, in one of the rooms there. It is likely that I will probably have quieter nights there than anyone in the main house anyway. Too much purring there and, even if the mages are not making the night noisy with other sounds, Theodora snores.

Chapter XIII

Ayesha

Ayesha had almost been the first person awake in the village and after she had undertaken the first two prayers for the day she just moved on to the next task. *This morning there is a small crowd outside the mage's door.* Ayesha and Basil decided to enter together and nothing they said would put little Fear off coming in as well. *It is worth it to see the look on the faces of the naked women as we all spill in with food and drink.*

"Enough...this we do not need," said Theodora, for once trying to hold the covers up around her chin as Rani almost hid under them. "Basil. You have admitted that you are really here as my guard. Good. You can be my guard. I am sure Granther will be happy with that. Ayesha. The same applies to you, and Miriam will still know you are doing your job. You both have other things you should be doing now rather than fetch and carry for us. For a start, Basil, today you need to pay attention to Astrid—and only to Astrid—but if she is willing, she can still fix my clothes ...but not now. She sews far better than you do. However you are marrying her today and she doesn't even have a wedding dress. Do you have a man to stand beside you? Ayesha you have women to train—actually you can both do that. But first, let the women of the village know that there will be a wedding. Astrid will probably find that she will be well-dressed by tonight. While we are in the village, little Fear here can do all that we need done. It will give her something to do."

Ayesha glanced down. *She looks smug, but she is spoiling it by turning and, thinking that the two on the bed won't see, putting out her tongue at Basil and me.* The adults all smiled and Basil and Ayesha took their leave. *I am happy with that.* Basil muttered that he thought that Astrid could be so happy with this arrangement that she might even decide to keep doing the sewing. *He is unsure that he can predict every-*

thing that his bride-to-be will do. She is like a cat in so many ways.

Allah forgive my pride, but the Christian priest is not as good at a call to prayer as I am. "The first Mass today will be straight after breakfast for those that want to come." *The bustle of a day in a busy village has started. If anyone is taking advantage of the changes to sleep-in, then I guarantee it won't be for long.*

Chapter XIV

Father Christopher

As the day started to warm up a little in the pale autumn light Christopher noticed that Dharmal's body had already gone from where it had hung and the gate to the outside was standing open. *Good. The corpse is being buried. The less reminders of the past that are left lying around the village, the better it will be for the women.*

He then noticed that Stefan still had that red-headed woman following him on his heels. *Did I see her last night for confession? No, I didn't...still, she might not be one of mine...I will ask Bianca to have a word with her and see what her intentions are. If she really can smell treachery, and I have heard of others who could, then we will see what she can find out. It looks like the two had spent the night together. I may be beginning to see how differently people move around each other when they are becoming one flesh. Hmm, Hulagu is looking contented and there are smiles on the faces of both of his...what are they? Again, I need to ask Bianca to find out what is happening there. I would have thought that women who had just escaped sexual slavery...well the last thing they would want would be another man. What are their motives? Why would they do it? I wish I knew more about such things but I am sure that I am going to have plenty of chances to find out.*

Just then Bianca came out of the stables, followed by the Khitan. The Khitan had a horse each and, of course, Bianca had three. Christopher smiled to himself. *Whoever married the girl had best have a large bed. There was a chance he would have to share it with the horses. Where are they all going before breakfast, and why?* He stopped and thought for a moment. *Am I the moral conscience for the entire village? Am I the one who will have to keep track of who slept with whom and why they did it?* He paused as he turned that over in his mind. *Yes I am...I am their priest. That is my job, tending my flock and interceding for them with God and explaining God and His wishes to them if they wish—perhaps even when they did not wish. It seems like over half of the people are Christian, so this is a Christian flock and I am the only priest, of any sort. I will need to make some sort of accommodation with the pagans and heathens, but at present I am the only spiritual advisor here and I am sure that God will want me to care for them all, regardless of their own gods; not push them, but to hope that the others would eventually see the light. Yes,* he nodded to himself. *That is right.*

Bianca

Bianca was woken up by someone entering her room. Quickly she pulled one of the blades from the arm sheath that she was wearing and was about to throw it when she realised that it was one of Hulagu's women—Anahita—the quieter one. *She has a look of horror on her face and just stands there looking at the blade about to be thrown. She is not even armed.* Bianca put the blade away.

"You are sleeping without clothes, but you have knives strapped to you—do your people always do that? I thought that you were all soft. Were you expecting to be attacked?"

"We attacked and killed the last person who slept in this bed. If he had been wearing a weapon we may not have. Not all of our people—" she stopped explaining. *I have a right to be grumpy at what just happened. The woman has somehow made me be the one who is defensive.* She said, "Now, what do you want? With us it is the custom to knock on a door before entering a room. You are not in a tent now and I suspect you do not just go into someone's tent without announcing yourself first. I don't know. I have only slept in the open with Khitan. Close the door." She began dressing. The girl closed the door, but stayed inside. *She must still want to talk. I will stay silent to give her a chance.*

"Are you the one who Hulagu will marry?" she eventually said.

Bianca smiled. "I doubt it. He has seen my breasts, and they are my best assets, and he looked past them as if I were his sister. He seems to have adopted me into the clans somehow. That is fine with me, I have never had a family and he is a good brother…Now then, seeing that I am now his sister, what do you want from him? He says that he cannot marry you, but I presume that one or both of you just slept with him. Do you just want to rut with him? If he finds the one he wants to marry, will you try and stop him?"

"We are his köle, his...slaves. Of course we sleep with him if he wants it...and last night he wanted it when we showed him that he did. He had just been through a battle; who does not want to celebrate life after there has been death?" She smiled. "Didn't you want to? We know we cannot marry him. He is of the wrong clan. But we will help him find a wife, just as he will help us find husbands. In the meantime we enjoy ourselves. Do your people only make love with their wives? Are you shocked because there are two of us? Would you prefer that only one of us slept with him? Where then would the other sleep? With you...his sister? Do you want one of us?"

She looks more than a bit confused. I feel more than a bit that way. "If you wish to share my bed you can if it gets too crowded in his...but it will only be sharing a bed. I don't think that I am interested in your body, except that I wish I had it instead of mine," both girls smiled at that, "but I am still a virgin...Now, apart from the fact that we need to be up, why are you here?"

"Hulagu sent me to you. He said that last night you saw your priest and were purified your way. Now, before the day starts and we might have to fight again, he wants us all to be purified in the way of the tents."

Bianca nodded. *I knew that I would see fires soon.* By now she was dressed. All of the blades she had worn naked were now hidden, but she was now picking up a belt and adding a shortsword and more knives, including in her boots.

Bianca saw Anahita's eyes going over her knives. "This is all I can do in a fight, throw knives and sort of fight with them—so I carry lots of them. I am not very good—yet—but I am getting better with them..." she slapped her side where the shortsword hung, "and Basil is showing me how to use this. Hulagu says that he will try to teach me how to use a mace, but until he does, all I have are knives." She looked around. *I think that I have everything I need.* "Well, let us go then and light a few fires."

They went down to the stables to find Hulagu and Kāhina already saddling horses. "I suspect that the horses may not get much work here," he said. "We will not be going far at all today, but we need to take every chance we can to exercise them."

Bianca nodded and started checking her mounts. She started to saddle Firestar and would have left the others behind, but they started to push at her. *It is less fuss to let them run free behind.* They went out of the open gate and noticed that the village men were heaping more earth in front of the wall. *It looks like Dharmal has already been laid to rest alongside his henchmen.*

"See," said Hulagu to the girls, "she is followed everywhere by them. You and I they would bite. Her they nuzzle." *Father Christopher had been right—from the faces of the Khitan girls, despite the other women being far more beautiful than I am, perhaps there are things that others envy about her.* With that thought in mind she gave a laugh and dug her heels in and headed off to the small patch of green woods that lay up the valley's river. The others followed, trailing behind her. *I have grown a lot since I left the nuns and I have a lot more growing to do, and...damn Anahita...I know that it is wrong but, knowing what Astrid has been up to, I did want a man in bed with me last night, even if it was only to hold on to.*

They rode behind a little patch of woods on the village side of the stream, where they would be out of sight of the wall. Dismounting and leaving the horses grazing together on the long grass they started to gather fallen sticks and limbs and to make two long piles of wood. *Hulagu keeps making them far apart and the girls are coming behind him to push them closer together. Will we all go through this? Oh well, Hulagu knows me for what I am, but his...köle don't and they are the ones who have to learn to trust me. I'll join them in keeping them close.*

When they had two hands of paces of wood piled up in rows Hulagu called a halt. They threw their last loads on and started to light them. Once they were all alight the attendees started to undress. *We didn't do this last time. We must be more serious now. Should I take my blades off? If I singe my skin it will grow again, but if I singe my leather straps and sheathes, I will have to replace them. It seems that, apart from being naked, nothing lewd will happen. That is good. I am sure that I am scarlet already. Saint Ursula, please forgive me. I will confess to the priest later...I forgot to mention the fires last night.*

Having stripped off all their clothes, the other three sat down cross-legged near one end and seemed to be quickly lost in thought. *I guess I will do the same...* She jumped a little. *I have never been tickled by grass quite like this before.* When the fires were well alight Hulagu stood up. He walked to the start of the passage they had built and slowly walked through it. *Even over the fire I can smell burnt hair.* He sat down again at the other end. One after the other the other girls did the same.

They really are beautiful. Each are taking longer than the person before them. Do I have to do that? What are we doing? Is it a sign of penance, of cleansing, or of courage?

Now it is my turn. Slowly she stood and approached the opening. *It looks very narrow now.* She screwed up her courage and began to walk. *Slow...slow. I can feel the fire lapping up my sides and smell the smoke now, mingled in, the stink of my hair catching alight—all of it.* Eventually, after what seemed like an hour, she had walked out. The girls rushed at her. *They are brushing ash and burnt hair off me and...I hurt in a few places. There is a look of pride on Hulagu's face. Why?*

"You took twice as long as we did," said Kāhina. *Is that awe in her voice?* "You truly are one of us." Anahita kissed her as a sister.

They slowly dressed and kicked the remains of the fires out and used water from the stream that they fetched in a leather bucket to dowse them thoroughly before riding back to the village. The smell of burnt hair hovered all around them. Firestar sneezed.

How funny. Half of the village has abandoned breakfast and are standing on the wall. It seems that Father Christopher prevented anyone from following, but they are all trying to work out what we were doing. I may be grinning inside, but I think we have to keep a straight face and not answer any questions.

Let the singed hair and the smell of smoke on us keep them all guessing.

Chapter XV

Ayesha

*A*ll of the Khitan, even Bianca, smell of smoke. I can see singed hair *here and there on all of them and, as the women brush each other's hair I can see little burnt bits falling all over. Bianca has perhaps lost a third. She looks smug. None of them are saying anything though. They are just deflecting, or even ignoring, questions.*

After a late breakfast and Mass the work of the village went on. With Verily in tow she went back to sorting weapons. The mages soon disappeared, taking a selection of the items that had been identified as magical up to the roof. *I suppose Rani is right. Until we know what is happening with the carpet and its mage, we cannot afford to be very far away from it. The mages will spend their time up there with the watch.*

That is funny. Astrid is trying to go out to the lookout, but she has been grabbed by some village women...I think her protests will be futile...One of them has fetched Basil and he is being sent in her place. It seems that, although they may have spent the night together, they are now not allowed to see each other...Astrid is still protesting as she is being dragged off.

Thord took Ayesha to the cliff and together they dragged up the miner, Harald Pitt and some of his tools. *You cannot help admire how quickly the stumpy Dwarf, who looks comical walking and even funnier on his sheep, has scaled the rock face. I would have had difficulty doing it half as well. Thord has just taken a hammer and some small metal objects from a pouch at his belt and, alternatively hammering and attaching a good rope, he has just gone up the flat cliff in no time at all. I just used the path he made.* She looked back down. *There are still no handholds I can see.*

"Can you teach me how to do that?" she asked.

"What?" asked Thord.

"Climb like that. I can climb, but I need something to hang onto or at least a small amount of slope. That is flat with no cracks and…well…hard."

"Yes. Good rock." *The miner is nodding in agreement.*

"Good rock?"

Now both of them are agreeing. Thord said, "Good rock. It's hard; fractures clean 'n' doesn't split 'n' shatter. Makes it easy to climb, if you know what you're doing."

"It's also better to mine," said Harald. "Yes it's hard, so it'll take longer to dig, but you know t'at when you have a tunnel it'll last. Nothing worse t'an being below 'n' worrying about whether t' tunnel'll collapse behind you." *Each is comfortable that the other knows exactly what he is talking about. They are nodding again.*

Ayesha shook her head. *Trust me to get side-tracked.* "But can you teach me to climb like that?"

"You want to learn? A Human?" *He doesn't have to be so obviously amazed.* "It's rare even among Dwarves for someone to want to learn to do this for fun. I am rare among Dwarves." He grinned before saying, "Of course I'll teach you; I'll take any chance I can get to climb. Good cliffs here…wait until I show you how to jump off'n them." *Jump off them?* "You do use rope," he added as if in consolation. *I feel scarce better at that. What have I just volunteered for?*

"Can I learn as well?" said the miner. "I've always t'ought it'd be good not to have to rely on ladders when you're down a shaft. Too many t'ings can happen t'ere."

Thord rubbed his hands together and chortled. "E'en better. Now, let's see about t'is way in." They set to work to see if they could close off the flaw in the valley's defences, at least temporarily.

Astrid

*W*hat *are these bloody women up to? I haven't been here before… one of the small buildings alongside the courtyard that is also our main street. Seemingly every woman in the settlement is in attendance. They have stripped me bare. I am being prodded and measured…at least they are nice about my size, my muscles and my 'marvellous' breasts…without a by-your-leave one has plumped in front* *of me and is lifting my boobs in each hand as if she is weighing them and judging them. I may have landed into a village of frustrated brides and they are all determined to take years of this frustration out on me. Why are they arguing about fabric and what colour it should be for? When did that start? I have to take a stand.*

"Enough…if I have a choice in this then I want red." *They are all looking at me…Aren't I allowed an opinion?* "At home red fabric…any red fabric is very expensive and so, if we get a chance we wear it whenever we can. We don't have special dresses to get married in so, if I am to have a good dress, I want it to be red." *Well that kept them all quiet for a moment…where are they going? There is a rush to the rear of the building. There is a lot of noise there.* Soon they emerged with a bolt of fabric. It was red. *It is also made from very deep pile velvet. I am sure it is the sort of material that is seen in a court, not in a dress in Wolfneck.*

"I hope you don't mind." *That was the girl who seems to be in charge, the one who judged my boobs…I have been told her name…what was it…something wrong…she is from Freehold…Fortunata, that is it.* "This was brought in for a robe for Dharmal, but he changed his mind for some reason." She handled the fabric lovingly before holding it up beside Astrid to show its drape and colour. "It will show your pale hair so well." *Several other women are agreeing. Last choice I get.*

Astrid felt the fabric. *Never had I felt anything so soft, so lush. The colour is a rich dark red, darker than blood. It must be worth a fortune. Theodora might be used to things like this, but not a working girl, even one from one of the richer families in Wolfneck. They are eagerly waiting on my approval. Look at the expression on their faces.* After a pause and with a sigh, she nodded. "It is just right. It is perfect."

On hearing this, there was a collective sigh and the women flew into action. *It looks like I am going to have a new chemise as well…white silk…something around my waist and lower chest that they have brought out already made. They call it a corset. Do I have to? I have heard about them. I might even have helped to catch the whale whose bone was inside it, but I have never seen one before, and am not sure I want to see one now. I am sure that it doesn't look very comfortable.*

She said so.

"It is not supposed to be comfortable," said Fortunata sternly. "It is to make you look like a lady, not like a hunter. You move like a cat all of the time. He expects the hunter. We will surprise him by giving him a lady." *Nodding like a bloody shelf of wooden dolls.* Astrid also had silk pants quickly produced for her with a drawstring to keep them up. *They, at least, feel good and I am allowed to keep them on.*

Astrid surrendered.

Bianca

After lunch Rani announced that Stefan would go out to replace Basil in the lookout. Father Christopher grabbed Bianca. "When Stefan goes out, make a pretext to detach that Bryony from him. I want you to find out what she is up to. She is not from his village, she is from the Swamp. I don't even know what religion she is. Stefan is one of our people and a Christian. I want to make sure that he is safe with her."

"And how do I do this?" asked Bianca.

"I don't know," replied the priest. *He is a bit flustered.* "I know little about women. Surely there is some women thing you can make an excuse about...and use your sense...whatever it is, when you talk to her."

Bianca thought a bit. "I have an idea." She had her lunch and quickly headed for the gate and climbed up to the wall so she could see when Stefan came out. *I don't have long to wait and, yes, the girl is beside him again. She is like glue. Even the two mages allow each other to get further apart than that...I am sure that the girl has not been more than a few paces from Stefan since I first remember seeing her...and it is hard to forget that red hair and cleavage. Should I unlace some more of my bodice? It will even make some of my knives easier to get to in a hurry. No, that is not the point. Saint Ursula forgive me, the point is to show off my one asset, my one claim to beauty. However, yes, the girl definitely needs someone to find out more about her.* They approached the wall and Bianca clambered down.

"Stefan," said Bianca, "introduce me to your friend. We haven't met yet."

"Haven't you? Bianca t'is be Bryony verch Dafydd. She be from t' Swamp. Bryony, t'is is Bianca of t' Horses. Despite her dress, 'n' her singed hair, she be from Freehold."

"You are about to replace Basil at the lookout, aren't you?" asked Bianca disingenuously.

"Yes, we be just a goin' —"

"Well, don't let me keep you. I just want a chat with Bryony." With that she linked her arm through the taller woman's and, before she could protest, turned her and started back into the village. A brief glance back showed Stefan standing there just opening and closing his mouth. She waved him on his way.

I have thought this out. I don't think my sense, whatever it is, will work if I am subtle. I have to be direct. The priest is up on the veranda. Good, I will have backup if I need it and the girl only has a spear and bow with her, neither of them are ready nor of much use at this range.

"Tell me about what you are up to with Stefan," she said bluntly.

Bryony pulled away and faced her. "Why do you want to know and what right have you to ask?" *She sounds indignant.*

"I ask because I am the one who asks questions," said Bianca. *Now, make sure she sees my eyes cross to where Dharmal had lain. I am getting the hang of this business of asking things and being... threatening. You have to bluff. Now I cross my arms, making sure my fingers are near two hilts...and wait.*

She suddenly looks quite agitated. "I meant no harm. I just wanted a man to hold. I was taken from my husband on my wedding night and kept as a toy by one of the women here. I miss my husband so much and Stefan seemed nice and there are so few men among you and..." She broke into tears and began sobbing. "I am sorry. We have done nothing yet except hold on to each other. I will leave him alone if you want me to. I meant no harm. Did you want to take me instead?" *There is fear in her voice. Two offers in one day. I wish my luck were as good with men. Still I cannot feel any funny feelings about anything the girl says. She might be honest.*

"There, there, that is not what I meant," Bianca said. "I don't think that I am interested in women...that way at least. I just want to make sure that you are not going to hurt him. Men are just so fragile." She reached up to comfort Bryony and soon had her leaning down and sobbing on her shoulder. Looking past her she could see Father Christopher and she gave him a quick shake of her head. "Do you want to marry him?"

"I don't know," Bryony sobbed. "We haven't even really made love yet. We slept together and we were naked, but all he did was hold me while I cried. At the moment I just need someone who will hold me and look after me and...and make me feel safe. I like him to hold me and comfort me, but I don't know anything of what I want past that."

"In that case, I am sure it will all be alright. Just remember, you are not to hurt him, or you will have me to answer to." *Time for me to sound grim. I may know that I am bluffing; she won't.* "Go along now. Go and do something in the village. Don't go after him. He should have some time away from you. That way he will find out if he does like you and not just lust after you, and besides, men are very easily distracted and he should be watching for enemies that are coming here, not just at your cleavage."

Bryony swallowed and tugged the gap in her top closed a bit as if to lessen its impact. She gave a quick bob at Bianca and fled.

*Well, a bob...just like Theodora gets...I may develop a reputation here. Several other women are looking at me as well. Let us see...*She began to softly sing a beautiful little tune. *Well, it is a beautiful sounding song until you actually listen to the lyrics. Once you listen for a while you realise that everyone in the song dies in one gruesome manner or another. A lot of the old songs seem to be like that.* She wandered up the courtyard looking about. Ahead she could see the Dwarf and Ayesha, with one of the village men climbing a cliff. *The village...they were always calling it 'the village'. Didn't it have a name? I should find out.*

She spun around to a passing Havenite woman. "Excuse me," she said. The girl almost dropped what she was carrying despite Bianca's quiet tone. *She must have seen what transpired with Bryony.* "What is this village called?"

"I...I don't know. It doesn't have a name," the girl stammered. "They didn't tell us. We just call it the village. That is all we have needed." *Again the girl, the woman really—she is sure to be several years older than me—gives me a bob and moves away.*

"Then we must give it one," said Bianca, and continued on her way, going back to her quiet song. *Would it be useful to be seen as fifteen hands of enforcer? There was a certain irony here. Astrid, who is nearly three hands taller than me and a lot stronger and far more dangerous, is being fussed over somewhere in the village while I, Bianca, the one who is almost useless in a fight, am scaring the women. If I take this role it will certainly distract from the others, but I have told them my story.*

What was in that? Have they seen more in my behaviour with Dharmal than I had meant to be seen? If I'm not going to have anything else to pass the time, unlike my new brother, then I will have some fun. Speaking of which, where has Hulagu gotten to?

Hulagu

Hulagu was on the roof with the mages. He had looked down and, although he couldn't hear what she said, he watched Bianca's little performance. *She certainly is playing up to the role of a Khitan woman in a walled village. I wonder if she knows that. What is more I am curious about what is she up to with the way that she is acting.*

Chapter XVI

Stefan

*W*hy did Bianca stop Bryony? Why did I just leave her behind without asking what she wanted? I know I am certainly getting used to having the red-head beside me, but why did Bianca want to step in? Now, I admit that I am glad to have some time to myself, but I haven't asked for it nor have I given any indication to anyone that I wanted it…at least I don't think I have. I suppose that I will find out what it is about when I get back.

He had gone through the gate and was about to climb the track up to the lookout when Basil came flying down it. "Quick, get up there and get your bow strung. I think the carpet is coming. I have to get back and tell them. He is coming from the north, not from the mountains." He pushed past. *He is off before I can say anything. Basil can certainly run fast. I might be a quick runner, but Basil could give me a good start and still beat me.*

Stefan moved up the path as quickly as he could and peered north. *I can just make out a dot in the sky. It is moving.* He picked up the magic detection device from the ground and pointed it. *Yep. It gives an indication. It could be the mage, or it could just be a carpet from the Caliphate straying down from the mountains looking for something. Still, I had better be prepared…an archer against a—no doubt powerful—mage on a carpet. What preparations can I make?*

Theodora

*T*heodora heard the spider chirp for the return. *Rani-my-love must have as well as she reaches into her pouch and does something absent-mindedly before going back to what she is doing. I'll keep* *working on the pentagram. It is ready now. Why am I still playing with it and showing Fear what I am doing? Why do I seem to have this effect on children? We cannot have children...Why hadn't that struck me before? You got married, or not, and you had children. Will my love mind not having offspring with me? Why do I suddenly want to carry her kaf-hued child?*

She was only half concentrating when Hulagu interrupted everyone's thoughts. "Basil is running here—fast. He wouldn't be that eager to get back for his wedding, he will be exhausted. It must be trouble. No sign of Stefan." He called down to the street. "Make it look normal. There may be something happening. Bianca...get to the wall with your sling and bullets...on the way see if my köle are in the stables and get them up there with their bows, but tell them to keep down until I call."

Theodora shooed Fear away and told her to go down the stairs into the building while she moved to the centre of the fresh-painted pattern. *I won't start my incantation until I know what is happening. If I start and miss with this spell I will have wasted our only chance and we have no idea how powerful he is, nor what he has with him. For all I know he might be able to destroy us all with one spell or one device.*

Basil is calling something as he ran. *Bianca, with her superb hearing, has heard him from the gate.* She waved at him and turned. "He said carpet," she called aloft, "from the north." She then went up the wall, followed by the two Khitan girls.

Still not time to start chanting, but it is time to mentally prepare myself. If it comes from the north I won't have much time to cast the spell and he would be much closer than I have allowed for in the casting. No time to change now. At least I feel stronger now. I think that I feel like I have more mana inside me than I did before we attacked this village. Perhaps I have gained back what I lost from the undead as we left Darkreach. After this is over, I will have to find out how much more. She mentally flexed her in-build senses on her capacity and nodded. *I can feel it. I have enough in me to cast this spell without any help from either my girlfriend or my store. Good, drawing over your limit was always risky. I think that I will risk having an empty store.*

I will let my store device charge the diagram at my feet. I'll have time for that and I will need every bit of help I can get. This is a new spell and while I have thought long and hard about it and written it down and practiced each phrase and gesture...a new spell is always harder than one you know well...and I am casting against a mage of unknown power. It is a long spell, and so harder still. I have to take action and stop worrying. Worry will only destroy my focus. At least I have his clothes here and some of his hair from a brush.

"Stand clear," she called. "I am charging the pentagram." *I can feel the flood of power flow through me to the diagram beneath. My entire store of mana is draining into the pattern to aid my casting. It is done. I have never used that much before just in charging a diagram. It is a heady experience. I hope no-one disrupts it. That would be disastrous.*

As she started to lay out his shoes, turban and the hair she looked down and could see that Basil had reached the wall and was now coming through the gate. *He is strolling and regaining his breath now that his news has been passed on...concentrate.*

We need to find a way to communicate with the lookout...one of these devices must do that; if not we have to build one. We should have asked Dharmal. Basil is a fast runner. I can hardly imagine Thord trying to run back like that. She looked around. *The street looks deserted. No-one is visible up on the cliff. Only Bianca is visible on the wall, the Khitan are crouched down behind its crenellations.* She was about to say something to her lover, when she noticed her grab Hulagu's arm.

"Come, Hulagu," she heard Rani say. "The way she is dressed Theodora looks like a man from a distance and one person on the roof could be understood, but we need to disappear. Let us get on the stairs and not be seen. Theodora can call us if she needs to." When they were at the stairs she called back, "Good luck, my love."

It is nice to hear that, but I am now concentrating. Theodora waved a hand vaguely in acknowledgement and started scanning the sky to the north.

All is quiet, the quiet before a battle, the quiet that tells you everything is in place and you are hoping that your planning is right and everything will take place as you want it to. The time when you pray and hope.

Stefan

*H*e is coming close. Do I stay upright or try and hide? No, he might have detected me already. They were expecting more men to arrive and I could be one of them. If he sees me I will just have to bluff. I am glad Bryony is not here, I couldn't have explained it to her.

The carpet is coming straight to me and moving lower. Is he going to talk to me? Why isn't he just flying straight in? He waved at the figure and the seated figure waved back and kept coming in. *Great, I have a spear in my hand and that is a mage. At least I had some company last night, if only that. I may understand the Cat better now.*

The carpet is getting much closer now. I can see the mage clearly. He is from the Caliphate. He must be the one from the bandit band. Should I speak first? What if they have a password? I know:

"You be late," he called. "We be gotten in yesterday an' Dharmal been expectin' you t'en. He be angry."

"The Masters wanted me to do something in the far north. I am here now. Who are you?" was the reply. *He looks angry at being questioned by a mere armsman and one he doesn't even know.*

"I be Stefan—I been a workin' in t' south. You had better be a hurryin' in."

The mage snorted and turned the carpet into the ravine and flew along the river towards the gate. *He flies but he still uses the gate. Because we see birds doing it all the time, that must mean that there is something in the valley or at least over it that stops a person just flying in. I wonder if Rani knows that.*

Rani

*S*uddenly the spider chirped. *The gate? Why would Stefan want to come in? Should I open it? Asvayujau, goddess of luck, please be with me.* She opened it. *I wish I could see what is happening. Should I tell my Princess, or will that distract her? She will not have much time and she needs to see the carpet as soon as she can.*

"He is coming from the gate" she could hear Bianca calling from the gate below.

Theodora

Theodora heard Bianca call out and changed her position. She started chanting before she saw her target. *There he is.* She looked back to her book and then, before the final phrase, she looked up at the target. *He is not looking at me, but he is a bit over ten times two hands of paces away and will soon realise that I am not someone he knows.* She said her last word and pointed at her target. *I can feel the spell flow along my arm and out along my finger. I can feel it strike home. I can feel him resist the compulsion. You are mine. I am far stronger than you and I have surprised you. Despite the unfamiliarity of the new spell, and all that means, I own you.* "Come to me now" she said softly. For the charm to work he didn't have to physically hear her. *I can feel the words resounding in his head as if it were a struck bell. He is screaming silently.* The carpet started heading towards her. She risked a quick break in her total concentration. "Come out. I have him." She returned to her focus. *He is no fool and he is fighting back. He has practiced this. He nearly slipped out there.* With her gaze fixed on the approaching carpet she only just noticed Hulagu emerge onto the roof, bow in hand, followed by Rani. "Set down on the roof and then get off." *Not only can I feel it, but now I can see the strain on his face as he fights my control. I can feel his hate, his rage, his impotence, his evil.*

Hulagu approached him.

"Stand still," she said.

"What do I do to him?" he asked.

My love looks from me to the Caliphate mage and back again. I can feel the strain and I am sure it shows on my face. He has a strong will to fight this hard. I want to scream out to kill the man, but even using my may be too much and allow him to slip free. Surely my lover knows that it is hard to hold on to someone like this, especially a strong mage. At any time he can break free. It would have been easier if he were bound and already helpless, but he isn't. It would be good to have Bianca talk to him...but that would give him a chance to break free. Oh relief.

"Kill him," said Rani.

I thought he was fighting hard before. *Now it is like fighting a storm with your bare hands.*

Hulagu is nodding and has gone behind him, taking out his own dagger. My victim is making an effort to keep track of Hulagu…to break free. It isn't working. For now I have his muscles under control. He will do almost anything I say at present…but for how long? Hulagu is in place behind the mage and has the tip of the knife under his chin. Above his hand the mage's face is covered in sweat. Inside he is snarling, but nothing can be heard.

Hulagu is looking at me.

Theodora nodded.

Hulagu drove the blade home and into the mage's brain and the top of his spine. *I can feel his screaming, his death. I must pull out and let go.* Luckily she caught herself and did not disturb the lines of her pentagram. *I have not been inside someone's mind as they died before. That is not an experience I want to quickly repeat.*

She saw Hulagu withdraw his dagger and lower the body to the roof. *It is moving again. A contingent cure has come into play. Hulagu is waiting and has thrust again with the blade as the eyes brighten and move again. The man's hands are coming up to grasp Hulagu's hand as he thrusts the blade in again. The mage's mouth is opening and closing and again he dies.* Hulagu removed the blade from where it was stirring around inside the skull, paused to see if he revived again and, when he didn't, wiped the blade on the mage's clothes and stood up.

Fear is running onto the roof. I can do little. She has dodged Rani-my-love's outstretched arm and run up to the dead mage. She has her sandal in her hand and is hitting the still slightly stirring body on the head with it. Why? She is turning towards me.

"Roxanna told me she wanted to do that to him. I don't know why. He used to do things to me, things that hurt." *Her voice is too old for one so young.* "I am so glad I got to watch him die. It was so good. The other girls will be so jealous." She said to Hulagu, "Thank you," and gave her little bob at him and then rushed over and hugged him around the legs.

Ahmed's body was disposed of and the carpet rolled up and taken below. *It will be safe there until we can learn to use it. I have never flown one before, but I should easily learn how to. I am an air mage after all.*

After killing the mage, the rest of the day was an anticlimax. The Khitan and Bianca had joined them on the roof and Rani asked Hulagu to let Stefan know what had happened. He nodded and called Anahita over to tell her to go.

"No disrespect to you," Rani said to Anahita, and to Hulagu, "but how do we know we can trust her?"

Oh dear. Rani-my-love...that was silly...you are getting identical flat stares from Hulagu, Anahita, the other girl...and Bianca. What had gone on where all the smoke was?...She has seen their looks.

"Sorry," she said, and sounded flustered. "I should have thought...it is obvious."

Anahita stuck her nose in the air and strode off to get her horse... she wasn't walking that far. Before Rani could say anything else the other three had stalked off the roof as well.

"I have a feeling you should not have said that," said Theodora in an amused tone.

"Whatever gives you that idea, my beloved? Now I have to work out a way to apologise...and Bianca is getting just as prickly as the Khitan are. What is going on? Are they all lovers? What is happening?"

"No, I was told that Bianca slept alone until they went out to set their fire. The other three didn't. Now, I have no mana left, so I am useless keeping watch as a mage. You have done nothing all day, so you can sit up here and look important and bored. I am going to have a dig around in the house and see if I can see anything interesting."

Theodora took Fear's hand and, with the little girl chattering at her, went down to the ground floor. *So far I haven't even looked around down here.* She wandered from room to room. *Except for a room that is obviously where the former residents relaxed, it is all basically unused. I would say that the place was once a tavern. The bandit's common room was the bar; it even has a small stage. There is a complete unused kitchen out the back and storage rooms for food. A trapdoor covered in dust leads down from one, presumably to a cellar. I will have to check that out later.*

Eventually she came to a door that was locked. *There are some keys hanging on the wall in our room...Dharmal's old room. I left them there for later. It is now later.* She sent Fear up to get them. When the girl came back they started trying them in the lock. One clicked the lock open and Theodora pushed the door ajar and entered. *There is a small room here with a table and a few chairs. This looks like the room under The Slain Enemy. Yes...it is very like the room under the tavern. It even has books on a set of shelves...quite a lot of them actually...maybe a hundred or more. They vary from huge volumes, such as are found in the library in Ardlark to small books that are of use to travellers. I wonder how many people have died to furnish this room.*

"Fear, go and get us some more light, dear. I am going to be here for a while I think, and when you have done that, please let Rani know that I have found their library."

Time to settle down, get comfortable, and start checking all the books.

Chapter XVII

Basil

After Ahmed the mage had been dealt with Basil started wandering around looking for Astrid. *How can Puss be lost? Whenever I ask one of the valley women they just smile and say they don't know. Yeah, right. One even sniggered as I walked away. I am getting a bit fed up with this. The smithy is back in operation. If the women won't tell me, maybe the men will.*

Everyone speaks some degree of Hindi, but the smith looks like someone from Freehold, so I'll practice my poor Latin on him. "Hello, have you seen Astrid the Cat anywhere please?"

The blacksmith paused in his work. "You're the one she'll be marrying tonight then," he said, throwing a hot piece of metal into a small pot that then gave off a plume of smoke and gave off a very bad smell. *It has to be some sort of fat in there.*

"That would be me. Do you know where she is?"

"Yes. But if I tell you I will be in trouble with the women, and there are a lot more of them than there are of me. At any rate, you should be getting your best clothes ready."

Basil looked down at what he was wearing. *What is wrong with padded black leather over hemp? It doesn't show blood very well and it goes with everything...well everything that I normally have to do. Actually, it is showing signs of my recent encounter and it does smell a bit...*"Umm," was all that came out.

"You don't have anything else, do you?"

"Ahh, no. I left home in a bit of a hurry and paid more attention to weapons and food than to having something to get married in. It hadn't actually crossed my mind when I left that this was something that I would do. I do have other clothes, but they are work wear as well."

The blacksmith laughed. "Come on, my name is Norbert Black. Let's go and raid the rooms and see if we can find something for you that works better than that outfit. What do you wear at home to get married in?"

"In my family usually uniforms...often on both sides. The Army has been our family career since before The Burning; well at least that is what we think. I haven't actually been to a civilian wedding, except when I was working, and then I was usually paying attention to things other than clothing and I just wore what fitted in."

The smith shook his head and led him off. Along the way they found Bianca, Hulagu and the Khitan women.

"Come on," said Basil to Hulagu. "If I have to do this, you may as well join in."

"We can help," one said. *I think that is Kāhina.* "We have been in most of the rooms after all and we can at least tell you if any have clothes we can adjust. I can sew a bit, so I might be able to help there as well." The two girls stood beside Basil and began talking in Khitan. *They are obviously sizing me up, with much shaking of heads.* Eventually they grabbed him and dragged him into the barracks.

They paused in front of Bianca. "Come on Bianca—you can help too—and we might find something for you if you want."

Bianca shook her head. "I am not comfortable in dresses. I haven't worn one since I stopped serving in taverns. They tangle your legs when you try and run."

"Come—even we wear them for festivals—you can as well," said Anahita. "You should not be fighting tonight, and you can still carry blades beneath them."

Rani

Rani agonised. *Should I set a watch and keep someone away from the festivities? It seems wrong not to, but tonight, of all nights, we should be safe. We have dealt with all of the threats that we know about. Ratri, goddess of the night, surely you will give us at least a few uneventful nights.* She eventually compromised and asked Ayesha to organise an occasional visitor up to the roof to look around with the magic sensing device. *At least the one I have to do this task will be sober all night. Surely that should do for the now.*

Father Christopher

F ather Christopher looked into the hall. *Astrid may not know it, but Sajāh has taken care of her wedding celebrations. I am Christian, but otherwise it is looking awfully like what I imagine a Caliphate wedding might be like. The hall smells cleaner than it did last night. When I wandered in earlier it had been stripped of everything and the floor was being washed, but apart from a few large chairs up the front, it now looks like everyone else will be sitting on the floor. They have added something to the washing water as there was a lingering fragrance to it. When I asked, being told 'tea-tree oil' left me none the wiser. It doesn't smell like tea.*

The floor is covered with carpets, and some even go up on the walls. Women and girls are running everywhere and all the rooms must have been ransacked. The men are curiously absent; I suppose they are on watch; someone is on the roof. There is a profusion of cushions around the room...big ones, little ones, golden ones, blue ones...they don't match in the slightest. Every few minutes one of the children appears with another. Are they making them somewhere? I wonder if we will be allowed wine tonight? I hope so. Even the candelabras have been hauled down and fresh candles set in place in them even though the room seems well enough lit with the enchanted sconces on the walls. At least I will be able to see well to read my words.

A few tables are set up along one side and heaps of clean plates, which mostly match, stand on one. The stage is bare and I suspect it will be used a lot tonight. I had better tell Sajāh what she might not know about several of the ladies of our party...she looks a little shocked at my information...not used to Princesses dancing like that I suppose...she had better get used to it.

Eventually, just before the Muslims had evening prayer, Sajāh emerged and stood with her arms crossed looking around. *She surveys her domain. That one is a beauty, when she gets older she will be formidable. Now she chases everyone away and tells them to have prayer, find all of the others, and to dress.* She then looked panicked and asked where the groom was.

One of the little girls piped up. "He is with the men and the horse women in the barracks. I don't know what they are doing, but there is a lot of music and singing and they are all laughing a lot...even the executioner." She looked around as she said that. "Shall I get them?" Sajāh nodded and the girl ran away.

The executioner? That would have to be Bianca, or was it Ayesha? No they have not seen Ayesha at work. At least that explains what I saw earlier. I wonder if I should tell her and how she will feel at that.

Ayesha came into the hall at the hour for her prayer. *She obviously knows what will be happening tonight, from the way she is dressed. She has scandalised a few of the other women with her clothes. They obviously already have their own ideas about how a woman holy warrior should dress for prayer. Ayesha, equally obviously, realises what is on their minds.* "If you are going to work after prayer, you wash, make sure you are clean and you wear your work clothes. I will be dancing tonight, so I am wearing my work clothes...at least as I wear them out here among the barbarians. Allah, the All-Knowing, knows what is in my thoughts. That is all that is important."

Stefan

Stefan came in from the lookout at last light. *It is nice to see that they have not forgotten the watch and the valley gate in their preparations. Why am I relieved to see Bryony at the village gate? We have done nothing yet. She has her dress back on and is carrying something. She really is very pretty, far too pretty for me to land normally.*

"I didn't know if you had clean clothes. These should fit you and everyone else is dressing up. It will be a big night. Come, I will help you."

Father Christopher

Eventually all is ready. Father Christopher took his place at the head of the hall, with Bianca's Testament in his hands, and looked around. *Most of the women are drawn up in two blocks with a gap between them. I suppose the rest are with Astrid or in the kitchen. A few are sitting on the stage with a variety of instruments. They are dressed in what are obviously their best clothes, even if a couple scarcely cover the nipples of the women who wear them, even with a pulled up chemise to help in concealment. The styles vary, just as do the places they come from. They look like a cross between some upper-class tavern and what I imagined a bordello might look like. This is what they have and at least they are probably the handsomest set of women I have ever seen. In my very limited experience, that is.*

He had a chair behind him and a table covered in crisp white linen where he had put a crucifix and his chalice and a silver plate that had been found for him. There were two stools and two matching cushions in front of him. *At least one of the women knows what is needed. I am not sure if this was exactly what the Abbot had thought of for me as a village priest, but you take what God gives. I am nervous. Apart from that rushed ceremony on the way into Evilhalt, I have never performed a wedding before. I have only seen a couple. Mind you, it is likely that no-one else will know if I err and I am sure that God will forgive me. I have chosen the text with care thinking about my audience.* He looked at Sajāh and nodded. *She sends two of the little girls running out of the hall. Fear is standing with Rani. She is shifting around to see what she can. Where is Theodora?*

There was a little wait with women nervously talking among themselves and shifting around. Eventually they could hear some drumming and then a flute. *The music sounds, well, wild somehow. The drumming surges and pulses and the flute sounds around it. A singer has joined in an odd fluctuating song. It is in Khitan. It is a wedding song. Well he supposed it is, given the context. I wonder if Basil knows what is being sung about him. It gives him a lot to live up to at any rate.* He smiled. It was not the sombre music he was used to in church, but it was full of life.

The men's party came into the hall. The girls came first. Anahita was singing and moving her arms and shoulders around, Kāhina was the drummer, playing a long drum hung on one hip with a small beater and two smaller skin-clad cylinders hanging off her belt on the other side, and Bianca was playing her flute. *That must have been the music that the little girl heard. They were teaching her the tune.* The three women moved in the same exaggerated steps as if a part of a dance and sometimes turned themselves around. He looked again. *Is that what Khitan wear to weddings?* The three girls, including Bianca, had jewelled veils and wore embroidered dresses that flowed low from the hips. Bianca had her veil lifted a bit to play. On their tops they only wore a brief and tight embroidered bodice with bare arms, a plunging neckline and a very exposed midriff to just under the breasts. *Well it is tight on the Khitan girls. They obviously had to adapt one for Bianca, and her smaller frame and...more generous other proportions does not just make it snug. I hope she does not fall out. Oh dear. She looks embarrassed and she skipped a note when she saw me watching her. I am certain she has never appeared in public wearing so little since she was born.*

He smiled at her to reassure her.

Is that a smile back around her flute and through the veil? I cannot see even one weapon on the three of them. This would give the village women a new view of their 'Executioner'. It certainly gives me a new view. I think that the Metropolitan was right. I was not meant to be a monk.

Behind the girls were the men. Basil came first. *One of the dead bandits must have been a Freeholder fop. I am positive that Basil has never worn so many colours in his life. He is basically still clad in black leather, but on each leg and each arm—and even on the chest—the leather has been slashed and cut in a different pattern and the lining has been pulled partly through to show off its colour and fabric. The lining on his left leg is gold, his right leg is a vibrant green, the leather on his arms is lined with blue and white, and his chest is lined with red. He is wearing a codpiece and even it was coloured. Half of it is red and half is green. He has hose on the lower parts of his legs in green and red, and on his feet are, of course, slashed shoes...black with gold lining. In place of the rapiers a fop would wear he wears his shortswords, but they are worn low, hanging on his waist in the Freehold style, his hands resting on the pommels...fingers with jewelled rings. On his head is a hat. It is a good pace across and has three huge feathers stuck in it, gold, red and blue. His vest is open nearly to his waist and he has a white undershirt that is so voluminous under the vest that it emphasises his wiry build. A golden chain is glinting around his neck. His normally homely features are transformed and he walks several hands taller than his normal height. He is strutting like a bantam rooster.*

Christopher heard a soft sigh rustle through his audience.

I suspect if Astrid says 'no' during the ceremony, I will easily be able to find a few volunteers to take her place.

After Basil came Hulagu. *It seems even Khitan men dress up for weddings. He also has an embroidered vest on, although he walks in a similar way to the women. He is fully armed and looks around as if expecting attack. His hand sometimes shades his eyes as he seems to look far away, even though he is inside. It all seems to be a much-stylised dance of vigilance. This must be what the Khitan expect their attendants to do for them. The four village men came behind in an assortment of clothes, all of good quality and, by the fit, with new owners. All wear hats of one sort or another.* The hats were swept off as they entered the hall together and then broke up to take a place to sit.

The girls moved up to the stage, but kept playing and singing until the men took their positions to Christopher's right. Basil stood behind a stool and Hulagu stood beside him.

Suddenly when they were all in place it went silent. On stage Verily began to play a harp, its soft liquidity contrasting with the wild exuberance of the barbarian music that had preceded it.

Three of the young village girls came into the hall, their faces wreathed in smiles and wearing ribbons through their hair. For once they wore longer dresses, even if they were all plain and similar in cut and fabric. *Had the women made those especially for today?* They came to the front and stopped. The next in were the rest of the village women, those who had been preparing Astrid, dressed as the other women in the hall were. They hurried to join the audience. Ayesha came next. *She is undulating more than walking. She is in her dancing clothes, but has found a lot more jewellery, mainly gold and silver bangles around her arms and around her ankles, but she also has silver bells braided into the ends of her hair. There are so many that even Ayesha cannot avoid making a soft tinkling noise as she moves.* She reached the front and took up a position mirroring Hulagu's. *Despite her dancing clothes, she still wears two of her blades. Is she supposed to defend the bride?*

The harpist changed tune and the joyous music became more processional. Theodora came into the room with Astrid on her arm. *So, the Princess would give the bride away, would she? The Princess must have hidden one of her Court dresses from home on her pack-horse. No-one here would have been able to produce such clothes on short notice...even if they had the materials handy.* He looked her up and down. *There is a long and voluminous floor-length robe in white silk, another over it, equally as full, in red with no belt, but a sash. The white one has a painting around the hem and a band of lavish embroidery around the end of the long sleeves that are just visible under the red. Another wide band of embroidered fabric is around the hem and cuffs of the red. Around her neck she has a yellow silk collar, over a hand wide. It is embroidered with gold thread and simply covered in jewels and pearls and golden beads. It matches the hem and sleeves of the red. It sort of looks like a Metropolitan's robe, only it is a lot more spectacular. Wound tight around her waist is a long sash of gold and purple and red and green with small gems sewn onto it. Over her heart is embroidered in gold the chi-rho symbol. That is a surprise. On her head is a band of metal three fingers wide, it may be gold, but I can't really be sure what sort of metal it is as there are so many gems, of different sorts, attached to it. Strands of pearls hang in loops from it along the sides of her head. The red robe is embroidered with pearls in many patterns. Red slippers are sometimes seen peeking out from under the hem. They probably have pearls sewn on to them as well, from the look of them. She is obviously of Royal birth, and she is showing it.*

Astrid does not look like a woman of Wolfneck. What is more, to my mind she only just misses out on not looking like Astrid at all. The few women from Wolfneck that I have seen have worn shapeless loose dresses with long aprons that go over the head to the back and front and with strings of beads of amber and jet and coloured glass. The Cat looks like a lady, a high lady, from Freehold. She has a long rich red velvet dress, also covered in pearls and with gold thread embroidered in it. It is cut low at the front and her breasts are pushed up and struggled to be contained by it. How had the women done this so quickly? On her head is an elaborate close fitting hat, also embroidered, covering her hair and from it, covering her face, hangs an almost sheer red silk veil. I can just see a feline smile through it. She walks very upright. She must be wearing a corset. That explains why her breasts are so pushed up. It must have been a fight to get her to wear that. Just visible under the veil there is a necklace. It must have come from among the bandit's loot. It is made of linked red crystals that match her dress, or are they rubies?...They couldn't be that...they are far too large and a single huge stone, in the shape of a heart, sat resting near flat between her breasts. In her hands she carries something that looks like a small bunch of flowers. They must be made of material as there would be no flowers around at this time of year.

Basil was staring at her, entranced, and with his jaw almost hanging open until Hulagu gave him a dig with his elbow and he closed it.

Astrid came to a stop in front of Christopher and looked shyly down at Basil. He reached out, equally shyly, and took her hand and the ceremony began.

With no-one to stand as Astrid's father, Theodora gave the bride away. *You would think that Darkreach still owned Wolfneck and she is giving the head woman of the town to a loyal noble. If any had doubted her claim to her heritage before, they wouldn't do so now.*

Astrid's and Basil's rings were also of a dark red stone. *I am no expert on such matters, but they do look a lot like rubies.*

I hope that I have given adequate thought about my text. I don't have the Gospels so I have to work with what I have. I hope that what I have will work, not just for the wedding, but for everything around me.

"Go thy way," he intoned, "eat thy bread with joy, and drink thy wine with a merry heart; for God now accepteth thy works. Let thy garments always be white; and let thy head lack no ointment. Live joyfully with the wife whom thou lovest all of the days of the life of thy vanity, which he hath given thee under the sun, for that is thy portion in this life, and in thy labour, which thou takest under the sun. Whatsoever thy hand findeth to do, do it with thy might." He stopped there, fearing that the rest of the verse was too gloomy.

It seems to be working...as is the rest of the ceremony...despite having a Khitan groomsman and a Muslim maid of honour. I wonder if I should tell the couple that it is traditional at Christian festivities for them to dance together afterwards. I may leave that to the people who have arranged everything else for the rest of the night.

After the ceremony was over and everyone had kissed everyone else, Theodora disappeared along with the kitchen staff, and the musicians started playing. *The party has started. The seats are for Astrid and Basil, me and Rani and, presumably, for Theodora when she returns, as that one is hard against Rani's seat. Two broad stools, probably more comfortable for both of them than chairs, were put opposite the bride and groom, and Ayesha and Hulagu have been sat down on them. All of us at the front have small tables in front of us.*

Servers began circulating with pitchers of wine, ale and water. Plates began to appear with small pieces of food on them. Sajāh stood up and announced that she would be running things tonight.

"What is new in that?" one of the younger women called out cheekily from the crowd. Sajāh glared briefly at the area the comment came from and continued, "Food and drink are coming around now. Many of our dishes will be served from common bowls and I ask those who are not familiar with the customs of the Khitan and the Caliphate to only use your right hands to eat with...if you don't know why, ask a neighbour. Bowls of rose water and towels are also coming around. Take your ease on the cushions. We should have enough room. I ask anyone who wants to entertain us tonight to see me and we will work out what time we are all going to get to bed tonight, if at all." This was greeted with laughter. "And for my sake, if any of you men," she turned towards them, "want to teach me the dancing of this side of the mountains when the dancing starts, then I am available to learn." This prompted more laughter. *Ayesha is surprised at that last comment.*

So, the village has installed the two mages as their headwomen, have they? I wonder if Rani and Theodora realised what role the women have given to them? I doubt it. I have noticed that the two are sometimes so wrapped up in magic and each other that, unless something serves to focus their attention, the world seems to pass them by in its more subtle moments...and that is from me. Even more important than them realising their role, who among the women had thought this through, or was it an accident? Unlikely when you consider that someone in a village full of women had chosen two noblewomen, each from different cultures, to sit in the position that would indicate a symbolical rule over them. They could have just as easily not had anyone there at all. Theodora has unintentionally reinforced this by being the formal Princess at the wedding and giving the bride away as if it is her right to do so. Someone here must have a big smile over that. I will bet on Sajāh. Whoever it is, it indicates that someone is planning for the village to continue as it is and for it to stay independent. If they can use their symbolic rulers to get guarantees from their homelands, then they should be able to hold this independence...that is if they can fend off bandits and the wild tribes and any attempt by these Masters to take them back. If they stay independent, unless I can get a replacement to fill in for me—despite my commitment to the others—in the long run I will be staying here. He smiled inside. At least I will be easily able to find the wife I will need as the village priest. I thank the Lord that the text forbids me from taking more than one.

If we all end up staying, how would Sajāh, if it was she who had done it, take that?

T heodora came sweeping back into the room. *From the way they are not reacting, the women of the village don't recognise her... now are they reacting. This time she is dressed very much as Ayesha in her dancing clothes. Of course she is three hands taller than Ayesha and has quite pale skin, but really it is only her golden eyes above her veil that give her away.* She went up to Rani, lifted her veil, and gave her a kiss before taking her seat.

There is scarce time for them to react before the food is out. Basil and Astrid are not used to being waited on, are they? As soon as they go to rise, two of the little girls pounce. It looks like they have ladies in waiting tonight. Another is before Hulagu and Ayesha and now here is mine, the oldest of the children, a Havenite lass who had not been in the procession and is dressed far more simply. Her name is Gurinder and she is quite shy. Rani and Theodora, of course, have Fear sitting at their feet. It looks like we will be eating mainly Caliphate food. That will be a relief for Ayesha and a new experience for most of the rest of us. Most of the meat seems to be goat or mutton...there is rice with nuts and fruit in it. Basil and Theodora know what it all is. They get to help their partners and point out things. Ayesha is doing the same for Hulagu...to the disgust of the Khitan women, who have taken a seat near the stage with Bianca. I get to find out for myself... Strange...but I like it. It is hard to eat hot food with your fingers though. I am glad of the bowl of rose water and the towel. I must not wipe my fingers on my robe. I suspect that this is not done.

Theodora

"**I** haven't had a chance to tell you," Theodora said to Rani, "but I have found Dharmal's library—and his diary. At least I think it is his diary. It is written strangely and I cannot make it out, but it is in Dwarven characters."

Rani patted her hand. "Later...as long as we have it. If you cannot read it, give it to Thord. Maybe he can puzzle it out. Meantime, look around you. We cannot leave these people alone until they are safe. We will have to go to Dwarvenholme but we have to prepare first and safeguarding these people could take all winter. I have thought of a spell for you to work on, this one I know we will have to do together. That should keep them safe and we will need to start working on it soon, if it is not already too late... You look...magnificent tonight. Did you bring the dress with you?"

Theodora nodded. "I couldn't leave it at home. It was made for my cousin's wedding feast and taking it seemed like taking a part of her with me. It has been rolled up in the bottom of my things, taking up a lot of one of my bags, but luckily it survived without problems. I never thought that I would have a chance to wear it."

"The gems must be worth a fortune, if you need them."

"One of the reasons I brought it, actually, but I suspect that they are not worth as much as what Astrid is wearing. Thord may say that he is not a typical Dwarf, but he cannot take his eyes off them. He must be the only one who is looking at the gems and not what lies underneath."

Rani laughed and put on a look of mock petulance. "Are mine not good enough then?"

Theodora blushed and changed the subject.

Astrid

*I*t is just as well Basil knows what I am eating. I have no idea. It is all tasty though. I must make sure I have enough. I am sure that I will need all the energy I have tonight. She licked her fingers.

After the first course was mostly finished, Sajāh stood up again. "It is the custom in the Caliphate to have certain dances performed first at weddings, for the bride and groom. They are supposed to ensure fertility for the marriage. I don't know about that, but it is obvious that they help men rise to the task." There was laughter.

She clapped her hands twice in command and Ayesha stood up and gestured to Theodora. Verily also stood up. *Those clothes have never seen the mountains of the Caliphate, let alone come from there. I suppose they are loosely modelled on what Ayesha and the Princess are wearing. They are just...well...much briefer, and also worn without a veil. I will bet the bandits liked to see her dance in them. She must also be naked below to wear something that brief. It covers very little.* Two other Caliphate women also stood, dressed much the same as Verily and Lãdi.

The Hindi cook came rushing out of the kitchen, leaving instructions behind her. Several drummers gathered on the stage along with Kāhina, who had also picked up something that looked a bit like a mandolin—a passing girl told her it was called an oud. There was also a girl with a sort of psaltery and another with two long reeds joined beside each other with holes in each of them for fingers. *I suppose it is something musical that I have never seen before. There are a lot of things like that.* The women moved in front of the married couple and others cleared a space for them. Jokingly the women pushed all the rest of the men to the front of the audience. *None of them are reluctant to go.*

Astrid looked to her right. *Hulagu's face is blank and his eyes are fixed on just one place... wherever Ayesha happened to be. With Rani watching Theodora it will be just like the last night in Evilhalt.* She gave a short laugh and felt the jewels at her neck...*well almost.*

The music started. Slowly at first with a soft drum beat...*and they are far better than Howard.* The women's upper bodies didn't move—but their hips did, the tiny cymbals that they wore on their fingers keeping time to their undulations, a different time to that their bodies were starting to take. Lãdi's dance was slightly different to the others, but it went to the same beat. *I am sure Basil doesn't know whether to look at them or at me...he is so funny. I point out the beauty of the dancers... particularly that of his Princess...That made him blush. I am fairly sure he is feeling feelings that he shouldn't feel towards one of Hrothnog's grandchildren...especially when he is in front of me, his bride.* His blushing made Astrid laugh all the harder. Casually she put her hand in his lap. *Yes, he is enjoying what he sees. It is supposed to be a fertility dance and it is making him rise to the occasion.*

"I am going to learn this dance," she said into his ear, "and make you compare us. See, Verily is not Caliphate and she can do it and she has breasts as large as mine. Will mine jiggle like hers, do you think? Like a litter of kittens under a blanket in a small basket?" She moved her shoulders to try and shimmy. *Basil has obviously realised where my hand is now. He is bright red, but he doesn't move my hand away.*

Astrid laughed again.

The night continued. *People are telling stories from all lands but I am glad when they stick to Hindi. I am not the only one who has difficulty with some of the others. Theodora, for the first time, is telling tales from her own land. I have heard some of these events...but hers are very different versions to those I am familiar with. Songs were sung.* More food came out. The dancers came out again.

Kãhina and Anahita have grabbed Bianca. *Why are they coming up to me? Bianca is blushing.* "We are going to dance for you a dance of the tents. Again, this is one with marriage in mind—although it is most often done when people are choosing each other. We have never done it here, and none of us are very good, but we will try." She started beating out a rhythm, a wilder, more insistent beat than the more languid and sensuous Caliphate form, and the three girls started dancing in a line. Kãhina was dancing as she drummed.

Bianca is having to keep glancing at the others to check where she is up to, but she is more or less keeping time...better than I would...and the other two are not so far ahead of her in skill that her lack shows too badly. It is not only a more urgent beat, but there is more hand and arm movement than during the Caliphate dance. They are telling a story! I wish I could read it. The dancing is more enthusiastic than smooth like Ayesha and the Princess, but the men in the audience seem to like it a lot.

They took a break and held hands and bowed, before running to where they were sitting and pulling sabres from under their cloaks. *What are they up to?* Kāhina handed her drum to one of the others who had been following along with the beat. "Same beat please," and she resumed her place.

Sabres? At my wedding?

Father Christopher

*B*ianca *looks very nervous. Well she might. Those are real sabres and the girls are spinning around and performing a pattern where Anahita, in the centre, is being struck at from both sides, fending them off, and striking back. The clash of steel echoes in time to the drum beats. I wonder if I will be needed as a healer…but the blows are not random, are they? There is a pattern to them that repeats and, as long as the girls don't forget their pattern, they should be safe. The dancers may not be as good as those that preceded them, but they certainly hold your attention. Why…I am tapping the beat with my foot…all of the men are doing that…some are thumping on the floor, and many of the women are doing the same and it is getting louder and louder. Other drummers are joining in…Anahita is gesturing at them. They are gradually increasing the pace of the beat.*

The girls whirled around, the blades flew and the noise got even louder. The girls' dresses started to rise from the floor and to form a circle around them as they flew around and up. The skirts showed now that the dancers had bare legs beneath the dresses but did not rise far enough to show any more. *Thankfully.* It seemed that one of the girls would surely die as blades flashed towards throats and bare stomachs and at legs, and the beat increased in speed. *Some of the Muslim women are starting to ululate, the wild sound a perfect counterpoint to the dance. I am sure that Bianca will soon burst out of that top. I don't know if I should keep watching or not.* Eventually Bianca spun out of the three and collapsed on the floor, her face flushed. *She can keep it up no longer.* She was gasping from lack of air, her chest was heaving, and Christopher found his eyes drawn to her. *I can feel my body stirring in a way that I am not used to. I should keep my body under control. I should not be lusting after her. It is so wrong. Oh Lord, give me strength.* Next it was Kāhina's turn to go and finally Anahita was left on her own, whirling her sabre and her body in a circle before collapsing.

The hall rocked with applause. *Bianca may not be the most beautiful woman here, but she can be very attractive when she forgets herself. I wonder what performing the dance will do to her reputation.... Blessed Father, how much penance must I do for my thoughts tonight?*

Hulagu

Hulagu went down and hugged and kissed all three. *I know that I have a big smile.* "Now they have seen something that few outside the tents have seen...Bianca, you did well, very well. One day we will take you back to the tents and get a good husband for you."

Anahita went back to talk to the other women. Kāhina and now Bianca had gone to join the musicians. Hulagu returned to his seat beaming. "I wish some men were here. The men's version is even more energetic. You should see a whole field dancing," he said to Ayesha.

"So, have you married Bianca now as well? Will she join your harem?"

Her voice is cold. Hulagu's face fell. *What have I done now?* "Married? I am married to none of them. Bianca is my sister and Anahita and Kāhina are köle. I cannot marry them. If I could marry them there would be no problem. I would marry them and they could leave and go back to the tents and in a year they would divorce me and regain their lives. But I cannot marry them and the only way to get them back to the tents is to be köle until I find them husbands. I could do that if I took them back, but I cannot and so they have to stay with me and they insisted that they had to be proper köle and sleep with me." *I am just moving my mouth and flapping air. Everything that I just said is probably nonsense to her.* He paused. "Did any of that make sense?"

"So they wanted to sleep with you and you had to because they are your slaves? It is not the other way around?"

"No...I mean yes...I mean...it would dishonour them if I refused when they had offered."

"But you do not love them, nor they you?"

"No, we just...enjoy each other as men and women do."

"Both of them? At once?"

"In this case, if that is their choice, and seeing that one is not senior to the other and neither has borne me a child, yes."

"But you cannot marry them?"

Where do I start? "You see, I cannot marry anyone from their clans. From my clan, if I marry into the tents, I can only marry an elephant, an eagle or a lion. But I may not marry into the tents. You know that my prophecy was to marry a woman from outside. I know it will not be Bianca. She belongs in the tents perhaps, but not with me as a husband. I am her brother and I will find her a good man as her husband if she lets me. She will have a very good herd as dowry and so she will be a good match."

Ayesha

I may be shaking my head in disbelief but no wonder people think that the Khitan are strange. Tonight, in a side conversation with Hulagu, I have learnt more about the way they married and bedded each other than my teachers had been able to tell me in all of my studies. He has two women to bed and it is the choice of the women! He doesn't really have a say in it? She smiled. That would shock the Mullahs, but I do like the sound of it.

"Let us see if others will dance," she said to Hulagu. *Face front and change the subject without setting his mind at rest.*

Astrid

"So," said Basil, "you don't want to learn that dance too?" *That question is just a little too innocent.*

"That dance? No, I am content to learn the other. I do not use swords. I would as likely cut myself as well as the person beside me," replied Astrid, "but you should talk to Hulagu. Maybe men can do it as well and he would teach you."

She stuck her long, slightly pointed, tongue out at him.

Father Christopher

It is time. Christopher stood up and raised his hand for silence. "Many of you would not necessarily know this, but in the western lands it is the custom, on such occasions, for speeches to be made and for toasts to be drunk throughout the night. I am going to make the first speech, but it will be a short one.

"Basil you have a jewel of a wife. I have only known her for a short time, but I treasure her. I have to. She saved my life." *At least I got some laughter.* "Astrid, you fled a forced marriage to a man who did not deserve you and I think you have made a good choice in his place. Basil is a good and gentle man…"

"I hope not," said Astrid. *Her voice is deliberately not quite low enough. It causes even more laughter, but is she ever serious? No…I guess not.*

"I am sure that he is, at least in the areas where it matters. Now, I want you all to get something to drink and join me in a toast to our bride and groom, Basil and Astrid, the first marriage of the village of…of…what is this place called?" *Damnation…I forgot to ask…now I sound all bewildered and they are laughing again.* Soon there were cries of, "Basil and Astrid," and, "to the first marriage of 'What is this place called'." Christopher sighed. *This really is going to be a long night.*

He gave up and took a drink himself before sitting down.

Theodora

"**S**urely that man who wrote the book came here," said Theodora to Rani. "There must be a name written down somewhere. We have to add it to the list of things to do before it really does become, for all time, the little village of 'What-is-this-place-called'."

Bianca

Before anything else could start Naeve Milker, Fortunata, and two other women from Freehold—whose names she did not yet know—came over to the musicians.

"Can you play a pavane?" Fortunata, the seamstress, asked. She said to Bianca, "Despite our long time here, and being allowed to play music, we have never had the chance to explore such gentle activities as a courtly dance. Our skills are used to accompany songs and only sometimes for Caliphate dances or things to excite them."

"I can," said Bianca. "I have worked mainly in taverns, but sometimes people wanted one. Will Lord Bar's do?" Fortunata nodded. "Good. It is a simple one for musicians to pick up." She stood from where she sat and moved up to the stage with the other musicians. "I will run through it now and the rest of you just follow me." *At least they obey me quickly.*

"In that case we will be back in a while when we have found out if we have to teach some men to dance," said Fortunata.

Bianca started giving the beat to the other musicians as the women went away. *I can see that the four men of the village are the first targets. They are still at the front of the audience. It is easy to hear what is being said.*

"Giles Ploughman. I hope that you can dance better than you can milk a cow," said Naeve. "You are going to do a pavane. I hope that you know how. The rest of you can stand up as well and we will go down the back and find out if you are worth keeping around."

Looking over her instrument as she played Bianca could see the men looking from one to another. *It is obvious that they had enjoyed the*

Caliphate dance and then the Khitan sabres on top of that, and had been hoping for more as the women competed with each other. They don't expect to be putting on an exhibition themselves.

Ayesha

Verily has obviously realised that her harp will not be needed for the pavane, whatever that is, and there are enough drummers already. She is sitting watching the others getting ready and is looking bored. Straight away she is up and pulling some knives from a bag near the wall. Now she is juggling them. Ayesha's interest was sparked. This girl does have potential. Let us see how good she is with the blades. She stood up and moved to stand beside Verily, facing her two paces away.

"Throw them to me," she ordered.

Verily looked surprised, but obeyed.

Ayesha plucked them out of the air and started cascading them and then sending them back to Verily. *Verily's catch is not as fluid as mine, but she is managing. She has obviously not done any throwing with another person before, but she isn't bad for a beginner.* They managed a few passes backwards and forwards. "Enough. We need to practice together. You keep going," and she made a last pass back to Verily.

Ayesha returned to her seat. "I think I will train that girl. She has some ability."

"Are you allowed to do that? She is a Christian, isn't she?" said Hulagu.

Ayesha laughed. "That is simple. I just have to ask Theodora if I can. She will not know why I ask and so she will say yes. I must follow her orders and if she says no, then I cannot—but, perchance by the will of Allah she will say yes and I will have to obey."

By the time Verily had sat down to applause, the Freeholders were ready. *They are clearing more carpet and people at the front. They must need a lot of room for this.* Fortunata signalled to Bianca, who gave the beat leading in with the end of her flute, and the musicians began to play. *The beat is very...stately. The couple moved back and forward and then around each other in pairs and then a refrain and then in fours, the refrain again and then all together before reversing the process. Except for Giles the men are obviously less skilled than the women, but all are enjoying it. Even I like it although it is wrong for men and women to dance together like that.*

After the dance Naeve kissed Giles. "That is the first time I have done that in seven years. Thank you."

Others are coming forward to learn. It may be a while before the men sit down again. They are short of partners. Stefan, Thord and Hulagu will be up soon.

"Go on," said Ayesha to Hulagu, when he was asked. "You wanted to dance." *I am enjoying sitting up front watching the interplay of people unfolding in front of me far too much. Who talks to who, who is flirting with another...it is like a training session where you have to just sit and watch and listen and then answer questions about the dynamics...only now I can do it for fun...or to work out how these people may act later...it seems that the mages are not the only girls who like each other, for instance.*

The women are looking around for their next victim. Basil declining in case his wife grows jealous that he dances with such obviously beautiful women on his wedding night is hilarious. Beside him his wife is laughing at him. Father Christopher gets dragged up instead.

"But I am a priest... I have never..."

"Then it is time you did," said Sajāh, who had grabbed him. "It will be a first for both of us. I have never danced with a man and you have not done anything with a woman." *She has him cold on that. He is lost for words.*

With two sets going the men get no respite. They just finish one dance and then are grabbed by another woman for the next.

A Freeholder, Eleanor, went up to Bianca. "Can you do any other dances? Perhaps a galliard or a tavern bransle or even a canarios?" *A dog? She is dancing a dog?*

"I can do all of them. Kāhina, get your oud, we have enough drummers. You can go back to the drum when we do the canarios, although I suspect you will want to learn to dance that one."

Eleanor called for attention. "We are going to learn more dances." *The women are cheering and the men are groaning. Father Christopher may try to cry off, but he is not going to be allowed to. He is very different from any mullah I know. They would all have gone off in a huff by now.*

The night continued with alcohol flowing freely and the dancing changing between styles. Speeches and toasts…many speeches and even more toasts…more juggling and singing and storytelling and yet more drinking. Except for her visits to the roof Ayesha managed to just sit there and watch and listen. *I am sure that, except for the children and even including the other women of the Faith, I will be the only fully sober person in the entire place by the end of the night…even including the priest…although he, at least, is moderate. Just as well Rani gave me charge of the watch.*

The dancing is stopping…of course…more food. Soup in two styles, bezelye çorbasi and havuç çorbasi, in bowls…hummus and tabouleh with flat bread, keftethes, and borani chogondar. I have not eaten so well since leaving home to start my training. The cooks here are absolute gems. If they choose to return home, I am sure I can help find them work.

Eventually everyone except Bianca and me have, willing or not, joined in the dancing. Once he decided to dance with his wife, Basil scarce has a chance to do so with his wife again and he and Hulagu are being passed from woman to woman in the same way as the priest is. At one stage they had three sets on the floor at once. Basil may be graceful, but Hulagu is obviously more suited to riding a horse than to capering on the dance floor. He balters. His legs are those of a horseman. That doesn't stop him being passed around among partners…

Stefan tries to dance as much as he can with Bryony. What is more, when she is not dancing with him she doesn't dance with anyone else, except once with Basil—as all the women have—and a couple of times with the priest.

Even Thord is having a good time, although his dancing is not graceful, may Allah forgive my laughter—but he is worse than Hulagu. As he gets more and more drunk, his laughter is getting louder and more infectious. His partners sometimes stop dancing to laugh with him.

Bianca

*A*ll of the other musicians, at one stage or another, have put down *their instruments and danced. I am seeing them all take turns with the men. I am the only one who hasn't. I want to dance.* She puts down her flute. "You all know the tunes well enough now. It is my turn to dance." She rose and grabbed Father Christopher. *Did I cut someone off? Oh too bad. She gave ground quickly enough...Lord pray forgive my temerity. Saint Ursula, patron of virgins, care for me and guard my thoughts. I am dancing with a priest and I feel that I am nearly naked. Lord, please forgive my lewdness... Mind you, it is fun. He is clumsier than me, and so much larger, but it is fun. Here am I worried about how I am dressed and the poor man doesn't know where his hands should go. He doesn't want to put them on my skin and I am mainly skin at present. He should put them where they are supposed to go.*

After that dance he insisted that seeing she had been without a dance, and all of the others had danced with him many times, he would dance with her again. *That is nice of him.* They had two more dances before she let him go.

Is it wrong? I like him and his eyes scarce look at anyone but me. But he is a priest...not even really mine. Will I go straight to hell over this? He is now even my confessor, so I cannot even raise it with him and seek help. He is gentle with me and he does have nice hands, and they feel good on my waist.

Astrid

*H*ello...*that is interesting.* Seated at the front, and looking out over the floor, the Cat nudged Basil. "Our priest may need a priest soon. I think he likes seeing Bianca like that." She grinned.

The last remove is all sweet and sticky things. Basil tells me they are baklava, kataifi and rakis lokum. Some smell of roses and some of oranges. As well there is also kaf, thick, hot and sweet. My husband...I like that word...blows on his to cool it down a little. I could easily get used to this drink. It makes you feel a bit more alive, without getting you drunk. I will have to watch out for the sweet things though. I love sweet things and they are far too delicious to be good for me.

*I*t is late enough...now is time to go to our bed and enjoy a few other *things beside food and drink. I will see if I can remind him of the first dances.* Astrid nudged Basil. He nodded. *He has taken my meaning.* They both rose.

"Does that mean that the party is over?" said Valeria, a young girl from the south coast.

This is my night. I can say what happens. "Only if you want it to be," replied Astrid. "You young things can continue as long as you like, but I am sure there will be some work to do tomorrow, or rather, later today. We old and married women have a bed to go to and a husband who we need to make sure is rested." She grinned. *There are cheers, whistles and more music as we leave.*

It would be fun to stay, but I mean to wear my little man out tonight.

Theodora

*I*t has been a long night. Most of the children have already gone to bed *and now Fear is asleep at my feet.* She pointed down and Rani rose. "I think it is time we put her to bed and went ourselves." *I am still feeling wide-awake, but I suppose that will wear off soon the bed is a good idea. My dark beauty is stronger so she can carry Fear.* "I don't know if we have gained a serving girl or a daughter," she said, laughing. "Get my light from around my neck and we will put her to bed."

*W*e made it back to our room and I may have had more to drink *than I thought. Let us look at that book again before I forget.*

Theodora got out 'My Travels Over the Land and Beyond' while Rani undressed. *We have never really looked in the book after finding its mention of Dwarvenholme.* She and Rani lay on the bed and Theodora began leafing through the book. *It feels good her trailing a finger over my back and bottom...and lower...no I want to concentrate.*

"Stop that...for now," she said. "Look what it says here. I knew that there would be something. 'After two days on the track at the base of the mountains we crossed a torrent coming from a gap in the hills by an old bridge. On the other side was a short and poor track that led to the hidden village of Mousehole...' that must be here. It means there is a way up to Dwarvenholme from close to here. We must have missed it."

"What else does it say?" asked Rani. *She has left off with her play and wriggled up beside me now.*

"Where was I...'There is a rock in the middle of the river with an old set of standing stones on its top. No-one knows who put them there or what they are for or even how to get to them.' See it is here he means. 'At the end of the ravine is a valley that opens up. There they run herds and have a mine for rubies of the highest quality...' so it might even be from here in the valley that the Cat's necklace came from...'Where the river lies quiet in the valley they also pan for antimony. This is one of the most pleasant places that I have been to. The cliffs and mountains that surround it make access difficult from anywhere but the ravine so the inhabitants live happy and secure lives. We stayed in their inn, the 'Hall of Mice', for the night. Next morning we continued south.' Well, it seems that we are now living in the Hall of Mice."

"Even better, the Cat now lives here among the Mice as well," said Rani, and giggling, they put the book away to concentrate on other matters for a while.

Ayesha

*T**he night is winding down; morning prayers are only an hour or so off. I am just heading off for a last look from the roof and two women start having a disagreement about a man. What will happen here? Of course...Sajāh is striding over and she grabs them like a mother chiding naughty daughters.* "At least for the present we are not going to have enough men for us all. We are going to have to learn to live together—without fighting. Life will work differently here to the way it works in other places for some time. You have both had too much to drink. It is time to go to bed for you. There will be more parties. While you are going I have something for you to think about. Ayesha was telling me about Hulagu and the arrangement that he has with his girls..." *Oh yes, I did. I know where she is going now. She can continue while I go up to the roof.*

Chapter XVIII

Stefan

Despite having had a late night Stefan woke early after only a couple of hours of sleep. *My head is still a little fuzzy from the night's festivities. Now if I can get my eyes open...someone is beside me.* He turned. *There is a head on the pillow beside me.* He checked. *Red hair— it has to be Bryony. I remember drinking a lot and dancing with her and...nope...after Basil and Astrid left the rest is a complete blank. I wish I could remember what happened and how she got here. This could be embarrassing. I can remember hoping she would come back. The first night we actually just slept, on top of the bed even, with a huge sleeping fur around us and she was almost naked in my arms—after she told me her story in full. By the time she was finished she had cried herself to sleep while I just held her tight. Did we do any more than that after the wedding? At least this time we are sleeping under the covers.*

He left her sleeping and snuck out of his bed and quickly dressed before grabbing weapons and going downstairs. *I wonder if anyone has thought about a watch...silence greets me in the courtyard...it is worse...I wonder if anyone else has thought about being awake.*

He heard some noise in one of the buildings beside the hall and wandered over to where it came from, which led him to the kitchen. There he discovered Lãdi and a couple of others hard at work. Lãdi wore an apron over her dress from last night and did not appear to have gone to bed.

"Good...you are starting to wake up...here...isn't it time for someone to think about guard duties? Take this basket with you...it is your breakfast."

Feeling chastened Stefan thanked her and headed to the roof. *Without the spider I cannot get out of the gate and without the magic detector I would be almost useless anyway, but at least I might give a bit of warning.* He sat down and looked in his basket. *Despite her tone, Lãdi had provided well for whoever came out. There are warm rolls and pastries, a little crude pottery tub of butter and another rough jar, a quite hot one, with a wooden lid, a leather seal and with a leather strip holding it all shut tight.* He opened it and smelt it. *That stuff from last night…what did they call it?…kaf. It smelt good in the morning, even better than the tisanes I am used to.* He inhaled appreciatively. *Even the smell clears my head just a little bit. I could get used to it its thick sweet taste.*

He sat on the roof. *I'm gradually seeing the village come to life below me. Bianca was off to the stables and is now back.* She soon joined him on the roof.

"I thought that you would be…occupied for most of the morning," she said.

"You obvious be a knowin' more t'an me. What be a happenin' last night? I mean did I…did she…oh damn. I canna remember a t'ing after Basil 'n' t' Cat left."

Bianca laughed. "You and Bryony danced some more and then she whispered in your ear and you led her off. There was a lot of cheering and after you left there were some toasts in your honour. If you appear in public too soon you will disappoint a lot of people." Stefan felt himself blushing. "What is it with the men here? We seem to be able to get you blushing easily. At any rate, how do you feel about her?"

"I don't be a knowin much. She be nice to be with an' feels good in my arms. I said I canna remember much else."

"I tell you what. It looks like you got that basket from the kitchen. I didn't think about that. I will go down now and get one myself and take it over here. I will also get another for you to take to her. When you wake her with it, the two of you can see what happens…I don't know if I should tell you this, but I have had a talk with her. She doesn't know what she wants from you either. At the moment I would say, and Lord please forgive me, I cannot believe that I am saying this, as long as you are both comfortable, do it and if you need to see Father Christopher, then you should do so then. I know for certain that he does not think that we can only enjoy ourselves in marriage if the circumstances are proper." *From her face she has just realised what she had said and how it could be taken and it is her turn to blush.* He smiled. "I mean, I went to him with a question and that is the answer he gave to me." *She did no better with her second try. It is amazing how quickly she just stood and left.*

Interesting...I may not be the quickest, but I think that our horse-girl Bianca has feelings for the Father and does not want them to be known. She may not even know them herself, or at least be allowing herself to know.

When Stefan went back to his room he took a refilled and augmented basket with newly baked hot pastries and jam. Bryony was still soundly asleep in his bed. Putting the basket down, he gently lifted the blanket and looked underneath. *She is naked beneath the covers and lying face down. Nice bottom. It has freckles on it as well. I don't think that I have seen it before. I am sure that I would remember.* He put the blanket down again, this time lower down her back. *Her back is very pale and also covered in freckles.* He started to gently kiss her back along the spine. *She is murmuring a name...not mine...it sounds like Conan...that is her dead husband. Shit...what am I doing...I should go.*

She came awake with a start and turned over. "I just had the most beautiful dream," she said sleepily. After a slight pause her eyes opened. *She has just realised where she is... Her eyes are looking down her own near-naked body...now she is fully awake and her hands are flailing about to grab hold of blankets.*

"Eeep," is all that came out as she grabbed the blanket and pulled it up.

"I be a bringin' you some breakfast," said Stefan, waving at the basket. *Try to avoid looking at her or saying anything else...God I sound more than a bit inane...a right idiot.*

"Did we...was I...I cannot remember anything," she almost wailed. "I am sorry."

What to do? He leant down again and lightly kissed her on the lips to silence her. *At least she doesn't try to avoid me. That would be a start. She has gone quiet.* When he pulled back he smiled. "I be likin' to pretend otherwise, but I canna remember a t'ing either. T'ere be several t'ings we can be doin' now. One is t'at I can be turnin' round 'n' you can be getting' dressed 'n' leave. Another be t'at I can take off'n my clothes 'n' climb in with you 'n' we can be havin' breakfast 'n' get crumbs in t'bed an' be workin' out where to be goin' from here. I t'ink I would like to be a doin' t'second if it be alright with you an' I hope t'at you be a wantin' to do t'same."

I can see her thinking. I guess she doesn't know what to do either. She wiggled to the side and looked under the covers. "Unless we did it somewhere else, I don't think that we did anything last night. So I now have two questions. What do you have in that basket that smells so good and what side of the bed do you prefer?" She smiled up at him.

She looks nervous, but it is a nice smile.

Hulagu

Hulagu woke up with the two girls beside him holding tight on to each other and sound asleep. *They are curled together like puppies. Well, they did more work than I did last night—even if I did have to dance a lot. Let them sleep. I will look after the horses. Some köle they are. They get to sleep and I do their work as well as my own.* He dressed in his everyday clothes. All of those from the night before lay tangled in an indiscriminate heap beside the bed. *At least the girls can sort them out...when they finally wake.* He grabbed his weapons and, buckling up, went out.

I feel a bit fragile this morning. Did I drink that much last night? By the Spirits of the Sky and the soul of the Clan I did...and I made a decision...now to think on it again...I wonder if anyone is on watch and who will be up. We still have a lot to do here before we can all sleep in as much as we want to.

Father Christopher

I *have done them so long I must have the Hours built into my system.* He got up and did his prayers before he was even fully awake. *I doubt that I will have anyone there, but I said there would be a daily Mass in the mornings, so I need to go and say it. The hall will still be set up for the wedding, but it will have to do. If I am going to stay here I will have to think about building a church...somehow...and the Church is not rich.*

Having thought that, his mind turned to the corollary. *I am badly in need of a confessor. Lord forgive me, I am lusting after a woman. I might be able to forgive it in others, but every time I see or think of Bianca now I am starting to have impure thoughts. I really shouldn't have watched her dancing last night in those clothes. It is just luck that my robes hid the reaction of my body and, when we danced later I was in better control...although when I had my arm around her waist...*He headed down the stairs still thinking about his situation. *I wonder what her reaction would be if I approached her. She might wish to join the Khitan...or she might say yes. I just don't know and I don't even have a clue about how to approach the subject. My lack of experience with women is...well...painful...literally. Her upbringing has, however, made her a strong girl and so much more practical than I am. Obviously, even if she said yes, we could do nothing about it until we are married, but she might not want to wait a year until everything is over. Perhaps it would be best to say nothing. Maybe, with prayer, I will conquer my lust.*

Rani

R ani woke up on being shaken. She looked on the other side of the bed. *Princess is there, but there is another head between us and Theo-dear is reaching over its owner.*

"Didn't we put her to bed?" asked Theodora quietly. *It is Fear. She must have left her bed in the slave barracks and come over to the Mouse Hall and climbed in between them. They couldn't allow her to do that too often. We are both sleeping naked as it is, but what if she came in when we are making love? She has already seen and experienced far too much for her six years. She doesn't need to hear me calling out to Devi and Krishna.*

They got out of bed and quietly dressed in ordinary clothes, each helping the other with lacings. "We have a lot to do today," said Rani in a whisper. "We need to look in this mine for a start and set up a guard. I forgot to do that last night and that is not good. If anyone thinks of it, they cannot even do a watch properly. We have the gate opener and the telescope and all of the other things. I think that maybe we need a bag to put them all in. That way we can just pass them from guard to guard."

Theodora nodded. "I need to think about a spell. It will be hard, very hard, but I may be able to hide the valley…well, not hide it…but at least stop people from looking in using magic. The Masters know where we are, and we know where they are, but they do not know what we are doing here. If we can keep it that way it will put us on the same footing as them. After all, we have no idea what they are up to. I also think we need to see if Father Christopher knows any miracles to find out something about all that magic. We don't have an earth mage, but a priest should serve nearly as well."

Rani agreed. "And we need to see how the others feel. I think we need time to prepare before we go further. I mean they may not wish to go further…particularly the men. Here they have a good home, we know from what we read that it is going to be a prosperous one and there are a number of good-looking women for them—why should they risk their lives? Even Thord might like the idea of a mine of his own and to give up on wandering." *It is nice that we seem to agree on things, even before we say them.*

By now they were both dressed and armed. Rani looked at Theodora and nodded towards the bed. Her lover shook her head and, taking her hand led her out of the door. They left Fear sleeping in the middle of the bed and went up to check the roof. *Bianca is there on watch. She is sitting on the edge of the roof with her legs hanging over. There is an empty basket beside her and a smell of kaf in the air.*

"About time you two got up. I am the second watch. Stefan was here when I arrived. Have you two taken to keeping Princess' hours?"

Theodora blushed. *She is grinning and…I think they say…pulling our legs. I must say that I did not expect that reply…I thought my lover was more…formal. She just stuck out her tongue like a little girl.* Bianca gave a short laugh. Rani gave Bianca the detector and the gate opener and the two mages left the roof.

"Breakfast is ready in the kitchen," she heard from behind her, as they went down the stairs, "and Lãdi has not gone to bed yet. You might want to send her there…she might listen to you. She totally ignored both Stefan and me when we tried to persuade her."

Astrid

A strid woke up in a bed…a big bed. *There is a man lying beside me, his hand is lying in place, but it is not quite able to cup her boob and there is something around her throat. Oh, that is right. I am married. That is Basil…my husband.* She felt her throat. *I am in bed naked and I still have my necklace on from last night.* She giggled to herself. *If only Gudrid could see me now. I am married. Last night I must have felt that I should keep the necklace on as long as possible before I have to give it back. I still want to. Where had it come from? I was dressing, or rather I was being dressed, and people were doing things to me and someone had come from behind me and put it around my neck…a man…I am sure it was a man…it smelt like a man…but I didn't even see his hands, let alone the rest of him. All I saw was the way the women's faces in front of me lit up. I didn't dare move with all the pins that were stuck into bits of my clothes. I didn't even dare speak.*

Astrid looked beside her. *Basil has a smile on his face. I have seen many men who are more handsome, but he is cute and brave and strong and he is kind and Father Christopher was right…he is gentle when it counted—and much more important…I have this warm feeling inside when I think of him…I guess that means I love him. Many women don't get all of those things. I am lucky. I have never had another man, but I have seen many in the sauna and I suspected that I might be lucky there as well. In addition, his wiry athlete's body has stamina…lots of stamina. I wonder if I should be up doing things. No, I was married last night. I have better things to do today.*

She rolled over and gave Basil a series of kisses on the side of the face and whispered into his ear: "It is time for you to wake up and make me purr," she said.

Thord

Thord woke up in his room. *Mine now…I have taken over a room that had obviously belonged to another Dwarf. Everything is the right size and even the clothing in the chest at the foot of the bed fits me. The day is good and I am happy. I am doing what I want and used to dream of. I am seeing the world and living life to the full. I don't have to get up and just worry about something taking one of my flock as its prey. I have enemies. I might have died easily when we took this place. This is what the stories are all about. Mind you we might be here for a while, but that is fine. Even here I have mountains to climb and people who want to learn how to do that and enemies who are going to come to attack us.*

What is more, there is a mine here. I am not much of a miner but, as with all Dwarves, mining is in the blood. You hear of a mine nearby, you want to see it. I wonder what it produces…those gems that the Cat was wearing. I wished that I had paid more attention in class and not dreaming so much of open sky and mountains. I have never been good at telling the value of gems, but I have a rough idea. What I saw around her neck, if sold to a ruler—and only a ruler could afford them—would be enough to buy the entire little village that she came from. I wonder if she knows that. If that came from here, a Dwarf could get rich…very rich if he was an owner of the mine. He would have prestige. It might even make up for not seeing the world, but anyway, even in that case someone would have to carry the gems elsewhere for sale. That would mean money, adventure, prestige and travel. He smiled and started to get up and see what had to be done…*and that means seeing the mine, for a start.*

The day is getting better and better.

Ayesha

Ayesha didn't get much sleep. She had not gone to bed until after sunrise prayer. She woke up and looked at the other side of her bed.

There was no-one in it. I know that I am feeling disappointed, may Allah, the Virtuous, forgive me. Somehow I had dreamt that I would find Hulagu there...and without his girls. It had all been a dream. I know that I was dreaming that I had Hulagu beside me. Allah preserve me...no...I had dreamt that I had Hulagu inside me...I am even damp. That dancing! The Mullahs were right. Men and women should not dance with each other. I only relented after the other Caliphate women had teased me...I danced with a man and I liked it. From now on I will only dance with women. I still have Hulagu on my mind and I was actually jealous when I thought that he had a harem already. Now I know what is happening I am happier. I don't mind if he has sex with his slaves—men will do that, even when they are married, but usually because they want to, not the other way around...it was the thought of him being married to a first wife that had...upset me. Maybe I could subtly see what Bianca knows about his feelings. If anyone knows it, it would be her. Mind you, Bianca obviously does not know her own feelings. She danced with the priest and grew clumsier and stumbled over her words when she tried to talk to him alone, and he did the same with her. She has a holy man to marry and doesn't realise it, nor did he realise that he has a bride eager and waiting for him.

She realised what she was thinking and was shocked. *My thoughts have gone back to where they should not. I cannot marry Hulagu...or can I? I have heard Mullahs argue that for a woman to marry outside the Faith, if she kept hers and raised her children in it, it means that the Faith grows and reaches new lands. On the other hand if I were to stay outside for all of my life, and keep others here of the faith, we will need a Mullah eventually and he would then be the right person for me to marry.* She thought about the Mullahs that she knew who were of her own age. *I would, at best, be a second wife with one of them and, more importantly, none of them appealed to me and I cannot imagine waking up damp from dreaming of them. That thought alone was funny. Unless they are very different men when they are in their homes, they are all far too serious and have no idea of what the word 'fun' meant...except to condemn it...and public dancing, of any sort, would shock them voiceless.*

Well, from the light outside the windows it could even be nearly Dhurhr and I have responsibilities to the other women to lead them in the prayer. It is time to get up again and to get on with the day.

Chapter XIX

Theodora

Theodora came out into Mousehole's courtyard holding Rani's hand. Father Christopher was going into the hall. "Time for Mass, I think. I want him to do something for me, so I had better keep him happy. I have seen more religion since I left home than I used to see in a year in the Palace. Mind you, I find it comforting. I wonder how he would take it if I asked him to marry us." She looked anxiously at her lover and tentatively smiled. *How would she take that suggestion?*

White teeth showed in Rani's brown face. *Rani love has the most gorgeous smile. She should do it more often. At least she is smiling back and she is leaning down to give me a kiss...a long kiss.*

When they had finished she spoke again, "Then we can be a proper family, since we seem to have found a daughter."

Rani

Alarmed and flustered at Theodora's idea Rani headed for the kitchen while Theodora went toward the hall. *I don't know how to take what my lover just said. Does she really want to try and marry me as if we are to be man and wife? Can we? I know that it is not just lust on my part. I love my exotic Darkreach Princess...and we are fated to be together...I know all of that...but marriage? Surely we cannot get our priest to do that for us...or can we...he is not much like the priests at home. How would my family in Haven react to that?...that is, if they ever managed to hear of it at all.*

Theodora

Theodora saw Verily standing beside the guardhouse. She was throwing knives at a well-used target with a look of determination on her face.

"I have had to practice in my room by throwing blunt knives at firewood before and I had to hide what I did. Now I can work at longer range and get better." *She cannot get much better. Standing nearly thirty paces from the target the girl is using both hands to draw and throw and is landing six knives within half a hand of each other at a speed I have never seen before. It took a mere count of three for an entire hand of blades to be on their way to the target. It is a blur of flying steel. On its own just one thrown knife blade will not do much but the way this girl throws, a person drawing a sword would have six in their body before their blade even left its sheath and only one of them has to strike an eye or cut a vein for it to be fatal.*

"I am going to Mass," said Theodora. "If you want to come with me, we can see Rani afterwards. She wants to start looking to see if she can teach magic to you. I mean, I could as well, but that is one of the things she does and she would be much better than me."

"Yes, I want to see this priest and talk to him again. He seems to have sense and I do not know what I should do and what I should feel. I just feel empty and sad and I should be happy. Before you came I had rage and revenge to keep me going...to make me feel alive. Now I don't have that," she said dejectedly, "and I have nothing to replace it with. It is as if there is nothing for me now. I am an empty vessel with just an ache inside and last night there was nothing to help me fight my dreams...I have very bad dreams." *Even her voice sounds hollow and far away. It is sad that this velvet-voiced and beautiful girl has been ruined in such a way.*

"Come," Theodora said. "You were raised in a different religion, but let the Mass wash over you. It is a consolation and there is a peace in it. I am sure that, if you offered, Father Christopher would teach you the songs to sing." She thought back to some of the castrati she had heard at home. "There is one that is called the Kyrie that you would sound beautiful singing and there is calm and contemplation in those sorts of songs. They may help you." She smiled. "Rani wants to teach you magic, Ayesha wants to teach you how to kill, and now I want you to get the priest to teach you songs. Your life is soon going to be too full to be empty."

Father Christopher

Christopher was setting up for the service when they started to come in. *Despite last night there are quite a few. The milkmaid is here with the farmer, the dressmaker sits beside the smith. On the other side of the smith is Sajāh. The three are obviously together. What is more Eleanor—what had she been?—oh yes, a guard, not only has the bowyer beside her, but is holding his hand. There are a couple of other women as well, even one of the Havenite girls, as well as young Valeria and four others whose names I do not remember and two of the children. We will have to organise something for them, a school, and someone to look after them. We cannot just let them run around. Now Theodora has come in...I will wait a little longer. I am not sure about the expressions on the faces of the women. Some of the women sitting with men just look determined while others look like a cat that has caught a mouse. The men look...I suppose stunned is the right word. Rani is now here. She is looking a little nervous as she sits beside Theodora.*

A last look around. *Yes the men all look...owned. I hope the women know what they are doing. That is something else we will have to do— find some more good men—although it looks like Sajāh and Fortunata have found one solution to that problem. I will need to think about that. It looks like last night will not be the last wedding that we will see.* He was just opening his mouth when there was another arrival...the brewer, Aine. *I wonder where the miner is. He is the only local man not present and not, apparently, claimed yet.*

Theodora

After Father Christopher had finished Mass Theodora stood up and turned around to all of those present. "After lunch," she said, "Rani and I would like to see you all and find out what you know and can do and want to do. Can you please spread the word through the village? Oh, and by the way…we know the name of the village now. It is not going to go down for us all as 'What-is-this-place-called'." She looked at her priest. *Father Christopher looks embarrassed, but everyone else is smiling.* "We have an old book from a man who travelled everywhere and he once stayed here for a night. He says that it is called Mousehole and the place where the bandit chiefs stayed used to be an inn that was called the Hall of Mice." *People are turning the name over in their minds.* "I will see you all after lunch…"

She said to the priest, "Father…Verily needs to talk to you."

After getting the rest of the day organised, Theodora and Rani sat down with a newly awake Fear between them. Theodora started to brush Fear's blonde hair to get the tangles of the night out. *I have agreed to let Rani do the speaking here. I will try and keep the girl calm.*

"Little one, I want you to listen very carefully," said Rani, sitting in front of her. "You have a choice to make. You have had many bad things happen to you here in Mousehole…things that a little girl like you should not have had happen to you. Theodora knows a way to make your memory of them go away — if you want her to do this. It will be as if they never happened. You will wake up as if you have just arrived here and the last year will be gone forever. You can have a childhood back. We will still keep you and look after you and love you, but the bad bits will be gone. It is your choice."

Fear sat and thought. Theodora had a hand on her shoulder. *I can feel the tension. There is a slight tremor in her body as her muscles tighten.* "So I would be here, and you would be here and I would remember only what was before?"

Rani nodded.

There was silence. *Fear must be thinking hard.* In a serious tone, one that was far older than the girl was herself, she said, "I will keep what happened to me. I hated the last year but I didn't like my life before much either. If I lose the last year I will not know why I love you so much for saving me." She reached out and put her arms around Rani's neck and hugged her and continued, now in the voice of the little girl that she was, "Will you be my mummies forever?"

Rani is now looking across at me. I can feel tears springing into my eyes. They are starting in my lover's eyes as well.

"Yes dear, we will."

The question that I asked myself earlier is now answered. Neither of us might ever carry a child, but now we have a daughter. Fear turned and hugged her...*and I...I don't know how to feel except confused.*

Chapter XX

Father Christopher

*W*ell, we are gathered, Christopher thought, as he looked around at people standing around and talking quietly. *I wonder where the mages are? Except for Hulagu and his köle, who are on watch, every-one in the village is gathered here. I was there when Rani spoke to Hulagu and so she knows the mind of the Khitan. Apparently his mind is also that of his köle, on this at least. He hadn't even bothered to ask them, although they stood right beside him.*

It was still a little longer before Rani and Theodora entered the hall, each holding one of Fear's hands as she skipped between them. They went up to the front. "Thank you all for coming," said Rani. "We must leave you to sit a little while longer though. Before we can speak with all of you from the village, we need to see our original band for a few minutes."

"Can we see you out the front please," continued Theodora, and they moved back out of the hall. As they were gathering he looked at them. *Astrid and Basil are clutching each other's hands and smiling. Stefan has brought that red-head, Bryony, with him, Thord looks, well, it is sometimes hard to tell with Dwarves, I know that I look grim at one end of the line, Ayesha has a blank face and Bianca stands at the other end from me and is shifting her weight from foot to foot. She is nervous about something.*

Theodora said, "What we need to know is who wants to stay here and who wants to continue on our Quest. We also need to work out, if we go, when."

"Where you go, I go," said Ayesha. Basil nodded.

"And where Basil goes…you will not stop me from going," said Astrid.

Thord looked more cheerful. "I'm going to Dwarvenholme. Many have set out for t'ere, but none have reported success. If'n I stay here I'll probably just be rich. If'n I go t'ere, win or lose, I'll live in t' legends. T'ere is no choice."

Stefan thought for a bit. "We have discussed t'is. I be not lovin' Bryony, nor do she be lovin' me, but we be wantin' to stay together for t'present. I left with you for t'is purpose. I canna be lettin' you down now. I admit t'at I would prefer to be a livin' a quieter life with a better chance of stayin' alive, but I be havin' a duty t'at I must complete."

They are all looking at me now. This is where it gets difficult. He looked around at them and started, "I have two duties now and I am torn. I was sent out to just see the world and charged with the pastoral care of any that I encountered that need me. Personally I want to come with you. I think that this is something that must be done, but I cannot leave this village of Mousehole without a priest. For other reasons, I need to talk to someone above me as well. Is there any way we can get to Greensin on the carpet? If we can, and I can get another priest to come here, then I will go with you."

The mages are looking at each other blankly. "We forgot the carpet," said Rani to Theodora. Then to the group she said, "Yes, we think that we in the valley should stay secret, and so don't want to use it much, but this is something that the carpet would be good for. We will get you a priest."

Next...Bianca. *She looks uncomfortable and is still restless in the way she stands. Now she has her arms crossed defensively under her breasts, almost hugging herself.* "Not long ago I had no family at all. I now have a sort of brother at least. What did Hulagu say?"

"He thinks that we should go," said Rani. "Whatever this means, he said that I had to tell you that he thought about it last night and reached that decision and he thought about it again today and still thinks the same."

Bianca is smiling and nodding. She looks far happier. I wonder what that means. I have no idea, but obviously Bianca does. Now her arms uncross and she is still.

Rani continued, "He still has his Quest and," she smiled, "he still doesn't have his bride. He said that if you really didn't want to go, he would take you back to the tents, but he hopes that you want to go on. He said that he thought it would be good for you and he knows your determination."

"Then it is decided," said Bianca. "We go. I suggest though that we do not go during the winter. The cold will be a worse enemy than the Masters. We should go in the spring."

"That is what we think as well," said Theodora. "Does anyone object?" They all shook their heads. "Then let us go and see what help we can get and what the rest want."

They re-entered the hall. *Sajāh is on her feet and facing the other former slaves who are all seated on chairs, benches and cushions. She has obviously just finished speaking to them.* She spoke before anyone else could, "Before you say anything, we think that you should hear what we have to say first." *Others are nodding.* "Until a few days ago we were slaves. We lived as long as we behaved ourselves and we died if we objected or if we lost our beauty or even just at a whim. One girl died because of a bet on who could better hit a running target. We existed for others as if we were things, not for ourselves as people. We were treated as no other slaves are ever treated. Now you have given us freedom. I presume that we may go or stay as we wish." She paused and looked from Rani to Theodora. They both nodded. "Then those of us here, we choose to stay. We have been talking about this since we were freed. This is our village now. What lives we had before here are now gone and in the past. In many cases our families are gone as well, and we all need to start again…this time together. However, having said that, we realise that without you we would have nothing and without you someone, anyone really who is determined, could take our freedom again. These are the mountains, the Great Range. We are far from anyone and even further from help. Several of us are from the villages of the north and south plains and they have argued that their old villages stayed independent only because they could draw on the Khitan as allies against whoever came against them. We have no-one like that to draw on here and we want you to be our safeguard and to teach us. We want Rani and Theodora to rule us, as our…we don't know what to call you… Princesses, if you wish. That would be nice. I think that we all liked having a Princess last night." *There is a fair amount unrehearsed murmuring of assent among the villagers.* "This will be a rich village. In return for freeing us and protecting and teaching us, half of what it earns from its mines and fields shall belong to you people, and your descendants, forever. The rest of us will still be wealthy and, more importantly, we shall still be free." Sajāh looked around her. *Even more agreement is being expressed. She must have been talking to them for a while. She didn't just organise this today.* She sat back down beside the smith. He patted her hand and Fortunata leant over him and gave her a kiss on the cheek.

It looks like the rest of us are astonished. I feel a little smug. It seems that I was the only one of us thinking ahead. Clearly I was right in some of my speculation…and I certainly am not going to be the one to start that conversation.

Theodora was the first to recover. She waved the others to seats, putting Fear between her and Rani. *She stopped momentarily in thought and glanced back at me. Something has struck her. Does she worry about my opinion on this?* She said, "You know that Rani and I are lovers." *There is nodding.* "Perhaps neither of our families will have us back." *There is more nodding.* "The rest have, for one reason or another, left our homes behind and we have a Quest to perform…a Fate that must be settled…before we can come to rest." *Again there is nodding.* "Yet you still want us to rule you, you want us to take your wealth?"

Good question, even though I suspect that I already know the answer to it…but it still needs to be laid out. Sajāh looked around at the other freed slaves. *The others are all looking at her.* "Some would be yours anyway, by right of conquest, at least the khums, the fifth. Most conquerors would take it all, including us. We count one half to be cheap against our new lives and our freedom. Oh, Father, the Christians tell me that your share is the…what is the word?" She looked down at her sister and their partner.

Fortunata said, "We are to be free of normal tithes, Father. Your share of the half is to stand as our tithes to the Church. Those among us that came here from the Brotherhood have always been sold to slavers by their masters so that they could pay tithes. We want no-one to ever be faced with that sort of choice again. If other Churches come here, you will have to share that with them."

Christopher stood up. *I hadn't thought about this part of it, but it does make sense.* "I think that the Metropolitan will be pleased with that arrangement. Tithes may be set at a tenth, but they are not always paid and the Church is always short of money and always has too much to spend it on." He smiled. "I think that I can say yes on his behalf. I thank you, my flock, and …" *I need to choose my words carefully now, something I will always have to do here…*"may the Blessings of the Most High be on you all for your wisdom."

He was about to sit down again, when he had another thought. "As your local priest, I am now free to perform more marriages if required." *Now for the next fireball.* He turned to the mages. "I will have to get back to the library of the monastery to look at something I once read there, but I believe there is a precedent for you to be married, if you wish. You would need to be joined in some way for me to install you as equal rulers, after all." *The expression on their faces is worth that. They must have already wondered. I really hope that I am not going to disappoint them, but I am sure that I came across something...just a line...many years ago in an old history, that would back me up, at least partly.* He sat down to cheers.

I can almost read the expression on Rani's face. 'Married? We can actually be married?' He tried to resist smiling.

Theodora's face is more controlled, but I can see the wheels turning behind her eyes. She jumped to her feet and ran over and kissed him. "Thank you," she said. *Well, that was a surprise. Sometimes I forget that for someone well over a century old she is almost a teenager in so many ways.*

Fear was tugging at Rani. "Why is mummy Theodora so excited? Why did she kiss the priest man? I didn't think she liked men?"

"She kissed him because he just gave us good news. She and I can marry and you can be our real daughter in the eyes of everyone." Fear then ran over and flung herself onto his lap, threw her arms around him and gave him a kiss as well, before running back and landing on Rani's lap.

"In case you had not guessed," said Rani, with Fear squirming around on her lap, "we have adopted Fear. She is now our beloved daughter. That is another thing we were going to tell you."

Theodora then took up, "Which means that we now need someone to look after us." *Without looking back she held up a hand behind her, with her palm facing the direction of Basil and Ayesha to forestall what we all know they are about to say.* "And that means not one of you two. We will accept you as our guards. That is your real task and why you were sent after us. We want someone who is worried about our hair and not whether someone is trying to kill us." *It is easy to see rueful smiles on their faces as they look at each other. It has brought some smiles and laughs from the rest.*

"Besides, you are now supposed to worry about my hair," Astrid said to Basil. *One of her deliberately-not-quiet-enough whispers adds more laughter.*

Theodora tried to get back on track. "We still need to find these Masters and stop them. It is their fault that you were enslaved. By now you all know this village is really called Mousehole, don't you?" She looked around…"This place, Mousehole, was rebuilt and became a home for bandits. We could ask someone else to do it or to help, but seeing that you have made the decision you have, this is the first test of our independence. We think we know where they are. We think that we have some ideas on what to do with them and, I actually don't want to say any more about that this week. I am not being secretive…well yes I am…but not from you. I have a spell I want to cast. It is a major spell and I will need at least a week to prepare for it. Once I have cast it then I will say more.

"We are going to stay here, perhaps even for the whole winter, before attacking. We need time to prepare and time to train you and to get things organised. I understand that winter is often a time for doing very little outside because it is too cold. I am from Ardlark—we don't see much cold weather there, so I am not sure. Well, this winter will be busy. We hope to test to see if anyone can become a mage. Rani used to teach at the Mage's School in Haven and she wants to see if anyone here can learn from her. We want to set up a school. This is not just for the little ones, and we need someone to take charge of them, but everyone needs to learn to read and write at least two languages. I suspect that a lot of us can teach some form of music or musical instrument. We are already a village of bards. I like that part. As well, we have many weapons skills to share and Thord, I believe, is going to instruct us how to climb like mountain goats. We need to find out what you can teach us and what you can do and who wants to come with us on the next part of our journey."

She has clearly finished and with her sitting down has just started the questions and talking…among the villagers and to the…Princesses. Looks like to me as well …

"This may be a silly question," said Naeve loudly, cutting through the rising chatter, "but what are we called? We live in Mousehole, but being called Mouseholers sounds silly."

"Why can we not just be the Mice, since we live in the hole?" the Cat asked quickly, before Rani could say anything.

It seems that everyone likes that idea.

*I*t is amazing how fast the day goes when you are busy. With looking *after* the animals, changes of guard, and people leaving to get food *and prepare for the evening meal, the rest of the day went by quickly. No-one got near the mine today. It is amazing how many people want to talk to the priest or the Princesses.*

Chapter XXI

Astrid

*T*he shared meal on our second night is a lot quieter than my wedding evening with a night watch now on duty. We have more people to share the job as guards now, but admittedly some are trainees and almost useless. We are now on the Evilhalt system; everyone is in the militia, regardless of what else they do. Mousehole is far too small a village to waste people. Unlike Wolfneck, it is also more likely to be attacked. Everyone has to be used. Most of these women have never handled a weapon seriously before. We just handed them arms tonight, more to give them confidence than anything else. Stefan and his woman…definitely his woman now…are sitting opposite us and it has gotten out that tomorrow the leatherworker, who is used to this sort of thing from Evilhalt, will start testing them and seeing what their skills are. Then we get to try fitting them with what armour we have. That should be funny. The women are generally very different in shape to the bandits. Stefan has already had a word with Norbert about what they would have to do between them. The smith and the leatherworker will be very busy for a while.*

Eleanor was quick to claim first place, although she thought that one of the women bandits might have some gear they could easily modify for her. "I want to stop guarding caravans and fighting. All that being an armsman got me was ending up here as a slave. Robin and I have started working on a family already." *That caused laughter.* "And Father…we want to book the next wedding, and I used to make jewellery at one time and that would be nice to do again, but I think that I might have one more campaign in me before I stop."

Despite it not being a festive occasion some of the women are bringing instruments and are taking turns making the meal more pleasant. It looks like this is going to be a Mousehole custom for a while, a communal meal with music. If it makes the place more like a tavern than a house, well, it will be an improvement on my home. No disrespect to the Brother Shield and Mist Home, but it is even a big improvement on our taverns in Wolfneck.

*My necklace...*She stood up. "When I was getting dressed for my wedding, someone gave me this," Astrid said, pulling it from her pouch. "I would like to thank them for the loan of it, it is really and truly beautiful, and I'd like to give it back to them." *Well that caused silence.* She looked around. *Still just the sound of crickets.*

Eventually Harald, the miner, gave a cough. "We...some of us a least ..." he looked around at the villagers, "sort of decided before t'wedding t'at it would be your gift from us. It did belong to Dharmal. He obvious wanted to keep it for when he became king to bribe someone to marry him. Giles is our authority on tales 'n' such things, 'n' he tells us t'at it was made here for some ancient king, but it never got to him because of T'Burning or before. Ask him if you want to know more. T'ere is a whole tale outside about it not reaching some lady across the sea." *Giles is nodding.*

"But it is too valuable! I cannot keep it," said Astrid. "I could buy a ship with this."

"You don't realise just how valuable it is. With t'at you could get enough money to buy your whole village...and all its ships 'n' everyone in it. If'n we sold it, we would have to cut it up. Nowadays only t' Princess t'ere's," he nodded at Theodora, "ancestor could afford to buy it whole...'n' it would be a waste to sell it in parts. It were meant as gift original 'n' seeing how you were our first marriage, we sort of thought t'at it could give us all luck and wealth 'n' all t'at if, rather t'an keeping it or selling it, we gave it to you 'n' sort of completed a journey with it. We don't think you should wear it away from here t'ough. Someone might want to steal it. As it turns out, what could be better, t' Mice give t'present to t'Cat...'n' it is not a bell."

*Surely it is too much...*She looked around. *The Mice are all nodding. There are smiles on their faces. I give up.* "I really don't know what to say...thank you." She sat down. *I don't know what to say. I am not really used to getting gifts of any sort and this is way beyond being a normal gift in any way. This is like being a Princess.* Her husband gave her thigh a squeeze. *And I am married as well.*

Chapter XXII

Rani

If I am to be their Princess, does this mean that I have to tell them what to do? She surveyed the tables. *Prayers and Mass and breakfast are over, but many are just sitting chatting. Luckily it only takes a few words to send all of them, except for those who already started early, such as the cooks and Naeve, off for their tasks or to see Stefan.*

A short girl with long brown hair and dark brown, come-to-bed, eyes is approaching. She must use makeup even now. What is her name? Valeria—that is it—she wanted to keep dancing last night. Her voice sounds shyer now. "I hate farming and I am only young and I don't have anything else that is useful to do. I admit that I like to party and to dance and, when we were slaves, I used to spend a lot of time in bed...one way or another. I can use a bow, I know that, but I want something else to do. I can look after things and clean them. I like playing with hair and I used to cut it and look after it for the others. I can use makeup. I can even sew and embroider a little bit, although I am not very good at it...but I can get better. It will be like being in a story being a maid to the Princesses. Please, if you have no-one else as your maid, will you have me?"

What does my Princess think? She is looking at me. We need someone and this young girl, not a lot older than a child really despite her curves, is their only volunteer so far. I am sure that Theo-dear is thinking the same as me. She will do. We can train her and if she doesn't learn from us Ayesha or Basil will have words with her. "Thank you," said Theodora.

"Can we ask you to start now?" asked Rani. "I am afraid that our room is a mess. We really are not used to looking after ourselves."

"I will just see Stefan and tell him that I can use a bow and then go up." She smiled and gave a curtsey. "Thank you Ladies," before dashing off.

Next to come up is a tiny, but well-proportioned woman with black hair, dressed in the fashion of Freehold. She wears a well-worn but once lush dark green velvet gown with, as it seemed all did here, a very low cut top, but she topped it with a matching close fitting square-topped hat that covered most of her hair. "We have not been introduced yet. I am Ruth. I am going to be the teacher here." *She said that with a quiet confidence that most of the women here seem to lack.*

"Why you?" asked a curious Rani.

"I was a trader and worked as such for a very wealthy merchant, and…well let us just say that I ended up with a lot of spare time and in a house with a large library and teaching his children for a variety of reasons. I think that you will find that I have everything needed…and I venture a lot more than you were expecting. I can teach some music, but I am going to need to learn more myself for that. I can draw, I have Latin, Hindi and Khitan, even a little High Speech. I know poetry, and a little of all the sciences and the geography of the Land. I even love running and will make sure the children have exercise." *She looks smug, reciting her virtues, but then her face darkened.* "I ended up here because I was stupid. I should have stayed where I was, even without the man. I enjoyed the teaching, but I thought that I should have love as well. We all learn, but sometimes the lesson is hard and the last three years have been very hard."

"Are you happy to teach the women that need to learn to read and write as well?" asked Rani.

Ruth nodded. "I will, however I need to learn things myself. I will need time for that. You said there is a library. I want access to that…and the book you brought with you."

"Agreed," said Rani.

"You sound as if you already have more skillsets than many of my teachers at home," said Theodora. "Sometimes I think that we learnt in spite of them and not because of them…Please round up the children and start…I think you will be able to use the big room downstairs at the Mouse Hall to start in…the old bar. It will be quieter than the hall. We will need to find slates and other things for you from somewhere, but see what you can do for now." She looked down at Fear. "Fear, you are going to go with Ruth and she is going to teach you how to read and write and all sorts of things with the other little girls. Won't it be fun?" Ruth put out a hand towards Fear.

Fear's hands clutched tight to Rani's sari. *We are about to have our first parent moment. A petulant look appeared on Fear's face as it screwed up and disappeared into the sari.* "No, I don't want to go. I am going to be a Princess too. I don't need school. I want to be with you all of the time."

Rani gently detached Fear's hands from her sari and knelt down. She took one of Fear's hands in each of hers. "Sweetheart," she said gently. "Your mummies are Princesses partly because we spent a lot of time in school. I was in school until I was twenty. It is what Princesses do. If you want to be a good Princess you have to learn many things. Sometimes it is boring, but most of the time it is fun and you get to find out many things. How else can you read something a handsome Prince writes to you if you cannot read?"

I think it worked. Fear thought for a bit. "Then I will go and learn how to be a Princess," she said in a regal voice, and she went off hand in hand with Ruth to find the other children.

*H*arald is the last one waiting for us. He has a leather helmet on his head. Despite him being Human, he speaks with a thick Dwarven accent and sounds much the same as Thord.* "I t'ink it is time t'at you saw t'mine 'n' Dharmal's special room t'ere. I am not sure if'n you can get into t'at. It is locked. Do you..."

Theodora dug into a pouch she was holding. "We just happened to find...these." She waved the set of keys. "We know the use of only one and we need to check what the rest do, but we found them in his room, so it is likely there will be one for the mine. I suspect that most are for the houses and the barracks. When we work them out we will give them to the people who are in them...I just realised..." she said, turning to Rani, "who owns what? Who owns the houses? Does Naeve own her cows and...whatever else she milks? That is yet another thing we need to work out." She returned to her conversation with Harald. "Will we need anything?"

"Do you have a light spell?"

"Yes. I'll give you one of your own later," said Rani.

"No more fussin' wit' candles." *It is not hard to hear the pleasure in his voice.* "T'ank you. I hope you don't mind t'ose clothes getting dirty," he said pointedly.

Rani gathered Theodora and they went to change.

They headed out of the gate and across the meadows along a path that was obviously made by small carts.

"We have a cart?" asked Theodora, pointing down at the tracks.

"Yes, usually oft it is used to collect firewood, or to carry rock to do repairs to t'village with, but sometimes Naeve or Giles use it. We ha' horse for it 'n' Giles has some oxen he uses for ploughin'. If'n you look up t'ere on t'slope you will see t'at Naeve has some sheep up t'ere 'n' some goats, as well as t'cows over t'ere. You've taken Valeria from her, so she is going to ha' to get someone else to help her... Don't worry about t'at. Valeria wasn't very good at it. She is much more suited to be lady's maid. T'ord may want to take up being shepherd again."

To their right, aiming away from the hen house and a small pond with ducks, the bandits had butts set up and Stefan was running people through their paces with bows. *From what I can see most of the village archers will need a lot of training to be of any use against anything smaller than one of the larger lizards. There is too much laughter and calls about the poor shooting. Stefan is shaking his head and you can almost feel his despair. Some arrows are clearing the top of the butts. Eleanor has found a couple of wooden swords from somewhere and has put some ill-fitting armour on two of the women and is watching them flail around wildly. Bianca is standing listening to Verily and Ayesha and it is obvious that they are talking about knives, as occasionally one flashes through the air.*

"Do you have a woman yet?" asked Theodora in an innocent voice. "We have not seen you with just one."

"Several ha' asked," replied Harald. *He takes questions at face value.* "but I told t'em all t'at I would wait until one showed t'at she was right for me. Apart from t'Father and T'ord, I t'ink I might be t'only man sleeping alone in Mousehole. Mind you, it is interesting having women courting me. I'm not too ugly, but I've never been rich, handsome 'n' courted either." He chuckled. "Being courted sort of makes up for years under Dharmal with choice between cooperation 'n' dying or at least losing me balls or even of watching others die in place of me." He shuddered.

After a while of walking in silence, Harald picked up the conversation again, "Do you know what we mine here?"

"Well, according to our book, before The Burning they got rubies from the mine and antimony from the river," said Theodora.

"Really?" *He sounds excited.* "I wasn't allowed to look at anythin' else apart from t' mine. Did your writer say how or where t'ey got t'antimony or do I ha' to go 'n' look for myself, 'cause I will."

"I think he said something about panning for it where the river lies quiet in the valley," said Theodora, pointing at the only broad curve to be seen. "That will not produce much, will it?"

"T'at depends how you do it...t'ere is panning 'n' t'ere is panning. You can actually pull a fair bit out t'at way, 'n' if it was panned t'ere, t'ere will be places outside t'valley where we can look as well, 'n' we can now look for where it is coming from upstream. We can even use some fleece to do it for us. Wait until I tell T'ord. He may reconsider his career...but you distracted me. We don't just get rubies...we also get sapphires 'n' other, less valuable, gems. When we get back I will show you where he kept 'em all. I'll bet you ha'n't found it. I only know by accident."

Eventually they came to the bottom of the ridge. The path went up and around it. Harald led them up as he waved his hands around in explanation. "In most places t'ey get t'eir rubies from t'rivers. Here, where t'best ones are, it is different and it is harder. T'is rock is granite, 'n' it is sitting over another rock—limestone. T'at is unusual for it to be like t'at. We can also use t'limestone for some of our building 'n' to make cement. For t'gems we mine into t' boundary of t'two, 'n' t'ere we sometimes find t'em buried in t'e rock. I am not even sure how t'ey found a mine like this. Must ha' used magic. See..."

Ahead of us is a tunnel into the rock. The path continues beyond. The tunnel is not very high and we will have to crouch to move and not hit our heads. That is why Harald has his helmet. They went in. *The rock is glistening with moisture that almost seems to ooze out of the rock itself. Above them the roof is dry. Is this normal? I have never been in a mine before.* "T'water comes t'rough cracks in t' limestone" said Harald. He pointed at the wet lower rock. "If t'ere are no cracks in t' rock, t'ere is no water." He then pointed up. "T'granite'll not allow water to pass, so it is dry when you dig into it."

Twenty paces in Rani pulled her amulet from within her top and opened it. For a small area around them it became as day. *Some of the rock have little crystals growing in it and smooth protrusions. Occasion-*

ally there is a white bump on the rock floor that glistens and is wet. A drop of water hit my head. Water is running along the limestone wall across the granite and dropping to the floor. There is a pale line of white rock on the ceiling wherever this happens. Ahead the tunnel continues and starts branching.

Harald took the first branch to the right and then the next to the left. Four paces along there was a door to the right. *It is made of solid iron and more glistening white rock run across it in trails, as if left behind by a myriad of stone snails. Why?*

Theodora produced the keys and began trying likely ones in the lock. The third opened it. As the door opened toward them it nearly blocked the corridor leading out of the mine. Theodora took the keys and held her hand out, stopping anyone from crossing the threshold.

"Traps?" asked Rani.

"T'walls 'n' floor look solid...hold t'light up please...so is t' ceiling. Unless it be magic one, I don't t'ink t'at I can see one." He reached forward with his foot and put it down. "It feels solid, but let me go first." He entered the room without any problems but he stopped well short of the centre. "I t'ink t'at you had better come in 'n' ha' a look at this."

Rani entered with her lover behind her. *Near the centre of the room is a complex magical diagram etched into the rock itself.*

"T'at must have taken some work to get it right," said Harald.

On the wall to the right is a mirror fixed to the stone with iron spikes.

Rani sighed. "Why is it always mirrors?" She said to Theodora, "You are the air mage. Why is it always mirrors?"

Being careful not to touch the pattern, Theodora peered at the mirror. "It is glass. It would work better to communicate if it were made of chrome. It wouldn't work as well as a mirror, but who cares? Usually they make it from glass because that is how they were taught to do it and some mages lack the imagination to think that there might be a better way to do it. If we had to make something to talk to the lookout, I would use chrome and amber. It only needs the flat surface if you want to see something clearly. See...they have even made it look like a normal mirror. It is a rectangle," she said dismissively. "Mine would be a hexagon...I don't want to go near that diagram. It is an involved one, and I suspect it is not to communicate so much as to control. Isn't that what Dharmal said?...The mirror may even be a hoax." She ran her hand, palm down, just over the surface of the mirror. "It is. I feel no magic at all. Do you?" she asked Rani.

Rani did the same. *There is no tingle at all. It is a bluff.* She shook her head. "No, nothing at all...so what do you think?"

"That they are subtle, but not imaginative. If you stand in the diagram it triggers a spell and lets them take over your mind. You think that you see them in the mirror. They made a mistake though by just using a normal mirror. Many would do it that way anyway, but this is a spell of power and a powerful mage should not just be working from rote. A non-mage, and many mages, would assume that the design is just for turning on the power of the mirror...that it is not the spell itself. If they had been more imaginative, they would have made the mirror as I would. That they didn't shows that they did not care or else that they lacked imagination. I think that they care so...at least we now know a bit more about them."

She thought for a while and then continued in a speculative tone, "We might even be able to get Father Christopher to do something to disrupt or dispel it. The Christian religions work through the element of earth and that is opposed to air. I will try and work out how powerful the spell must be and we will see if he has enough power to do anything. Dispelling is dangerous, but if we do it right the effects are more likely going to affect them, than they will be to affect anyone here, particularly if we stand ready to counter any free magic that is released. As well, if I can work out the power of the spell, it gives us a lower limit on what power they have to work with.

Rani smiled. *It appears that my lover is not only far more powerful than I am, but she also had thought more about the theory of magic than I am accustomed to doing, even though I used to teach it. I wonder what the school she learnt in was like.* "Seen enough?"

"Yes, now it is time to sit down and make some calculations." She said to Harald, "Can you see if you can find some chrome and amber please? I doubt if there will be any elm wood, but that would be nice as well. Father Christopher uses frankincense. I can get some of that from him when I talk to him about getting rid of this. I will need to make something for the lookout anyway and it will help me think about the problem. I will get Eleanor to help me."

Harald is just looking from me to her. From his face, I can see that everything that we have just said is all just gibberish to him. "Do you want to see where we get t'gems?"

"Sorry to disappoint you, but not today," said Rani. "I think that I need even more sturdy clothes to go further and, just as we know our business, I am sure that you know yours and are doing everything right. Let us go back now and I will go and encourage our new militia while Theodora gets to work. Tonight you can show me where the hiding place is."

"You won't help her?" He nodded towards Theodora. Rani looked at her. *Princess is standing there with an abstract look on her face and her eyes a little unfocussed. Her lips are moving a little. She is talking to herself and one arm holds the other by the elbow with an upright forearm and one finger tracing patterns in the air.*

"No, I am a Haven battle mage. My element is fire and I specialise in either teaching or in killing, in fire and light and in warfare. My love is an air mage. I am sure that she knows all about the mind and control and weather. This spell is all about using the mind of another and controlling it to see, or not see, what you want, and I am an amateur in that field. If I tried to help I would just distract her and get in the way."

Re-locking the door they started to leave the mine. After a few steps Rani slipped and saved herself from a fall, but as she did so her hand landed in the puddle of water that had caused her to lose her footing. "This water is warm," she said in surprise.

"Much of it is. One of t' bandits told me t'at t'ere is a hot spring t'at enters t'rivulet from t'mountain upstream."

"That is interesting. I will make sure I tell Theodora that when she is thinking about other things again. I have a feeling that I know what we are going to spend some of our income on."

They emerged again into the sunlight and headed for the village. "Where does the path go after the mine?" asked Rani.

"T'ere is quarry t'ere around for t'limestone t'at most of t'buildings of Mousehole are made of. Lucky for us t'ere was a lot already cut 'n' lying around when we arrived, but we still had to cut some special pieces. Soon we'll ha' to cut more when we want to make repairs or if'n we want to build somet'ing new."

They wandering back across the meadow and past the stone walled fields. *Princess is quite lost in thought. She just waved vaguely and continued on when I gave her a kiss. I will go to the butts and she can continue on her own.*

*V*aleria is still at the butts. She can go off to our room to get my padded top, bow and arrows. The sun is pale here in autumn, but it is warming. She turned her back on the men of the group, stripped off her top and quickly put the padding on. *Valeria wants to stay and watch, but we need to see she can do the job. She needs to tidy up and see what needs washing...with strict instructions not to interrupt Theodora if she sees her.*

Rani then headed off to join in the practice and see if she could lend a hand and also to try out Eleanor using a long and short stick, instead of her sword and main-gauche. *I am a little better than the guard...but not by much.* "You use a kite shield, you must usually fight mounted," she said.

"Yes," Eleanor said, "the idea is to fight to cover the traders getting away and that often means charging attackers to give the carts a breathing space and then returning quickly. If you are on foot you are trapped and static and have to defend. I am so badly out of practice..."

Rani nodded. *Eleanor is showing her ability to think tactically.*

The bowyer, Robin, is a good archer, though not as good as Thord, the only other member of our group here, so he will not be as good as Astrid, Hulagu or Ayesha, and a long way short of my Theo-dear. However, he is certainly good enough. He shamefacedly admitted that all he could do was use a bow. He had to do that to test those he made, but had been able to get no excuse to use any other weapon here and he didn't get enough practice with a bow to get much better than he had been when he arrived. *He and Thord can take on training the archers. Robin's bow is taller than the Dwarf, who being a cavalryman, favours a horse bow.*

A lot of the villagers can throw things; everything from knives to the big double bladed axes and javelins. It was a skill they could practice secretly or that they had learnt before being caught. At least that meant we can fiercely defend the wall if someone gets inside our valley. Apart from that though, it is all fairly dismal, with few exceptions. The blacksmith is leaning on a two-handed hammer as if he knows how to use it and Giles, Bryony and Eleanor had a bit of a play with long spears that they had to use reversed to avoid injury to each other. We obviously need more practice weapons. Bryony is also competent with a bow...still she was once a hunter so you would expect that. Otherwise this session is more to be noted for the eagerness that people show rather than their levels of skill. Still it will help us to work out how to make up the watches to best effect. I can see that Stefan is taking notes on a wax tablet he has gotten from somewhere...although he does look worried.

One aspect of training is going well. Ayesha has taken Bianca and Verily aside and is teaching them how to attack from behind and pointing at target points on the body and showing how to aim at them. The other two are rapt. They are being drilled over and over on using two daggers for attack and defence. She is driving them hard. It is a shame they are only working with daggers...oh...that is not quite right is it? I have already seen Verily throw hers to effect...and Ayesha killed several with her blades...and I suppose Bianca has already proven herself. You never know, maybe Ayesha can show the other two some of the things she has learnt in her hard school. Several other women, when they are not doing something else, are watching this session, but if any try to join in, Ayesha sends them away. This session is obviously for advanced students or those who Ayesha thinks will benefit immediately.

Rani was watching the three women at work when they stopped and Bianca and Verily put the sticks they had been working with down and both took their jerkins and chemises off. *They are comparing breasts? It would be a close contest then. Neither is a small girl in that regard, both would rival Astrid, although Bianca has a better shape to hers than Verily...am I allowed to admire their breasts now as the men no doubt do?* As Bianca finished taking her top off it became obvious what they were doing. *Bianca carries knives in two rows of three strapped under her breasts and two others on her back between her shoulders, and she is showing them and their harnesses and then getting Verily to try it on. It did not look to be of the most professional make, and the knives do not match in it. Bianca must have made it herself. The two are oblivious to the onlookers. The men present have been either forgotten or ignored. They were there though and as Bianca turned she noticed them, but after a brief pause she is carrying on, as I am sure a tribal woman would, when she becomes aware that the priest is one of the men and, turning red, she spun around again and grabbed her top. The others are almost ignoring her, but the priest isn't turning away...ah, on being noticed he is also turning red.*

I knew it. Now which of them will have the sense to make the first move?

Chapter XXIII

Father Christopher

Tonight we have our second wedding although for a while there it looked like they wouldn't. During the afternoon Eleanor and Robin had approached him with questions. For once Eleanor was not taking charge. "Eleanor now doth ha' doubts about a marryin' me and a makin' me an honest man," said Robin. "She saith that she be eight years older than I and that she shalt grow old afore me and that I shall not be a wantin' her and so it be I should just have her now to bed and marry a younger woman who canst a bear me more children." *Eleanor looks close to tears.*

I don't have to think about that one. "Do you love her and want her to be your bride and bear your children?"

"Aye, that I doeth, Father."

"Do you love him and want to marry him and to bear his children?"

"Yes Father," she said quietly "but—"

"There is no but. When you marry you promise to do so until death do you part. In this vale of tears there are no guarantees as to who will live and who will die. You must trust in God to look after you. If you wish I can include in the ceremony a prayer for a miracle. I can guarantee that you will become pregnant straight away...if you take the proper steps of course...You are taking the proper steps of a man and a woman who want to have children aren't you?" *My look of false seriousness had brought a smile to Eleanor and a laugh from Robin.*

"Yes, Father," "Aye, Father," they said together, and Robin squeezed Eleanor's hand.

"Then I will marry you whenever you wish."

They looked at each other. "Then tonight it is, please Father," said Eleanor, regaining her composure. "I think my time is coming on."

"Then you had better tell Sajāh and Lādi and get it announced properly. Everyone will be upset if we surprise them. You are not giving them much time as it is. Like our last marriage I will dispense with the banns. I have never thought that they were much needed if people knew their mind."

*N*ow we do it. I need to get this right. He checked the symbols drawn around where the marriage would take place so that it would be easier to include his prayer for pregnancy in the ceremony. *I may have sounded confident, but this is my first time doing this prayer. It is a prayer that all the novices are taught and rehearsed and automatically written in their prayer books, but even a few weeks ago I would not have been able to perform it. I am growing and changing in many ways.*

*T*he feast may not have been as well prepared as the first, but it is *obvious that Lãdi knows what she is doing as the food is nearly as sumptuous. This time it is more western with roast meats and vegetables, animals stuffed within each other, jellies, fools and frumenty and other delights. Eleanor must have insisted on foods from her homeland. That would have been interesting to watch, especially given the short notice. I wonder what she will produce when we give her a week to prepare. This time everyone sits at tables and benches. It looks like most of the chairs have been gathered in from rooms. They are certainly mismatched enough. The benches however are mostly new and obviously just knocked together with wedges. Come to think of it, I have been hearing hammering and sawing all day. The tables look to have been stored somewhere, perhaps only brought out on large occasions. Even with everything set up there is still plenty of room in the centre to dance. This hall was built to have far more people than this in it...at least a couple of hundred. Indeed, it may hold more than the village can be populated.*

Again we have our mages at the front, this time with Fear at their feet and Valeria looking after them. The bride and groom have pride of place with Giles and Naeve as groomsman and maid of honour. One of the other, younger, women is the flower girl. They are using the same cloth flowers. Each bunch has a couple more in it this time. It is obvious that they are not going to be wasted. None of the clothing is new, but it is all well cleaned and has obviously been worked on over the last few hours. The bride is beautiful. Usually that is just a saying, but it really isn't possible to have it any other way among the Mice.

*W*hy am I being told that the first dance this night is a pavane with Eleanor and Robin as the first couple, Giles and Naeve as the second, and the Princesses as the third. Oh, I am to be a part of the fourth. Bianca is already being placed as my partner by Ayesha. This is awkward given this afternoon.

They both blushed as they took each other's hand.

Our dance is a little stilted as Bianca has only danced it a couple of times before, and not in the men's role. She keeps trying to head the wrong way and then laughs about it. At least everyone applauds when we finish. The entertainers are more confident about each other now. Anahita, Kāhina and Bianca again did their Khitan dance. Verily stands aside from everyone as they dance and she looks at them and is walking through the moves on her own. Perhaps at the next wedding she will be dancing it as well. Bianca is more poised doing the furious dance now. Lord, please forgive my thoughts. Please help me stay distracted. If he does not keep my thoughts busy my mind keeps drifting between what is in front of me and back to what I saw this afternoon, and imagining how her breasts would feel, and indeed she would feel, beside me. I know she does not think herself beautiful, but I think she is, partly through her inner strength. Lord I promise a night spent on my knees in prayer. Let this stand as my penance.

*W*hat now? Robin is in front of me with two of the younger women and Eleanor is hovering in the background. There is an expression of concern on his face...on all their faces that is at variance with the night.

"Father," he said. "This doth be my sister Goditha." He indicated the taller girl. *She is the flower girl from the wedding; she has pale skin and brown hair like Robin, and for the women here, a strong and athletic build. Once you see them standing beside each other the relationship is obvious.*

She gave a bob.

"It be because I was a tryin' to save her from bandits that I be captured," Robin said. "Luckily they doeth found out my trade and brought me with them instead of a killin' me out a hand, but they made me suffer by forcin' me to look on as she suffered. I hast always only a wanted the best for her. I ha' known for some time now, since she were a child really, that she hath no interest in men but it seems that she hath found love anyway.

"This be Parminder." He indicated the second girl. *She is Hindi, not all that far from childhood herself, perhaps fourteen years of age.* She also bobbed up and down. "She were a brought here as a little girl and, like Verily, hath lived most of her life here. She doth love Goditha. Thou told Rani and Theodora that thou would a marry them. Please, will thou also a marry my sister?"

I made my promise to the Princesses, but I am still unsure as to my own thoughts and feelings on this issue. Contemplate the passages on love. He took the outer hands of the two girls and drew them forward. He looked from one to the other trying to read their faces. *I can only feel good in both of them, nothing of the taint of evil at all. At least that helps.* "Do you love one another?" he asked seriously.

Goditha took hold of Parminder's left hand in her right. "Aye Father, that we do. In my arms Parminder canst sleep and she doeth not wake a screamin' and if she be troubled in her sleep, my kisses and my voice they doth sooth her. We doeth be well used to each other's bodies. It doeth start as a joke for them, one of us pale and the other so dark...one of us big and the other small...the bandits would ha' us make love on the stage there, while they watched and sometimes they doeth take one or both of us while we did, but they doeth also make us to share a room. That be how we discovered that we doeth want and need each other."

Christopher looked at the Hindi girl. *I have not talked to her yet at all nor have I heard her story. It does not sound to be a good one.* "And this is your desire as well?"

She looked up at her lover and shyly smiled. "With all my heart... Father, and we promise that we will look after my sister as well."

"Your sister?" said Christopher, surprised.

"Yes." She waved towards the children. "Gurinder, she is the oldest of the children, if not the biggest, she is my sister. She was brought here four years after I was. I nearly did not recognise her. We wish to look after her and make sure she gets a good husband."

"That is good. That is the right thing for you to do and I am pleased that you wish to do so. You will give her a family again...I need to ask this question though. Do you mind being married by me, a Christian priest?"

Parminder glanced at Goditha briefly before turning back. "We have talked about this together already. For Goditha's sake I am willing to become a Christian...that is, if you will have me after what I have been," she hurriedly added.

I am elated. Of course we will have you. I cannot seem to be making demands though. "It is not as easy as that. You will need to want it yourself, not just for Goditha. I will need to instruct you in what we believe and to make sure you understand what you are doing, for it is a serious thing for your soul that you will do. I need to check on a few other things for your ceremony, and so will not be able to marry you, or even Rani and Theodora, for a while yet, but I look forward to it and my blessings are already upon you both, my children."

"Then," said Goditha, "we doeth be goin' to choose one of the empty houses tomorrow and I be goin' to start a repairin' it, and then ..." she turned to Parminder, "thee and I will move in...I am sorry for thee my sweet, but my hands art goin' to be a gettin' all rough agin as I will ha' to get stone and timber and work them...but then it be belongin' to thee and me...not just a room, but a house of our own." She leant down and kissed her much smaller companion and they hugged.

The happy pair had left to dance and Christopher was standing there watching them go with a smile playing over his face. *Robin and Eleanor have not left.* He said to them, "It is your wedding feast, why are you not enjoying yourselves?" he asked.

"We have another matter as well," said Eleanor. "It seems that Sajāh will be looking after Ruhayma and Roxanna," she waved towards the children. *These must be the little girls from the Caliphate.* "So act surprised if she asks, although she may just ask the Princesses. With Fear and Gurinder taken care of, that only leaves Gemma and Aelgifu without a family to care for them. Would you object at all if we started out with our family by asking them if they would like to be our children?"

"Are you sure you wish to do this? It is hard enough to start a family of your own without the additional strain of added children who are not yours. I am sure someone will look after them."

"They doest be ours if we a make it so," said Robin. "Family is as family doest. It beseems us that it doest be a best if they stay together, so that they always doeth have a sister who doth know what they ha' been through."

"So you are of the same mind?"

"Yes Father," Robin smiled. "My house and workshop doth have room for us all and some extras, and I believe that a good husband is always of the same mind as his wife on such important matters once she has ha' told him what it is."

Christopher smiled at this and Eleanor slapped Robin's hand playfully.

"Then my blessings on you and your marriage are threefold. It will be certain that the Father and my namesake will both smile upon your union."

The two left to draw aside the two little girls and talk with them. *It is apparent that Fear might have been saying something to the other little ones and it is evident that being adopted and having a family is a popular idea with the children.*

Chapter XXIV

Rani

Harald showed Rani the secret compartment. It was in the library. "I am miner. My life oft depends on seeing rocks t'at look wrong. I was doing repair here 'n' t'ought t'at I would check what was hidden and it was…" He pressed two rocks an arm's length apart as Rani watched. A section of timber panel on the next wall gave a faint click. He went over and pushed on one side of the panel and the other side swung open. It was a small door a pace high and another wide. Rani looked in. There was a deep shelf and some drawers there. They began opening them.

"There is a fortune here," said Rani after a while. "I suggest that we tell no-one about this. We can use some of the jewellery as wedding presents and keep the rest to sell as we need. Some may even be magical, but I doubt it, unless I have completely lost my touch." She looked through what was there before taking a necklace of jet from one tray. "This will look good on Eleanor," she said. Harald nodded approvingly.

Rani looked at what was in front of her. *That has to be beef. They serve me, a Kshatya, with cow?* She looked around. *Other Hindus are eating…Lakshmi and Shilpa are obviously enjoying themselves. Parminder and Gurinder were taken away from Haven too young to know better, but the cook, Lādi, is even Hindu. How could they?* She went down to where the rest of the people were and moved to behind Shilpa. *She had been a trader, and so should be Sudra.*

"How can you eat cows?" she asked. *I hope I sound shocked. I am shocked.*

"It was easy," Shilpa replied casually. "They punished us if we refused to eat anything. They liked to find excuses to punish us. Eating beef is far better than being whipped. Now we are used to eating anything. If you look around, you will see that this beautiful roast pork is being eaten by the Muslims as well." She pointed. "See...Ayesha has noticed. You can see the look of horror on her face." She dug Hagar, a Muslim woman and the butcher for the village, who sat beside her, in the ribs and pointed out Ayesha's face. They both laughed. "You said we would have a lot to explain to the priests if we ever went home. This is just one of them."

Hagar joined the conversation. "So, we eat whatever is in front of us. The Hindus have had their caste broken thoroughly. I kill and eat what I was taught to think unclean according to the way that meat should be treated. Will that change your idea on what you will do here? Is that too much?" *She sounds worried.* "If we ever get a Mullah here, I do not think that we will be forgiven what we have been forced to do anyway."

"And I will worry about the priests and my karma if I ever get back to Vinice," added Shilpa. "Coming back as a lower form might be a relief after the punishment of this incarnation. In the meantime, I eat beef and I meditate."

"Thank you," said Rani. *I am shocked to my core, but the women are right. Surely other people who have left Haven have faced the same choice. Why haven't I heard of this issue? Did the priests at home just ignore it until people came home, and then purify them?* "It doesn't change my mind. I have made a promise. I will however, as you said, have to meditate on it. In the meantime I think that perhaps I should talk with Ayesha, before she explodes like a fireball."

The other two laughed again and Rani moved away to do as she said...*Quickly.*

*H*arald *is right. Women keep approaching him but he does not favour one over another and he has gone aside with none. They flirt with him and he flirts back with all of them, and is careful to detach any hands that try to grow intimate, and if he kisses any it is lightly and on the hand or cheek. He is enjoying himself immensely.*

I wish Theo-dear didn't make me come to her priest's service. It makes me uneasy. Mind you, if the man is offering to marry us, I suppose it is the least I can do. He is not even hinting that I convert. At least the incense is familiar, even if that is all. Someone has put seats at the front and to the side for us. Matching chairs no less. Everyone else sits on mismatched chairs or benches. Looking out it seems that everyone is here, even those who are not Christian, except for Thord and those on watch. I am certainly not the only Hindi woman. I have only dressed in normal clothing but, others haven't. The Cat and Eleanor have their wedding dresses on and the others are generally in good clothes as well. Maybe I should think about some better garb to wear on Krondag since my new people are marking it as special.

The priest is still fussing around at the front and Princess wants me to look at how there are little clumps as our growing number of families sit together in pairs, sometimes with a child or two.

A fter Mass, Rani stood up. *More work for me as a ruler lies ahead.* "Today, as we agreed, is going to be our day for training and teaching...I want every one of you to see Ruth now and prove to her that you can read and write in at least two languages, one being Hindi, to her satisfaction. If you cannot do that then you will be spending every Krondag morning, at least—and probably a few nights—learning how to do it." She scanned the crowd. *Several of the women, particularly the younger ones who have been here some time look...reluctant and about to object. They would have found no need for writing as slaves. I have to kill that reluctance before it is given voice otherwise it will be much harder later.* "If we are to stay a free village, we all need to be as skilled as we can be. What is the use of being a guard if you cannot read or leave a message? Outside this valley even slaves can usually read and write. You have decided to let us be your Princesses and this is our decision." She looked sternly at them. "Once you have done that test, and made any arrangements that you need to make, you may practice with weapons, or with riding, until lunch."

She continued more lightly, "After lunch we will continue our testing of what people can do. We already know that most of you could use a little help with weapons," that caused laughter, "but today I will also be testing people to see if they can become mages. Hulagu and Verily have already approached me and have started some training, but I would love to start our own little school. Unlike the way it was in Haven, I will teach any of you who want to try to learn regardless of caste. If you do not want to try to be a mage, then go back to training with weapons. I am sure we will need all the skill we can gain in that area."

R *uth has eight students and all of them have glum faces except for Parminder, who appears to be happy most of the time, and Verily— it is hard to tell what Verily thinks of if she doesn't want you to.*

A *lot of good it does reminding people that Krondag is to be, gener- ally and as much as possible, their day of training and teaching, when Lādi snorts at it.*

"For me every day is work." *I heard that. The woman may want to work herself to death, but everyone needs some time doing something different.* She sighed. *If I am supposed to be their ruler now, I had better do some ruling.* It took some stern words to convince Lādi to take the whole day off. Others could look after the kitchen on Krondag.

She still had to be chased out of it several times. I need to have a few more words with her.

A *ll of the Mice who were former slaves are here. I have them sitting around thinking about things and concentrating on bits of fluff, candle flames, grains of sand or water. From the expression on their faces it may not be what they are expecting. Do they seriously expect to cast a spell straight off? It seems so for at least some of them.* Some were sent away and some decided that this was not what they thought it would be and left on their own accord. *By the end of the day, I am more than happy. Some of my students are a little surprised to still be here, but it is not a bad start. I have Verily, Naeve, Fortunata, a pair of young Caliphate girls—Fātima and Bilqīs—and both Goditha and Parminder.*

That is interesting. With Fātima the last to make it into the class, three of my potential mages have been brought here as children and have managed to survive the experience. Is that significant?

She studied her new students. "Naeve, I cannot be sure at this stage, but I feel you will never be a strong mage. Having said that, you are free to continue if you wish and there is no reason that you cannot be successful. Remember that we are now going to be studying as in a real school and some mages that I have known, much weaker than others, have risen much further than the more talented because they have studied and worked hard."

"Oh, I will stay," Naeve replied. "Are you joking?...I am a milk-maid... My mother was a milkmaid...As far as I know every woman in my line has been a cursed milkmaid. Now, to be honest I do not mind being a milkmaid. A few days ago...God it seems a lifetime ago... milking a cow certainly used to beat spending every day underneath a hairy and usually unwashed and smelly man pretending to enjoy whatever he did to me, while I thought Giles, whom I knew loved me would never have me even once. But the chance to be a mage...I am not passing that up. All of the women of my line will be so jealous."

Rani nodded with a smile. "Verily, Fātima, Bilqīs, Goditha and Parminder: Ruth tells me you are all working on your reading and writing with her. This now becomes much more important. It is essential for a mage to write... Do any of you wish to stop now?" She waited a little. "Good. She will now add an extra lesson for all of you one night a week." There were a few groans. "Hulagu does not know it yet, but he will be joining you. You are all going to learn High Speech. Ruth will start on teaching you the basics and then either Theodora or I will take over. Verily, you are going to have to work very hard, because Ayesha wants to work with you as well and train you in her ways of fighting. She tells me that you and Bianca have potential and by the end of winter she wants to see you almost fully trained. I will want to spend as much time with you as she does, so do not count on too much partying." Again she paused. "Does anyone have any questions?"

Fortunata raised her hand. "I don't know anything about being a mage and...you hear stories...will it hurt my life in bed?"

"I hope not, and if it does it is news to both Theodora and me."

Fortunata nodded. "While I am learning, before I get control, will I be dangerous to anyone who is in bed with me if I have a bad dream?"

"To be honest," said Rani, "I have heard of it happening. But it was only the one time. Most of the time it would be like going to sleep and then accidentally firing a bow in your bed and hitting someone." This caused smiles at least. "Is there anything else?" She looked around. There was a shaking of heads. "All right, then go and put on some old clothes and hit things…and Verily dear, try and avoid taking your top off again like you did yesterday." *Now that I have acknowledged to myself that I like women, I had best not mention that I had been more distracted by what I saw then the men seemed to be.* Even Verily had to smile a tight smile at the weak jest.

That night in bed, Rani, over the sleeping body of a child, quietly told Theodora what she had found out. "If all three of the girls who survived a childhood here have the potential to be mages do you think that perhaps Fear might—"

"Hush dear. She is still getting used to being our daughter. She is still far too young to test. Even the oldest of the children is a couple of years away from puberty. We will have plenty of time to find out if our daughter will become a mage. But speaking of our daughter, I know she likes sleeping with us, but I want some time with you…alone. I think that it is time that we had a house of our own. How are we going to organise that?"

"Father Christopher told me that Goditha is planning to rebuild one as well. According to Robin all of the girls—as well as being used for sex—had to do almost all of the work themselves. Apparently she had to train herself to become a mason and a bit of a carpenter—she sometimes even used to help Norbert. Perhaps we can get her out of other work and make her our village builder and book her services."

"Good idea. Now you need to get your sleep. I am going to start with my big spell tomorrow and you and I are both going to need rest beforehand."

The next day, before breakfast, Theodora began preparing for the spell to protect the valley from magical inquisitiveness. "Dearest, have you seen a piece of jade anywhere—any piece will do. Is there any in that treasure cave that Harald showed you?"

Rani thought for a bit. "There is just the piece. Do you want it now?"

"The sooner the better."

Rani went down into the hidden cupboard and brought back a small piece of jade, half a hand long, carved in the shape of a mouse.

Theodora smiled. "Better and better," and, wrapping it carefully, slipped it into her pouch. "Now I am going to make an odd request to them all at breakfast. You will understand why. Back me up if I need it, please."

A s they were all finishing breakfast Theodora stood up. "I am going to ask you all to do something that will be…distasteful for many of you. I do not ask you lightly. I am going to try and cast a spell that will protect this valley and everyone in it from prying magical eyes. This is a spell that normally only someone as powerful as my Granther, Hrothnog, would do. I would normally die if I tried it, but I think I have found a way to cast it safely. If I am wrong I will still die in front of you and you will have to watch. I think that it is worth that risk…if you will all help me."

She looked around. *The matter of fact way that she said the words 'I will die' caused looks of horror to appear on faces. I am relieved that the new mage apprentices mainly look curious rather than fearful. I probably look more worried than them…and she didn't even warn me…but I am her lover and they are not.*

"Outside the hall are a large number of small pots that Lãdi has found for me. I want you each to take one, and take one for everyone who is not here… This is where it gets messy. I want each of you to put into a pot a small amount of you. I want each of you to…go to the toilet…in both ways…in it. I want you to spit in it. I want a clipping of your hair in it and I want a clipping of a finger or toenail in it. I have an extra request for the men. I would also like some of your seed in it. I am sorry to ask this of you, and I will take care of what you give me and destroy them safely when I am done, but this is the only way I can cast this spell. Naeve and Giles. I want more from you. There are some larger pots. In them I want seeds of the plants here. I want little bits of wool, little pieces of grass, some of the earth, the water. I need some of the timber of the wood to burn. In fact, if it is charcoal already, that will be even better. What I want is the essence of the entire valley." She stopped and then had a second thought and blushed a bit. "Father Christopher, obviously I cannot ask for your seed; forgive me."

"There is nothing for me to forgive, my daughter. We have already been thinking here about the vexed question of doing things that are normally forbidden in the name of good." He looked significantly at Bianca, who shuffled in her seat. "You are obviously serious about dying if you do not get this right."

Theodora acknowledged him with a nod.

Sri Ayyappan, wise protector, I pray to you. I know I am unhappier than I was before. Don't let my exotic Princess die. I have just found her.

"In that case I will give you of my seed and will ask forgiveness later. It is good for us all to help you help us. Thank you for asking us."

"Thank you Father. Oh, and for all those studying magic, Rani will have you watching what I do today and tomorrow when you will give me your pots. I suspect your next few lessons will focus on why I am doing what I am doing. It should help you learn the theory if you see it in action on a scale that few in the entire Land will ever see." She briefly gave a tight and forced smile. "That is, if it works for me."

Asvayujau be with her, at least it will be a good lesson…one way or the other.

L ater that day Rani trooped all of the apprentices to the roof and explained what they were seeing; the charged diagram and the jade statue being prepared as the receptacle for the real spell that would be held within it in a matrix. "The spell preparing the jade lies in the realm of earth. Theodora is an air mage, so this bit will be hardest for her in some ways, but it is a charm that is well within her limits for the day."

They are impressed as Theo-dear casts the spell. "That was the easy part," she said, as she picked up the jade mouse and carefully re-wrapped it. "We now have to be careful what spells are cast near this as it is empty and wanting to be filled. A prepared holding spell like this is greedy and will take in any spell that it can into its store until it is filled and locked. It would be best to do the rest of the spell straight away, but

I cannot do that. To be cautious, none of us will cast another spell or even practice any at all until the spell is complete."

I am not sure how I feel about my growing domesticity. My lover is taking me to choose a house. I only have to approve one that my Princess has already chosen, a large empty building at the head of the courtyard against the cliff, and directly behind the spring. It is the one that we originally came down on from the cliff. Given how small most of the houses are in the village, I think it is very roomy for just the four of us. We have a kitchen and rooms for each of us, including Fear and Verily. There are two spare bedrooms, another two rooms that we can use as studies, and a courtyard at the rear. Off that are storerooms and a washhouse. There is an area for toiletries, a flat roof to put pentagrams on, a large room for dining, and a larger reception room at the front.

"If we are going to be Princesses here, we will need areas to work and then we will need to receive people at some stage," said Rani.

"I am sorry that it is so small," said Theodora. "Apart from taverns, I have never had to live in anything as tiny as this. Even where I played as a child was bigger."

"Yes, but you grew up as a real Princess — and with an Empire to look after you. We now live in a very small village. Look around you, dear. We have taken the largest house in Mousehole. It is the biggest by many rooms." *My Princess may know this, but she still expects more.* "We still need to get it repaired. We can move in before it is finished, but with winter upon us, and being at the foothills of the mountains, we need it to be as weatherproof as possible. Having some doors will be a start, and some leather or waxed cloth at least to fill in the windows. Whoever built this village had some interesting ideas with plumbing."

"You mean that you do not have them like that in Sacred Gate?" asked Theodora.

"Like almost everyone else in the world, my dear, we used pretty buckets. You mean these are normal for you?" *I may ignore such things, but I am sure that I have never seen or heard of such pipes and levers that let water run through them before.*

The next day—Deutera—the second of the week, the students stood in a line on the roof waiting for the start of the fourth hour after noon. *It is back to basics as I explain the times, how mana storage devices work, how the now-full and covered pots are placed and why, and show them all of the other correspondences.* "We will go into more detail later. Remember that what you are about to see is a large amount of potential mana converted into bound and constrained mana by a spell, which is controlled and focussed mana. We will also be using the bound and restrained mana of the diagram to aid the success of the spell." She studied their faces. *I am seeing only blank looks.* "Never mind, I will show you what I just said later. Now just be quiet and watch. Theodora may be the most powerful mage that you ever get to see. She is a lot older than I am, so she has had far more practice. There will be some in Pavitra Phāṭaka who are more powerful than her, but I think not that many. This spell should be beyond even her powers, it is the sort that only Hrothnog, of all living mages, would normally do. But my clever Theodora has worked out a way to, hopefully, safely do something that a mage of twice her skill might perhaps question." *Does that sound hollow? They seem happy with the explanation. Why is it not obvious to them that I am trying hard to sound more confident than I feel? Oh my dear Princess, I hope you are right. I cannot lose you. Sri Dhatr protect you!*

At the propitious time of four in the afternoon, Theodora started reading her newly written enchantment from her book held by the apprentice Goditha. *I wait in my new, smaller, and uncharged pentagram to pass on my mana when she needs it. The spell is taking a very long time to read. She nods at me.* Rani chanted the few needed words of passage and pointed her finger at Theodora. *Now all can see my love shudder as my mana, her own mana, and the mana from our storage devices combined in her head. Now it is real. Now is the time things can go most wrong. She is saying the final words and pointing at the jade mouse...*

It has gone quiet. I can hear murmurs from the people going about their business below, but here on the roof my students are as quiet as... well...mice.

She nervously looked around. *There are no manifestations of free magic that I can see, all the colours are still the same, the bricks are not bulging, there are no odd shadows moving in the air, my Princess is still standing there seemingly unharmed, so she seems to have made no bad errors and her careful preparations seem to have overcome the massive penalties of such a cast for her.* "Beloved, can you hear me? Did it work?"

Very carefully Theodora moved outside the charged diagram. "I think so; I felt as if it did. I may have even been lucky and done it better than I expected to. I felt…elation when it was done." *She is able to move towards the door.* "Now I need to rest." *She is collapsing.*

Rani moved to catch her. "Goditha, Naeve, help me get her to our room. We will need sweet drinks for her. Hulagu, take the others and pick up the pots and clean them carefully, make sure you disperse what is in them in the river so that nothing remains together. Take particular care that when you move to pick up the pots, that none of you touch the lines of the diagram. Come back to me when you are finished."

A fter a day Rani took Theodora outside the valley and attempted to probe it just with their normal senses and then with actual castings. They couldn't and Theodora came back very pleased with herself. She insisted on celebrating that night and enjoyed so much of it over the success of her casting that she had to be carried to her bed. Rani spent the night beside the bed with a very concerned Fear and a bucket.

I suppose it is fair that Goditha and Parminder shall use our guest room instead of staying in the barracks, in return for working on our house first. She admitted she wanted to be out of there as soon as she could. "Parminder and me art still in our old room and it hath too many memories for us both. I doth hope that bein' away from there wilt help with Parminder's dreams."

It seems that others need to work here as well. Now we have Dulcie, a woman in her twenties from the Swamp who, like Goditha, has taken a trade by default. Dulcie is the best carpenter among the Mice. She is also one of Harald's suitors. Soon the sound of our village has become one of the two women working, with the blows of hammer on iron or of a bolster working on stone echoing sharply through the air.

*ire is good for killing and creating light and I am good at both. My
lover favours Air and that is best for spells affecting the mind and
for flying. Information is the province of Earth and we have no earth
mages yet, but some priests work in that area. Our priest just needed to
be shown need and the idea. Father Christopher has developed his first
major prayer that lay outside curing or protection. He seems to be very
pleased with himself as he is reporting that he can now find the function
of up to sixteen of the magical items they had lying around.* "It will be
every second day anyway, even for just one, so I may as well do more
when I do. While we just sit here I have no problem with using a small
storage device. I have already made that."

Isn't smugness a sin?

*It is with relief that it turns out that we have a device in a small box
with five little stones inside it all of the same size and as big as a small
fist. Each is been pierced and can be worn around the neck on a string.
Using it, up to five people can talk to each other. I think it needs to be
called a Talker. If we leave one part with a mage, one with the lookout,
one with the roof guard, and one with Naeve, or whoever was going
away to the furthest field or to the mine, that will work. I have no use for
the last one as yet. It would have been nice to have sent Thord out with
it.*

Chapter XXV

Thord

Thord saddled Hillstrider and set out to find where the path behind the village went. *I have missed this. Looking back to a village slowly waking up after the wedding of Eleanor and Robin I can see a slowly stirring settlement. It is so much a part of the cliff and the valley that it can almost be Dwarven. Breathing in I smell the smell of sheep. Beneath me the saddle feels solid. A snuffling noise tells me that Hillstrider is more than glad to be out of the stable.*

They went down the gentle slope that led to the rivulet and around and up the slope on its right flank as it curved beneath them. *I will go up ridge or valley, once we find the way. To me the river looks too flat to go properly up a pass. I wonder…* He pushed through the vegetation. *Going up the ridge, we are following what is an old path. Now I am past where it curved around to the mines and the quarry, it probably hadn't been used since Mousehole was abandoned. The start of it is even harder to see. Now that I am through that screen of scrub I can just make it out. The path abandons the ridgeline completely and begins to make its way along the increasingly steep slope… Now I am travelling along a path set into a natural ledge in the face of the cliff and it is quickly narrowing.*

I can see that in places it has been partly carried away at the edges, but in other areas it is still solid and flat, even if overgrown. As the sheep and rider climbed they had to cross a stream that steamed in the cool autumn air. Hillstrider snorted at the heat from it. The water course went another two paces from the path and then curved through the air as it fell into the rivulet below. Dismounting and checking his footing, Thord edged forward. *The fall is sheer and is already around forty paces. This is the hot spring.*

The path curved to the left as it followed the rivulet below. *It is more evidently a path now, cut into the more steeply sloping hill that looms above it. The track way is damp and slippery with undisturbed mosses and small plants.* Hillstrider snatched mouthfuls and grazed as he moved. *I am content with the path. It will be wide enough to drive animals along, even to pass someone coming the other way if both parties are careful.*

Below him the valley had become uncultivated. At first there were patches of thick woods, and boulders that had slid down from the slope opposite and landslides of scree. As they had climbed for some time, the path reversed its curve and went to the right around a spur of the hill as the valley itself bowed around. *Ahead of me I can see that the valley narrows until all that is below is the rivulet forcing its way through and under fallen rock. It is just as well I decided to follow the ridge rather than the valley.*

I am around the curve I can now see where our rivulet comes from. Some way ahead there was a waterfall above him and falling at least four hundred paces in a couple of drops to the rivulet, which was now two hundred paces below him. He looked ahead. *Where is the path? Can I get up? It cannot just disappear. What I am riding on must, after all, go somewhere.* Excited, he pressed ahead to discover that the path ran damply beneath the falls through a moss-covered cave and continued steeply up the other side of the valley. After another few hundred paces it changed direction again at a flat wide spot and ran back towards the falls, stopping well short. It reversed and did this again. This time it almost reached the falls and he could feel the dampness from its flow, the rock beneath the feet of his sheep was wet and the top of the falls was now a hundred paces above him. Here it again changed direction and headed away from the falls. *We have bays cut back into the rock. This must be where you pass something that is wide. At the sharp bends there are even shelters that will hold a few people or a rider and a mount. Unless you knew how to look, they are almost invisible from below, cut into the rock behind the roadway. Someone had once done a lot of work on this way up the cliff.*

At last we are at the falls...I wonder where that side path goes. Thord dismounted and went down a few worked steps to a carved platform. There he looked down over a stone rail and the edge and saw the drop ahead. *What a climb it will make to come up that.* He chuckled. *So they want to learn to climb do they? Wait until they see what their graduation from my school will be.* Turning around and going up the last piece of slope he found himself at the bottom end of a new valley, one that was much larger and far flatter than the one below. The rivulet disappeared winding into the distance on a wide plain. *This has to be where the original Mice grazed their animals in summer. Even now it might be worth bringing them up here for a few weeks. I wonder if we can get the cart up here. The grass, heavy with seed, is rippling in the gentle breeze. It is long and lush—not grazed, except possibly by some small animals. Looking over the upland plain there is no sign of any grazers at all. Why not? Whether or not the mines are successful, here is the real long-term wealth of Mousehole. If I show this valley to the people of Kharlsbane, they would likely want to move here. Their grazing is in many small valleys and animals have to be shifted from one to the other by shepherds. Behind the valley is the first chain of the real mountains and behind them somewhere, but probably in front of the taller peaks behind, lies Dwarvenholme. Mousehole lays at least a thousand paces below him.*

It is just as well that I said I could be up here for a week and that they should not worry until then. It will take a lot more time than that to explore everything here. I'd better get to work.

There is a lot to see.

Towards the end of the last day of his allotted six, Thord returned down the valley. As he came down the path he waved at Naeve, who was out with her flocks. *She has spotted me and signals back. I will go over.*

On being told of the secret trail, Naeve confided that, in all of the time she had been in the valley, she had never realised it existed. *Even though I have had just come down it, the path is really invisible until you know where to look for it.* As they chatted they gathered the flocks and brought them back to their folds.

That night as they sat at dinner Thord told everyone about the valley. Thord, the Shepherd, was in his element. He and Naeve wanted to move some of the flocks up there for some late grazing starting tomorrow. *I can see that Giles doesn't like the idea, but Naeve is glaring at him and he is relenting. It seems, unlike most of the Human places I have heard of, the women have the situation well in hand in the valley.*

I am glad they are all pleased with what I have said. My other report, just for the Princesses, will not be as good. If some attackers are good climbers and have motivation, then I have found places where they could enter the top valley and so come down the trail.

"We have to assume that these Masters know of the top valley," said Rani. "That means whoever is up there must have the last Talker. As well, when they bring the flocks down for winter we will need to put something up there to alert us to anything coming through the back door. We need to go up to see how far the hiding spell reaches anyway. So my dear, you know what your next device is, if the Father cannot find something useful with what is left in the magic horde."

The next day Thord left again for the top pasture. This time he had Naeve with him. Behind they left it for others to take over caring for the flocks that were being kept in the lower valley. They took the whole flock of sheep with them and some of the cattle. Seeing that he was no longer exploring, Thord rode at the front of the flocks and tried to stay in the middle of the path. Across his saddle he had tied a stick. *It is a little longer than the width of their cart. This will give us an idea if the cart will make it up and back. If it can't, then we cannot bring many of the milking animals up.*

There had been a lot of talk last night about what we need. Giles told me he had made cheese before being brought to Mousehole and some more since. Now that he can do as he wishes, he wants to make and set aside a lot more to give us added winter supplies for next year. He is already making some of the soft and easy cheeses, but they don't keep for long. Now he wants to cheddar some. The bandits didn't trust the slaves much and brought a lot of their winter food in from raids, but Rani, after talking with some of the Mice, had decided to try to avoid having to rely on the outside world if we possibly could. Some food had already arrived for the winter before we freed the valley, but we will perhaps still be a little hungry this year. She does not want that to continue into the next year. I approve of that. I don't like being hungry and, although we still have plenty of dried food, that is best kept for the trail. Dried food tastes better when you have to just bolt it down.

Chapter XXVI

Father Christopher

Over the next few days Father Christopher found time to finish looking at the magical items they had horded. *Most of these are, of course, weapons. It is sad that people are much more eager to kill each other than to be charitable, but we also have a few more interesting objects. I have told the Princesses about a few and given some to people who could use them, and yet others I have put aside to go with us next spring. Several are very hard to place. What do we do with a hall-runner carpet that, when it is unrolled across a gap turns rigid and acts as a bridge? How can we use this? At the very least I can let people look at the other side of their little river without getting cold and wet. Astrid likes looking in their small patch of forest. How she knew that it had been untouched for five hundred years, and probably at least twice that long, I still don't know.*

Others presented a different puzzle. *Thord and Astrid are the two strongest of our people. Do you give them the pair of leather arm bracers that adds to their strength, or do you give them to someone who is weaker and would gain more advantage? Should the crystal pendant, which protects its wearer from major spells by turning them back against their caster be given to a mage, who has some natural resistance, or to someone like Ayesha, who might be sent to attack a mage or to Astrid, who took the lead on foot? Any of them could use a copper ring that spits out big lightning bolts that covers a significant target. So who could best use it? Or the magnesium and jade ring which helps protect the wearer from evil. They might all need one of those, the same with a woollen cloak that always protected the wearer against cold.*

Some, at least, are easy to work out. Ayesha was immediately given the bronze lock pick that opened magic locks and an amber and chrome ring which concealed the wearer from sight, sound, hearing and magic. She maintained that she did not need it, and it should go to another as she was silent enough anyway, but she was overruled by the rest of the group. One of the best items was found in Dharmal's room. Christopher realised that the Dwarf Bandit leader must not have had a chance to put it on or else Thord would not have stood much of a chance. It was a gold arm torc that made the wearer weigh only half as much as usual and also increased the speed at which they were able to attack and defend. Astrid was given that precious item. *From my sparring with her, she is terrifying with that spear; now, attacking at twice the speed made her even more formidable. No one could face her on foot.* She immediately put it on and, after trying it with a practice weapon, swore it would not be taken off except in practice.

Even I realise that some of this magic had obviously been with the wrong people from a tactical point of view. The ring that shielded against mages and the one that fired lightning had been in Dharmal's room while the carpet runner, which is very beautiful, was actually on the floor. It is possible that the bandits were just like us; they couldn't think of a use for it either. Some people just like to display powerful magic unused as an expression of their wealth. Perhaps Dharmal had been like that.

After consulting with Stefan, Christopher started to share out enhanced weapons as they were identified. *I know that Hulagu is insisting that I need to learn a new weapon rather than just a staff, but do I need a magical mace? I am sure that it is unkind to refer to my staff as basically just a very good stick. He wants me to learn how to use a horse mace and a shield and the Princesses back him.* He sighed. *It is not as if I have wasted much of my time with the staff. I have very little skill to forget. Still, I am not sure as to whether I like it or not. Our village is becoming an armed camp. Rather than put their past behind them it seems as if, when people are not working on chores or rebuilding, they are practicing with weapons or spells. What I am forced to do, they want to do. Rani even wants them fitter and stronger.* He considered Theodora's efforts and smiled. Stefan insisted she could scarce move if she had all of her arms and armour on. *It is hard work convincing her that her partner is right in what she said.* "You have been a Princess for too long and need more muscles, my love. I will join you if that makes it easier." The nights after dinner tended to see people finish their eating and go straight to bed exhausted unless they had more lessons. It was now only on Krondag eve that they were sitting up and dancing and singing.

One night at dinner, after Parminder had been baptised, Father Christopher was joined by Robin. Behind Robin, and remaining tactfully further away, were the three women in his life, his wife, his sister and her partner. *Robin looks embarrassed. This does not look good...for Robin at least.* The bowyer sat down and promptly started a conversation with the priest that went no-where. *I need to cut this short.*

"Robin," he said, "from the expressions the three women hovering behind you have, I suspect you have something on your mind. It does not matter how strange or embarrassing it is. I am sure I have heard it, or its like, before. If I have not, then it is as sure as the Resurrection that it is going to come up soon. I have decided that nothing in this village is ever going to be straight-forward."

Robin cleared his throat and looked back to the women, who all stared back with a flat look. Eventually he said, "Now that all doeth believe that I hath a made Eleanor pregnant, Goditha and Parminder have decided that they doth want a child of their own."

Christopher nodded. *Alarming as it may be, at least I have already thought about where this particular conversation is going to go. I hope my prayers are good enough and pray that the Metropolitan will forgive me for what I am, I think, about to say.*

"Goditha hath a decided that, seeing that I art her brother, I shouldst be the one to father the child with Parminder so that it be as much like my sister as any wilt be a knowin'."

Christopher sighed and nodded. *I was right and this is the only solution. I may as well go ahead.* "Yes, it is clearly your duty, that is, if Eleanor agrees."

A spluttering noise came from the other man and it was a moment before he could speak. "What doth thou mean that it be my duty? I be a married man now. I cannot father a child on another woman without it shall be a sin."

"That is normally true, but also the Bible does state that if a brother dies without having a child, a man is obliged to take his brother's wife and give her a child that shall be regarded as the child of his brother if she so wishes. One of the few sensible parts of Deuteronomy, I have always thought. By analogy the situation is the same here. Here, clearly, your sister cannot father a child so, in my opinion, and at this stage it is only my opinion, it is your duty to father the child for her. When the child is born, remember though that it is not and will never be your child. It is your sister's. Again though, I would urge you only to do this with Eleanor's consent. I have no theological grounds for that, it merely seems to me to be common-sense."

"Her consent? It were her as suggested it to Goditha."

Christopher smiled. *I thought that would be the case.* "She struck me as a sensible woman. In that case, if Parminder is in agreement, remember what she went through as a child and be very gentle with her. You do not love Parminder, but you love your sister and she loves Parminder very much. Do you wish me to bless your union? I can do it without a marriage ceremony and it will guarantee the fertility of your coming together so you only need do it once."

Christopher was handy when Naeve used the Talker and asked for Giles to be sent up to the top meadows with the cart and a scythe, and someone to help him, and volunteered to fetch him from his fields. It was decided that Hulagu, who wanted to see these prodigious fields that Thord was so impressed with, would go. The two came back two days later with a cart loaded full and high of hay to put away for winter. It was so full that Giles walked to the horse's head and the load of hay near touched its rump and reached high into the air while Hulagu rode behind. They were all gathered to hear of what they had seen. *The fields around Greensin may be fertile, but that is one of the largest cartloads of hay I have seen.* Hulagu was as impressed as Thord had been. "You could house a whole tuman up there over summer," he said, "and not run out of grass. There are even rabbits and small deer to eat. There seem to be no predators, so your herds would just keep on growing. What I don't know is why there is nothing large up there already. You would think that over the years some larger animals would have made it up there."

On his return Giles asked Father Christopher if he might have a quiet word with him. "Father," he said very diffidently, "Naeve was wondering if you could marry us the night after she comes back from the top meadows?"

"Gladly," said the priest, cheerfully. "It appears to be my main duty here, and to think that I had never presided over a wedding before I set out for here." *Giles has a silly happy smile on his face, but he is also still looking at the floor and shuffling his feet, as if not sure what to say next.* "You don't want me to?" Christopher requested curiously.

"No, no, that I do, but—"

"There is a 'but'?" asked Christopher.

"Well, it's like this…Naeve and me; we worked most with Goditha and with Dulcie. We was going to have them both as maids of honour, but then…because we was locked up so much, we men never got to know each other real well and I best knew those two girls and I says to Naeve that I didn't know who to have as my groomsman…well she says…'I'll have Dulcie, why don't you ask Goditha?' and…well, apart from Naeve…she's my best friend here…but she's a woman. I know, I know, she doesn't like men, except as friends, and she is with Parminder but…is it right? Could I?"

Father Christopher paused briefly. "I have already agreed to marry Goditha and Parminder, once I have checked with the Metropolitan. Now if what you tell me is right, then she will be asking you to be her groomsman next. Go and ask her. Don't be surprised if she breaks her own rules and gives you a kiss when you do."

Christopher was pleased to later hear that he had been right. Parminder heard the news as he was asking and excitedly headed straight out of the door to organise 'something for Goditha' and a dress for Naeve.

Theodora

I wonder if I am the first to have noticed this custom. Goditha has started work on our house. She arrived and has taken off her dress, carefully folding it out of the way and keeping on just a short leather skirt she had worn underneath the longer garment and no top. Over this she has put a leather apron. Now she has explained, it does make sense. The bandits didn't bring in much for the women and used to make them work without giving much support. This meant that they were given no work clothes and they had to 'make do' with what they were given. If they tore their good clothes while they were working they were punished so this had led to the women doing their heavy work in less clothes than they normally would use outside the valley when engaging in tasks that would be rough on their clothes. It seems that Astrid, when she was watching the village on the first day, had forgotten to mention this. The village men are used to the custom. Harald, who was helping bring in stone explained to Theodora, when she asked his opinion, that the girls with larger breasts, such as Verily, would sometimes wrap leather around their chests, but this was not out of modesty, after all the bandits had seen everything they had, but just to avoid being hurt. The women who were less well-endowed would just work as men did when they worked in the fields on a hot day.

Theodora kept watching the rest of the rescuers to see how they took it, and was rewarded with the sight of Basil being confronted by Dulcie with a load of timber, to little reaction and then Stefan who saw his own Bryony helping Goditha with some stone. Stefan's eyes nearly dropped out and Bryony burst out laughing and nearly dropped the stone as she pointed him out to Goditha. She smiled and gave an ironic bob in his direction. Bianca's reaction was more matter of fact when she saw Anahita and Kãhina getting ready to ride out to the river to wash all of the horses in just loincloths, but she immediately went over and there was an animated three-way conversation incomprehensible to anyone who couldn't speak Khitan. Anahita left the group and ran up to Hulagu's room and came back with something under her arm. Bianca went in to get her horses and Esther for a wash as well and re-emerged bareback and dressed in the same fashion as the other two. She was trying hard not to look embarrassed.

Some time later the three were returning with the horses. *Bianca has quickly adjusted and, despite looking more than a little nervous, is laughing and joking along with the other two. Oh...this is interesting. Father Christopher is coming out of the hall. His face is priceless. His jaw may hit his knees. Now Bianca turns and sees him. I have never seen anyone blush from the waist up before. Bianca is trying to sound calm and failing. Father Christopher is trying to reply and is not saying a single intelligible word. Everything is coming out in a garbled fashion that starts with almost a squeak. Now the girls are taking the horses into the stables and there is a storm of laughter. But is it at Bianca or with her?*

Father Christopher

The sight of Bianca nearly-naked is almost too much. I saw Aine, the brewer, working earlier in leather trousers and an apron and then Goditha working with her stone. I asked Ruth and she explained. I do understand the necessity that had driven the women to this situation, and Ruth told me that most of the women preferred to work that way, once they were used to it, particularly when reaping and gathering in the fields in hot weather—a loincloth or kilt, a straw hat and a pair of sandals were all that most wore. I do accept that, and I accept that the circumstances of the Mice are unusual, but I don't lust after my parishioners. My thoughts have been struggling with the possibility of this. Seeing Bianca out in the open and somehow wearing even less than she does in her dancing clothes is now real and in front of me. What do I say? What do I do? Oh Lord, I will be speaking to you tonight at length about this on my knees. Can I get the image of her breasts out of my mind?

He realised that he was fleeing as he returned to the hall.

Once he had recovered his composure he went off to see Theodora, whom he had noticed standing on the veranda of her house and gazing over the courtyard. He made sure his eyes were averted from the stables and hurried up the courtyard.

"I really do need to see the Metropolitan," he said urgently.

The Princess is looking more than a little amused. Oh Saint Mary Magdalene, did she see what just happened? How can she respect me as her priest, poor sinner that I am? At least she is tactfully saying nothing even if it is written on her face. "We have the carpet. I think that it is time that we let someone else know what is happening in case we fail... If you saw your Metropolitan, would he keep your confidence?" Father Christopher nodded. "Would he let you bring a priest back with you if we promised to return him?"

"I think so"

"Could you find Greensin from the air?"

"I am sure that I can do that...now I can at least. Ruth has shown me a map. I couldn't have found it on foot when I started. Remember, for me, this all started with me getting lost."

"Then I will take you there after they bring the animals back down from the top valley safely. We will fly at night and we will rest during the day and continue on in the next night. We should not be seen by anyone and we can have a word with the Metropolitan and I am sure we can fix your problem at the same time."

My problem...yes, she has seen my reaction. I am shamed. Saint John Chrysostum, patron of priests, aid me. As soon as we can then...oh wait. "If it cannot be now, it will have to be two nights after they come back. I have another wedding to perform."

Chapter XXVII

Rani

It is odd to be involved with things I have never had to think about before. The animals are still away and it has been seven days. Giles and Hulagu have made another trip for hay and also with large earthenware pots with tops that could be firmly tied-down. They have returned with them full of sheep's milk. Ayesha is headed to the lookout for the morning.

That is the Talker operating..."Someone is coming down the path from the north. They probably won't be here until tomorrow, they are still having breakfast, from the smoke, but I thought that I should let you know so that you can work out what we should do."

"How much smoke?" Rani asked.

Following a short pause, "Enough for a small fire, no more than a hand or so."

"I will think about it. See if you pick up anything else from them and we will talk tonight."

I don't know. I will ask my Princess. They discussed the options and decided that they wanted to stay secret from casual passers-by for a while, perhaps staying that way until well after winter unless someone actually sought them out.

"It is a little late in the season for traders to go anywhere but here. I would rather fight Shiva than bet against any innocent traders that went along this road not being waylaid. If these people are innocent, then I want them to continue past us to report that the track is clear. That way, next season we might find a ready supply of traders starting to use this path. I think we should not go out to them. If we did we could not avoid inviting them in and anything that they see could get back to these Masters."

The next day the lookout was to be manned by Astrid, Bryony and Stefan. For today Stefan was given the lighting bolt ring and Bryony was given the ring which protected the wearer from evil. Astrid had her day made for her by being given both the arm bracers and a loan of Ayesha's invisibility ring. She immediately put it on and moved behind Basil, easily picking him up and squeezing him playfully.

"Astrid, put your husband down and listen," said Rani, as she prepared to give them their instructions. Astrid took the ring off and reappeared with a grin on her face. "Stay low," said Rani. "If they turn up the path, let us know, otherwise let them pass. Keep an eye on them until they are out of sight. In case of need: Astrid you may have to get down the path fast and any extra damage you can do will be useful if you are fighting alone. Bryony, stay with your bow and hold the lookout, taking out the stragglers. Stefan, as you need to—use the bow, the ring or your spear. If they come up the path, then we do the same as last time, but we will take them captive. If it is possible, find out what they know. Understand?"

All three indicated their understanding.

"Then off you go. You all need to be out there soon in case they are moving quickly, but you may be there all day. Let us know when they actually come into sight so that we can move to the gate."

Astrid

*W*e have had to wait all day and now we see it is just a small trade caravan, so I don't even get to have the excitement of combat. One man is on foot leading three laden packhorses, and with one guard out at the front and another at the rear looking around as they go. The rear packhorse has a spear stuck through the pack frame, while the front animal has two. All three men are wearing swords and they have round shields on their backs. The two guards walk with bows strung and are looking all around them cautiously. No wonder they are travelling slowly. The guards are clad in mail. The horse handler is wearing more normal clothes. The magic detector glows. From the way the man in the front is moving and checking his surroundings he has not been along this path before. He keeps moving ahead to look over crests and then waving* *the others forward just as I did, but he is not really a hunter. He seems to be at least as good as many I have seen at keeping within cover, but he walks on the pathway too often and leaves tracks. He must be from what my husband calls the Army.*

Astrid reported their presence with the Talker and, despite the ring she wore, kept low. As the visitors drew closer she took a better look using the telescope. *The one with the animals actually has mail under his clothes and his garb looks to be of more than reasonable quality. The two guards...well they are ugly...they are part-kharl, just not as cute as Basil. This must be a Darkreach trader and he is either heading for the village, or he is in search of a market.*

Quietly she used the Talker, instructing all the users to be as quiet as they could be until one of the watchers on the lookout said otherwise. She received acknowledgement from the other four and then handed it to Stefan and went back to her task of watching.

She observed the group move down the track. They stopped when they saw the bridge and then, after a short discussion, continued. Astrid had an idea. *This would make up for the boredom of the day.* She pulled back from the edge and appeared to the others as she removed the ring. "They seem to be innocent," she whispered. "I am going to see if I can hear anything from them. If one of you takes over watching here, I will be back as soon as I can be."

Stefan

*D*amn, *what is she up to?* She had disappeared again and he felt her brush past. He waved Bryony forward. *She is the more experienced hunter, after all.* She wriggled forward with the telescope that had appeared when Astrid had put it down and left. She didn't need to use it to see the traders cross the bridge and then continue down the old road past the valley, but she whispered back all she saw. The visitors had barely glanced at the ravine and its two disguised paths. After crossing the bridge they continued down the path and past where the initial assault had gone up the hillside. Once they were well away, Stefan reported back to the village.

"She did what?" said Rani. "Is there any sign of her?"

"She *is* invisible," interjected Bryony from the side.

"Then finish the watch and come in. Hopefully she is back by then. Come in when you see their campfires."

U ncomfortably Stefan held position. *Now, how long do we wait?... They have set up for the night. At least I think that is how that small column of smoke should be read... It is growing stronger...we will keep waiting...at least we can take comfort from the fact that no-one has gotten on to the Talker to ask what is happening.* He and Bryony discussed how long to wait and they looked at the path time and time again. *There is still no sign of Astrid.* He waited until the last of daylight was fading before motioning Bryony down the path. With a last look down the path she went down and he followed the track to the path up the ravine. He felt a wave of relief when, just as they reached it, Astrid appeared, taking off the ring. She was panting.

"I stayed with them as long as I dared and then ran back. They are Darkreach traders, one Human and two are insakharl, hoping to sell herbs and spices in the Swamp. If they get a good price they will come back north in a few weeks with what they can buy and come back again next year with a larger supply or whatever they think will sell. They want this to be a regular trip and for them to get rich. They found this road by accident and are congratulating themselves with saving a week on their journey and avoiding any tariffs on the way. This ring makes being a scout almost too easy."

Together they returned to the village.

Rani

" T hose were not your orders," said Rani uncomfortably.

"I know," said Astrid, with a grin. *Damn her. Couldn't she take these things seriously?* She continued, "But I suddenly realised that this was possible. If I had asked then, they might have heard your reply and that would have spoiled everything. As it was we know all about them and can talk to them next season. I even know that the trader is called Carausius and his guards are Festus and Karas. I am the scout. It is my job to use my initiative and find things out. That is what I did," she concluded stubbornly.

"She is right, dear," said Theodora. *Her hand is on my leg.* "She found out exactly what we need to know. If she can do the same when they come back we might find out even more. She also safely gave us a good idea how well the magic works."

I am used to being in an army where people obey orders and there are plans to be followed, not this madhouse where people do what they think best...however. She sighed. Chagrined, she admitted that Astrid had been right. "But try and obey orders. If you had gone missing I would have had to explain it to Basil."

"He would have found me somehow," declared Astrid loyally. "Can you make us another of these?" she asked Theodora. "It could be very useful for scouting and I have more jewellery like my cloakpin that you can use, if you want."

"We will see," was the reply.

Thord

I am used to bringing the animals down from meadows to town, but not quite like this. Here I am the only Dwarf and the adventure has only just begun. We have been taking milk and hay back; now it is time to bring the rest—one Dwarf, Giles, Naeve and our Khitan.

"Last night we had light snow..." said Thord, when they had returned, "'n' we decided t'at it was about time to come down. I explored further while we were t'ere, 'n' t'ere was no sign of anyone up t'ere, but I found what may be an old path leading further into t' mountains. T'ere are some faint signs, in t' way of displaced rocks t'at it may have been used, perhaps year ago, but I'm not good enough tracker to tell for sure. It could've been animals, it could've been people. It is too hard for me to tell."

"Go, wash and rest," said Theodora. "Tomorrow I will go back up with Hulagu and set two warning traps, just in case. Naeve, go and see Giles and Dulcie. You have a wedding to prepare for."

Rani

*T*he third wedding has been better prepared than the second. The groom and his groomsman both stand there in new trews, tunics and vests. Goditha has her hair held back in a braid and, if you ignore the swell of her breasts beneath the tunic, looks more like a very attractive youth rather than a woman...unfortunately. The bride is wearing a new dress of fine pale yellow wool to go with her hair and her maid of honour has a new dress of green.

Rani said, in an aside to Theodora, "I am betting that the most successful merchants coming in here will bring either men or cloth...or both."

Her partner giggled behind her hand.

Our priest is more polished in his delivery this time and, at the request of the bride and groom, includes the prayer for pregnancy. The girls here regularly used herbs for some time to try to avoid pregnancy, not always successfully. Pregnancy could be a death sentence with the bandits if things went badly and Naeve has said that she is not sure if her body was working right yet. At least there is little sign in her demeanour of the terrified woman who had huddled in the mage's house screaming on the night of the attack.

That necklace of citrine from the store well matches the bride's colour. The food is again more to the Freehold style, but there is greater variety and the night is being the success that everyone hoped it would be. From up front you can see and hear all that is happening. Verily still lacks the confidence to dance the Khitan dance but vows she will be ready for the next wedding. Ruth has also joined in learning the dance, but then I notice she seems to want to learn everything.

Father Christopher

*V*ery late in the afternoon of the next day the carpet took off bearing Christopher and Theodora. They had the cloak of warmth to share on the trip and they took the Talker from the top meadow with them. They would now have a chance to find out its range. In front of him on the carpet Theodora was dressed as if she were a mercenary in mail, not her own rich armour, but she did wear and carry her own helm, bow, sword and shield. She was also wearing her amulet to disguise her eye and hair colour. Father Christopher sat behind uncomfortably. He was in his new, matching apparel. *Did Hulagu and Stefan have to find a set of magical mail and a helm that fit for me as well as the enhanced, mace and shield?* The mace hung at his side and the round shield was slung on his back. *I know that I try not to think too much on the previous owners of these things and what they have seen. At least I am far more likely to survive a fight now than when I set off on a trail wearing a cassock and sandals and with a staff in hang. I was armoured in my ignorance and faith then and can only thank the Lord that he helped me find Astrid. Now I might, with all the practice that Hulagu is making me take, be getting less incompetent at using these weapons. Not that I am competent, mind you. That is still a very long way off, but at least I am unlikely now to be a danger to the person standing beside me.*

They still had not worked out why the bandit Ahmed had entered along the valley and through the gate, but decided that it was prudent to do the same. Getting to the gate, Christopher hopped off the carpet and had it opened, closing it behind them. They flew down the valley and up to the lookout. No-one appeared to be there. They waited for a while.

Theodora lifted the Talker and was about to call Rani when Astrid appeared, grinning.

"Sorry, I couldn't resist that," she said. "You should have seen the look on your faces. Ayesha and I are trying to work out which of us is best to use this one. When I have it, she bears the new amulet that you have made for me with my old cloakpin. It seems safe for you to go on. I have seen nothing besides the usual eagles that hunt to the north and some hawks out over the forest."

I feel relief at that. Even if I now bear arms, I am not relishing having to fight at all… Now, as we fly the sky is lovely and peaceful and the view is disturbingly vast, but I am running out of things to say.

He had been talking constantly to Astrid, and she to him, and they had gone half a day's fast ride when the Talker stopped working. It went from being as loud as ever to a whisper in a few heartbeats. *We now know its range.*

In silence they sailed quietly through the rapidly chilling night sky. *There are some patches of light to our left…that must be Erave Town and its surrounds…and then the light of the moons reflect off a flat area…Lake Erave. We have the patches of lights of different sizes that should be Evilhalt and its hamlets. Is it silly to be pleased that I remember the positions of some of these places to the north?* They continued until the sky behind the mountains, which were moving further and further to the east, started to gradually grow lighter. In the growing paleness they looked below. *At least we can see more to navigate by now. To the north and west are some tall hills and below them is a river.*

"Ruth found an old map in the library," said Father Christopher, as he tapped the Princess. "If we are right, those should be the hills of the Dwarves, and it is where the river ends that joins onto the water way which enters Lake Erave. Greensin should be north of them, half way to the sea on the Ogunbil River. I know there is a path to the Dwarves and another that leads to Evilhalt and another, if you take the wrong turn as I did, to Wolfneck. I think that we should land near the river for the day and go on tonight until we see clearings and villages around Greensin. We should walk in rather than fly. I will do the talking."

"That is best," said Theodora. *She is probably glad she had been working on her fitness since we will have to walk some way.*

They did as Christopher suggested and early in the morning on the second day walked through the fields of the hamlets around Greensin. *It will be a goodly day's walk before we draw near to the monastery or the village.* The carpet weighed him down. He had it rolled and folded over his shoulder so that it came down to his knees at front and back as if it were a very bulky blanket. *This is heavy.* His shield strap hung off the other shoulder. *I am glad that this autumn air is more than a little chill.*

I asked for this meeting and yet now I dread it. I can only hope we find the Metropolitan straight away and we are not delayed. That is a relief. We have a file of the Basilica Anthropoi moving down the road towards us on a patrol with their horses. It was only a brief moment of relief. *Oh dear. We need names. I am not very practiced at this lying business.*

Theodora

Theodora watched the file approach. *This is interesting. I thought most westerners wore the same motley collection of weapons and armour as Freehold do and have the same lack of discipline. These could be some of Darkreach's best...they even bear the Chi-Rho on their shields and the leader has an icon painted on his shield. I wonder how many there are in Darkreach who know that the Church here may be militant.*

Father Christopher

As the troops drew near Christopher halted and waited for them to approach. *I know this patrol leader. I have met him many times. I hope that my disguise holds and that the monk will not be seen in the mercenary.* The leader held up his hand and the file stopped. *Their bows hold arrows nocked but pointed down. He is coming to us.*

"Greetings in the name of the Metropolitan and the Holy Church," said the leader. "Who are you and what is your business here?"

I have to bite my tongue to stop myself blessing the man. "I am Georgiou and this is Helena. We bear a privy message for the Metropolitan. Can you tell me where he is please?"

"You can give it to me and I will be sure that he gets it," said the leader.

"Praetor, if I could do that, it would not be a privy message now, would it?" said Christopher chidingly. "I was given a mission, I took an oath. I will fulfil it. We have lost one companion and our horses, and we are eager to complete this task. Can you tell me where he is please?"

The leader, *Michael, yes, that is his name*, grinned. "One always has to try. I believe that he spends the night at the monastery tonight. Seek him there. Do you need a guide?"

"No thank you. I have been here once before," replied Christopher.

The Praetor nodded and gathered his file behind him and rode off behind them.

"For a priest, you lie with facility," said Theodora, when they were out of earshot.

"I am glad you think so. I will add it to my confession when we are seen," said Christopher. "I may be busy most of the night. You may have to stay in a guesthouse outside the walls, but I will try and lure the Metropolitan out to us. In other words, I will probably spend a bit more time on my knees for my sins. Follow me and do what I do if he comes out."

E ventually they approached the monastery, threading their way through a large village and the people in it, passing the guesthouse and the outbuildings and the homes of the monastery servants. *People are looking at us with only mild curiosity. I may have been overly worried. I suppose Greensin is enough of a town for strangers to be fairly commonplace.* On reaching the gate Christopher knocked and in a short while the door opened...*Another shock—that is Brother Petrus. He has filled out in the time since I last saw him and the few stray wisps of hair on his face are now starting to look a bit more like a beard. I hope that he does not recognise me.*

"I am Georgiou and this is Helena. Could you please tell His Eminence that we bear an urgent message for him from Father Christopher, whom he sent away to the east? We will both wait here until we can see him."

It seems that the eye rims and the nasal of the helmet are sufficient as a disguise. He is not seeing past the armour. He does not even appear to have noticed Theodora's disguised black eyes.

"You may enter and I will take you to him, but the lady must stay here."

"I am sorry, but we must both see him. We will wait here until he is free."

"I will see if he can come then," said Brother Petrus. "From Br... Father Christopher, you said?" *At least he is interested in my name.* Christopher replied with a simple nod. Petrus quickly closed the door and left them standing here. Theodora made a move to speak, but Christopher held his hand up. *Her accent is wrong.*

"We will wait in silence," he said.

After some time the door opened again and the Metropolitan appeared, framed by the gate, with an expression of curiosity on his face.

Christopher immediately made a bow by reaching down and touching the ground with his right hand, rising, then placing his right hand over his left with the palms upward. "Bless, Your Eminence," he said. Out of the corner of his eye he noted that Theodora followed his lead. *The way she does it so easily must mean that she is used to it.*

"May the Lord bless you," said the Metropolitan, and blessed the two with the Sign of the Cross, before placing his right hand in their hands in turn. First Christopher and then Theodora bowed and kissed his hand. "Now then, what news do you have from Father Christopher for me?"

Christopher looked behind the Metropolitan. *Brother Petrus has tactfully withdrawn out of earshot while staying in sight.* "That I am here in front of you in disguise, Your Eminence, and we need to speak privately with you," he said cheekily. He was rewarded with a brief look of surprise as the Metropolitan took a longer look at the man within the armour and then studied longer his companion. *He has quite obviously noted her eyes.*

"Brother Petrus," he called out without looking back. "Have refreshments sent to the guest house and organise for two rooms to be prepared there. We will be proceeding there now and will be in the reception room while that happens." With that he strode off.

While we just trail along in his wake.

They walked there slowly, talking of the weather. They entered the large wooden guesthouse. *I have been here many times to tend to visitors. The familiar polished timber walls and floor, the plastered ceiling, the rugs to ward off chill; they are all comforting.*

When they were seated and refreshments had arrived and servants had left, the Metropolitan began in earnest. "So, Christopher, you seemed to have been much changed by the world you entered so reluctantly. I certainly did not recognise you, nor did Brother Petrus."

It was only once he heard the door close that Christopher removed his helmet. "Your Eminence, neither did Praetor Michael, who directed us here."

"By your dress, are you still a priest or are you now a soldier? Who is this part-kharl woman and what news do you bear for me that cannot be said publicly?"

"I am still a priest, but now I bear arms as well. This lady is not a part-kharl called Helena, but I will let her tell the story as she has more part in it now than I do and she is one of the leaders of a free village. After we have spoken I crave that you hear my confession and that you also give me advice and, if I may ask, lend me a priest."

The Metropolitan nodded agreement and Christopher indicated to Theodora that she should begin.

She stood and removed her helmet and then took her amulet out of her right ear lobe. Christopher saw the Metropolitan's eyes grow wide. *He obviously understands the significance of her appearance. That will make it easier.* "Your Eminence, I am Theodora do Hrothnog, I suppose that I am now a former Princess of Darkreach and also, by right of personal conquest and acclamation, I am Princess of Mousehole." *Curiosity flickers across the Metropolitan's face.* "I will explain..." and Theodora sat again and launched into a short version—for a bard—of what had transpired.

"...so you see, before we venture on this expedition in the summer, we felt we should tell someone what is happening in case we fail. I will also try and send a message to my ancestor. If we fail, between you and he, something should succeed. As well, and this is part of why we need a priest, Father Christopher will not abandon his new flock without someone to pastor to them. I said that this is part of why we need a priest. No doubt Father Christopher will tell you of the other part himself." She smiled.

Christopher looked at her curiously. *What is she talking about? If I am to do that, would someone please tell me what the other part is?*

"So all of these lost traders that we have heard of, some of whom have had their remains discovered, their loss is all down to this lair of iniquity? These so-called 'Masters' have some sort of evil secret plan and have agents to aid them all over the Land?"

"Yes, Your Eminence. We have a few ideas about them, which I would prefer not to share where magic can spy upon us, but none as to their goal."

"Well, one thing they have done is to nearly cause war over most of the Land. Freehold is blaming the Khitan for the death of traders. The Brotherhood blames everyone and appears ready to boil out of their misguided land in revenge. Haven came close to doing the same but, for some reason, backed off. I now know the reason for that. Obviously the rulers of Haven have not told Freehold what you first found out or else have not believed what they were told." He paused in thought. "Princess, you are sure that your land is not involved in any way?"

"My land is now confined to a few days' movement around the little village of Mousehole, Your Eminence. However I am as sure as I can be about anything my ancestor does. He does not consult me about his plans, but I am certain that he would have stopped me if I had interfered with one of them. My guard, who was sent directly by my granther to look after me, is even more certain."

"Then I will give you a priest to take back with you. Need he be a soldier?"

"No, Your Eminence, just a man who is tolerant of the ways of the world. If you will pardon me, I will use myself as an example of what he will face. I am sure that the good Father will inform you once you are alone with him, but I love another…who is also a woman and I seek the blessing of the Church on our union. Father Christopher has told me that there may be precedent for this. I hope so as we love each other. We have another two women in our village who have suffered much and have sought solace in each others' arms and we have another arrangement where there is a man and two women…one of whom is Muslim and I think they might all wish to marry. This is the choice of the women, not of the man." She drew breath. "While I tell you of these, I will also mention that many of our women are accustomed to working with their tops bare. They do this out of practicality, not lasciviousness and I might mention, that the Holy Church at home…sorry, I mean Darkreach…tolerates this under some circumstances as long as it does not lead to evil. My partner and I have already adopted one of the children of the village and, with Your blessing wish to raise her in the Church and find her a good husband and our other two women are already raising the sister of one of them in a similar way. The younger of these two women, who was a Hindu, has just been baptised by Father Christopher into the Faith in anticipation of Your blessing. The elder was raised in the Faith already."

This string of information surprised the Metropolitan more that the earlier story had. "I think that I will let you retire to your room for a while and I will talk with Christopher alone now. I may see you before I go tonight. If not I will have answers to your many questions tomorrow. Go in peace and with my blessing, my child."

When Theodora had left, the Metropolitan said, "She then really is who she says she is and everything she says is true."

"Yes, Your Eminence," said Father Christopher, "although I am not sure what else I want a priest for. She is a good woman, as is her partner, who, although she is a Hindu of high caste, attends all of my services, and encourages others to do so. As a matter of fact, the whole village usually attend when they can, even the Muslims and the Khitan. Ayesha, she is a woman ghazi, tells me that her people like that I only preach from the Old Testament, for that is all I have available to me to use. The Muslims come to me for their sermons and then do their own prayers. God alone knows why the Khitan attend."

"Did you say a woman ghazi?"

"She is the first and so far the only one. As Theodora said, our village is an unusual one but, for all of the suffering it has gone through, it is full of Christian love for each other. I have already performed three marriages in a few weeks and will hopefully have two or three more when I get back. After that we will have run out of men…we also need more good single men who are not afraid of work…and of being ruled by women, as I think that will ever be the way with Mousehole."

"And yourself, what are your plans?"

"Your Eminence, I should make you aware of my failures during my confession."

"Then, my son, if you have no more to add to your story at this stage, let us proceed to that…"

Looking firmly at the floor in front of him, Father Christopher began the litany of his sins. He began with the usual small sins that everyone has committed, or at least imagines that they have committed, but then he moved on and began to detail his relationship with Bianca and his growing lust for her at the first wedding. He concluded with the story of the bare-topped Bianca riding the horse and his reaction to it. It was all too much for his superior and, despite his long experience in the Confessional, he finally burst out laughing at the change in the man in front of him and his imagined sin.

Christopher looked up in surprise. *I can feel the shocked expression on my face. I have never been laughed at by my confessor before. It is even the Metropolitan that I am confessing to and he who is laughing at me. What have I said that is funny? I was accounting my sins!*

When he was able to control his mirth the Metropolitan put on a sterner expression and addressed the priest. "This woman," he said, "you admit that she is the plainest and least beautiful of all of your parishioners?"

I am squirming like a young novice caught out pinching apples.

"Except in her heart, Your Eminence. She has a good heart and I do not see her as plain. I hope I see her as she is."

The Metropolitan nodded. "So, apart from the fact that she fits in with the odd habits of her adopted home, and the fact that she has tortured evil-doers to get the truth from them—something that she has consulted you about and on that point, and I suspect that more has been said in the confessional that you can not mention on this point—" Father Christopher nodded, "then, apart from these points, she is a good woman?"

"Yes, Your Eminence. She has a strong faith and is disturbed by the way she feels she has had to act. I worry that I cannot go back there to be exposed myself, and what is more to further expose her, to further temptation."

"And you admit that you have seen others of your very attractive parishioners dressed in a very similar fashion and, indeed, far more frequently, and yet you have not entertained the same feelings towards them?"

Christopher swallowed hard. "Yes, Your Eminence. I admit to sometimes having admired their beauty, but that is merely an appreciation of God's handiwork, for they are all indeed beautiful and they have managed to keep their beauty through great hardship. However at least I can honestly say that I have felt no lust towards them."

"Then your path to penitence is clear. Your other sins I will talk about soon, but in regard to Bianca, when you return, and you will return, you must immediately remove temptation from you both by asking her to marry you."

My mouth has dropped open. Yet I have no words.

"Close your mouth. I mean immediately. It will be your first act upon going home. Listen to me. You are going to be the priest of a village. It is a small one now, but I suspect it will grow. Because you are a priest and not a monk you must marry anyway. What you think is lust is another emotion that you...because of your lack of experience with the world... have failed to recognise. You silly man...you are in love. You do not need Absolution over this, but another Sacrament. This is the other matter that Theodora said you needed a priest for. She obviously saw what you did not. It does not matter to us that your wife to be is of the schismatic rite. As well, although their Pope rails against us in Freehold and persecutes any of us they catch, they pragmatically sanction their people attending our services when they are on the peripheries of their lands. Their traders all know this. It is the same for our traders going to their churches, even if ours may be a little circum-spect in the confessional. Their Church would rather keep their habits of worship than that they be prey to heathens and pagans. I am sure that she will agree to marry you."

He finished with the rest of Christopher's penances and gave absolution. "Now fetch the Princess back while I compose my thoughts."

When he arrived back with Theodora the Metropolitan addressed them both. "To be blunt, there is no precedent that I can think of for two women to marry." Theodora's face fell. "However, there are several precedents that are in the diary of events that is passed down the line of Metropolitans, for the marriage of two men. Although such has not been done for a long time, the precedent exists. If we can marry two men, I see no logical difference in marrying two women. Christopher tells me that you are in a loving relationship and are already making good Christian provision for a child. I give you both my blessing and I hope that Christopher may, in time, convert your wife as he has already converted this other bride-to-be. I am very pleased with his efforts."

"Now, as to the other matter of the priest to go with you... I may have to ask around on this, but be assured that I hope to send one to you tomorrow. I will also need to brief Brother Theodule, as he should be the most suitable, if he agrees. He has been a priest before, but his wife died and he returned here hoping for a quiet retirement, but he is the only person that I have at hand who is suitable for this. I do not want to send a younger man. Having already been married and had children, and being an older man, he need not marry again, unless, and given your unlikely village it is always possible, he does desire to venture it once more. He can stay with you as long as he is needed, for all his life if he is happy to. Father Christopher will stay in his role as the senior priest among you, but Theodule will look after the flock while Christopher is away helping in your holy fight against these 'Masters', and he will also perform that second service by marrying Christopher and Bianca...that is, if you think she will accept."

Christopher looked at Theodora. She returned a smile. "I think it very unlikely indeed that she will refuse. Like our Father, she does not know her own mind and she feels guilty, as does the Father, at the feelings she has. She was raised schismatic and..." she shook her head. *I can hear the disbelief in her voice.* "...they disobey direct scripture and do not let their priests marry for some reason. She cannot reconcile that history with her feelings for the man before her...feelings which are evident to all of us except our Father."

The Metropolitan clasped his hands. "I thought that you understood. As long as Christopher asks correctly," here he gazes at Christopher. *I am...feeling flustered...again,* "I am sure he will succeed in his petition." He stood up. "If that is all, the night is now late. If he consents I will send you Theodule tomorrow morning. If I have to seek further you may have to wait here alone. It would be suspicious if I saw you again." Addressing Theodora he added, "At some stage I would also like to talk to you about the state of the Holy Church in Darkreach. Please feel free to visit me again after this is over." He gave them a blessing before leaving.

When he was gone, Theodora grinned at Christopher. "I am going to get married," she said joyfully, "and so are you." She gave Christopher a kiss on the cheek and hugged him.

I am not sure how I look, but I feel...stunned. There is nothing I can say.

They were breaking their night fast next morning when there was a knock on the door. Theodora answered it, after putting on her disguise. Christopher stood to the side in shadow where he could see without being as easily made out.

A monk stood there, a mature, but handsome man far shorter than either Christopher or her. The hair around his tonsure and his beard showed more than a touch of grey. He was dressed for travel in leather trousers and a thick tunic with a long sleeveless buff leather jerkin over it. In his hand was an old forward-pointing leather cap, like those the Khitan wore. It was lined with fleece. He had a belt that bore a dagger and an old looking, but serviceable sword. He looked her up and down.

"Bless you, my child. You must be Helena. I am Theodule and I will be leaving with you and...Georgiou. I have here all that I will take with me." He waved towards a large backpack and then towards a sack, "and food for our journey, and some more things. I do not look forward to carrying all of this a long way on foot and I believe we have a long way to go."

"Come in, Father," Christopher noted that she gave a bob, as they were used to doing in the village—although usually she received them. "We need only travel for a day and then it will get much easier. We are just finishing breaking our fast and then we will be off."

Theodule came into the room. He looked at Christopher in the shadow. "You must be Georgiou, whom the Metropolitan has told me so much about." He smiled at Christopher, who had already dressed in his armour, but had yet to put on his coif and helm. "He told me that you were a shepherd, but you are well-armed for such. Your sheep must indeed pasture in a dangerous area."

Christopher smiled in return at this word play from the older man and returned his greeting before they finished their food and set out. Theodora took the backpack while Theodule was given the carpet and Christopher slung the sack over his shoulder. As they walked away their conversation stayed an apparently innocent one such as would occur between strangers going on a journey together. This did not change until they were well away from anyone or anything that might harbour a listener.

Theodule checked his surrounds before saying, "So, Christopher, you have been changed by the world. You cannot have your way and be a monk and so you drag me away from the monastery as well?"

"It was not my desire to rob you of your rest and contemplation," said Christopher in apology.

"Do not be alarmed. To tell you the truth, after having cared for a village and taken part in raising our six children to where they have their own families now, and having lost my beloved Kale, I thought that a contemplative life would be good for me. However, I find that I miss life in all its richness. Not only do I miss the teaching, but I also miss caring for everyone and, to be frank, I was getting a little bored and I am glad that you have brought me out." He smiled. "You are about to marry—do you have a wife for me as well?"

Christopher heard Theodora laugh from behind them. He began to splutter. *I don't know what to say to that.* Theodora laughed harder. She said, "Father, you will fit into our village very well. You have a sense of humour that will be appreciated." She paused with perfect timing. *I am being made fun of. I am the butt of a joke.* "Now that we are speaking frankly, you realise that ours is not the most conventional village?"

"Young lady, the Metropolitan told me that you would tell me more of yourself when we were on our way, and that it was your story to tell. He also told me that he had blessed the arrangements that I would find as being in the best interests of the ecumen. I said that I wanted to get out in the world again and, if I am going to leave my contemplation, it would be boring to have only the normal issues to deal with."

Christopher glanced behind. *From the expression on her face*

Theodora is obviously thinking about what she should say next. She checked all around to see if any were close by. "I cannot prove it to you here where we might be seen, but Father Christopher will vouch for the truth of what I say. I am not a young lady." Christopher looked sideways.

Theodule stopped and turned around, his eyebrows were raised and his eyes were studying Theodora hard. *He is trying to think of Theodora as a man. It is my turn to smile.* Theodora eventually realised his confusion as well and said, "I don't mean that, I am fully a woman, even if I do love another woman, but I am not young. I am over one hundred and twenty years old and will live for many more centuries. I am a descendant of Hrothnog, a Darkreach Princess, if you will." Theodule searched for Christopher's assent, who just nodded. "That is one of the more normal things about our village," she added.

As they walked Theodora and Christopher began to acquaint Theodule with the life that lay ahead of him. They stopped talking if anyone, or any cover that might harbour a listener, drew near.

They had reached the first large area of trees and were about to look for a place to wait for night when Theodule had a thought. "So, you might then have another wife for me after all," he said in a semi-serious tone, but he spoiled it by adding, "or at least a member of the flock may have a mother of suitable age who comes seeking her." They all laughed and settled down.

When night fell they took off with the carpet and retraced their route. This time, seeing that they were over forest and there was little chance of anyone seeing them in the region, they did not bother to stop for dawn. After all, if anyone did see them they would probably mistake them for a Caliphate patrol. Flying low to avoid being silhouetted for the Darkreach watchtower, they pressed on and came to the valley before lunch.

"No-one is to be seen in the lookout post," said Christopher. "So it will be either Ayesha or Astrid there."

Theodora pulled up at the lookout and said, guessing, "Good morning Astrid."

Astrid appeared. "You guessed. I suppose I am getting predictable. You brought a man with you." She looked closer, "Oh, I am sorry, Father," and bobbed.

Theodule studied the woman in front of him. It seemed that he was weighing her up. "You must be the woman called the Cat," he said. She looked pleased. "We will talk later, but I am Theodule. I have come to help Christopher with all the problems that he tells me you have given him."

Astrid opened her mouth and was about to say something and then she realised that she, who was usually doing the teasing, was in turn being teased. She laughed. "I will talk to you later then, Father. Welcome to the Mousehole." She bobbed again.

As they flew up the ravine, Theodule asked Christopher, "Do they all do that sort of curtsey thing?"

"Yes. Most of them didn't know how to greet a priest and I didn't have the heart to tell them otherwise. It is now our custom. It is all Fear's fault."

"Fear?" asked Theodule.

"My daughter, Father," said Theodora, as Christopher dismounted at the gate. "She was named 'Fear the Lord Your God' by the Brotherhood man who sold her to be a slave. We just call her Fear. She is one of the children who were brought here for the truly depraved and knows nothing about the world outside except in stories. She had heard about bowing and this is her version, which everyone now have adopted, alas even me," she said wryly. "My old teachers of deportment would be most horrified."

Theodule was brought into the village and introduced.

Christopher looked around and innocently asked where Bianca was.

"All of the Khitan have taken the horses for a gallop and they are to go to the river for a wash, Father," said Valeria.

"Then it seems that to the river I must go," said Christopher. He doffed his mail and weapons leaving him in just loose trews and a tunic. *I may lack experience on such matters, but I don't think that weapons are appropriate for a proposal.*

"Good luck," said Theodora, as she allowed herself to be led away by an excited Fear, who obviously wanted to show her what she had done while her mother was away.

Christopher walked nervously towards the river upstream near around a bend and past the trees. He heard the noise at the same time as he saw the herd and their four attendants. They didn't see him until he was nearly upon them. *Those two girls are obviously far too amused to see that Bianca is again blushing on seeing me. From what I see she was probably comfortable in her state of undress until now. Now she is embarrassed.*

"Hello Father," said Hulagu. "How went your visit?"

"Well, very well indeed," replied Christopher. *Now I am confused.* "Ummm...I was wondering...if it might be possible...if I might have a few words with Bianca...alone that is." *Three sets of dark eyes fix on her and then immediately switch back to looking at me. I can see the two other girls turn and grin at each other. Despite the state I am in I can see she is worse. She is so beautiful.*

"I am sorry if my dress is not seemly," she said, approaching Christopher. "I did not think that it hurt to...all here dress this way...I will get a shirt and a dress if you wish."

"That is not what I wish to see you about. I told the Metropolitan about our...unusual habits in the village and he has given leave for them to continue here without them being counted as a sin. I need to say...the Metropolitan told me...no that is wrong...I want to say..." *Now that the time has actually come, I have completely lost my composure. I am completely tongue-tied. I should have thought this through on the way home. What should I say? Bianca is staring at me. She is unsure what I am on about and even whether to cover her breasts now that she is alone with me or whether to continue as she has been. Her hands are moving up and down, up and down and she is now crossing her arms under her breasts. She doesn't realise that this only serves to emphasise them even further as it pushed them up and together. I was not this close earlier. I must look at her face. I suppose that it is the cool breeze blowing from the river that is causing her nipples to change like that. Oh no, I can feel myself reacting to her as well. Look up. Lord, give me strength. This close I can smell her as well, she has just washed her hair and there is a faint herbal aroma from her. Saint Bridget, patron of poets, lend me the words.* "I mean..." said Christopher. *I am still struggling for composure. I still do not know where to look. Try her eyes...*he drew a deep breath and continued, the words coming out in a spurt, "I was made to realise that I love you and I now want to ask you to marry me. Will you marry me?" *There. I have asked it. Now it is up to her. What if she says no?* He heaved a sigh and waited.

Bianca stood there in shock. "Marry? Me? But—"

"She says yes she will, Father," said Kãhina. *She must have followed up behind Bianca without either of us noticing.* She called back to the other two. "He has finally asked her and I have told him that she will."

"That is for her to say, not you," said Hulagu.

"Then we will all be here for the rest of the day," added Anahita, coming up to join them. "Yes, Father, she loves you very much and she will be your wife and she probably will not admit this, but she has been waiting for you to ask her the question for weeks."

If anything Bianca is blushing even deeper. "I think they are right," she said very quietly.

"Is it all right then if I kiss you?" asked Christopher. "Will they be shocked?"

She seems to have regained a tiny measure of composure. "I think they will be shocked if you do not."

I am holding a nearly naked woman in my arms in public. She was three hands shorter than him and he had to bend down as her arms finally went up and around his neck. *It does feel good, very, very good. Where do I put my hands? Perhaps like this...her skin...it is so very soft and warm beneath them. Her lips are soft and warm as well and...what do we do with tongues?...Now I can taste her and breathe in her perfume, and it is divine. Oh no, she can feel that I am responding to her very physically...she is pressed hard and almost rubbing against me and...I suppose we are getting married so it is no longer sinful. Now I will just enjoy the warmth and the feel and the taste and the smell of her. I am glad that what I am wearing will conceal my weakness from others.*

It was only when he let her go that he noticed the applause from the other three. *Oh yes they started that earlier...some time earlier...and that odd voice-call that flutters up and down. I was lost in the moment.*

Christopher walked beside his bride to be as the others rode back to the village together. As they did so they found that the Mice were gathered and waiting for them with more applause.

Bianca

*M*y wedding will be the day after tomorrow. What is Theodule giving to people? Cannot Astrid stop distracting me? Soon she was being dragged over to a group of women. Fortunata stood there with Parminder and both were looking her up and down. *Astrid is still behind me and I am trapped between them, and all three of them are giving me the once-over.* Suddenly she realised what was happening.

"I don't need a new dress, there are clothes that will fit me," she proclaimed. "I am only an apprentice trader and I am not used to new things."

From behind her Astrid snorted. "Get used to it. You are no longer the orphan Bianca. You are to be Presbytera Bianca and must dress appropriately. At least you must do this at important times. I think that Christopher will be secretly proud of your breasts when you go to wash the horses." She grinned. *Why do I blush so easily?*

"What is 'Presbytera'?" asked Bianca, changing the subject.

"Your new title," replied Astrid.

"Why do I have a title? I am his wife, not a priest."

"You are the wife of a priest. I think it works like this but you will have to ask your husband to be sure…you are joined in marriage as one flesh, therefore part of him is you, so part of him being a priest rubs off and you get a title." *Astrid appears happy with her explanation. It may make sense to her but, as is often the case, the northern woman doesn't make the slightest bit of real sense. I will ask Christopher, or at least Theodule, if I am not allowed to see my betrothed.*

"And that is why the Metropolitan sent this." Fortunata waved some braid, a simple repeated design of gold on white silk. "And this…" Fortuna raised a small bolt of white silk for the braid to go on. "Let us get to work. We do not have much time and after you are finished here with us, Eleanor needs to see you."

"What—"

"You will see. Do not be impatient."

W hat Eleanor had was a wedding crown, similar to Theodora's in some ways, but not as elaborate, made of filigreed silver rather than gold, and lacking the gems. Eleanor was working to fix that last. "The Metropolitan sent this for the brides of the village to bless us. I managed to miss out," she said ruefully. "Here, let us see if it fits you or if I have to change something."

Father Christopher

I am sure my wedding is going to be our most formal so far.
Christopher stood up the front of the crowd in his new ceremonial
robes of white and gold. *A wedding looks very different from this side of
the ceremony. Beside me are my groomsmen, Basil and Stefan. At least
they seem to be as nervous as I am.*

Eventually they heard drumming and Khitan-sounding music.
Looking behind them they saw the musicians entering: Aine, Verily and
Naeve playing drums with Hagar playing a buzuq and Bilqĩs blowing on
a naq, a small flute. Anahita and Kãhina, as maids of honour, were both
dressed in their dancing clothes, but wearing as much jewellery as they
could find or borrow. Each had a belt on with their sabres and bows and
arrows hanging off them. *My betrothed has finally left her origin in
Freehold behind. She is being brought to marriage as a Khitan bride,
but dressed almost as one from a Darkreach court from the look of her.*
Behind the other attendants came Hulagu, again fully armed, bringing in
Bianca as was his right as her brother. Bianca was wearing a long white
robe, similar to Christopher's, but of a lighter silk. It was very full and
promised to be almost circular if she twirled around in it. It had the gold
braid at the hem, half-way up and around the neck, in a fashion similar to
Theodora's neckpiece. She had no necklace, but blue sapphires--
matching her eyes—were embroidered into the braid of the neckpiece.
On her head was the wedding crown. It was mostly concealed by the
white veil covering her head. *She is so beautiful.*

Hulagu gave the bride away in a speech in Khitan. *Does he have to
speak in his own tongue? I only have scraps. Is he stating her wealth in
horses? That bit I get: he, as her brother, stands by her side in all things.*
Theodule must have realised that he had to explain to everyone what
being Presbytera meant as he addressed Bianca in the ceremony.

For the first time Verily danced the Khitan dance, in Bianca's place,
and the music and entertainment had a distinctly more Khitan flavour.

There was a mild moment of confusion when Christopher and Bianca realised they had not worked out whose room they were going to, which was resolved by the maids of honour who escorted them to bed in favour of Bianca's. On entering they found that it had been cleaned and there was sandalwood incense burning and the sheets had been sprinkled with rosewater and other scents.

For a brief moment Christopher thought that the other girls were going to stay and stand witness until Bianca firmly ordered them out of the room. Soon he discovered that his imagination had not lied to him about the woman he loved. *If anything it has not been rich enough.*

For the first time since their arrival in the village Father Christopher was late to Orthos, the morning service. Theodule had started without him.

Chapter XXVIII

Rani

The attack came the next night. It was just after dinner when Basil, who had the watch on the roof, called Rani on the Talker, waking her from a deep slumber. *This had better be important. My Princess, beside me, is still slumbering on, softly snoring as is her wont.* "The first crystal for the path above is glowing blue," he said. "I will call again if the second one glows." She peered at the oilcloth covering the window. *Not a hint of light out there and yet I have to think.*

Best to be ready, it is time to wake Theo-dear. They dressed, Theodora grumbling as she did so. *If I am not good at doing mornings, my Princess is as bad as an elephant with indigestion. She needs her kaf.* Soon they were waking others and sending a wave of movement spreading through the village as people found their weapons and took themselves to their stations. *Sleep is still being rubbed from eyes as the first kaf starts to appear. My love grabbed the first quickly.* Those who only had daggers and little skill to use them she sent to lock themselves in the guardhouse with the children. Rani was on the way to the roof as Basil let them know that the second crystal was glowing.

"That delay means they are moving at walking pace," said Theodora. "We have a few hours yet, they will not be here until midnight. I would say that the bandits did not know about that path and, with our screen in place these Masters did not know that we found it. This means they intended a surprise attack. Instead we can surprise them." Rani gestured up the cliff behind the village to where they had entered the valley. "Thord, get up there and keep a watch on the entrance we used...we really must block that more fully...in case this is a diversion. Take your bow and get as many arrows as you can up there. If needed you are to be the cover for all of those below."

Rani looked at the sky. *We are well into the Moon of the Fish, the first moon of winter. September is almost ready to slide into October and*

281

the moons, Terror and Panic, are nearly at their least visible. Luckily there is very little cloud and at least Krishna, the largest of the wanderers, adds a little light as do a couple of the others as they stand bright among the stars. Information...we need information.

"We will see what we face," she declared. "Valeria, run and get the carpet from the room please. Astrid and Basil, you have the best eyes between you, you are going to get a carpet ride. Now, pay attention to the task and do exactly what Theodora says. No sitting up there thinking that this is a romantic moonlit ride. Basil, you take the telescope and hang on to it. Astrid, you will also have the magic detector. Do not point it at them if they are likely to hear it." To Theodora she said, "My dear, stay well out of bow range and travel very high until you know you are above and behind them. Then I would suggest coming down the opposite wall of the ravine and staying in shadows as much as you can. The moons should aid that."

"You are telling me how to use illusion to hide?" asked Theodora with amusement.

She is waking up. "Sorry dear, it is just a worry sending you out."

Astrid

The carpet arrived and they set off. Astrid gave a squeal of delight at the sensation. *This is fun.* "Don't do that up there," said Theodora, as she headed up as steeply as she dared without them sliding off. "Or that," she added, as Basil made a suppressed noise behind her. *I will need to circle a few times to gain enough altitude.* "I hope that we don't run into whatever, perhaps, stops people flying in or out. I dare not climb too high." Eventually she headed off to the left of the valley and the left bank of the river.

It didn't take long to reach the ravine and, hugging the wall near the top of its cliffs, to go up it slowly. After five minutes Astrid leant forward touched the Princess' arm and pointed down and to the left, still well ahead of them. The first of the intruders had just started down the cliff path. "There they are," she whispered, pointing towards the path down to the falls. Theodora looked down as she heard a 'beep' behind her. "Well, we know they have magic. I will put that in my pouch now.

Basil, what do you see with the telescope?"

"Nothing...my lady, can you hold this thing still for a while?"

Theodora brought the carpet to a stop and they sat, rocking gently.

"Now I can see. They are large, like boyuk-kharl but bigger, not anywhere near as big as an insak-div though, and with shields and carrying curved swords. Some have long bows like Astrid's. I think their colour is wrong, but there is not enough light...I cannot tell...I haven't seen their like before."

"Give me the telescope, my love." He handed it over and Astrid used it. "Where are they?" He pointed. "They are hobgoblins. I have seen them sometimes in the northern forests. There is a tribe of them in the far north and they sometimes raid far afield for livestock. I have never seen so many. The most you see is usually a hand. There must be at least three filled hands of them there...All have armour, some of it metal. They are fierce, very strong, and hard to kill. Some say that they eat people...but then some say that of kharl as well."

They watched for a few minutes more. "Are you seeing anything new?" asked Theodora.

"I think some have ladders, or at any rate, some long things that might help them over the wall. Maybe three of them near the middle are dressed differently. They have the skulls of animals bound to their heads. Do hobgoblins have shamen?" The others both shrugged. *No-one knows. Few know much about hobgoblins. It is said that sometimes you can trade with them, and sometimes you get eaten. It is best to stay clear.*

"Well, that would explain the tracks that Thord thought he saw," said Theodora. "They might come out of their tribal area to hunt the plains and to see if any larger animals have moved in. Mind you, he saw no sign that they had ever come down this path. Astrid, from what you know, do you think that the Masters would have sent them?"

"That is most likely the case. The wild tribes I know rarely leave their area, except to hunt. That is not a hunting party. If there is nothing else, we should be going back," said Astrid, and Theodora turned the carpet towards the village.

Rani

R ani watched the carpet flying away and started giving orders. She
sent Eleanor to the wall with those who only had missile weapons,
while Norbert, with his two-handed hammer, was told to sit and hold the
gate. That cleared most of the people off the roof. *Do I get Naeve to
bring the animals inside the wall or not? Let us wait until the carpet
returns. We may not need to and it would be wasted time if we didn't.
Everyone can sit down and rest until we know more.*

Everyone reached their assigned places and waited.

"The carpet is coming back," said Hulagu.

She peered out into the pale light. It took a while to see it, but in a
few minutes it was back.

"We have hobgoblins, a large war party with druids or shamen of
some sort," said Theodora. "If they get off the path they can use cover
and move around through the animal pens to the wall and we will not be
able to stop them. There are far too many, possibly even three hands of
hands. I know we have the advantage in defence, but they would just
overrun us."

"Any ideas?" Rani asked.

"I will take Ayesha's invisibility ring," said Astrid. "I will use it
and my strength and speed enchantments and I will meet them on the
path where they can only come at me one or two at a time. They have
bows, so I will need to find a corner to wait behind. If they want to come
down then they have to come through me and I will be trying to throw
them over the edge with my spear as much as fight them."

"And if you fall? What then?" asked Rani.

Astrid shrugged and grinned.

She obviously relishes the challenge. Rani flicked her gaze to Basil.
He looks concerned but is staying quiet. He already knows his wife.

"Send some backup then," Astrid said, "Basil with his short blades
and Eleanor. If I am hurt I will get back behind them, take the ring off
and take some healing draughts and they can hold them until I am ready
to return. You can make it easier by putting some archers with all of
those arrows you brought from Haven on the opposite wall. You make

better ones yourself now, so we can use those ones up. It will be a long shot, but the archers will have a height advantage and it will be hard to shoot back at them. They can attack the centre and try and take the druids at the same time. I haven't been up, but I am told the path goes around a big corner. If we hide behind that then only the one that I am killing will actually see what is happening at the time…and hopefully he won't do that for long."

Not bad for a start. Ayesha said, "If I am one of the archers, I speak their tongue. Not well, but enough. I can try and make them turn back. If they are stopped from going forward and are just staying in place and dying, they will not want to just stand there and let it happen. Hobs are wild and fierce, but totally without patience. They like to attack and kill and they will have little stomach for just dying without a good reason and for someone else. If they are not killing others as well then it will be even harder for them."

It comes together and becomes a plan. "Valeria," said Rani. "You wanted to be our maid. In a combat you will be doing a lot of running and fetching. Get the bag with the potions and the bags of betterberries and quickly." Valeria headed downstairs at a run. She addressed the others, "That should work. We don't want to damage the path, so we should not use too much magic… Astrid…get on the carpet with Basil…pick up Eleanor at the wall and fly up the path to a good spot. Try and be well ahead of them so that Theodora can get archers in place before you hit them." She addressed Theodora, "My dear, you are going to be the most exposed with your runs. Take my helm. You know its enhancement. It will stop at least some arrows if they see you."

They swapped helms and Rani gave Theodora a kiss. "Good luck."

Basil

I don't like this idea, Basil thought to himself, as they headed off, stopping to pick up Eleanor at the wall. *I can see that Puss is convinced that it will come off and she is fast with that magic and strong as well. I just wish I am as certain.*

Better pay attention, the Princess is talking, "I have a sort of invisibility device, and would give it to you," she said, "but, when I made it I was escaping Darkreach, so it only works for me. I think that I need to try and make a better one once we get time. At the rate we are going, I am going to run out of the ability to take on new spells before I run out of things I need to make."

They flew up the path this time. *I haven't been up here either, but the spot to make a stand is obvious. The river's long left curve abruptly reverses itself around a tight turn. It is well down the path, but the path curves most strongly here and, unless the hobs can shoot right around corners, even their druids can do little to whoever is attacking those at the front of their war party.*

Theodora set out back to the village for the first archers. "Don't start shooting them until you see that they are starting to come around and die," Astrid reminded Theodora. Once the carpet had left, Astrid said to Eleanor, "Unless you wish to get jealous, close your eyes." *I can feel her lips, and the rest of her, as we hold each other. She can make me stiffen that easily.* "Even our leather gets in the way of everything," she said in a mock grumpy voice. "Still I am now getting all randy and I need to keep my mind on the job. Wish me luck. We can continue this later." She slipped the amulet on and disappeared. *Her hand rubbing on my trousers...her butt should be...*He gave a slap and was rewarded with a familiar feel and then she was gone.

*I*s that the carpet? I think it is. It is only two hundred paces from here to the other cliff, but with the cloud the way it is the moons are only giving a quarter of their best light and it is tricky. The Princess will be using the shadows as well. Their bows will not do much damage from that range, but then, seeing that they are a good fifty paces above the path, the hobs probably would have a lot more difficulty hitting the ambushers, if they see them at all—despite what Puss said about their strength and what this meant for the power of their bows. I will just have a quick look around the corner. I am better able to take advantage of shadows in a city, and in the wild I am no match for Puss, but I am far better than most. The hobs are easy to see. The last of them will be out from under the waterfall very soon. The first of them is already well past it. We have at least ten minutes before the combat begins.*

He passed the telescope back to Eleanor and kept watching. She nodded and sat down against the mossy wall for a few minutes. *Once a fight starts you crave a rest. She may as well have one now.* She put the pack with the potions and other healing herbs and bandages in it down against the cliff wall where they both could reach it.

The hobs were one hundred paces away when he felt a push backwards on his chest. *Puss wants to get ready for them out in front.* He moved further away from the curve and gave her ten paces to work in, nodding to Eleanor as he prepared. He didn't draw his shortswords. *I may have to help Puss back before I can attack. I hope not.*

Eleanor stood up and took her kite shield off her back and put it on her arm. She took the outside position with the shield near the edge and her horse mace resting on her shoulder. Basil took the inside, slightly ahead of her, his back almost to the wall. He reached back. *I can feel its roughness and some damp moss.* They waited.

Soft footfalls from around the corner...some deep and rough-sounding voices talking... They aren't worrying about stealth. Who would? They will be thinking they have the advantage of complete surprise...up here they can't even be seen from the village... Is that the carpet again? Is this its second or third trip? Aren't the hobs paying attention? Are they that confident? They think they have the village at their mercy, but the tables are turned. I may not be trained for normal battles, but I know, from talks around the family table, that in a well-prepared ambush—and this is—unless those who are attacked are very lucky, most of them die. Surely some of them have to be feeling uncomfortable with all of us watching them and about to attack. I suppose that might even be what the voices are talking about.

T he first hob appeared around the corner. *He is large and very ugly and wearing mail. For an instant his shape stands out clearly against the paler sky behind. Almost straight away blood is gushing from his neck...no time to cry out...over the edge...the same for the second. The third is close to the second and has time to cry out before he is clutching his chest and heading for the edge. He is trying to keep hold of the spear in his chest. I hope he fails. He is only lightly injured by the spear and...that scream...that thud cuts it off... It is a sickening thud.*

Basil heard explosions from around the corner. *The Mice above us must have decided to use magical arrows after all, probably for the druids. The next hob just peers around the corner and is rewarded with a spear thrust that goes into his toothy mouth — not nice cat's teeth like my Puss but snaggly and large, meant to take a throat out and rend raw meat.* He reeled back and disappeared, his head a ruin.

A babble of calls and screams erupted from around the corner and there was a rush towards them. *Not sure what Puss just did, but three hobs run around the corner together and they keep going straight over the ledge. They tried to turn, but failed and so fall screaming...arms and legs flail in panic, weapons and shields discarded, as they comically try to fly or run on the air and so prevent their fate. They fail...those cries now end in thuds. There is not even a single groan from down below.* More explosions sounded loud from around the corner. *Rani and Robin will be hard at work through the winter replacing all of these shafts.*

He heard a woman's voice, *it must be Ayesha's,* calling out from above them on the cliff as arrows continued to rain down and hobs tried to come around the corner. *The ones coming around the corner are obviously expecting someone with a sword because they are swinging as they die and they are swinging in the wrong spot for where Astrid is...I hope.*

There was a gap then another hob came cautiously around the corner with his shield held high and just his eyes visible. He was calling something out when Astrid's spear took him in the stomach and she pitched him over. Next a pair came around slowly. *Blood spurts from the inside of one's leg...now from the outside one. They crouch, trying to protect legs...the outside hob has Puss' spear in his face... The other calls...tries to back up...trips...he gets a thrust to the groin as he falls...he is down and screaming in pain and rage and holding his parts...trying to crawl back around the corner...Ayesha is calling something out...the combination of deaths and screams and what she is calling must finally have been too much for the hobs...there is a lot of noise from around the corner, but no more attackers.*

Basil waited. *Is it over? Apart from the injured hob trying to crawl away ahead of them as he staunches his own blood, the calls are growing fainter.* Basil sensed something behind him and turned to see Theodora, on the carpet, coming up the road.

"We forgot to give you a Talker," she said, a little embarrassed "Sorry...They are just running now. We are still shooting at them as they climb towards the falls, but I think they are finished as a menace. We will harry them as they go. Astrid, you can appear now." She looked down at the wounded hobgoblin. "I see you brought a wedding present for Bianca. Now, at least we can find out why they attacked us."

Astrid appeared with a smile on her face and a bloodied spear in her hands. Basil felt relief run through him. *She doesn't look to have been hit at all.* She smiled down at the wounded hob and blew him a kiss. He tried to back up further. He didn't appear to be able to rise. She must have severed something vital in his leg. She waved the spear at him and sweetly said in her native tongue, "No kitten, stay there so that mother can see you. That is a good hob." He was a large person but he looked confused and terrified by her. She said in Hindi, "I don't know what the archers were doing and Ayesha was calling, but it worked."

"We got their druids in the first two volleys," said Theodora. "Everyone fired at them at once. By the time the rest had a chance to recover, what with no-one coming back from your corner and not knowing what was here, and with their leaders down and more being hurt or killed by arrows, they just broke and ran. I think some even dropped their weapons. It was lovely."

The hobgoblin spoke then, in broken Darkspeech. "I stay still...help me. We told easy food here, treasure, bandits gone. They lied to us." *He sounds bitter. Not a happy and willing soldier then.*

"Well he speaks," said Theodora, also in Darkspeech. She took her helmet off and leaned forward so that the hob could see her eyes, which glowed faintly in the night. *If anything he now looks even more terrified.* "Give him a few berries and keep him alive. He has already told us that they were sent. He might be able to give us more yet. You stay here and I will start ferrying everyone back. We will follow them on the carpet, but we should regroup first."

They brought their captive hob back with them. It turned out that his name was Saygaanzaamrat. "A bad choice for coming here," said Astrid, with a laugh, when they had reached the village to a series of blank looks. "Oh, in Darkspeech it means something like 'pillager of emeralds'. It may be the same in Hob." She checked with Ayesha, who nodded. "Well, we mine emeralds and the pillaging didn't quite go according to plan, did it. Jokes really lose something when you have to work them through a couple of languages. Why cannot you lot all speak Darkspeech like normal people. I'll bet more people speak it than this entire gaggle of western languages all put together."

Basil stood guard with his wife. *Saygaanzaamrat is very eager to answer anything we ask, particularly after Father Christopher healed his injuries. He asks to be let go, but that is not happening. He speaks in broken Darkspeech. Now I am a translator. The Masters sent someone to the village, a Human. He had come several times before when they were told not to come in this direction. When they had not obeyed what they had been told to do, bad things had happened to the tribe, hunters had not returned from the hunt, avalanches had thundered down, the crops had failed and floods had swept people away. The shamen of the village had proved that they were useless against them.*

Yesterday they were told that the village had been left open and the slaves were theirs to do what they wanted with. They were told that there were only a few defenders and much treasure. He looks around at that. "Yes," said Theodora. "There are very few of us, and yes, there is much treasure. That much is true."

He swallows and continues. *They were told to come down at night. They were told everything was theirs except for a few things. He said he didn't know what they were—their leaders did, but he didn't. All he knew is that they were supposed to leave the gate open when they returned to their village and to hold it open with a rock.*

"I guess," said Theodora, "that the Masters had new tenants in mind. We need to be very vigilant over the next few days, although we know that they are expecting to have the door open and will probably go away if it is not. We need to look deserted. That means only someone who cannot be detected can go to the lookout."

"Then I am off to bed," said Astrid. "That means Ayesha and I have some sleep to get, after I burn some of the excitement off." Basil felt his hand grabbed as she left, to much laughter as she dragged him away.

Although he liked the idea of what was to come he tried to salvage a little dignity. Quickly he blurted out in mock terror ,"Help me. Won't someone please save me from the ferocious insakharl woman." Behind him he could hear a lot of laughter, cut off by a closing door.

Rani

R ani ignored the byplay and kept looking at the Hob. *His hands are now tied, his leg bandaged and he is looking around him at the varied faces. It is clear that he has not gotten the joke from the blank incomprehension on his face.*

When the hilarity had subsided, Rani asked, "What do you know of the Masters?"

Saygaanzaamrat's eyes switched quickly from left to right, as if one of the Masters might be in a shadow nearby. *He sounds very nervous.* "We know very little. Only our shamen have seen them. They say they walk like men, and reek of evil. They say that they think that they are some form of undead, but none that they have ever seen or heard of. They once tried to find out more in the spirit world, but there has been a fog over much of it for many years. The fog is growing and growing deeper. The shamen convinced our headman...I cannot say his name...we cannot speak the names of the dead, and he led us earlier and was the first to die...there are many names that will not be spoken for some time...they convinced him that the growing fog meant that the power of the Masters was growing. We either had to leave the valley where the village is or else become one with the fog and the Masters. We should have left."

What should I say to answer that? She looked at Theodora.

"No." Her lover took her hint and interjected. "You should stay. We are going to destroy these Masters in the summer and then the fog will be gone. We will even trade with you in your village. It can again become strong. You know who I am, don't you."

"Yes mistress. You are one of his." He jerked his head towards the mountains, and then looked abashed. "We don't normally say his name either, but you are one of his children."

"That is right, and what I tell you is true. We cannot let you go yet, because when the Masters catch you, you will tell them what you have seen." *He looks scared again.* "Don't worry, we will let you go...but not until after the Masters are finished. Then you can return to your village and you will tell your village this. The valley above is ours. You may not hunt in it without permission. Anyone who enters armed will die. Anyone who enters without arms, to trade, will be allowed to do so. Do you hear me?" The hob nodded. "I am the Princess Theodora and this is the mighty village of Mousehole and we will enforce our will on our area and the area around it." She switched back to talking Hindi. "Does anyone have any other questions?" She was answered with a chorus of shaking heads. "Then put Saygaanzaamrat in one of the cells in the guardhouse. We now have to look after him all winter. Ayesha, better start teaching some others how to speak to him or he is all yours to look after."

Rani said, "Dearest, you and two others should go to make sure the other hobs have left the valley and you need to reset your alarms." She thought briefly before pointing. "Hulagu and Ayesha, you will do. If you find other hobgoblins you may need to talk and they may not have any Darkspeech."

They climbed on the carpet and headed off.

Ayesha

When she went to sleep the next morning Ayesha was thinking, *Damn Astrid burning her excitement off.*

When she woke up it was to... *Where is he? Hulagu should be here...Shaitan take these dreams that I keep having. This time I haven't even been dancing.*

Chapter XXIX

Astrid

A strid spent the morning at the lookout trying her patience as a hunter. Excitedly she had used the Talker to report smoke to the south when she arrived, but that was it. *If there are some hard-riding bandits coming up this road, there is no sign of them. They cannot just disappear.*

It was that afternoon before the Darkreach traders went past again. This time they were in a small hurry. Now, as a light drift of snow presaged the hardness ahead, they were heading north and going home for the winter. The packs on the horses were very full and the trader looked to be in high spirits. *I guess they will be back.* She smiled. *This time I won't go down, but Carausius, Festus and Karas were due for a surprise when they return next year.*

Theodora

Theodora felt a bit smug as she spent the day making a new device with Eleanor's help. It was a very special copper ring inlaid with seven amethysts that, when completed, would make the wearer invisible, but not silent. *This is a big improvement as a spell from my first device that I had made at home. Being able to talk while invisible, either to say what was happening or to call for help may be more important than silence. Not that I could afford to add that in anyway. Changing the spell from aiding just me to anyone had cost. That little bit of extra would have made it impossible. You can never have everything you want. Tomorrow I will put in the actual spell and lock it. I would not have been able to do that without drawing on a store when I left home. Now I can. I am growing a lot.* She was humming a little as she worked alongside the jeweller, but she could hear her lover explaining what was happening to the apprentices and why the spell was being cast as the ring was made instead of later when it was complete.

Eleanor complained she had never had so many people watching what was, even with the tools that she had, from her point of view a very simple operation. Theodora just smiled. *She will need to get used to it. I suspect that we have many more amulets and other things to make before this adventure is all over.*

Ayesha

The next day was different. Ayesha had the morning duty and when she arrived she saw some faint wisps of morning smoke lingering in the sky to the south in the growing dawn. *It betokens someone who is trying to be surreptitious and who has instead been a little clumsy in putting out the fire just a trifle too late. They might not even see the smoke from below it, but the light is just catching the wisps and revealing them.* She reported this and was told to let them know when they came in sight and if the travellers turned in to the valley.

"Above all, stay undetected," Rani said. *This from the Queen of Stealth...as if she would teach a mouse to like cheese.*

Eventually three riders came into sight. They stopped some distance away when the lookout came in their sight and one gazed through a telescope at it, while another looked at his hand. Ayesha used the Talker to describe what was happening: "I think that we can be certain that these are bandits. I bet they will come up here. I will try and make it look like no-one has been here for a few days. I will let you know when they leave."

She started trying to make the few tracks look a little wind blown and used other artifices to age them. By the time she was content, and standing very carefully on bare rock beside the small shelter, the three were below. *Again one is consulting his hand as he looks up at the lookout and along the path. He is dressed in dark green cotton clothes that anyone out in the wild could wear and he has a sword at his side. I guess that perhaps he is from the Swamp. He might be a mage or a warlock as he has no armour. The two with him are very obviously arms-*

men. Both wear mail, with coif and helm, both bear kite shields on their backs and have lances stuck through their saddle girths. Both even have swords at their hips and light crossbows hanging down off the saddles on their horses…and both are looking very nervous. They keep looking around as if they are expecting to be attacked at any moment. Ayesha kept up her commentary on what she saw, unconsciously whispering despite the magic that protected her. The three rode up the valley with the possible mage in the centre. When they reached the path to the lookout Ayesha's guess was confirmed. They stopped and the man in the centre ordered the armsman at the front to climb up and look around. *He is using Faen, the language of the Swamp people.*

The front rider dismounted. *He is still looking around.* Ayesha grinned. *His sixth sense is telling him he is going to be ambushed and he can see no evidence. This is making him more suspicious, not less.* She passed this on. The rider came up to the lookout. Sure enough he stooped to look at the ground.

"No-one for a couple of days, by the look of it," he called down.

"Right, well have a look around to see if there is anyone else visible and then come back down." The man up at the lookout grunted and muttered to himself as he inspected the small area. *He doesn't even seem to be aware that he is talking.* "That bastard just sits there and gives orders… Bloody wizards, think they own the world…I'd love to stick one under his ribs one bloody night. I wonder if any of the girls are still here or if we will have to get a new lot in. I hope that redhead from home is still here. I missed her wedding night; she turned me down for him and I turned her in. Now I get up here and hopefully I get to have her anyway I want." He grinned smugly, finished his look around and then went back down the track muttering something else Ayesha could not catch.

Ayesha reported this and said, "Better tell Bryony in case she does something rash when she sees him…oh…now he has been sent on to the gate…is it open?"

"Yes," said Rani. "None of us can be seen, most of us are in the village laying low."

The rider returned to his horse and the three set off up the trail.

Rani

After Ayesha first reported in, Rani called everyone together. "We need to prepare for these men. These Masters obviously have their people everywhere…and lots of them. I want to capture as many of them as I can so that we can question them. Astrid, you will need to get to the gate and latch it open with a rock. Make sure you are not seen. You still have the device Theodora made you when you set out?" Astrid nodded. "It is important for you not to be seen, but you must prevent any leaving and close the gate when they are through and out of sight. Theodora, my dear," she looked around. Theodora was not there. "Theodora?"

"Mummy, Theodora is on the roof," said Fear. "Will I get her?"

"No, little one, Valeria can do that, she runs much faster." Valeria headed off.

Rani waited. Presently Valeria came back with Theodora.

"What is happening?" she said.

"More bandits are coming. Can you do the control spell that you used on Ahmed again?"

"Oh dear, not today I can't. I was just completing the spell on the new ring." She held it up.

Rani sighed. "In some ways that is a pity. Oh well, we now have it and it cannot be filled by what we do now. Can you give it to Astrid please?"

Astrid took the ring and put it on and disappeared. *I know exactly where she is yet, even concentrating hard, I can only make out a vague shape, almost like heat haze. With her skill, it will work well.* Astrid took it off and re-appeared.

"Well, it works. You may as well head off now. You will still need to hide—despite the magic, mages can sometimes tell if something invisible is near them. I can just make you out wearing it."

Astrid kissed Basil and ran towards the gate.

"Wait,' Rani called after her, "this time take a Talker. Let us know when they are through the gate and it is closed, otherwise keep silent." Astrid took the Talker and kissed Basil again.

"Feel free to call me back. I enjoy saying goodbye," she said, and headed off again.

"Does that girl think of anything but sex?" Rani asked Basil.

"It is not only sex she thinks about, but she also thinks about food, hunting, drinking, killing and sleep. I won't say in what order she thinks about them though. She is the Cat, after all." He grinned. *He is always more than a little proud of his bride and somehow surprised...*

"We need to take the mage out of the battle quickly. Ayesha can you...damn. We should have kept Ayesha here. No-one else can attack from behind like she can." There was a cough.

"Actually," Lakshmi spoke up. *She is one of the young-looking girls from Haven who is always one of those who stay quiet and so tends not to be noticed. What did she do that was special? There is something...*she remembered. *What could a girl like that do to help us here?*

"Most of you will know what I can do with men," said Lakshmi. "Before I was brought here I worked in Sacred Gate and I learned some of those skills from my mother and my sisters. I was reluctant to mention this because you," she looked at Rani...*her voice is a touch bitter...*"will probably shun me now." She paused, gathering words. "I worked on the streets as a prostitute and a thief. I lived in the shadows in several ways. I was born into it and used these skills to stay alive there and here in this village. I can jump on the mage as he comes through the gate and, if I can get behind him on his horse, he won't be doing anything. Keeping him alive is harder, but if I put a knife to his eye, he should stay still...as long as he doesn't spell me."

Rani nodded at the harijan girl, keeping her face controlled. *I thought she is untouchable, but I did not know how much so and I was careful not to ask. Her entire life has been crime and sex and...I will deal with my thoughts later.* "Thank you. If you can control him, we should be able to get the others to surrender. Those that do not have bows or a sling will go away from the courtyard. When I call out everyone must stay as still as they can. Ruth, this includes the children, but most importantly it means those of you who now have magic on them. Lakshmi, you go to the walk above the gate. Yours is the most important role. The rest, with bows and slings, go onto the roofs. Lie down and stay still. They will expect to pick up magic, but they will also expect it not to move. Only appear when I call out, then aim at the two armsmen. Now, Basil and Harald, once they are through the gate and Lakshmi has leapt, you must close the gate and bar it. You can stand waiting hidden behind each side of the gate. Once it is barred—Basil you are experienced with this sort of thing—do what you have to do to disarm and arrest them." Basil nodded. *Yes, he is used to that.* "Now does anyone have any questions?"

"I have my storage device," said Theodora. "If I really need to I can cast a sleep spell."

Rani said, "Fine, but wait and see if it is needed. Now everyone go to your places. You can talk and move around a bit until I say so. I will wait here until Ayesha tells me that they have arrived. Valeria, stay with me for the moment."

Everyone dispersed and Rani and Valeria took a seat on the veranda. It fell silent.

I now need to consider what Lakshmi has just said. She has volunteered for a very dangerous job, knowing what she has said might bring her down in everyone's eyes—especially in mine. Previously I only had suspicions, and I have to admit I was not eager to clear them up, but now she has confirmed she is harijan—untouchable. She had been the healer for the village when the bandits had it. Here she has used her skills to help the women and children and she has been looking forward to becoming the midwife and a healer and all this while she has kept her past as a street thief and criminal secret from everyone. I have touched her many times. We all have. Can I now cast her out? I know what my Princess will say if I do that. Yet how can I accept her as she is? What am I doing to my soul? Am I already condemned to a lower form? Need I worry at all? I have some hard choices to make about my relationship with the girl.

Eventually Rani heard from Ayesha—the bandits had arrived. She sent Valeria racing through the village alerting everyone to be still and silent and observed the three at the gate, who were all ready to move into position. She made her way to the roof.

Basil

Basil looked up at the girl on the ledge. *She looks very downcast and distracted when she needs to be concentrating on her job. If she fails, we could all fail.* "Don't worry," Basil said, "I won't hold your past against you. Yours is a recognised and respected trade where I come from, not the thief part I mean, we punish them. Prostitutes are licensed and those that are skilled can get very wealthy. If it doesn't work out here I will give you a recommendation and some names in my service to help you get set up in Ardlark. My Strategos...my General, will help you out if I ask him to. Of course you will have to learn Darkspeech and a few other tongues and all your customers may not be human—but then Astrid and I are not fully human either."

"Thank you," said Lakshmi miserably, as she looked down over the edge. "I was hoping to have put all of that behind me, but I think that what I know is needed."

"Yes it is," said Harald from beside Basil. "What you did was very brave, 'n' what you are about to do is near as brave. Did your past afore t'valley have anythin' to do with t'fact t'at you are near t'only one not to have tried to court me?"

Lakshmi nodded despondently. "I am alive, but it is my entire fault what happened. My karma is working itself out on me still. I am not worth anything." Just then the word came from Ayesha and Basil waved them all to their places and checked on them before patting himself and making sure he had what he needed—some lengths of rope knotted on one end.

"You did right. Just do your job and I will make sure you come out well." She smiled weakly back. *I think I can safely promise that. I can send a letter if need be, but I am sure the Princess will not stand still and let the girl suffer. At least she looks a little more cheerful.*

Rani

R ani hoped she was well hidden on the roof and in some shade. *I can just see over the wall and I have a good view of our little open plaza where everything should happen. Hopefully none of them below can see me in the shade.*

It was not long before the riders came into her view. The mage stopped and checked his device. He waved the others forward. They moved towards the village. *I hope that it all looks deserted enough. The armsmen keep looking around. They are acting very suspicious...expecting an ambush.* Both had their hands on their blades. First one, then the other, put their shields on their arms and drew their blades. *They are looking intently at every vantage point but, apart from me, I hope that no-one is watching them.* The mage spoke to them and waved them on. They slowly approached the gate, looking about them as they did so. In the fields untended stock wandered about and even the chickens had been left out to run around as they wanted to. *The whole village is meant to look as if no-one was at home and I am sure that it does.*

Basil

*W*aiting *is hell. Speaking of putting your past behind you…the number of times I have been in this situation, waiting for someone to make a deal or come home or…any number of things. Who would expect that I would still be doing it here?*

The first riders came through the gate…the armsmen…riding side by side and looking up the long courtyard towards the spring, but thankfully not backwards to where two men waited still and silent in the shadows. He tensed. *They are looking around ahead of them and to the sides, but see nothing. They are tense and still sensing attack.*

The mage then came through and, from above him, the little brown-skinned woman leapt. Ignoring whether she had succeeded or not Basil sprang to close the gate. *The key to these operations is teamwork. You do your job well and trust everyone else to do theirs in the same fashion.* As his side closed he noticed that Harald had moved as quickly as he had. He heard Rani shout as loud as she could. The gates slammed and, leaving Harald to lock them, Basil turned ready to throw something or to draw his shortswords, or to leap onto someone.

He wasn't needed. Lakshmi was sitting on the withers of the horse behind the mage with one blade against his neck and the other further down. *It must be in his groin. The horse is plunging and she is using the two blades to steady herself. That must be uncomfortable for the mage. The top blade, at least, has drawn a little blood. The armsmen are moving around in circles, swords in their hands, looking up at the roofs. Everyone up there is now standing with bows drawn, pointing at them.*

Basil moved. *If they have to fire, I hope they hit the men and not me.* He moved first to the mage and drew his sword and dropped it on the ground and then, reaching across him, his dagger and two wands that were also on that side. Those he tucked in his belt. Lucky it was a short horse. The mage glared down at him, a thin line of blood was starting to trickle down his throat from where Lakshmi's dagger was held, its point dug into his flesh. *I was right in my guess. The other blade is planted firmly in the groin.*

He went to the first armsman. The man had already dropped his sword, so Basil only had to remove his dagger and untie his crossbow. "Down" he ordered. The man obeyed. Basil slapped the horse away up the village street; people were emerging up there. *They can deal with it.* "Lie face down, legs apart, arms held out straight." He obeyed. Basil knelt and felt for hidden blades. *None I can find.* "Now don't move. There are archers aiming at you and they have exploding arrows."

He went to the next. The armsman still held his sword. "Drop it," said Basil, out of caution drawing his left hand blade. It was just as well. The man slashed at him. Basil blocked it and grabbed the man's arm with his free hand, pulling as he did so. The man gave a cry as he came off his horse. *There is a shaft in his back. Someone has felt confident enough to fire.* He hit the ground hard and Basil kicked his sword out of his hand and then quickly used his feet to spread the man's legs. The man tried to struggle, so Basil kicked his groin...hard. The man screamed and tried to clutch himself. Basil dropped on his back with his knee and forced him flat, his breath whooshing out. He was now kneeling hard on the man's back beside the arrow. "Stop moving." He pulled out the man's knife and patted him. *A knife, no two, down his back,* he felt lower, *one in each boot.* As he pulled them out he threw them away. He then put his shortsword away, still kneeling on the man, and checked his arms...*one blade up each sleeve. That seems to be all.* The man now lay there groaning. "I am standing up now," said Basil "and you make a fine target for the archers. Spread your arms and legs and stay still." This time the man did as he was told and stayed still.

He now turned to the mage and drew his right hand shortsword. He placed it in the man's groin. "Now you get down...and do not try and say a word." The man started to dismount and Lakshmi came after him. As soon as she was down she reached up and again placed her daggers hard against his throat and groin. This time she stood in front of the man. *She is smiling at him like a hungry beast. Very disconcerting it is indeed; that sort of smile on such a pretty face. It is a grimace that is barely human.* He pulled his sap out and brought it down hard on the base of the man's skull without warning. The man collapsed as if he were boneless.

"Right," he called. "We are clear. Someone call Astrid in please." To Lakshmi he said, "Well done girl. I might give you a recommendation to my Strategos for my old job instead." He turned to the two on the ground. Harald was already standing over one and he took a place beside the other. Soon the courtyard was full of people looking on. Just like crime scenes at home, he thought. *Rani has gone up to Lakshmi and openly given her a hug and a kiss…well, it looks like I won't need me to write a letter after all.*

He turned to stripping the mage, and as he did so he yelled, "Valeria…get me the gag from that woman's room…and bring some of the restraints there for the other two. They are better than this rope." Valeria caught Theodora's approving eye and raced off. Once the mage was stripped and Basil had searched him, Basil lugged him towards the whipping frame and securely trussed him there where he could not move.

Rani

"Why is he doing that?" Rani asked Theodora.

"You told him to do what he did at home. I imagine that this is how you would treat a captive mage. I don't know. I didn't go out with his people on things like that. He is just doing his job I suppose." *She sounds a little shocked at the casual brutality she is seeing.*

Chapter XXX

Basil

By the time the mage was fast in place Valeria was back and Basil tied the gag with its leather ball in place on him. It forced the man's mouth open and prevented him biting himself when he woke, but it also stopped him talking or casting a spell. Basil checked that the restraints were tied tight so that the man could scarce wiggle and turned to the other two. Father Christopher was tending the one with the arrow wound, so Basil went to the other.

"Stand up now and keep your hands away from your body." The man did so with fear in his eyes. He caught sight of Bryony and looked even more scared. Stefan was holding Bryony back. She had obviously heard what Ayesha had said and she was crying and trying to get at the man. "Now strip... Don't make any false moves...Lakshmi, get behind him." She did so. "If he tries anything, take a kidney...either one, but I want him alive afterwards." The man looked terrified as he hurriedly began to strip off his clothes and his shoes. He was staring wildly around. He finished stripping and stood there naked with his hands covering his groin. "I would imagine that a few of you ladies," said Basil, "will enjoy this part. Here is rope and some shackles...Tie him up...hard."

He turned to the last bandit. "Have you finished, Father?" Christopher nodded. The arrow had been removed and the bleeding staunched. "Now it is your turn...Lakshmi, get ready...now stand and strip. Remember, a false move will not be your last, but it is going to be painful, very, very painful and, even if we decide to heal you, you will be pissing blood for a long time." The man grunted and stood. Defiantly he removed his clothes and stood naked. His hands were clenching and straightening at his sides. "Ladies, you get to tie him up as well." The man struggled at this, but stood no chance, all it got him, in the end, was a knee in the groin from Verily and a punch under the small of the ribs from Anahita that left him gasping for air.

The men were left trussed and lying naked on the ground.

Basil said to the mages, "Criminals apprehended and restrained, ma'm. I await orders as to their disposal."

"You seem to have done this a few times before, Basil," said Theodora.

"All part of the job," he said smoothly, and with a smile. *This is the most normal I have been for quite some time and damn, it feels good.* "Even at home we had enough low-lifes to keep us busy. Now you will want to question them." He said to Bianca, "Will the Presbytera be doing the questioning herself this time? Might I suggest that we start with the mage? Once you have broken him, these two will be easy."

He saw Bianca go white and clutch Christopher's hand and had to listen hard to follow what they said. "You don't have to if you do not want to, my dearest," Christopher said to her quietly. "Although, and I hate to say this, you are very good at it from what I have seen. You get the information more from what you say than what you actually do. I am sure that Basil's people use much rougher methods."

Basil nodded, and kept his voice low. "Unless we have someone around with some truth spells. A good truth spell makes everything else unnecessary."

"I am sorry, my dearest" said Father Christopher. "I am not strong enough to pray for one of those yet."

"I can, though," said Rani. "I don't know anything at all about that area, but if anyone can give me the principles...I am sure we can manage."

"If you can get the truth from the mage...with these two watching...then I will handle them both," said Bianca. "I am sure that they will be more...open once they have seen him talk."

"Let us prepare then," said Basil, and he raised his voice. "Can you ladies take these two gentlemen over near the whipping frame please? You don't have to be too gentle with them but—" *Bryony is drawing a dagger. Stefan has to be quick.* "Stefan hold tight to Bryony." *He grabs her. She is trying to get at the bandit who talked about her. Tears are streaming down her face. She is incoherent and she is seeing nothing but the man, the nemesis that has destroyed her life. Stefan is trying hard to holding her tight...he is suffering scratches and cuts and even a stab from her knife as she tries to break free.* Basil moved quickly over and, pinching the nerve in her wrist, disarmed her. Stefan gathered her up in a sobbing bundle in his arms as other women came around to help. *Several are kicking the man in whatever part presents to them as they pass by.*

Basil bent down to him. "You are going to tell us absolutely everything, aren't you? Otherwise, if you think she would be bad, well, you should see how quickly the Presbytera Bianca broke Dharmal. I have never seen better before and I work with Darkreach law enforcement." He smiled evilly.

The man looked up at his black eyes two hands away and flinched back. "I'll talk. I'll tell you everything. Conrad, the mage, he organised things. He just got us to do things for him and find out things and we would be well paid. I just told him about the wedding and he arranged the rest…told me not to go, he did. I just work for a living, really I do."

You just have to push in the right places… "Be quiet now. We will talk about your work later." Basil patted the man's cheek. "I am sure you will be able to remember more then, lots more. I hope you are not too attached to all your parts." Basil straightened up. "Ladies, take him away." He went over to where Rani, Bianca and Christopher were. "If it helps in the spell, his name is Conrad."

Conrad

Conrad woke up with a head and neck full of pain in an uncomfortable position. *My groin is on fire from where that bitch stuck her blade. My face and body ache as if I have hit the ground and the back of my head…it feels like straps are running around my head…something is lodged hard in my mouth…I cannot close it and it is hard to breathe properly.* Cautiously he ran his tongue over it.…*a sewn seam in a leather ball…the taste of leather and blood and spit.* He bit…*it gives a little, but not enough to let me do more than gurgle. I cannot move my mouth enough to cast anything.* He flexed. *My arms and legs are tied fast and my fingers are forced straight by splints and held apart. I can feel the wind on my skin enough to know I am naked. Whoever has done this to me has done it before. I have no chance of casting…it will be hard to resist. I can hear the murmur of women's voices around me.* He opened his eyes. *Gwillam and Cuthbert are lying naked and trussed up before him. No aid there. The rope is cutting into their skin and*

Gwillam is bleeding from his wrist and his feet look to have little circulation. Cuthbert has lost control of his bladder. He lies in a pool of his own piss that made mud of the dirt he lies in. Someone must realise I am awake…they have hold of my hair and are forcing me to look at the other two on the ground and around. By Morrigan that hurts as well. We are well and truly fucked.

"Hello Conrad," the man said in Hindi. *He has an odd accent.* "My name is Basil and I work for Darkreach law enforcement. Have a look around you." *The roots of my hair really do hurt as he moves my head around to see the women…some of whom I have sent here and many of them I have used as they all deserve…they are all staring at me. I know what is in my mouth…one of the women bandits owned it, but would loan it out if you didn't want to be distracted by screams or pleas. There is also a woman with gold eyes watching…her eyes are…oh shit…gold eyes…Darkreach…another, obviously Havenite, preparing a pentagram. I am bound to the bloody whipping frame and there is at least the edge of a pentagram drawn in the hard dirt around it. Bryony is sobbing in a man's arms. I remember her body well. I took her first on her wedding night and her husband had never ever gotten to it. Bloody hell my groin is responding to the memory of that. One of the women is pointing at my manhood and…now it shrinks…this is not a good idea. I will have to fight with my mind to stay alive…not give way.* His reminiscences were cut short by reality. "Payback is a bitch," said the man who said he was from Darkreach. He felt his hair released as the man moved clear. His head dropped and now he had to use his own muscles to see. *My neck is in pain…a lot of pain.*

The Havenite woman began to chant. *I must fight to…shit…he stuck a blade in my arse…resist…oh Morrigan that was in my ball sack…I cannot concentrate…shit…I cannot focus to pray, let alone…not my balls again…everything is muffled by the gag…I can feel blood starting to run down my legs…I have never felt pain like this before…much more fun giving…fuck…I cannot even make out what she is saying…shit…she has stopped…so has my tormentor…no new jabs or cuts are happening…everyone ahead of me is just looking…some of the cunts ahead look like starving dogs as they watch me.* The Haven mage has said to remove this cursed gag…*rough hands are untying the releases…it is being pulled out of my mouth…*he sucked in a lung full of sweet pure air. *Now a quick cast…I cannot frame the words…my mouth* *is no longer mine to speak with. The woman must have taken complete control of me while that bastard was sticking me.* With dread he waited for his instructions. They soon came. *I can try to fight, but the words just come tumbling out, one after another, to condemn me. I can hold nothing back. My mind can still think and want me to be silent, but my body is eager to please the woman who now owns me and it finds new things to volunteer.*

"I work for the Masters...I recruit for them in the Swamp and Haven and tell them things about caravans and prime women to bring here... I told them of Bryony...I paid for that one," he nodded towards Lakshmi, "in Sacred Gate and then organised for her to be brought here... The young one there," he nodded towards Parminder, "and her sister and the one holding her...and they brought her brother as well... The one who cooks here... The brewer here and that one," this time he indicated Dulcie, "and another child and that one, Valeria...and others that are not here now.

"I told them about when rich caravans were leaving and I told them about people they asked about. They paid me well and I came up here at least once a year to enjoy the women."

"How did the Masters talk to you?" asked the woman. *My mistress' name is Rani. Has she told me? No...it is stamped in my brain like fire.*

"Sometimes one would come and see me. Sometimes I had a note slipped under my door. Sometimes I used a mirror that is set up in a house that I rent in Sacred Gate. That is how I gave them information."

"Did you set up the mirror or did they? Does it have a diagram in front of it?" asked Rani.

"They did and yes it does. I stand in the diagram to activate the mirror."

"Tell us all about the Masters. Everything you know about them and what they want and what they wanted from you," commanded Rani.

I can feel the sweat standing out on my brow as I try to fight the commands...it makes no difference. "They are not really alive, I don't think, but they are not really undead. I have touched one accidentally and I lost nothing. They are all magicians, each more powerful than I am. They want to be fully alive, one told me that. They want to cause the Kingdoms to break up and then they will come out and each of them will rule an area. The one I met most, I think it was the same one, was going to rule Sacred Gate. Once he had control of it he was going to organise his re-birth into a body. I was looking for a suitable man to take to him when I was sent up here to take control. It was supposed to be empty otherwise I would not have been sent. I am too valuable to risk in the field. I had to find something…they thought it would be made of jade and hidden and I had to either destroy it or to take it out where someone would get it from me."

So it continued. *There is major harm to me and others in what I have left…in what I am saying, but they are writing lists of places where I hid things in Haven and other short lists with the names of agents, contacts and people I work with. I have met some of the people who organise other areas, but don't know their names. Still I have given it all. Now Rani…dark-skinned cunt…beloved mistress…cherished owner is forcing me to cast my mana into a storage device until it is used up…now she is draining me into deficit…it hurts but my body and my hind brain want to please her…I am so far in deficit it is a wonder I am still alive. I feel foul…defiled. I have done this to others before, and especially to a couple of female mages. Now I am telling of that. To have one doing it to me now…I can feel my manhood almost shrink into me. I find it hard but I have to try and fight to do something. I must concentrate. I must ignore the pain even as my mouth still betrays me. I must ignore that my brain feels like it is being torn apart as memories spill out to condemn me…The control has left me. It may have even just run out of time for all I know…I may have done nothing, but I can stop speaking.*

He came out of the control spell swearing and cursing futilely and weakly from being drained. *My head pounds …my neck is on fire and other places hurt in brief stabs.* He started to swear aloud in his own language. *Curse my bitch former mistress. Now the man in black, Basil, is stepping up to me…his hand back…he hits me in the mouth…I can taste blood…he made me bite my own fucking tongue.*

"Shut up or you will be gagged again." *I don't want that.* The man turned to the mages. "So, what do we do with him? I would suggest letting the ladies that he named kill him. They can take their time if you want. Otherwise we should either let them lash him until they are sick of it, or just slit his throat. At home a person like him would be soundly whipped and then, while he was still alive, tied to a post and smeared with a thick layer of pitch and set alight. It serves as a good example to others…a shining light if you want. You are our rulers though. It is your decision."

"Nooo," screamed Conrad. Without really looking at what he did, Basil casually back-handed him again across the mouth to shut him up. Conrad hung there sobbing...broken. *I had been hoping to work my way free somehow...that they would want to find out more from me... anything.* He felt another wave of uncontrollable sobbing and tried to stop.

"He can wait for a while," said Rani. "He cannot do anything now. Let us see what these other two can tell us first."

Conrad watched Basil go over to the two men. *I can let myself hang limp in the frame...use it to help hold myself up against the spasms and weakness I am feeling in my legs. I shouldn't feel relief that he is leaving me like this, but I do, even if I hate myself for it*

"What are you going to tell us to add to our tale," the man in black said. "We are eager to hear. You..." *he just casually kicked Cuthbert in a kidney...he ignores his screams and spasms...*"can start by telling Bryony why you had her taken and letting her see what a worm you are." *He turns. He is harder even than Rani. I am so screwed.* "Stefan, bring Bryony closer so that she can see." *Stefan is obviously the solid man who is still holding Bryony tight. She is clutching his shirt and sobbing on his shoulder. Stefan is making soothing sounds and stroking her hair as if she is a small child or a startled horse. Dried blood covers part of his face and still trickles from his arm where he has taken a wound somehow. He just ignores that and holds her tight as he brings her close. A short woman in white also there is trying to get clear so as to get Stefan to sip on something. It must be a healing draught. The quicker it is taken the less scarring there will be.*

Cuthbert started to speak. *I want to tell him to be silent, but what does it matter? We are all dead.* He felt contempt for Cuthbert as he snivelled: "I loved her and she rejected me. I was getting wealthy." *Was he always like that?*

Basil broke in, "You mean from working for Conrad?"

"Yes, I was working for him. It was good work and I was getting rich. I would have been an important man eventually. I am even handsome and yet she rejected me for that peasant with only years behind a plough to look forward to."

Basil kicked him in the ribs. *From the sound of it, something just broke.* The man screamed and kept screaming for some time. *Maybe he won't mention me again...please Morrigan...let him just talk about his own sins.*

When Cuthbert stopped making a noise Basil said, "Be polite to her husband that was. She loved him, not you. A real man would have accepted that."

Cuthbert grimaced and swallowed. "I told Conrad of her beauty and he said that he would have her taken and brought up here for me as a reward. Her father had to die anyway. He was one who stood in the way of war between the Swamp and Haven." Cuthbert saw the people looking on. *From his face he is trying to work out whether to tell the truth or lie. He has decided. He has always been bad at cards.* "My reward would be to come up here this winter and to use her any way I wanted. He said I could do anything I wanted to her. I loved her. I just wanted her to love me. If she didn't, I was going to kill her so she could love no-one else." *Shit. I know that I said it, but he wasn't supposed to be so possessive about the bitch. In the long run she is just another hole to screw. Now there are eyes looking at me again. I can feel the hate in them...be quiet...look innocent.*

Basil nodded. "Do you have anything you can say that is actually useful?"

"No, please let me go, I did it out of love. You must understand...I love her."

I can see the absolute contempt on Basil's face. At least he had a blank look towards me...professional. Basil's look towards Cuthbert shows that the man on the ground is far beneath that. It was like he was looking at a chopped up dying gut worm. Basil looked over his shoulder, saying, "Bryony, is there anything else you want to hear from this thing?"

Bryony shook her head. "No," came weakly out.

With relief Conrad watched Basil turn to Gwillam. *At least Gwillam won't say anything stupid.* He looked back at Cuthbert briefly, "At least this one showed some fight. Stupidly, but he tried." He said to Gwillam, "At home you would be put in the arena for one hundred fights. You wouldn't live through a sentence that long, but you would at least entertain people in your dying. It would take a couple of years. Here your life will be much shorter. How well you talk will determine how long you live. If we don't like what we hear when I talk to you, then the Presbytera Bianca will take over. She broke a Khitan called Koyonlu...oh, you know that name do you?...anyway she, little girl that she is, defeated him in battle and then tortured him until he talked and told her all about this place. Then, when we got here, she broke your boss Dharmal and we found out all about these so-called Masters. Now it will be your turn to be broken. I have to admit that I look forward to watching on and learning much more from her. I do this for a living and yet I manage to learn something about the job each time that I see her at work."

Gwillam's eyes have grown wider and wider and they are flicking from Basil to the little woman, dressed in a white dress who looks like she is celebrating...she is even holding the hand of a priest.

She smiled. "Hello," she said sweetly in a sexy, husky voice, "please tell him that you will not talk so that I can go and change. I hate to disappoint these ladies." She waved a hand towards the mass of former slaves.

Gwillam looked from her to the faces of the watching former slaves. *I can see the taut wildness in them...Gwillam is seeing it as well...I can see that...it is as if they were some of the animal women of the Wild Hunt going to rend him with their teeth...Gwillam can see his fate in their eyes...damn...he is going to break as well.*

He did. He begins to talk in a frantic babble to try and avoid the attention of the women he sees before him. He is telling everything he knows. Unfortunately for him he does not know much except for one thing that brought another woman to stop him. She is a big woman with braided hair like those of the north. She has teeth like a cat and she strikes quicker than a cobra...her hand is on Gwillam's throat so fast and so hard that her nails are digging in. One broke the skin and blood begins to trickle over her hand...he is screaming in terror...I don't blame him.

"Repeat what you just said," she ordered. *Gwillam is telling again how he had come to this village more than a few times before and one time had gone further to take a message to Wolfneck and to meet a man there.* "Describe him." *Her face is suddenly more animal...more a feral snarl of a beast about to rend.*

I can see Gwillam looking at the teeth and the tongue licking the lips around them. He is trying to swallow but she has his throat too tight. Who is this woman? What is she? Gwillam starts describing the man he met and how he had to take the package further to the north. Gwillam didn't know where to, but the man seemed to know. I remember that package and the description of the half-man. They hadn't asked me about that. I know where it was going to. I still have something left.

"Was his name Svein?" asked the woman. *Gwillam is just staring at her pointed teeth only a hand from his face as he tries to shrink into the dirt under him.*

"Yes, that was his name, yes." *He stopped and looked again at the woman above him. He obviously thought of something that might help him as suddenly he blurted out,* "You must be the one he was boasting of having snared. He was going to marry you and have you and then he was going to have you sent down here to be tamed to the way he wanted."

"I knew it." *She is glaring at the Darkreach man.* She spoke again to Gwillam, "This is my husband, Basil, who is asking you the questions. He is so glad to hear from you about my betrothed." She spoke to Basil in Darkspeech. *They don't know that I can understand them. I have had dealings that way. That is another thing I have.* "Apart from…well apart from…you know…you haven't given me a wedding present. After this is over, can we go back to Wolfneck and you can get me Svein's balls to dangle in front of him. I want him to still be alive when you take them."

"Yes, my love, I think that would be suitable if you are happy with something I would like to do anyway," he replied in the same tongue. *So casual they are about it. I know that I am going to die. What little I have will not keep me alive for long, but somehow I am glad that I am not Svein.*

He turned his attention back to what was before him.

Basil is squatting down to address Gwillam from near his level. Who would have thought that he would break like that? "Do you have anything to add? Do you have any apologies to any of the girls here? Would you like to confess your sins to God and ask forgiveness? Would you like to plead and cry?" The man went silent.

Basil straightened and addressed Rani, and the golden-eyed woman, the one from Darkreach. "My ladies, I think we have all that we are likely to get from these two. If I may be so bold. I would suggest giving Bryony her knife back and letting her kill Cuthbert, and find out which girl here has the biggest grievance against Gwillam and then let her do the same."

"That would be me." *A girl…who is she? A Brotherhood slave bitch…Verily something…she is pushing her way forward.* "You know how he has all of those knives. He likes to use them on people and, because I didn't react the same as some of the others and because I am…I have no hair below, he used me and hurt me every time he was here. What is more, I claim his blades…all of them. They are part of my blood money." *I remember her now. I have only had her once. She is not normal, even when you fucked her body her face was always a mask. It was as if she was challenging you to try and make it change. It put me off my stride.*

Basil is looking at the brown bitch. Rani is indecisive. I cannot believe it. She thinks this is harsh. I would have taken far longer myself, but I am grateful for a quick release. I am not going to say anything. The man in black seems to be impatient at her indecision. He turned to the other woman. "Princess, you know this is merciful for them. They should take a lot longer than this to die, but we do not have the facilities to keep them."

I am right. She is one of Hrothnog's get. She nods…my death is about to be announced. "You are right. Have that one," *she points at me,* "whipped to death by anyone who wants to do so. Make sure they share the use of the whip. If he has run out of people to whip him and is still alive, cut off his manhood and let him bleed out the rest of his life." Conrad began to wail. *I know I am broken. Damn I was hoping to die quickly with a cut throat. Oh shit. I am not as brave as I had hoped to be. Now my bladder has let go and I hurt already. I wish I had known what my fate was going to be when I chose my direction. Perhaps if I can get my mouth to work properly I can trade what I still know for a quick death.* "The other two, make them watch and then let it be as Basil suggests." *I need to form sentences but my throat and tongue are still not fully under my control. What can I say? Why is my will having no effect? I was drained so much that I am that weak? Obviously.*

One of the Khitan cunts…Kãhina…I remember taking her…it was good at the time but now I regret everything…she has won the race to get a lash with many thongs on it from the room upstairs…oh Morrigan…my body is screaming in pain and fear…and she has not struck yet.

The pain of that first blow made the rest of his aches disappear and he felt his voice rising into a shriek of sheer agony and despair. His thoughts of bargaining fled.

Chapter XXXI

Theodora

I have given the judgement, so it is up to me to sit and watch it carried out. Their deaths will not be as much fun here as they would be in the Arena in Ardlark. Here it is harsh and immediate and brutal...not at all entertaining. I can almost feel pity for the men and what I can see in their eyes around them.

Verily has fetched Gwillam's blades and has taken station beside him, working the harnesses for the blades off his body. Now she is stripping naked in front of him and putting the harnesses and blades on her own body before squatting down to wait. Her beauty is displayed in front of him as a reminder of why he is about to die horribly. She sits on her heels and has her knees splayed apart near his head. Her groin is only a cubit from the man's face and I can see that he keeps staring at it, licking his lips nervously and swallowing, attracted to the sight, even though it means his death. Throughout Verily is keeping her usual composed demeanour, ignoring the man's gaze fixed on her womanhood.

Bryony is still crying as she takes the knife that she is offered...she is shaking...and sits down to wait with Stefan's arms around her as he continues to try and calm her. He says he doesn't love her, but he obviously cares for her.

Kãhina has won the race...she has never used a whip before but blood is flinging off Conrad's back and his legs as his screams and pleas rise. Each woman is giving five lashes and then handing on to the next before going back to the end of the queue. He will die soon and horribly.

Bryony killed Cuthbert by simply cutting off his manhood and putting it on the ground in front of his eyes. She then wrapped Stefan's arms around her while she watched him bleed to death as he cried and thrashed and howled with pain in front of her. As she was cutting he tried blaming others, he tried pleading, he tried claiming bonds of love and affection, but finally he died crying and cursing Bryony, Conrad, his gods and everyone and everything else. He died quickly and badly.

Eventually Verily has stopped just sitting. She is leaning down. Even listening hard I can only catch snippets. Don't understand a word of it but she must be saying what she is going to do...he has turned white and the pleading in his voice is easy to hear. You don't need the language that the two are talking in. He may as well have been talking to a rock. Not a flicker of expression is crossing the girl's face. Not a smile, a snarl, a sneer or a look of compassion. She is putting a knife into his rear end, doing it almost gently with the aid of a stick. She is taking care that she does not cut too much until she wants it to. A small, barely human, smile flickers across her face as she seems to savour his screams.

Now the blade is fully inside him and she pulls out the rod...my God...she is flaying him alive. Her face has a parody of a smile, but her eyes are blank. If he moves he hurts himself even more on the blade that is lodged deep inside him...blood is running out of his rear. She is not very good at skinning. He died, screaming continuously almost right until the end, after less than half an hour. *Now her face changes...while she was working she was smiling, but it was more like the static rictus of a corpse than a real smile...her eyes as they watched what they did were as empty as the windows of a vacant house. Now he is dead all expression has left her face...her eyes still show nothing. How much pain is inside the girl? Would she ever recover...could she ever recover...if she did...what would she feel about what she had just done?* Theodora was glad when she was able to verify that all three were dead and the bodies could be disposed of.

Theodora noted that Ayesha went up to Lakshmi at dinner. She was sitting at the side with Harald, and they were talking quietly. Curiously she moved over to hear what was said, trying not to be too obvious with her attention. She missed the start, but heard, "...what you did. You will be joining Bianca and Verily for my extra lessons now. You should have told me that you already had some experience and I would have had you working with them from the start." *It appears that it is not just my lover who is re-evaluating the girl.*

Tonight's meal is a quiet one. No-one feels much like entertaining.

Stefan and Bryony are not here. I sent Valeria up with a tray of mostly cold food to leave outside their door in case they get hungry later. She has reported knocking softly on the door and receiving no reply…at least she had the sense to leave the food there, just in case.

Stefan

*S*omeone is knocking, but I am sitting up with Bryony lying in my arms on the bed. I cannot let her go…I rock her and try to calm her as she sobs and softly cries her dead husband's name, and then her father's, and back. They stayed that way for most of the night until she fell asleep from exhaustion. Stefan slowly and gently disentangled her and laid her fully clothed on the bed, covering her up before fetching the tray and having something to eat. *It has warm food still on it, so it must have been replaced at least once without me hearing it.* He left the tray with half the food on a stool and then crept under the cover to take Bryony in his arms again and fall asleep.

Stefan awoke to see her sitting in her chemise on the side of the bed eating the rest of the food, now assuredly cold. He watched her for a while before she realised that he was awake. She turned around and kissed him on his healing cuts. "Thank you for what you have done," she said, "now I need you to make love to me…slowly and softly. I am alive and they are not. I am empty…so empty. I want to feel the little death and have it wash over me to make me feel real again…to remind me that there is something to live for."

He gently began to comply, feeling her skin smooth but chill beneath his hands and tongue. Soon she began to sob softly, but would not let him stop when he went to just hold her. Eventually the salt tears he was kissing away stopped, her skin and body warmed and her cries changed.

Rani

"It is time we are married. Your priests have said we can. Our village has had a lot to deal with and it needs us. We have new traditions to establish. Lakshmi made me think. Here many traditions are being broken. Caste is just one of them. I will have to talk to the Father. I don't know if I will follow your religion yet, but I will talk with him." *Theodear is rolling over to kiss me...passionately...so passionately...so...oh Krishna preserve me.*

It was some time before they began to discuss who would be in their wedding party.

Father Christopher

On his way to Orthos, Christopher noticed the grass outside. *This is the first time since we arrived here that it is all covered in a thick hard frost. I suppose that I felt that chill outside our warm nest of blankets and feather throw last night. Winter is well on the way. Not the winter I am used to, mind you, but a mountain winter. The work of repairing the houses will have to take on an extra urgency. I wonder if I can use the patronage of St Amos, of maps and surveyors, whose day it is, to seek aid to our work? Can I make that work?*

After he had finished Orthos Christopher received a surprise. He had been distracted by the events of the day before and unusually did not notice who had been sitting with whom. When it was over he was approached by Harald. He had Lakshmi by the hand.

"Can we ask'n you to perform a wedding for us please," said Harald, "'n' Lakshmi wants to talk to you about conversion."

Christopher felt a little stunned. *How did I miss this?* He found himself saying, "Of course, yes, but this is sudden."

Harald shuffled his feet. "You know t'at I've been lookin' for t'right woman?" he asked. Christopher nodded. *That is true.* "Well

Lakshmi, because of how she used to earn her living you see, she understands jewels 'n' I want someone who knows what I do 'n' she is strong 'n' she can help me if'n I need 'n'…well have you ever seen such courage. First just telling her past 'n' then taking out a strong mage armed only with pair of knives. T'at is all real courage. I like t'at even more in a woman t'an her beauty…even though she do be beautiful." He added the last hurriedly.

That is almost Dwarven logic. Christopher addressed Lakshmi, "This is what you wish?"

"Yes…Father. I do not love Harald, and he does not love me, but most marriages start that way. He is a good match for me. We have no-one to arrange a marriage for us and he is right, we have a lot more in common than many others here do and I think we will grow old and learn to love each other as we age. I am very happy in our choice. Much happier than I ever thought I would ever have a chance to be. I will have a man, one who knows my background, and I have made him fully aware of it, and yet he still wants me for what I bring and not just my looks."

When you look at it that way, the pair are right about their prospects. It is a very good match for them both. "In that case, my blessings are on you both. If you wish to talk to me about conversion, we had better wait for a week or so for the marriage, but we do have all winter ahead of us."

The next day at Hesperinos, the Mass at sundown, Christopher announced that Theodora and Rani would be married in two days and he announced the engagement of Harald and Lakshmi, with the wedding to take place in two weeks. After the service Goditha and Parminder came up to him.

"Can thee allow us to have the week in between please?" said Goditha. "We want to be married after the Princesses, but not too much after. We want our baby to always know us as always being married." *In this place of death and long-suffering there is now the new hope of marriage and children.*

This is good. This is the way it should be in a village…in my village.

*B*y their request Theodora and Rani's wedding will have a mixture of all of the cultures in Mousehole represented in it. Basil and Astrid have even taken over a section of the kitchen to assist by making Darkreach food. Astrid has been missing from the village all of the morning and came back with a large something hidden under a cloth. Once she returned, from what Christopher could hear as he moved around, this assistance mainly means Basil smacking his wife with a wooden spoon as she tries to taste everything he works on. I didn't think that it would take long before she was relegated to working on her own dish. Seeing that Basil will give the bride away and Astrid is a maid of honour, the kitchen is…a little confused.

What do you do for a wedding between two women? You make it up as you go from a normal wedding. I am glad that the two women had readily acceded. It was not surprising to anyone who watched them together, to find that Theodora has declared that she is the bride. We have Astrid, Bianca and Ayesha as maids of honour and Hulagu, Stefan and Thord as groomsmen. Astrid has declared that it is all a plot to make sure that no-one sat with their partners, but fell to work anyway.

Christopher found himself continually having to try and bring order out of chaos. Astrid not only had to help Basil with his cooking, but make sure that all of the clothes were ready by helping Fortunata sew. Valeria's day had been spent running between two rooms. Theodora had been installed in Christopher's old room but had insisted on wearing her own clothes that she had brought with her. Rani had not brought anything formal and the Havenite women in the village had little idea what a high caste woman would have on. They had to keep asking Rani.

It is with relief that I now contemplate the sight in front of me. Rani's party are installed in the hall to the music of Parminder playing a sitar with Shilpa playing a tamburi in support and singing. Kāhina is leading on percussion with Naeve and Hagar. They are a mixed lot. Rani wears a formal sari, probably not the right one, but at least it is a formal dress of some sort. She has her hands and feet painted with henna and silver chains hang from the rings on her face and in her ears. The red dot on her forehead is new and vivid. Hulagu wears his Khitan clothes with mace and bow. Thord wears full armour, even with his shield, insisting that this is what Dwarves wear to a wedding. In Christopher's eyes Stefan looks like the only one at a wedding. *He wears a long belted dark blue silk bliaut with silver trim over paler blue fine-woollen hose. As he stands there he keeps glancing with a worried expression at Bryony who is very silently sitting near the front with her eyes not really focussed. Verily sits with her holding her hands and, when she notices him watching, indicates to Stefan to pay attention to the wedding.*

Now the musicians change. Danelis takes the stage with a crumhorn, Eleanor with a lute, Elizabeth and Tabitha have shawms and Dulcie has a sackbut. Kāhina is the only drummer. The music starts. I was sure that there were more people in the wedding party and doing music than in the audience, but I am wrong.

The door is opening and Fear comes in as the flower girl, trying to look like a little princess herself...Ayesha is undulating up the aisle, as much dancing as walking. Astrid follows, stalking as she does. She is dressed in her own wedding dress as is the next girl in, my own beloved wife Bianca, and finally Theodora comes in. She has left her own coronet in her rooms and is wearing the village wedding crown except that the strings of pearls from her coronet now hang from this one. Basil is beside her wearing his own marriage clothes.

*I*t seems to me, in the eyes of almost everyone here, the wedding is *going superbly. The now traditional Khitan wedding dance has four dancers, which means that they dance in a square. Bianca is wearing her Khitan dancing clothes under her own and makes a simple change. Ayesha sits with Hulagu, Bianca with Stefan and Astrid with Thord. The same couples, along with the bride and groom, lead the dancing. The evening progresses well...I look at Bianca; she looks back. Stefan still shows his concern for Bryony, but Verily is looking after her. Astrid and Thord just stare at their tankards and are getting very drunk together.*

So, Astrid's big surprise was a huge fish that she had caught in the river that morning. "I knew that he was there, and I was keeping him for something special. I have been keeping my eye out for where he liked to be and this morning I tickled him out."

Sitting here, the soberest of them all bar Ayesha, I wonder if Astrid and Thord will actually get thrown out due to their drunken behaviour. Looking at Theodora, I am sure she is thinking of it. Astrid makes her first try at entertaining by relating to the village how the bride and groom came together, including their behaviour in the bath and admitting her own part in it all… It is hard to tell with Rani, but Theodora is blushing. It is not the most skilful tale that I have heard, but Astrid's humorous rendition, complete with running around to places in the hall to play the various parts as she told the tale had people laughing out loud. Her baltering rendition of Theodora's dance nearly had them all explode with mirth, and then when she ran down to be Rani looking up at her bride to be, the whole hall erupted. Oh dear. Even the groom has a small smile on her face. That is obviously all she will allow herself, to try and keep her dignity…although after tonight that may not be possible. The bride is still blushing and trying to deny it all. That only confirms it. Looking at the normally calm-faced Basil, it seems he was near choking with trying to control his expression as Astrid adds their own exit, playing both sides of it. Astrid sits down to cheers and stomping feet and reaches for another tankard of ale…which Thord already has handy for her.

I wonder if Basil will ever let his wife sit near the Dwarf again. They are definitely a bad influence on each other.

Rani

*I*magine my delight. I will have time together and alone with my Princess. Fear is with Valeria all night. It looks like our house will be repaired enough to be liveable before the snow sets in and I am already grateful for that. Do we have to put up with the whole village showing us to our room? It seems so. Behind us the door closes… "One day I am going to kill Astrid. I doubt if either of us will have a shred of dignity left after tonight."

"Except for Granther's, I believe most courts have a clown, my husband. They have license to poke fun at those who are in charge. It gives release and reminds us to be humble in our role. It looks like Astrid has appointed herself to that role. As well, people needed the release after the hobgoblins and then yesterday. Now, for once we do not have Fear between us. Come to the bed for your bride." As she lay naked she reached up with her arms. *I am married to this beauty…*

Ayesha

*A*strid will never be a classic storyteller, but she is certainly good at a comic tale. She has a sense of timing in it and is willing to let herself be the butt of the humour as well. I was glad of that interruption. I am finding it more and more difficult to even sit with Hulagu and, being part of the ceremony, as it were. I could not even politely avoid the dancing. He seems to have some problem. He was very quiet...far more than usual. His köle were not missing him. They were with Goditha and Parminder and of the four only Parminder is to be counted as being sober. However he was not watching them. He spent most of the night just staring off into space. If I say something I feel like I am interrupting his thoughts.

S he woke up the next morning. *At least this time I did not wake expecting to see Hulagu beside me, even if he was in my dreams. I can hardly have a night's sleep lately without something inappropriate happening in my dreams and on nights like this, they are not only inappropriate, but are...well outright sinful. However, I have to admit they seem good in the dream. Not that I have any experience of the reality to judge by... Everyone goes to the infidel priest with their troubles. I really might have to do the same.*

Goditha

*W*ho would have expected my wedding to be an anti-climax? After the Princesses', though, anything was bound to be. I looked at my brother earlier. We are now nearly twins since I have now cut off most of my hair and we wear near identical clothing. It is a plain brown tunic and green woollen hose and leather capelet. Only my boobs beneath my tunic say that I am not a very handsome young man. With my *brother's archery and my stonework, even our shoulders are filling out to near the same size with muscles. Giles stands next to me and he is dressed near the same as well.* At least, for once, he doesn't have a straw stuck in the corner of his mouth.

The music swelled and she looked behind her. Goditha felt her heart near skip a beat. *I am getting married...to my beautiful little girl lover and by a real priest.* Parminder's sister, *Gurinder, is the flower girl and first in. Naeve is the maid of honour in her best. Robin, of course, gives away the bride.* She looked at Parminder and suddenly could see nothing else other than her beloved. *She may not be wearing as fine a sari as that of the Princess, nor does she have the jewels or the red dot, but who cares. She is just so delicate...so beautiful...and she is mine...forever.*

Afterwards, she made sure not to drink too much. *I nearly mucked everything up last night. Giles and Robin got me far too drunk and my little one, and indeed the other women of the village, were not impressed. Once I recovered from my hangover, I defended them.* "That is what always happens at home—and yes, the women always are mad at the men all day—until the wedding starts, that is." *I was forgiven. Still, it is best not to press my luck as a new married husband.*

It rained during the wedding. "This is considered a good omen in our village. It means fertility and prosperity. We will manage the fertility part somehow." *Robin is nodding, so is Valeria—she comes from our area too. The only thing that would have made my marriage perfect would have been if my mother could have seen that her daughter is now not only still alive, but also married. Somehow we need to let her know. She will have difficulty with me marrying a woman, a girl really, but in time perhaps she will accept it.*

Bianca

During the days the pace of life continued. Bianca, having been raised as an orphan that few regarded, had to adapt to her role as the priest's wife and being deferred to and, at the same time, staying as an adopted Khitan and the executioner. *From an almost invisible role as a lowly stable hand and server I am now one of the most noticeable women in my village. My life has turned completely on its head.*

Looking around on Krondag I can see that the same sense of change is spread through the whole village. The training in weapons continues. Stefan swears that the women of the village have been waiting for this opportunity. They are soaking up what they are given and some are on the way to being almost fair in their skill. He and Hulagu are competing as to whether the women with swords will be better or whether it will be those who use maces. "One of t'em would no stand up to an experienced armsman on t'eir own yet, but t'ey will do so one day soon," he declared.

Thord had Ayesha and Harald, and now Lakshmi, climbing the cliffs around the village and Norbert was hard pressed to keep up with his demands for equipment. If you looked for rope in the village you would likely find it with one of those four.

The women are even being introduced to the horses and how to ride them, instead of just using one for the cart. Eleanor has even started to work with Theodora's Esther. For a warhorse, she is patient. Life is settling into a routine with the traditional slow down for winter that most places enjoy replaced by hard work, which went on well into the long night, especially for the trainee mages.

The day of Harald and Lakshmi's wedding was the day that Rani and Theodora moved into their house with all those who would be accompanying them. It was a clear fine day and they thought that they did not have much to move, but they were annoyingly distracted at the start by Naeve with questions about the wintering of the herd. They had to go down to the pens to see what she meant. When they returned they discovered that everything had been moved...and they had a new bed and many other new things. *That had been fun to plot. The whole village had been preparing for this move by secretly making things for their house, although it was not all theirs. Some of the items there would be moving on when Goditha and Parminder finish their house in a few weeks.*

The days were growing chilly and the nights were far colder. Astrid declared happily that she could smell snow in the air. *Why should that be good news?*

Chapter XXXII

Father Christopher

T he morning of the marriage Lakshmi was baptised and had her first confession. *This may have been the longest confession that I have ever done in my life or will ever do, even counting those that had been done after we took Mousehole. Lakshmi obviously thinks that she has a lot to be forgiven for and she is glad of a chance to unburden herself of it. It also shows that she has a very good memory. Instead of confessing such general sins as theft, she can still remember where she had stolen things, what they were and often how much she had gotten for selling them. She went into particular detail with gems. It is obvious that one of the reasons Harald has decided to marry her was that some of her skills complemented his. Her memory is, unfortunately, excellent. It extends well back into an early, and it turns out, very criminal, childhood. I am glad she didn't go into such detail about all of her other activities, just numbering customers. I am left wondering if she will have time to get dressed. I can see Goditha, who will be giving her away; and the maid of honour, Elizabeth, waiting at the back of the hall, but it is Lakshmi's right to give a full confession and she is taking it.*

W e made it, it is delayed...but we are here. Thord is Harald's *groomsman and the two are in front of me as we wait... The music has a lot of drums in it. Bilqīs with her naq, her flute, is the only melody. It all sounds very Dwarven, but then Thord is a Dwarf and Harald was been raised in a Dwarven village and may as well be one. The two are both in full armour. There is a shield on Thord's back and hammers at his side. He has a couple of throwing axes stuck into loops on his baldric and Harald has a pouch of martobulli hanging from his*

belt and his two-handed hammer over his back. They both look dressed for battle rather than a wedding.

Finally the women...the sound of harp and lute, with only a low and soft drumming behind it as a steady beat sounds like a female version of the same music that had been playing for Harald. I wouldn't say soft, but still it is feminine. Elizabeth is in first. She wears leather, but padded combat leathers rather than work wear. She has been training in sword and shield and bears the one on her hip and the other on her back, but the only thing she is actually good at is throwing knives, and those are strapped on to her as well. The bride is dressed the same, but with two shortswords, one high on each side as well as her knives. A horse bow is in a case at her belt and a quiver is on the other side. Goditha is giving her away and she continues the martial theme. She has found a mail hauberk that fits her. No shield, but there is a sword hung on her left side with a long dagger on her right ready to be cross-drawn to parry. To me it looks like a Dwarven wedding party and could turn very ugly if the participants have too much to drink and grow belligerent.

Lakshmi's present is a silver necklace set with citrine. She is the only bride so far to take her necklace off during the feast, but it is so that the bride and groom could sit with their heads together evaluating the workmanship and its value. This is almost automatic for both of them and they are not thinking about it or realising what people will think until their action is noticed and people started to laugh at the Dwarven reaction. Even Thord is laughing. Lakshmi sticks out her tongue at her wedding guests and the two continue until they finish, and Harald again fastens the necklace in place.

Interspersed with other melodies and dances the musicians reprised the two tunes and added another couple. They were proud of themselves. None of them were dwarves, but Fātima, who seemed to know something about every culture's music and was the musician playing the harp, had known a few tunes and had taught them to the rest of the players. Apparently they had been practicing these secretly, and often late at night, in one of the most remote of the abandoned buildings and it had been very cold, but it worked. Both Thord and Harald had congratulated them, more than slightly drunkenly and very tearfully.

When the village had escorted them to Harald's workshop and residence, Harald opened the door and, before Lakshmi could enter, swept her up in his arms and kissed her before carrying her into the house. He kicked the door closed behind him with his boot.

*W*hat with everyone else getting married, I have been waiting for this question to come up. I was not sure when it would come, but I knew it would. What is surprising is how it is being put to me.

After Mass had finished Sajāh and Fortunata came up to speak to Christopher. Norbert was waiting near the door. Sajāh took the lead. "You are probably aware that Norbert has been sleeping with both of us. It was our decision and our choice. He either had us both or he had neither." Christopher nodded. "Do you have a problem with that?" Christopher shook his head.

What will happen next? The two women are looking at each other.

Sajāh said, "It has worked for us very well until now. We think that he has gotten us both pregnant but he will not marry us. In my culture a man is proud to have two wives, or even more. Norbert said that in his culture this is not acceptable. He shouldn't live with us both, but it was not unknown, but he couldn't marry us both. He said he would marry one of us, and he wants to, but he will not say which one he wants to marry and the other could live with the married couple as a leman, a concubine, but we said this was not acceptable to us. We want you to help us in this and make him marry us." Fortunata nodded vigorously and both glared back at Norbert who stood near the door trying to look defiant.

It has come. Time for me to steel myself, take a deep breath and gesture to Norbert to join us. When he had, Christopher said, "Norbert, these ladies want to marry you and they say that you have refused to do so. Is this true?"

"Yes Father. I cannot marry two women at once, for that is wrong. I will marry either one of them, and they can choose which one as I love them both equally and would like to make them happy, but you know that I can only marry one." *The women are glaring at him and he has crossed his arms and put on an expression that men who are in trouble with their partners for no cause that they can see are all familiar with. I have seen that look a few times, even on Rani.*

I do know the way out of this, but I had been hoping to avoid it. "You are not quite correct in that, Norbert."

He is looking blankly at me as the words sink in. He is visibly deflating with his air of injured dignity punctured. "Not quite right?" he asked.

"No. The verse in the Bible that says that priests must marry goes like this: 'Choose your priests from amongst men who have but one wife,' so your problem is solved." He proudly looked at the three of them. *The three of them are looking back blankly. I am expecting too much of them.* He sighed. "If you must choose your priests from among men who have only one wife, it implies that there are men in the congregation who have more than one wife. There is no condemnation of these men, they are just forbidden to become priests." He looked directly at Norbert. "Are you planning on becoming a priest and have not told me yet?"

"No," said Norbert, surprised.

"Then congratulations on getting engaged to two women with the blessing of me, as the local representative of the Church. In fact I specifically mentioned your circumstances to my Metropolitan and he, reluctantly, agrees with me." *I feel smug. It is not something that the Church points out to people, but it is there for them in the Gospels if they choose to read it. Few choose to read the actual words, or have the chance to. Most take what they are raised with or what they are told by others. There is still little reaction from them. What I said seems not to have sunk in.* "I have solved your problem. When do you want to be married?"

Now the women look at each other. Now they look at me. Lastly they both look at Norbert…it is taking them enough time…there it is. There was a sudden cry of delight from the two women. They hugged each other and then Norbert. Norbert looked out of the hug and said, still a trifle dubiously, "I think, seeing there are two dresses, that we need at least two weeks Father, that is if Sajāh wants to be married in a Christian ceremony."

Sajāh responded by hitting him playfully. "I have spoken with Ayesha on this already. I can marry you, but my children must be raised as Muslim." She said to Christopher, "Do you have problems with this?"

This, in turn, gives me pause…"May I suggest something? I will marry you as a Mullah would, instead of my ceremony. You shall raise all of the children in the knowledge of both religions and, when they become adult you tell them that they all must choose between them. Whichever is most true should win them over."

Now it is Sajāh's turn to think for a bit. She nodded. "It is a deal."

Rani

The day came when the first of the trainee mages made their first cup of tea. Making a cup of tea was the name of one of the standard learning spells that involves heating a cup of water with herbs in it until it boiled. *It is one of the few spells that works equally well for the opposites of Fire and Water, although they approach it differently. Most trainee mages take a long time to make this first vital step as they spend a lot of their time running around as servants for their masters. The longer it takes for a student to learn how to be a mage means the longer it is that the mage has a free servant at hand. My apprentices have a lot less other duties and so they can spend more time learning. I am a good teacher. I am hard on them and keep them working hour after hour. Few have even a clue to when they were born, so I have been teaching them all four elements to see which of them they work best and worst with. Hulagu has taken advantage of this duality. He had been born on the third day of the second week of the sign of the Lizard. He is going to be a Water mage. I am so proud. He has adjusted his thoughts so quickly to the task.* Hulagu had called her over as all of the other students gathered around. *There in front of him is a steaming mug of tea. He looks very proud, but very tired with the breakthrough that he has made. Casting spells takes a lot of effort, and the first casts you make are the hardest as the mind twists around to learn a whole new way of doing things. Most people after their first successful cast are as drained as they would be after a full day of very hard work. It takes a long while to get more relaxed with the effort.*

With that incentive in front of her, Verily was the next to partly succeed and she did it later in the same session. *Her water however, does not boil. It has flashed, almost in an instant, into steam to envelop her. She sits proud, ignoring the pain.*

"Call Father Christopher...she is scalded." *It seems, from the strength of the spell, that she might be a fire mage, a powerful one of some sort, and that she will have to learn a lot more control before she can go much further. She will be my true apprentice...a battle mage.*

Over the next week the others showed what they could be. *I am not surprised that Naeve favours Earth. Fortunata turns in the same direction. Tiny Bilqīs, the smallest of all the women, has, as a child, been taught some glassblowing and is now again taking it up. The reason for her early easy success with such a task was now obvious. She is also going to be a fire mage and has empathy with any attempt to work with that element. Fatima follows Water. I am also not surprised that the mason Goditha shows that she is another Earth mage. She is already thinking ahead of ways of using her magic in the service of her craft and has been hoping that this element is the one that she will favour. It is good when fate follows our wishes. I am worried about Parminder. She has picked up the simple spells of each of the four elements. She is not strong in her casting, but she can perform them all with equal facility.*

More than a little concerned, Rani sat the girl down. "You have reached the stage of being a real apprentice in that you can cast your first spells. By this stage, like the others, you should have some idea what your element will be, but I still see you, each day, casting from all four. Is there no area where you feel more comfortable? Is there something about yourself that you are not telling me?"

She is looking unhappy as she shifts in her seat. "What do you mean?"

"Well let us look around. Lakshmi did not tell us of her upbringing until it was almost too late. Are you sure that there is nothing at all in your past that you need to tell me?" *She looks uncomfortable.* "There is nothing...unusual...nothing that, say happens to you, but does not happen to Goditha?" *She has opened her mouth as if to say something and then shakes her head. I think that she is lying to me.* "There is something that you want to say, but are scared to, isn't there?" asked Rani. "Would you be happier if you talked with Father Christopher about it?" *Her head is drooping. She is going to—*

Suddenly the words came tumbling out. "It is just that... sometimes...when I am near them...I think that I feel what the horses feel...and there is a cat that lives in the stables. I know when it is hunting and when it is being combed or happy and...and once I looked up and saw an eagle and for a while I thought that I was the eagle looking down at me. Am I going mad?" *She looks very unhappy indeed.*

"Really?" *I know that my voice is showing my astonishment. How much more is there ahead of us to discover?* "How many more surprises will Mousehole give us? You are not going mad. It is possible that you may have something that is very rare. If I had known about these...feelings...we would be working on them as well and, if you were born among the Khitan they would have been praising you...ask Hulagu...you would have been raised as a shaman among them. Some people can, without using any magic at all, read minds. None know how. You may have the ability to do that with animals." *She still looks worried.* "This is very good, little one. You do not even know if these are all of the animals that you can do it with yet... Did this just start to happen when we started working?" Parminder nodded. "...I wonder. It is rare, very rare...we will keep training you. It is possible, just possible, that you are one who is born into the realm of the Spirit. Most of those who are born into this realm become priests as they are often more...spiritual perhaps...than they are connected to magic. Those who become mages have no particular affinity with any of the elements...regardless of when they are born. They can use all realms in the same fashion. I know of none in Haven who are Spirit mages currently and there are no records of them that we have going back into The Burning. I once read some old writings that spoke about this. We will work on your ability with animals, which may have been triggered by your touch with the Spirit world, and we will assume that you are of the Spirit realm. This is very good little one. Go and be happy and tell your husband. We have been lax in this. We must start to look for any other skills that may be hidden amongst you."

We began with only a few buildings lived in, but now as winter begins to set in, my village is starting to spread out. All of those who are married are in their own houses now and the old slave quarters are abandoned. Those who want to live together have moved into the bandit barracks for the larger rooms and the better beds that are there.

Having had the attack from the hobgoblins as well as the proof that the Masters wanted to retake the valley, weapons training has become even more focussed. The progress of most of my people is swift...even among those who will be going on to Dwarvenholme have to improve, even if it is just to stay ahead of their students.

The children are getting on with their lessons and now that some are starting to show signs of literacy, I note that Ruth is now able to go beyond the basics with them and started teaching calligraphy and reading them poetry. It helps that Ruth writes her own poetry, as does my Theo-dear, and now the children are starting to work on their own and I have to admire Fear's attempts.

I wish I could appreciate music, but drums I can take and I am glad that one of the successes with the children was when Kāhina brought each of the girls their own drum that she had made for them. I may be tone-deaf, but even I can enjoy rhythm.

Father Theodule is often in helping with the children, but he has conceded to me that Ruth, as a teacher of the young, is far beyond his skills. We have been lucky.

Father Christopher

I *should have been on the lookout for this indulgence, I suppose, but such customs do little harm and help bind people together. I missed it, but Fortunata forestalled Norbert being hung over for his wedding. She had been sure that this was being planned, so she cornered Giles. He tried to look innocent, but she insisted that anything that take place must be at least two nights before. This time the number taking part was larger with not just Giles, as Fortunata had suspected, but also with Thord, Robin, Harald, Goditha, Stefan, Basil and Hulagu taking part. At least hangovers* made the repentance more genuine next morning at Confession.

The wedding itself was different to all of its predecessors in many ways. The groom, in tunic and trews, was attended by Harald and the women having decided this between themselves, was first married to Fortunata. She was attended by Parminder and given away by Stefan. The first bride then took a pace back and Sajāh was brought in wearing a white dress under a white canopy that was carried by Fātima, Umm, Hagar and Bilqīs, and accompanied by Ayesha. She took her place up the front and seven white dishes, each containing something white, sugar, cream, yoghurt and so on, were placed in front of her.

Here we go. I now have to preach a sermon on marriage that does not mention Christ or, in fact Christianity, and with all listening. I then ask each of them if they want this marriage. Three times I ask each of them and, after the third time they each answer, "Yes".

Then Sajāh said, "I, Sajāh, offer you myself in marriage and in accordance with the instructions of the Holy Qu'ran and the Holy Prophet, peace and blessing be upon him. I pledge, in honesty and with sincerity, to be for you an obedient and faithful wife."

Norbert drew a deep breath and replied, "I, Norbert, pledge, in honesty and sincerity, to be for you a faithful and helpful husband."

"I pronounce you man and wife," and, while the two brides embrace each other and then their husband, the attendant women begin to ululate. Some of the onlookers join in. Evidently the Khitan women are used to this practice, and they have, obviously, trained my wife how to do it as well as dance.

The feast began. In deference to the history of one of the brides it was the first wedding that had occurred in the village at which no alcohol or pork was served.

As the winter progressed, more of the married women, freed at last from restrictions, and with the aid of Father Christopher's prayers, reported that they thought that they were pregnant. Also, as the year advanced much of the training had to be moved into the hall as the weather grew colder and colder and there was the occasional day when the fields outside the wall would lie under a light cover of snow. Only archery would take place outside on those days and even that had to be cancelled on one day. Those who were doing duty out at the lookout were very glad of the cloak of warmth.

Astrid

I am the only one glad about the snow. "It is only a light coating, but it should be enough," she said. Now we amaze them with my skis that Dulcie made for me. The snow is deep enough. I can cover our whole valley and have even climbed through the snow up the river track so that I could launch myself back down. I have not had so much fun in a long time.

Astrid ended near the wall, sending up a shower of snow over the watchers in front of her. She did this every day if there was enough snow. Try as she might though, the only person she could convince to try this was Basil and he did not show any great aptitude for the practice. She was so glad of the snow that she would eagerly swap a sentry duty on the roof for one at the lookout so that she could ski back and forth. She even had Fortunata make her some loose white clothing, to wear over her normal clothes, so that, even if she lacked one of the rings, she would be hard to see. "What use is a ring like that, when everyone can see the tracks I leave?" She also made some things to attach to her feet, which, while they looked comical, allowed her to run over snow where others sunk in up to their knees. She preferred these if she was avoiding tracks and used to carry them with her on her back—when she took the skis off, she put them on, until it was time to climb.

It is mid-winter. I want to feel a bit at home with a Wolfneck celebration. With the help of Anahita and Kãhina, who understood the tradition, she cleared some snow away and fixed a pole—really a small tree—into the frozen field outside the gate and then dragged fallen timber up to it to build a cone of timber. At midnight of midwinter, when everyone had been celebrating in the hall she made them all come out. *With my husband's magic rod I light the pile into a Bale-Fire to banish the winter and usher in the spring, as is right.* The resulting blaze lit up the whole valley. *There are some things of home that I miss.*

As the advent of spring became more pressing, the village began to think about who would be going on the next stage of their adventure, for good or ill, and how it would be done and what they would take with them on it.

Glossary

Anne, Saint: Orthodox Christian patron of those who slay the undead and protect against evil and those who return from the dead. Her Feast Day is 25th October.

Asvayujau: Hindi goddess of good luck, joy and happiness.

Ayyappan: Hindi god of wisdom and protection.

Balter: to dance with no style or grace, but with a certain enthusiasm. The author admits to liking the word as it is how he dances.

Basilica Anthropoi: A Holy Order of warrior monks of the Orthodox Church west of the mountains. They are heavily armed and ride as kataphractoi or kynigoi depending on their role. They will bear the Chi-Rho on their shields and the leader of a group will often have a painted icon there as well.

Betterberries: one of many magical herbs, if picked at the right time each Betterberry will have a tiny amount of healing power. You can eat a lot of them.

Bezelye çorbasi: a smooth blended minted pea soup.

Borani chogondar: a chilled dish of diced beetroot and yoghurt.

Bridget, Saint: One of the most universal patrons. She has responsibility for dairymaids, compassion to the poor, and blacksmiths, as well as poets and bards. Her Feast Day is the 10th of Sixtus.

Buzuq: a Caliphate stringed instrument not unlike a mandolin.

Chi-Rho symbol: the two Greek letters joined together signify Christ. The Roman Emperor Constantine, when he was converted to Christianity is supposed to have seen a vision of this and heard the words: 'With this sign, conquer'.

Cosmas, Saint: always associated with Saint Damien as the Orthodox Christian patrons of healing. Their images are always dressed like men of the Caliphate and they have medical tools around them. Their Feast Day is 7th Duodecimus.

Crumhorn: a double-reeded wind instrument from Freehold with an upturned end. It makes an unusual nasal sound.

Damien, Saint: always associated with Saint Cosmas as the Orthodox Christian patrons of healing. Their images are always dressed like men of the Caliphate and they have medical tools around them. Their Feast Day is 7th Duodecimus.

Devi: the Hindi mother goddess and female principle.

Dhatr: Hindi god of health and magic.

Fergus, Saint: Orthodox patron of the Kharl races. His Feast Day is the 27th of November.

Ganesh: elephant headed and rides a mouse, the Hindi god of knowledge and divination.

Harijan: one of the castes of Hindi society that you are born into and cannot leave. This is the lowest of castes, often referred to as 'untouchables'. They deal with unclean acts such as handling dead flesh, dealing with garbage and sewerage and so on. Touching one can render a person of a higher caste 'unclean' and requiring cleansing.

Havuç çorbasi: a smooth blended carrot soup.

Hobgoblin: a grey-skinned humanoid and one of the Kharl-related races.

Homobonus, Saint: Patron of Cloth Workers. He shares a feast day with St John Chrysostum on 13th November.

Hummus: a dish made of mashed chick peas made smooth, usually eaten with flat bread.

Insak-div: a humanoid who is part Kharl and part-human.

John Chrysostum, Saint: Patron of Priests and those seeking a simple life. His Feast Day is 13th November and is shared with St Homobonus.

Jude, Saint: Orthodox Christian patron of the desperate and those who forlornly hope. His Feast Day is 17th Undecim. His icons always show a man in robes holding a book and an oar.

Kataphractoi: fully armoured riders on armoured horses who ride into battle in very tight formation using lance, sword, mace, bow and martobulli.

Kartikeya: Hindi god of war.

Keftethes: a spiced meatball dish usually of lamb eaten either on its own or with rice.

Kharl: a race of humanoids with several distinct subspecies. They can breed with humans.

Kindjal: a long heavy fighting knife with parallel edges that is generally close to a short sword in size and can be used the same way.

Köle: a Khitan word meaning something between 'prisoner' and 'slave'.

Krishna: Hindi god of love and carnal activity.

Kshatya: one of the castes of Hindi society that you are born into and cannot leave. This is the caste of warriors, mages and rulers. It is the second highest caste.

Kukri: a thick heavy-bladed curved knife with a blade 30cm long. It will readily cut through bone and even more easily through joints. It can also be used defensively to catch another blade.

Kynigoi: riders with any level of armour riding unarmoured horses. Their primary role is skirmishing and harassing as well as scouting. They mainly use bows in combat.

Mary Magdalene, Saint: Patron of sinners and those hoping for redemption. Her Feast Day is the 4th of Quinque.

Maskirovka: a Darkspeech word from Wolfneck. It means a big deception, usually of a military type.

Month: The months (all of exactly 36 days) are most commonly given in Latin: Primus, Secundus, Tertius, Quattro, Quinque, Sixtus, September, October, November, December, Undecim and Duedecimus.

Naq: a Caliphate flute.

Paradēśī: Hindi for an outsider, a foreigner, one outside the caste system and so automatically ritually unclean.

Pesh-kabz: a knife 15-20cm long with a thin straight blade, t-shaped in cross-section. After the first 5cm all three edges are only mildly sharpened. It is needle-sharp at the point and widened in a curve into a normal blade-width at the hilt. It is designed to penetrate mail and the padding under it, forcing even riveted mail to open up. It is an assassin's weapon.

Ratri: Hindi goddess of the night and dark.

Sackbutt: a Freehold instrument not unlike a trombone.

Services (Christian): Holy Day is Krondag. The traditional daily cycle of services is: Hesperinos or Vespers: performed at sundown, this is the beginning of the liturgical day. Apodeipnon (literally 'after-supper') or Compline: performed after the evening meal prior to bedtime. Midnight Office: Usually observed only in monasteries. Orthros or Matins: First service of the morning. Usually starts before sunrise. The Eucharist service or the Divine Liturgy: This is the celebration of the Eucharist. Although it is usually celebrated between the Sixth and Ninth Hours, it is not considered to be part of the daily cycle of services, as it occurs outside the normal time of the world. It is not celebrated on weekdays during the preparatory season of Lent or during other fasts. The Hours: First, Third, Sixth, and Ninth — Sung either at their appropriate times (usually only done by monks or priests with lots of free time), or in aggregate at other customary times. If the latter, The First Hour is sung immediately following Orthros, the Third and Sixth prior to the Divine Liturgy, and the Ninth prior to Vespers.

Services (Muslim): The holy day is Dithlau and the hours of prayer are: Fajr (an hour before sunrise), Dhurhr (just after midday), Asr (hour and a half before sunset), Maghreb (a few minutes after sunset) and Isha (an hour and a half after).

Shawm: a Freehold instrument, a double reed woodwind with a small barrel part-way up the stem and a conical-shaped mouth. It has a piercing, buzzing sound that is much louder than a crumhorn.

Shiva: Hindi God, one part of the Trimurtri, the Hindu trinity.

Signs: there are twelve zodiacal signs used in magic. Each takes up the last half of one month and the first half of the next. These start with the last half of Primus and the first half of Secundus (the month of the Tiger) and go from there. The fire signs are Tiger, Dragon and Rat and their time marks Summer. The Air signs are Monkey, Bird and Butterfly and their time marks Autumn. The Water signs are Fish, Dog and Lizard and their time is Winter. Spring is marked by the Earth signs of Horse, Goat and Spider.

Sitar: a Havenite long-necked stringed instrument with a gourd like sound-chamber and twenty-one strings, only six of which are played.

Shri: Hindi for Lord (or Lady).

Sudra: one of the castes of Hindi society that you are born into and cannot leave. This is the caste of the makers, traders, tradesmen and such.

Tabouleh: a salad of parsley, mint, tomatoes

Tambouri: a small hand drum with inbuilt zils (small cymbals) in Havenite music.

Week: each week on Vhast has six days. Generally, across The Land, these are given the names: Firstday, Deutera, Pali, Tetarti, Dithlau and Krondag. Kron is the name given to the sun. The definitions and roots of some of these names are unknown.

Zils: small cymbals, usually used on the fingers in Caliphate and Havenite dancing.

Cast

Adversaries: name given to the members of a space-faring race on the surface of Vhast. They are the enemies of Gamil's people.

Aelfgifu: 7-year-old child-slave of Dharmal's bandits. She was born somewhere in The Swamp.

Ahmed: air mage and bandit. He controlled a flying carpet.

Aine: from Bloomact in The Swamp, she was a brewer with some ability to make wines and distil drinks. She was kidnapped and became a slave of the bandits at Mousehole, but also continued her trade. She is the oldest of the surviving female slaves.

Amin Ramanujan: junior battle mage at Garthang Keep and part of Rani's escort north.

Anahita of the Axe-beaks: Khitan girl from Mousehole. Later she becomes Hulagu's köle.

Astrid Tostisdottir (the Cat): A part-kharl girl from Wolfneck, in the far north of The Land. She is fleeing an unwelcome marriage to Svein. Experienced at sea and as a fisher, she became a Ranger. Attractive but for a strong jaw and lengthened incisors (she has a strong bite). She is tall and statuesque, with pale blonde hair. Her mother has been dead many years, her father is Tosti. She can lap up drinks and purrs when having sex. She marries Basil Akritas.

Ayesha: A ghazi or assassin of the Caliphate. She is one of the rare women of that culture who is allowed independence and has received an education at Misr al-Mãr as a ghazi (holy warrior). In return she must obey any order of those who are placed above her. Part of her education is to maintain her cover as an entertainer. She is the minor daughter of Hãritha, the Sheik of Yãqũsa. She is short, slim, very attractive, bright, ambidextrous and good at it and has superb senses and a beautiful soprano voice. She has black hair and eyes and a tiny waist. Good at climbing and tracking, can ride well. Usually uses knives (including to parry); can use bow and horse mace.

Basil Akritas or Kutsulbalik (nickname from great-grandfather): Is a mostly human (one sixteenth kharl) who appears as a youth just out of his apprenticeship (although he is ten years older). He is an experienced member of the secret police (or Antikataskopeía) of Darkreach and of the Orthodox faith (as it is practiced in Darkreach). He comes from Southpoint from a military family.

Bianca: foundling from Trekvarna. Vagus, can sing well and play a flute, good at working with horses (and horses love her), can cook. Intelligent and average appearance, uses daggers and sling. Can smell treachery. Swore an oath to St Ursula to avenge the death of Rosa. Horses are Sluggard, Sirocco and Firestar. Sings husky contralto.

Bilqīs: a tiny girl, from a trade background in the Caliphate, who was kidnapped and became a slave of the bandits. She later becomes an apprentice mage.

Bryony verch Daffyd: from Rising Mud in the Swamp, newest captive at Mousehole. Her husband (Conan) and father were killed at her wedding and she was brought to Mousehole as a slave and kept as a pet by the bandit, Miriam.

Christopher, Father: A newly graduated Orthodox priest. He was born in the north of The Land at one of the hamlets of Greensin. Has a staff enchanted against evil.

Dharmal: Dwarf and leader of the brigands who attack Bianca's caravan. He rules Mousehole and acts as the main servant of the Masters in The Land.

Dulcie: From Bathmor in The Swamp. She became a slave of the bandits and the village carpenter.

Eleanor: caravan guard from Topwin in Freehold who becomes a slave of the bandits in Mousehole. She becomes the village jeweller, marries Robin Fletcher and is left in charge of defence of Mousehole.

Fãtima: comes from an unknown background in the Caliphate, she was kidnapped as a child and made a slave of the bandits. She becomes an apprentice mage.

Fear the Lord Your God Thatcher (Fear): 6 years old, child slave of the bandits in Mousehole, becomes servant to Rani and Theodora and then is adopted as their daughter.

Fortunata: bandit slave in Mousehole and skilled dressmaker and embroiderer. Marries Norbert as his first wife.

Gamil: comes of an un-named winged space-faring race. She works on a space station. Her very long-lived people created Vhast as an experiment in breeding 'magical' abilities. She is the Chief Predestinator (Project Head) for the planet below her.

Gemma: 8-year-old child-slave of Dharmal's bandits. She is from somewhere in the north.

Giles see Ploughman, Giles.

Goditha: sister to Robin Fletcher and former slave of the bandits. She has never had an interest in men, marries Parminder and becomes an apprentice mage.

Gurinder: 10-year-old child-slave of the bandits at Mousehole, sister of Parminder.

Harald Pitt: miner at Mousehole. He marries Lakshmi.

Hãritha: the Sheik of Yāqūsa in the Caliphate and father of Ayesha.

Hrothnog: The immortal God-King of Darkreach.

Hulagu: A young Khitan tribesman with ten toes. His tribe and totem is the Dire Wolf. Skilled bushman, tracker and hunter, very intelligent, he has very acute senses. Uses bow, mace and shield, lance and darts. He can teach. Has a destiny predicted by Nokaj. His horse is Kirghiz, plus two horses from bandits.

Kãhina of the Pack Hunters; slave of the bandits in Mousehole, she has ten toes and is a cousin of Malik. Later she becomes Hulagu's köle.

Lãdi: slave and chief cook at the bandit village of Mousehole.

Lakshmi: Havenite slave girl in the bandit village of Mousehole. She was a prostitute in Sacred Gate before being captured. Converts to the Orthodox religion and marries Harald Pitt.

Malik: a hunter of the Pack Hunter clan who helps Bianca and Hulagu defeat the bird demons and then escorts them to Evilhalt. He is also Kãhina's cousin.

Masters: A group of undead mages of unknown power who have control over Dwarvenholme and other areas.

Miriam, Princess: many time grand-daughter of Hrothnog and cousin of Theodora. She is married as first wife to Hassan, third son of Sheik Abdul Mohammed ibn Hasid, ruler of the Caliphate.

Naeve Milker: Former Freehold dairymaid, slave in the bandit village of Mousehole. Can become catatonic under stress, she becomes an apprentice mage and marries Giles.

Norbert Black: male slave of the bandits in Mousehole. He is skilled as a blacksmith, weapons smith and armourer. Marries both Fortunata and Sãjah.

Parminder: former child slave of the bandits in Mousehole, she marries Goditha and is sister to Gurinder. She becomes an apprentice mage and is a xeno-telepath.

Ploughman, Giles: farmer and one of the few male slaves at Mousehole. He marries Naeve.

Rani Rai, Shri: A woman of Kshatya (warrior) caste in Sacred Gate, capital of Haven who is both an astrologer and a battle mage. She has a minor post at the University. Her grandmother is a fortune-teller and her mother is a minor water mage. Destined to love and marry Theodora. Horses are Lakshmi and Juggernaut.

Robin Fletcher: one of the male slaves of the bandits at Mousehole, he is kept as their fletcher and bowyer.

Roxanna: 8-year-old Caliphate slave of Dharmal's bandits in Mousehole.

Ruhayma: 9-year-old Caliphate slave of Dharmal's bandits.

Ruth: Merchant from Ashvaria in Freehold, captured by bandits. Becomes the teacher of the village children in Mousehole and marries Theodule.

Sajāh: from the Caliphate, chief domestic of the bandit village of Mousehole, marries Norbert Black as his second wife.

Sanjeev Dahl: Subadar (junior officer) of cavalry at Garthang Keep, Rani's escort commander on the way north.

Shilpa: Havenite trader captured by the bandits and kept as a slave in Mousehole.

Sparetha: mother of Hulagu, master horsewoman and trainer, fletcher, very skilled archer. Her mother is 'from the east' and was a thrall.

Stefan: A young soldier from Evilhalt. He is sick of seeing the world pass through his village and instead he wants to pass through the world. From a craft background (leatherworker) he has an inherited magical sword called Smiter.

Svein: man of Wolfneck, suitor to Astrid. He is an ugly (kharlish appearance), violent drunkard and around 40 years old. He owns a ship and is a rival of Astrid's father. He is most likely the Northern agent for the Masters.

Theodora: Great-great-granddaughter of Hrothnog. She is not entirely human, a mage and, at 120 years, is far older than the late teens that she appears to be. She is also experienced (and is usually disguised as) heavy cavalry, a kataphractoi. She uses, as an alias 'Salimah al Sabah'. Her horse is called Esther. She falls in love with, and marries, Rani.

Thord: A shorter and broad humanoid of the species locally known as a Dwarf. He comes from Kharlsbane in the Northern Mountains. He rides a sheep called Hillstrider.

Thorkil: an outlaw from Wolfneck in Dharmal's brigand group. His hands, although usable, are more like bear claws. He is a paedophile.

Togotak: father of Hulagu, master horseman, married to Sparetha. He is a better rider than her.

Tosti: father of Astrid. A shipowner and widower.

Valeria: 16-year-old from Deeryas on the south coast, bandit slave in Mousehole and farmer. She becomes the maidservant to Rani and Theodora.

Verily I Rejoice in the Lord Tiller (Verily): A former Brotherhood slave and, since the age of six, a slave of the bandits of Mousehole. She is now 16 and traumatised. Among her other skills, she is a talented entertainer and skilled linguist. She can 'smell' magic and becomes an apprentice mage and then marries Aziz. She has long eyelashes, pale skin and black hair and a very smooth and sexy contralto voice. She has no hair on her body naturally.